# TALES FROM WAXLING BEACH

Mark Rasdall

Copyright © 2017 Mark Rasdall

All rights reserved

The characters and events portrayed in this book are fictitious. Any similarity to real persons, living or dead, is coincidental and not intended by the author.

Published by Burwell Web Communications Ltd

No part of this book may be reproduced, or stored in a retrieval system, or transmitted in any form or by any means, electronic, mechanical, photocopying, recording, or otherwise, without express written permission of the publisher.

*This book is dedicated to three women: Vera who loved me first; Elizabeth who was my first love, and Michelle who will love me last.*

# CONTENTS

Title Page
Copyright
Dedication
PRESENT   1
MONDAY 4th JUNE 2007   2
TUESDAY 5th JUNE 2007   18
WEDNESDAY 6TH JUNE 2007   31
THURSDAY 7th JUNE 2007   49
FRIDAY 8th JUNE 2007   63
PAST   70
SATURDAY 9th JUNE 2007   71
SUNDAY 10th JUNE 2007   89
MONDAY 11th JUNE 2007   98
TUESDAY 12th JUNE 2007   105
WEDNESDAY 13th JUNE 2007   132
THURSDAY 14th JUNE 2007   144
FRIDAY 15th JUNE 2007   162
SATURDAY 16th JUNE 2007   169
FUTURE   187

| | |
|---|---|
| SUNDAY 17th JUNE 2007 | 188 |
| MONDAY 18th JUNE 2007 | 212 |
| TUESDAY 19th JUNE 2007 | 252 |
| WEDNESDAY 20th JUNE 2007 | 317 |
| THURSDAY 21ST JUNE 2007 | 367 |
| FRIDAY 22ND JUNE, 2007 | 399 |
| Mailing List | 430 |
| About The Author | 431 |

# PRESENT

# MONDAY 4TH JUNE 2007

The sun was beaming down on the sea, a deep blue now that the clouds had finally been blown away. Warm and direct, the rays glinted off of the mast of the tiny ship way out on the horizon: dividing lines between us and them, even as we drew nearer. I could hear the bell, just as she said I would do, and strained my ears to hear voices, even whispers from unseeing villagers. But my concentration was interrupted by a cry from the living, a chilling wail that even the ceaseless waves could not drown...

\*\*\*

"The government is today urging the public to continue to be vigilant at all times and reiterated that we face a summer of intensified security checks, especially at major sporting and cultural events such as Wimbledon, the first stage of this year's Tour de France and the Live Earth concert at Wembley Stadium.

The UK National Security Level remains 'critical,' he said. An attack is thought to be imminent, possibly to coincide with the second anniversary next month of the 7/7 London bombings in which fifty-two innocent people died and more than seven hundred were injured.

An Opposition spokesperson, echoing the all-party view on defence at home, was this morning quoted as saying, 'No individual, young or old, should set out on their journey at the start of a day, never to return to their loved ones because of the actions of others.'

**BBC News. It's 7 o'clock"**

"Do we make history or does it make us?"

His sleep has been inundated by dreams, sweeping into his mind and colliding with real events that had taken up residence as seemingly reliable memories. He isn't sure if he is still sleeping, turning cartwheels across the stage.

"Well, Daddy; what do you think?"

His ten-year-old daughter, Rowena, is sitting on his side of the bed with an A4 pad in hand and an alarming amount of white space.

"About what?" he uses this ploy to both buy time and hide his astonishment when clients ask surprisingly sensible questions. With Rowena, it is usually just about buying time.

"History of course! Our teacher told us to think of chickens and eggs."

"Battery or free-range?"

"Nick!" His wife, Nora, wearing a blue dressing gown which is slightly frayed around the edges, marches towards him in that purposeful way of hers and shoots him one of her commanding looks which confirms that he must indeed be awake.

"Mum's here. She's the expert on those kinds of things."

"But I wanted to start with you - I don't think it would take very long. Please, Dad!"

Who does she think he is: Adam? Why isn't she more concerned with the volcanic spot that seems to have settled on one side of her face, ready to erupt at any moment?

"Let me think about it today and I'll let you know later." Another tactic he's perfected over the years.

"But it's got to be finished in three weeks."

"Plenty of time then, " Nora closes down the conversation. "Daddy's got a busy day ahead - let him think about it and you can ask him tomorrow when he gets back from work."

"But..."

"No buts, Rowena."

He turns towards his wife who, if he is not mistaken, turns away from him slightly in response.

"American video conference tomorrow, don't forget; assuming they don't take us all out with Agent Orange first."

Why has he used such an ancient noun now; one describing the carnage beamed into his childhood front room when he was very young? Perhaps it is the talk of death and destruction on the radio which, in every other way, he still loves? Barry McGuire was right: the world was on the eve of destruction then and seemingly still is.

Nora is listening to the radio while observing him avoiding their daughter's questions as usual.

She remembers the 'Light Programme' becoming 'Radio One' during that summer they are all reminiscing about and watches him for a signal. But he has tuned out or tuned in to something a long way away from either of them. Probably still for the best, she thinks, even as she witnesses the clouds of hurt rolling over Rowena's face. At least it isn't raining.

Rowena walks out of the room, just a little too slowly, her long auburn hair perfectly combed. He hadn't noticed how long it had become - practically down to her waist. Maybe she is rehearsing for the part of Rapunzel in the school play? He remembers her mentioning something about a school production now and is peculiarly glad that the endless fairy tales are about to be left behind or extinguished forever and ever.

Nora closes the door gently behind her. At one time he would have been quietly thrilled by this gesture but now it signals only interrogation against a ticking clock.

"You were shouting in your sleep again."

"Like a sort of hard-core Crystal Gale then?"

"You could at least listen to what Rowena is asking you for. One word from you is the equivalent of an encyclopaedia from me. You might live to regret the passing of these years, you know."

He considers whether this is what history will record - that he was there all the time but unplugged and useless. Like Eric Clapton in his later years?

"And you'll have to make some kind of excuse to get away from the Americans…"

"Most of Europe's been trying to do that since the Marshall Plan!"

"On Wednesday. The dinner party!" Her voice is firm and uncompromising. They're coming for eight thirty so I need you home by seven at the latest."

"I'll certainly try but…"

"No buts from you either. We've re-arranged this twice now."

"Third time lucky I suppose."

"No, Nick, not luck: intent and resolution."

"Sounds like a spinning big top!"

"Spoken like a clown who's forgotten how to make people laugh."

She turns away from him, perhaps recognizing the same old stalemate that he does. It seems that the only games they play these days are end games.

\*\*\*

"23 days until Tony Blair leaves office: 'a good job too,' say some, as taxpayers may not be able to fund so many goodbye trips for much longer. With him now in Germany ahead of the G8 summit and Deputy Prime

Minister, John Prescott, in hospital, we ask: Who is in charge of the country at the moment?

And, as promised, we'll be giving you details of those live broadcasts from Norfolk, later on in this programme."

Nick contemplates his work schedule for the week ahead which will keep him away from home for the most part. It isn't the thought of entertaining, just that the reality usually isn't. The truth is that most of Nora's friends would be much more interesting if they were actually stoned rather than predisposed to discussing them endlessly.

The television has taken over broadcasting duties in the kitchen.

"**History and Mystery returns to our screens and radio waves next week for a two-week series of live broadcasts and analysis by our history experts...**"

"There you go, Rowena, if you tune in next week you might get some clues to life's great mysteries..."

"**We'll be on the North Norfolk coast trying to unravel a local mystery, set against a global tide of change.**

**This dramatic coastline has witnessed innumerable wrecks as storms have battered it into near submission – so much so that it's almost impossible to land boats on the beaches; only the strength and courage of human endeavour have enabled life to continue here.**

**Join me later in our main bulletin when I'll be**

giving you more details and, don't forget, if you'd like to volunteer we're still looking for people to help us: you too could be on national television. Just go to the main BBC website, select historyandmystery, then follow the links."

"Do you know him, Mum?"

"His name is John Squires, darling, he presents this programme every summer."

"Praise the Lord that they bury his remains for the other fifty weeks of the year."

"At least he has proved himself determined and hardy enough to re-invent himself after the Air Force."

"I can see the glowing obituary already."

"And his tombstone will have a credit on it."

She means it as a joke, surely? He watches her scoop up a vast mound of ironing and leave the room.

Rowena barely looks up and isn't waving from the lounge window a few minutes later as he heads off for the Tube. He feels strangely comforted by the thought that she may not have done so for a long time.

\*\*\*

"Hello!" She winds a renegade curl of hair around her left ear, one leg raised on the kitchen chair revealing a long, still slender leg which she rubs gently, slowly from foot to knee.

"Of course I haven't!" She's a bit put out that he should talk about this so early in the conversation she has looked forward to so much for so little time.

"There's no need to."

It isn't what he wants to hear and she can understand his reasoning. She needs to be positive. Her future may depend upon it.

"Yes. Yes, I will. Before tomorrow night: that I can promise. We've got people coming over the next day so best he knows before then otherwise he might just fall asleep and forget it all."

But will she tell him everything? She knows that she will not. It's not just him she would be letting down.

\*\*\*

He takes the long escalator up from Leicester Square station, smiling knowingly at the losers peeling off to his right for the Northern Line. They'd called it the 'Misery Line' when he'd moved down to London more than twenty years ago, while Jim Packer, their Group Creative Director, famously declared it 'even more squalid than south London.' Jim makes a lot of sweeping statements. In his autobiography, *a single white line*, he prefers: 'breadth of vision.'

He approaches the floor-to-moon glass frontage of Prindle Massey, aware that sweat is already pouring down his face. Mondays are bad but not usually this bad.

Katie and Jen are manning the Reception Desk in tight white blouses and short red skirts over long, brown legs (as Marmaduke would say: 'The Receptionist is your best thirty-second slot').

"Hi Nick"

"Hi, Jen. Good weekend?"

"Not really. Friday night drinks at Barbie's turned into Saturday lunchtime rugby theme bar down by the river. Didn't see Putney High Street again until I came in this morning."

Julian Bannister is seated at his rectangular table of smoked glass in the space at the far corner of the second floor. His lovely white laptop with the way-above-average, nineteen-inch screen, sits patiently in front of him showing a screensaver image of Richard Branson. Every so often, planes in the Virgin livery silently fly across the screen's vast sky but Bannister isn't planning on going anywhere.

He glances over in Nick's direction but, discovering nobody of interest, continues to read his copy of *Persuade* as though Nick is a momentary aberration: a trick of the light or just one of the cleaners perhaps? Bannister is more than twenty years younger than Nick Golding but is the uncompromising adult to his indifferent child.

After an hour's well-observed silence, the Bannister Group weekly meeting begins. The first item on the agenda is a celebrity PR piece for which they paid a small fee. Celebrity pieces are the only placements the agency ever pays for; the rest is free and up to the whims, largely, of tired, over-worked and often hostile journalists – and Prindle Massey's techniques of persuasion of course.

While Bannister updates them all, Nick regards Vic - the intern - who sits across from him now, eagerly making copious notes – probably verbatim – of the meeting. Vic is 'quite brilliant,' according to everyone he speaks to, including Vic himself.

What is it with these geeky little nerds with their floppy hair and shirts with tailored collars? They speak in impossibly posh voices about Double Firsts and Magdalen and 'educated guesses' suggesting that those not in their (very) select club are ignorant through exclusion.

Bannister has paused for effect.

"You're very quiet, Golding; not that there's anything unusual in that!"

"I find that the sound of silence can be very effective at certain times."

"If you were Dustin Hoffman, perhaps, but you're hardly a graduate trainee anymore! I assume everything is running smoothly on Blackout?"

Blackout is a new analgesic drug the agency is helping to launch this year. Nick hasn't received any texts, emails or 'phone calls from his main client over the weekend (for the first time in weeks) so simply nods, knowingly.

Bannister always seats himself according to the sun's positioning – as though he were in Versailles rather than Soho (as Marmaduke would say: 'Control the seating plan and you control the meeting').

He continues to patronise as befits a king. "It's critical that we spend every waking moment, every seeing and hearing hour on our clients' businesses. Without our input disaster could strike at any time."

Petra, the other Account Director on the team,

leans forward, hoping the upper slopes of her tanned-to-order breasts might encourage Bannister to believe she would be the go-to woman in a crisis.

He locks on to the naked flesh, as he always does, talking to the tell-tale swellings of both nipples simultaneously.

"I don't want any trouble this week - not with the Yanks invading."

"Is Marmaduke himself coming, Jules?" Martha is their budget controller. She wears so much slap she looks like a mannequin but, at forty-something, is old enough to be no threat to Bannister so he tolerates her.

"No, darling. I confirmed with him in New York this morning that he would just be appearing by satellite. He is going to talk about our new social media division but I'm not allowed to share too much at present."

"It sounds like a great step forward for the agency" Petra toes the party line, as ever, exposing her gleaming teeth by *Colgaterri*.

"Indeed. They've decided that the change can't wait."

'Tell that to Martha in a couple of years. See how the bottom line looks then?' Nick is dazzled, but only by the sunshine.

\*\*\*

Nora cradles the telephone receiver under her chin as she reaches out for the soap. The bath water is warm and full of deliciously scented bubbles. She doesn't usually do daytime baths but she feels the need today; not to wash but to wallow.

"He doesn't seem to, no. The radio doesn't help but you try to keep him from listening. Even if I switch it off or remove the batteries he tunes into a station online – about the only thing he does do online I reckon."

The caller laughs and so does she. She leans back again, letting the water cover her body, the bubbles like little white markers on a dig. But there is no great discovery to be made here. She knows what lies below and doesn't like what she knows. Nick doesn't seem to mind but, then again, Nick would see only bubbles.

"No. Not until the weekend. We'll all come up on the Saturday if that's OK with you?

Two weeks, but Rowena will only be there for the first of them. Nick will bring her back at the end of the half-term. Yes, she will. She always loves coming to stay … well that's no problem, is it? She'll be able to help you with the packing. She likes to be useful."

She could have said 'noticed' instead of useful. That would have been sufficient. Rowena spends far too much of her time alone, usually reading in her room. Nora worries pretty much constantly that it isn't just the quality, or even quantity, of the stories that keep her there. She considers tomorrow's meeting and places the soaking flannel over her face, but it doesn't shut out the scene still playing in her head.

Her face feels flushed and she turns on the cold tap but it doesn't cool her.

\*\*\*

Nora greets him with such a loud 'Hi' from the kitchen that pilots of planes overhead in the Heathrow stack could have taken it as confirmation of their elevated positions.

"I've got a bit of news!"

"Fine. I'll just grab a quick shower and then you can tell me."

An hour and a half later, Nick returns to the kitchen but Nora is no longer there. She is instead sitting upright on the sofa in the lounge, surrounded by what looks like pocket guidebooks; a battered, purple OS map is sprawled out on the carpet in front of her. Nick can see a lot of blue beyond.

"What are you doing?"

"Planning my next dig."

"Dig! I didn't know there were any coming up – or down, obviously. Was this the news you wanted to tell me about?"

His voice is contrite but he is aware that there is an edge to it. So is she.

"It was - is. I got a call from Lizzie at lunchtime."

"Was she hungry?"

Why can't he just listen to her without making stupid comments all the time?

"She's asked me to join the excavation next week in Norfolk."

"Not History and Mystery?"

"Why not? I have a life too, you know. I don't choose to spend my days here hemmed in or running around after you and Rowena just hoping that the 'phone might ring."

"What did Lizzie say, exactly?" He sits down beside her but she makes no move to clear a space for him. He recognises one of the books: 'Seahenge - a personal journey.'

Eventually, Nora lifts her head and glares at him.

"She said that they were still looking for volunteers, as John reported on TV this morning, but now one of the history experts has had to pull out."

"Better post-mortem offer?"

She ignores him as usual. It's easier that way, especially since she stopped finding him funny.

"Lizzie thought of me, especially given my background."

"The discovery of those Phoenician ships in the Med?"

"That, but also the work at Holme-next-the-Sea."

"Seahenge? That was only a couple of years ago, wasn't it?"

"No Nick, it was eight years ago, but I did get to know that part of the coast quite well which John thought would provide some good experience for the rest of the team."

"Of course, it's all about the team with John, isn't

it, not at all about him?"

"I don't know why you have such a hang-up about him; he's genuinely interested in the subject matter."

"I bet he is."

She closes the book on her knee with such unanticipated force that it makes him jump.

"You think everything's a joke, don't you?" Her voice is icy. "Well get this for a laugh. Ask me where I'm going to be spending next week?"

He has no choice. She already has all the answers. "The North Norfolk coast?"

"Correct. We're going to be at a little village called Waxling - just along the coast from Happisburgh."

She stares at him as if waiting for some kind of reaction - any kind of reaction - before heading for the kitchen.

He finds her a few minutes later, hurling dirty clothes into the washing machine with all the velocity that can be achieved with only cotton-based socks and knickers.

"I thought it was Rowena's half-term week?" he feels like a truant.

"Funny how you can remember some things when you choose to do so! You don't need to worry about having to do anything. I 'phoned your mother and she'd love to have her come and stay."

"You did what?"

"She's lonely - especially with your father being

ill. I thought it would be good for both of them."

# TUESDAY 5TH JUNE 2007

She hadn't meant to even mention the place; not yet anyway. He hadn't wanted her to work at Seahenge and had made that very clear, the longer she had been away, but had never bothered or been able to tell her why he was so opposed to it. She assumed at the time that it had just been about John – some kind of primitive male jealousy thing.

"Can we open a window, Susie?"

"You OK?"

"I'm fine, thanks. Just a bit warm."

Mercifully Susie is too preoccupied with that day's sandwich-making to notice or maybe she doesn't have time for this today.

"They say it could hit the high eighties later. Good job I got those extra packs of spring water in!"

Nora has popped into the Spice Café, just before the triangle at Palmers Green, for an early coffee and croissant. It isn't especially spicy and neither is she in need of caffeine. Nick makes coffee round the clock when he is in the house and always for them both (always forgetting that she prefers tea) as though the kettle would steadfastly refuse to boil sufficient water just for one. No, she is already wired at nine o'clock in the morning. She just needs to not be on her own today.

"I imagine Nick's just communicated out by the time he gets home."

"Or maybe by the time he gets home to me?" She fingers the packets of sugars and sweeteners, neatly stacked in the little glass pot that sits between their cups.

"What do you mean? Where else would he go?"

"No, I didn't mean that," she sometimes forgets how sharp Susie can be (how could you run a café in North London and survive otherwise?). "He just seems to have less and less to say. He's gone into himself again and neither of us can find out where he's hiding."

"Who would he need to hide from?"

"I don't know for certain that he is. The agency people don't seem to respect him. Julian Bannister never has done for some reason: that I do know for a fact. At the same time, he won't do a thing about it."

"Maybe he doesn't know how to? Some men are so locked into a daily pattern that they've forgotten where the life key is, haven't they?"

"Under the mat that everyone else just wipes their feet on now."

"Wow. That's a bit profound!"

"Sorry, been having deep thoughts and, before you say it, I know that's what archaeologists are supposed to have most of the time."

Susie laughs dutifully but looks anxious. "As long as he's happy, though: as long as you and Rowena are happy?"

"That's just it. I don't know whether he is or not."

"We see a lot of blokes like that - middle-aged usually. They come in all smarmy and full of themselves but within a couple of minutes, you see them staring into space and wonder what it is they're really looking for. Stay in here for ages some of them do; sad really."

"Now who's being deep?"

"I know. I must get on. Maybe Nick has just settled for a quiet life? How's Rowena?"

"She's fine. Working hard at school."

"Nose in a book, as usual, I expect."

"When is it not? She's OK but I think she spends far too much time on her own."

"Could be worse I suppose, given the company some of them keep – even at that age! I hope you're not expecting to travel up there by train?"

"No, there isn't a station at Waxling."

"Good thing. According to the paper, this morning, passengers have never been so unhappy with the train companies. Apparently, a quarter of people complain about overcrowding and can't get seats."

"You only pay for the journey from A to B, I think, not an actual seat."

"Try telling that to all the tourists this summer! You ought to get Nick on to it. He understands what people want."

Or what they need to hear, she considers, unfaithfully.

\*\*\*

The Prindle Massey boardroom table's surface is glazed from the sap of a Canadian maple tree that the Mounties had had under surveillance for years. It is not a fancy piece of furniture but very long and imposing and rubs off on those who have graduated to sit self-consciously around it (as Marmaduke would say: 'Resting places are for those who would be stationery').

Bannister strides in, confidently. He is wearing his new light-blue Boss suit (formal yet sufficiently familiar, designed to engender respect).

"So, what's on the agenda today?" Nick tries to muster as much sincere interest in hearing the answer as he can manage that early in the day

"I imagine you'll find out soon enough." Bannister loves secrets and fully embraces Al Gore's notion of an information superhighway where data makes the difference. The problem is that his understanding of social networking is still limited to the exchange of business cards over lunch or dinner, and bed and breakfast if things go particularly well.

Just over two hours later, they are all still seated or standing in the boardroom, watching a live web link with New York in which the face of a bronzed and relaxed Marmaduke Prindle fills the wide screen and is summing up, like a modern-day god:

"Not since we merged PM Commercial with S.H.O.U.T. Public Affairs to form Prindle Massey, as we know and love it today, has there been such a common thread running through the business. Social Media in harness with the Word of Mouth tool is the most powerful armoury we've had since nuclear weapons were developed.

One American in ten tells the other nine how to vote; where and what to eat and what to buy. These are the new 'influentials.' Social is the new sex and we need intercourse; lots of it. Decisions will be based on conversations and we need to reach the people starting those conversations. We need to learn how to listen all over again to see what is going on.

However, we need a test bed and one which won't damage our commercial reputation. If we get it wrong let's do so where few people can see and even fewer really care. Charity cases are where we will try out our new skills; those in need are great for us because even if they start with little, they cannot complain if they end up with slightly less. I commend this new opportunity to all of you."

Hank Bummerman closes the browser window and looks slowly around the room, taking in every face, as his previous life in security camera equipment taught him to do.

"Gentlemen, Prindle Massey has come of age. We need to give the appearance of caring for the poor, even if it's the big bucks that are still driving us to do so. Marmaduke wants this to happen and so do we. Think of the press coverage this will generate for the clients that matter to us; think of the spending that could come out of this!"

Nick is barely taking anything in now. This cynical ploy under the guise of 'helping them but helping ourselves' is truly breathtaking. He has no direct experience of working on charity accounts and feels no affinity with do-gooders in dungarees looking for handouts. Surely Bannister doesn't either? He'd once flamboyantly dismissed the cardboard city of homeless people under the Waterloo arches as 'a boxed set of Lilliputians.'

Jonathan Massey, tall and resplendent in a gold silk suit, calls the summit to a close in his most clipped English accent. He rises gracefully to escort Hank Bummerman and his attractive female accomplice from the room.

Bannister passes close to Nick and whispers, "You have the lead appointment on this: on Thursday. It would be really useful if you did not mess it up completely," before fluttering after Massey and Bummerman, like a white butterfly on cabbage.

Nick gets back to his desk – at least he still has a desk – to find a yellow Post-It note fixed to his screen (Petra then) with just the single tag in bold, blue letters: #cartridgepensaredead on it. Nick has used his ancient Parker pen since first starting in the agency nearly twenty-five years ago. It was a present from his mother and he still loves to write with it, though not to her, obviously.

He makes a note with the said pen – Blogs,

Forums, Communities – before, remembering the strained conversation with Nora the previous evening, idly plugs 'Waxling' into the Google search bar. The place name looks strangely familiar - as if from a childhood story – but then it would do, he grimaces; after all, 'we're all connected now.'

\*\*\*

She sits to attention in the well-worn armchair opposite Ed Lerner's desk, more upright than she normally would, as befitting a meeting with the headmaster.

"And you're quite sure she hasn't said anything to you or your partner…"

"Husband"

"My apologies; to your husband about this?"

Ed is beyond upright, he is leaning at an alarming and surely unsustainable angle towards her. In his early fifties, he is greying on the sides of his head which only serves to make the jet-black, and so obviously dyed, top hair look like a charcoal beret.

"No. Look, I don't know if any of this is true, but it seems pretty disturbing to me," she allows herself to lean back in the chair now but, feeling a slightly sticky patch where any number of other heads had temporarily resided, quickly sits forward again. "You know better than I do what children are capable of."

"Capable, yes, but not necessarily culpable. We see everything as children, of course; very little is hidden from us and, if I may venture further, the more we try to hide things from them as parents, the more likely they are to seek them out; to dig things up."

"I'm not sure what you are suggesting?"

"Just that children tend to write or draw about what they see. They express their true feelings without any social, economic or political restrictions - they will instinctively tell the truth. Nobody has 'educated' instinct out of them yet."

He pauses for ironic effect but, seeing that this is wasted on her, quickly moves on.

"However, a child might also be blessed with great imagination – as Rowena clearly is – or, indeed, there has been some great trauma in their lives which they either choose to escape from or meet head-on. Perhaps that is what is happening here?"

Nora says nothing. What can she say? She is as speechless now as the moment she discovered the drawings on Rowena's notepad; unfinished sketches of a dark, terrifying figure rearing up above a young girl, who is lying on an island, surrounded by water.

\*\*\*

The first search result, complete with a picture postcard thumbnail is effectively an online brochure for North Norfolk covering holidays in Cromer and on the nearby Broads, along with downloadable photos of windmills and the sea from various points along the forty-three miles of coastline.

There is then the usual collection of forum entries from struggling companies – in this case, mostly specialist suppliers to a once-buoyant boat-building trade.

Next, he is introduced to the pubescent miseries of a girl called Amy who is ten years old and writing about her school days; how much she is looking forward to getting home in the evenings to tend to her beloved rabbit – Snuffles – which is, apparently, the only one who listens to what she has to say...

Finally, there is a blog called 'Abbots_Home.' Not a very subtle disguise for monks and mead, he thinks. Perhaps they're not supposed to be online at all? It has a sub-title (if that makes any kind of sense on the web?) of 'they think we're invisible but we're not.' Definitely, monks craving attention then, and not from God.

It appears to have been written by a madman who may never have been to school and has certainly never lived by the rules of grammar. The first entry is from April of that year:

**'Taking words from peoples' mouths?**

**They're looking to step up the 'save our village' campaign then. A bit late for that if you ask me. Of course, nobody does. Want people to have their say on the radio or even on the television in Norwich. Bet the main man don't mention the 1997 disaster. As I recall, the coxswain didn't turn up for duty when that Dutch trawler went on the Palling Rocks. I don't see them advertising that. Paid the coastguard off and that nosy reporter from the North Norfolk Gazette; let some other poor soul take the blame didn't they? Must have been good blood money as that little tale's been buried ever since - like them eight poor fishermen in**

**the graveyard. Try telling them about good causes - was nothing but evil that caused their early deaths.'**

He laughs out loud at such drivel and, more than that, those sad people with nothing better to do than to read it – which just encourages the no-hopers to write more of it.

\*\*\*

She opens the door to him before he even has a chance to get his key stuck in the Yale and utter his daily curse. She needs to talk with him; needs to make him see how important it is and how things are drifting away, apart.

"You're earlier than I'd expected!"

"Sorry, did I not give Mr Squires time to hide in the wardrobe?"

Not this again. She has been planning out what she will say for most of the afternoon; since she got back from school, in fact. She might have anticipated this kind of flippant response.

"That's neither farcical nor funny." She bangs the front door shut behind them, perhaps a little too loudly but, hey, who cares anymore? Not her husband that's for sure.

She heads into the kitchen where the aroma of freshly made coffee, enticing just a few minutes earlier, persuades him to join her.

"Did you hear the news?" she has chosen a neutral subject to break the ice

"What's happened?"

"No need to be alarmed, just that they are now saying that a video of the London 2012 logo is causing migraines and even fits."

"Who are they?"

"' Epilepsy Action' I think they're called."

"I know that designers are up in arms about it. You wouldn't believe sport could be so divisive, would you? I did read that someone had said it looked like Boris Johnson's hair!"

"Might be nice to try and get some tickets for the Games though. I think Rowena would love it – she's been talking about it ever since we won the bid."

"Has she? Well, I wouldn't want to raise her hopes too much. Someone in the office took over an hour to get in today because of signal failures on the Jubilee Line extension. It never used to cause them problems supposedly. They reckon it can only get worse as more and more people try and get out to Stratford. The whole network will probably grind to a halt and we'll have a diplomatic crisis of Olympic proportions!"

He seems quite relaxed and she lets him enjoy his witty asides but these don't seem to appease his desire to get under her skin.

"So, are you all set to bed down with those virile young diggers again?"

"What's the matter with you? Too many pretty girls seeing you as a father figure?"

Nick lets the blow wipe the smug grin from his face; adding it to the bruises that are barely skin deep. "I take it you're all set?"

"Of course. Opportunities like this don't come up very often and I need some space."

"That's what Hitler said when he annexed Czechoslovakia."

"He also said he was acting in the best interests of the people."

"And Rowena, what kind of half-term is she going to have?"

"One where she's surrounded by peace and quiet I hope. Nick…"

"Peace. You think staying in a house while my father coughs his guts up and my mother packs up her rubbish is peaceful?"

She turns to face him, the vaguest line of moisture below her eyes.

"Have some compassion for goodness sake; if not for us, for him. This may be the last chance your daughter has to spend time with her grandfather."

"Exactly. Her lasting memories of him should be good, not bad."

The words sound hollow even as he spits them out.

"Why do you have to judge everybody and everything according to your own experiences?"

"Because I'm a human being, not a computer. I

can't be programmed to forget."

"I thought that was exactly what had happened."

"What do you mean by that?"

She's gone beyond the limit - that acceptable boundary of mutual respect. She knows it and senses that he might too.

"Nothing. I'm sorry. I just wish you could be more excited about my having the chance to do something instead of throwing up obstacles all the time. That's all."

But it isn't all, not even a significant percentage. They haven't begun to discuss the main topic; she's barely even started the research into all their pasts.

# WEDNESDAY 6TH JUNE 2007

She has woken up early with a jolt and knows that Waxling has been on her mind. She has done some follow-up research since Seahenge: helped out on a couple of excavations up in the Lincolnshire Wolds and then down on the Somerset Levels. How she loves the old names. So much is changing these days, causing the old, reliable signposts to disappear.

This is why she is so excited about her expedition to Waxling, to the east of her last dig on that part of the coast: an opportunity to experience again the adrenaline of the new in finding out about the old.

The telephone rings and she picks it up quickly so as not to wake the other two. She is downstairs in her study, wrapped up snugly in a dressing gown and comfy slippers, though she still feels the morning chill in the house.

"Connie! How marvellous. I was just thinking about the dig next week."

"You're up early my dear!"

"You too but then I remember you being up with the dawn on most days!"

"Still am. The early bird gets to worm through mud and clay first as it were."

The caller, Constance Breeve, laughs out loud and she joins in, forgetting now about the need to be quiet - to be secretive. Larger than life and straight out of a St Trinian's sketchbook, Constance – or Connie to those who have ever bought her drinks at the end of long days in the field (often quite literally) – is sharp and very direct. And yet, she has an endearing capacity to listen to others and knows precisely when they have something to say; to share with her. Nora can't wait to see her again.

"I hope you're OK with my joining you. Lizzie thought my local knowledge might be useful?"

"More than useful and stop restricting your sphere of expertise to a Doorstep Doris! It is a significant dig with far more underwater elements than you or I have ever investigated. This isn't just a ship at the bottom of the sea, it's an entire village."

"Another drowned village – like Dunwich?"

"Indeed, except that ours disappeared in the early Seventeenth Century. Obviously, deaths in coastal areas have occurred throughout history - about a hundred and fifty people still die on the coast each year, which you may not have known - but this was truly an inundation of Biblical proportions. Practically nothing of that poor community remains."

"Wasn't there a church tower still close to the surface?"

"How on earth do you know that? Yes, there was

and still is. Lots of rumours about that tower and the church bell that still rings when the tide runs in a certain direction ... several hundred folk were drowned – most because they gathered in that church, thinking it would be safe.

Nobody knows why but it's a populist theme that John is keen to look at over the next two weeks. About two thousand acres of land and a thirty-acre wood disappeared. Much of the land was put over to sheep by then but not too many animal bones were discovered, though plenty of branches from trees. Sand has been good for us up there. A lot of things have been incredibly well preserved."

"Such as?"

"The usual Roman pottery in deep wells; day-to-day medieval items such as shoe leathers and buckles. More remarkably, the remains of some of the original cottages can still be seen down there and one can see cartwheel tracks and impressions of horseshoes, even gardens where the tree stumps and roots of fruit trees still protrude.

All quite eerie, according to the reports we have from previous explorations, and disturbingly so: not at all peaceful. The last expedition in the 'Twenties has descriptions of divers refusing to go back down there. Apparently, they had to keep bringing new people in. They're also long dead now so we have no way of corroborating any of this but, as I said, it's served to fuel local folklore even more than usual."

"So is this our focus for the dig?"

"Not really, we'll be on dry land throughout, but you have to admit it will capture the imaginations of a fair few viewers! No, our focus will be on the remains of a Priory, above ground and just along from where the old village had its boundary. We're keen to see what connection, if any, it had with the disaster. The obvious question is why the villagers didn't head there, to higher ground, when the storms came.

There is also a useful modern-day angle. The threat of flooding is still there today; only the settlement and the way man is trying to deal with this have changed. The villagers are trying to get EU funding to help build a more effective flood prevention scheme."

"Haven't the local authority or central government tried to help?"

"Twenty thousand tons of Derbyshire rocks have been deposited and special matting along the foot of the sea wall to replace the clay substrate but it isn't nearly effective enough and won't be a long-term solution."

"It doesn't sound like two weeks are going to be long enough for us either!"

"Quite right. Better warn that husband of yours that we might be making a return visit!"

She replaces the receiver gently and considers her last sentence, and his.

\*\*\*

'I wandered through my playing cards...' Nick hums the familiar tune as he tiptoes down the stairs and out of the house, closing the door behind him on a presumably sleeping Rowena and a wife who must have been in the shower as she wasn't in bed when he awoke.

He and Nora had barely spoken for the rest of the previous evening, though she had tried to broach arrangements for the weekend several times before giving up and going to bed before him. He'd allowed enough time for her to fall asleep before going up himself; it worked on most occasions.

\*\*\*

He now sits in one of the third-floor meeting rooms watching the 'in crowd' chatting inanely and communicating meaningfully through their assorted body languages.

Jim Packer, Executive Creative Director of the UK network, has called a meeting of 'cross-disciplinary teams' where suits and boots can find out about and practice some of the creative processes enjoyed by his own department. Jonathan Massey had suggested this, the previous day, as part of the new sharing mantra for the agency: 'Let silos be pulled down by common assent.'

"Thanks for coming along today," Packer is standing up at the front of the room, wearing a white Armani shirt over light blue, stonewashed jeans that are so tight he is speaking in a voice at least one octave higher than would be expected of his middle-age. The pretty, young creative things lap him up adoringly, and he adores their adoration.

"I thought we'd kick off this session with some mind-mapping techniques, yeah. The purpose of this is to take words and phrases, yeah, that might relate to a client product or a particular campaign idea and then map them out to see what's in our hearts, our minds, our sub-consciousness beings."

The three heads and you're out approach, obviously.

"For example, if we start with the keyword 'pudding,' you might then think plum, yeah, then Christmas, then brandy then matches and so on. Alternatively, yeah, you might have thought dull, then boring, then old then fart…you get my drift." He is addressing Nick now and, of course, the pretty, young creative things love him even more because of it.

Twenty minutes later, Packer is presenting some results from the starting point of 'tree' and comparing approaches in a caring, sharing kind of way.

"Now, Annabel, yeah, has suggested leaves, blowing, wind; Steve has come up with branching, fingers, gnarled, history. Nick Golding, on the other hand, came up with wood, timber, shelves, books. I think that shows our differences rather than our similarities, yeah."

'Have I really come to this?' Nick thinks as he stares out of the window until the laughing has subsided and sees only sky, clouds, no silver linings.

\*\*\*

"How are the hidden persuaders, Nick?" Mike's detestable wife, Belinda, has been prodding and probing since he first took her little black jacket to the tiny cloakroom under the stairs and feigned similar slashing actions with a (sadly hidden) knife.

He likes to think that Mike got Belinda a job as an 'executive officer' in the hospital up in Enfield somewhere because she was useless at everything else. Mike the doctor is alright. True, he used to fancy Nora but that was back in Basingstoke years ago now and he has Belinda now as a constant penance for having done so.

She wears a light-green, cotton jumper over beige linen slacks, reminding him of a chocolate pistachio ice cream he'd once eaten while on holiday with Nora and Rowena somewhere. While standing on the doormat she had declared herself 'quite exhausted.' Presumably administering financial cuts and lengthening waiting lists has made a casualty of her?

He doesn't answer her question so she moves quickly on to her next potential victim.

"Nora isn't a name you hear very often these days is it?" she sniffs.

"Not often, no," Nora replies levelly as per the old-fashioned politeness her old-fashioned name might expect her to display.

"It's an old family name. Nora was also the name of my mother's aunt. She was a bridesmaid to her when she got married and she never forgot the occasion – nor the aunt who asked her to share her big day."

"What a perfectly charming little tale; quite the Jackanora …" Belinda lifts her cruel head very slightly as if to show mercy to the body she has been pecking, expecting some kind of appreciation of her wit.

No sound is to be heard but there is a collective release of breath as Nora replies easily: "She knew the value of charm, not the price of it."

Applauding his wife inwardly, Nick simultaneously betrays her by gazing at Nora's friend, Suky, and her partner, Tristan. He is a journalist with BBC Home Affairs and she is just gorgeous; oh, and a social worker or something. Nora met her at a local history meeting up in Enfield and she is one of her few acquaintances who doesn't live in the past or smell of it. Far from it. She is very much of the present but sadly not of the future.

"Do you write stories in your work or just tell tales?" Belinda haunts the present tense too.

Nick has never considered himself to be especially 'creative' (Jim Packer and his luvvies would heartily agree to that) but hears a quiet version of his voice reply.

"I have to deal with facts and situations as they are. I imagine fiction writers can write things as they'd prefer them to be – they are the authors of them after all. I believe that poets too use writing as a technique to understand everything and everyone around them better but, most importantly, to explore and make sense of their feelings."

"Rupert Brooke's last love letter was printed in the Mail this morning." Nora is either bored with his treatise or assumes that everyone else will be.

"Who was it written to?" Nice Mike is probably just being nice.

"To someone called Cathleen Nesbitt. She was the love of his life."

"Was this just before he died at Gallipoli?" Suky purrs.

"It was, yes. He died just over a month later. What a waste."

"Of love and life," Suky nods and shakes her head at the same time which gives the rather weird impression of somebody head-banging to a heavy metal track.

"The blank page as therapy rather than tyranny?" Tristan has clearly been given a little nudge by his partner. He sports a trendy, silver waistcoat and an open-necked black shirt. The outfit is completed by a flash of red silk around his neck, not unlike the kind of 'neckerchief' worn by cowboys. He has an annoying goatee beard which Nick longs to cut off with a pair of kitchen scissors.

"Our agency is going to be working with charity clients in the future – some of the neediest and deprived in society." He sounds as if he is quite proud of it – and would be if the real reasons for doing so weren't so monstrous.

"But the message is still everything, right?"

There is a stifled giggle from his partner, who is leaning over the table provocatively, the valley between her large, swinging breasts appearing and then disappearing by converging milky flesh, to reach the glass milk jug. As she pours the warm, white liquid into the hot, black mass below, she looks up at him.

"Sorry, I thought he said the 'massage' is everything. I love a good massage don't you?"

"Nick's much too tired for that sort of thing; aren't you darling?"

Nora's voice fills the small room, though she has barely whispered the words.

"Are things hard for you right now?" Suky purrs.

"He's stressed. Too much work as usual." Nora lands her coffee cup into its saucer a bit more loudly than strictly necessary. The warm Rioja is undoubtedly an accessory to the crime.

"I know all about stress," retorts the goddess. "We've got a serious case on at the moment with a young boy. He was admitted to North Middlesex in April and then again last month. Scratches and bruising I'm afraid and it looks pretty bad."

"Not that long to build up a case though," Mike offers an empathetic, professional viewpoint while his unlovely wife is more concerned with the painting (a print of open Lakeland countryside) on the wall opposite her and just above his head. It's possibly similar to one on which she has just spent the wages, saved from some poor nurse's job, and re-invested in 'long-term value.'

"But that's the point." Suky is viewing a far less tranquil picture in her mind's eye. "The case file goes back to last December. An arrest was made at the family home but the police had to let the suspect go because there wasn't enough evidence."

Thick silence fills the room, so much so that a passing night bus outside makes them all jump.

"Nora wants to move out of London, to escape this kind of late-night interruption!" Nick has meant it as a light-hearted comment but she is staring at him, darkly.

She opens a window before sitting back down to face him, and them. "I'd just like to live in the country again, as would Rowena."

"Leafy lanes of Berkshire preferable to the yellow brick road eh Nora?"

Nick wonders if Mike was born sporting an agreeable grey beard. Although Nora has been complaining about transport, pollution and queuing - in shops or when stuck in traffic - for some time now, he wasn't aware that Rowena was similarly frustrated (if indeed she is).

Homely Mike, the doctor in the sensible dark jacket, over a white shirt and nice sky-blue tie, does the ever-so-decent thing and gallantly tries to plug the lengthening gap.

"I have been treating yet another PTSD case this week; that's four in the past fortnight. Some of my colleagues think that it's the anniversary of 7/7 that triggers events such as these. It seems that relatives of 9/11 victims express similar symptoms each autumn. Well, that's what the journals say..."

Nora has been listless throughout the evening and worries that this has been noticed. Nick is too busy staring idly at Suky's breasts to help her with the conversation, to keep it flowing. He delivers answers to questions as he does when they are alone together but the art of conversation, if there is such a thing, is completely lost on him.

As for the lust, she knows it's all in his head and rarely makes it further down. In fact, she always has known this about him but it would be nice if just a little of it was aimed in her direction; just occasionally would be good, adequate, and kind.

Certainly not 'kind,' no. That sounds like something Judy Dench might come out with at a much more glamorous dinner party than this one. If he'd had any other secrets, she'd have found them out long before now; after all, that's what she does, right? That is what her life is all about: uncovering the truth.

The meal has all gone pretty much as planned. The rice was on the edge of being pudding-like but she couldn't help them arriving late. She removes her blue silk cardigan and watches as Nick fails to notice. He might have noticed once upon a time and requested, insisted even, that she wore that and nothing else. But that need; that natural desire, hasn't lasted (in any definition of the word) and she feels more exposed now than she would have done then. At least she feels cooler with the cooking being finally over.

"I'm off on a dig next week."

They all look up politely.

"Is it the History and Mystery project that keeps being advertised on the television?"

Mike, bless him, is trying to be serious despite

being goaded by Tristan (what a dick!).

"And radio and web and social media I expect." Nick didn't need to respond. She didn't want him to respond. This is her moment. Why is his timing always so interruptive; so faulty? Her face is flushed but who cares?

"That's the one, yes. I haven't been up there for some years and looks like it's going to pose quite a challenge?"

"You worked on Seahenge didn't you?" Mike can do this, so why not her husband?

"I was part of the Seahenge team, yes, but Waxling has contemporary as well as historical connotations. I suspect that's why they've chosen it really – to capture a wider audience. The current residents of the village are concerned about sea defences and are trying to raise EC funds to bolster them, whereas the local authorities are trying to remove themselves from the debate.

Back in the Seventeenth Century the defence system also failed and there was a huge inundation: the village was literally swallowed up by the sea."

"How very interesting!" Belinda chooses words to mean what she wants them to mean and isn't so very different to Humpty Dumpty.

"It certainly is," Mike always means what he says, "and it starts on Monday doesn't it?"

"You must come round one evening then," Suky is licking her rouged lips by *Botox* as she simpers in Nick's direction, "I'd love to have you. Keep you fed and warm while Nora's away…"

"Can PTSD happen, just like that?" they all look up, startled but, sod it, she's fed them so they can have few complaints, "I presume the triggers you mention have to be really strong and personal to the individual."

"It depends on how the patient is treated at the time of the accident or whatever bad event has occurred in their lives – and age of course. There are quite different schools of thought on this. Talking about things at the time is part of an old-school way of looking at things. It was felt that by letting it all out as it were…"

Childish smirks from Tristan and Suky. What is the matter with these people?

"… and describing in some detail, almost being interrogated if you will, would enable the healing process to start earlier.

We think now that this could just establish firmer memories in the victim's conscious mind which ironically might increase the likelihood of flashbacks or even nightmares. The brain often takes in seemingly random pieces of information out of context and from years earlier – even if its owner isn't concentrating or even actively listening or reading.

It then tries to make sense of them – a bit like poets I suppose or, more likely, a clean-up program on your PC - and tries to file them away in their proper places. Unfortunately, it often attempts to do this too quickly if the person is already suffering from stress.

Everything heats up and speeds up and

unexpected collisions or connections occur. This is why we so often 'see' people or experience events in our dreams which have at least partially occurred but put together in a funny order or the wrong time or location so that they appear to our semi-conscious minds to be all jumbled up.

All of this could be avoided if we didn't feed the brain with these pieces of information in the first place, especially repetitively through so-called therapy. The victim has to be ready and sometimes a period of 'denial' may subconsciously help them to recover much better and return to long-term health."

"I thought that bottling up stress could do more damage internally?" Belinda again. "Stress responses are natural, aren't they? If you suppress them for too long people have no way of handling future stress. Isn't that what leads people to alcohol or drug addiction – because their natural resistance has been eroded?"

For some administrator at a local hospital, Belinda seems to have plenty to say about patients' conditions, Nora thinks. Or is she just trying to prove that she is every bit as clever as her partner?

"We have to be very careful here," Mike is in diagnostic mode, undeterred and unfettered, "stress is a term that's bandied about all too easily these days, though it isn't a new phenomenon – a new buzzword if you like – far, far from it.

Ancient scrolls revealing soldiers' accounts from Mesopotamia around 1300 BC have been discovered in which they talk about being visited by 'ghosts they faced in battle.' This is very similar to stories coming out of Iraq over the last four years or so. The symptoms are much the same and undoubtedly the cause of them; only the name of the location has changed over the centuries.

Sadness or feelings of unhappiness are often found to be caused by nothing more than imbalances of serotonin or adrenaline being produced out of context to cause panic attacks and feelings of anxiety. 'Time of life,' 'midlife crisis,' you've heard all of these labels by way of often quite incorrect explanations for people's seemingly abnormal behaviour patterns and," he looks accusingly at Nick, "the media hinders far more than it helps here."

After a short pause, for effect or gathering himself for the big finale, she isn't quite sure, he continues. "In truth, medical science can treat or manage the effects of most of these. PTSD is altogether more serious though. It isn't just about mood swings; it's a condition which can, in its most extreme form and especially in cases of warfare, lead people to even kill without remembering what they've done."

She drops her coffee cup into the saucer. It fractures and brown spots appear on her white cotton blouse. Her knee-jerk reaction is to stand and Mike does so too, the gentleman that she has always known he is.

"So clumsy of me, please do continue, lucky I'd finished…"

As she pats her tummy with her napkin she is aware again of Nick looking at her, following her fingers and catching her eye. A chill sweeps from the back of her neck and down her spine. For the first time today, she doesn't feel insufferably hot. But the chill isn't pleasant. It does not cool her. She finds that she is gripping her chair. Still, Nick stares.

She forces her gaze back to Mike. She had been so looking forward to seeing him again. In truth that was probably the main reason for having a gathering. Fate had done the rest by bringing the subjects and the subject she needed to talk about together.

"You mentioned age; do stress treatments vary a lot for children?" She directs this pointedly at Mike and doesn't even look at his wife.

"It can do. It depends on the nature of the trauma and the family background. Some children will talk to therapists where they absolutely cannot talk with their parents or any other family members. Others will 'talk' in the abstract in a diary perhaps or I suppose, these days, a blog?"

"Nick knows all about blogs and social stuff now, don't you darling?" Nora sits back in her chair which is reassuringly solid and far more reliable.

\*\*\*

Later that evening he enters Rowena's room to say goodnight. He isn't sure if she's asleep or not as her face is turned away from him, towards the window and the darkness beyond. What he can see is that she is cuddling her furry animal's big ears and sweating profusely as a result; her pillow looks damp and crumpled, even in the half-light.

The extra light from the landing seems to unsettle her and she turns suddenly to face him, flinging an arm across her eyes and squinting over the top. When she sees him she seems to grip the toy even more tightly.

"It's alright. Go back to sleep. I didn't mean to wake you."

"OK."

"See you in the morning."

He is aware of her half-open eyes on his back as he steps softly over to her bedroom door and pulls it gently shut. As he does so, she turns back over onto her side, the light no longer dazzling her.

\*\*\*

Holding the receiver at arm's length, he allows his mother to breathlessly fill in every detail of the days and weeks that have occupied her life since he'd spoken to her last. He isn't at all interested in the new bungalow, the twin beds, or the wet room that will be such a help to them…

"I suppose you'll be following Nora's dig on your computer?"

Like Prindle Massey's U.S. evangelists, his mother seems to think that everyone uses computers for everything these days - or maybe it is just an old person's fear of the new.

"If I follow any of it, I'll be doing so on the radio," he hears the sharpness in the tone of his voice and knows it is aimed as much at his transatlantic colleagues as her. He finishes on a softer note, "Nobody uses a computer to do that."

# THURSDAY 7TH JUNE 2007

He takes in the South London landscape of dilapidated factory buildings and run-down tower blocks with mostly rusting balcony railings.

Nick is visiting the 'Battersea Union' – a loose collective of volunteers who are trying to make a difference to lives in their community while their feet are kept firmly concreted to the ground. This is the first piece of Prindle Massey's social outreach in the UK but feels as foreign to him in both purpose and perception as being south of the river always does.

Being more than half an hour early, he looks for a café where he can at least grab a cup of tea or coffee while he waits. He soon spots a dark maroon door with tiny 'Café' lettering on it in once-white paint that is now peeling off, as is much of the coating on the scratched and badly warped wooden frame. Why am I here, he thinks, despairingly.

It is warm and light inside, in sharp contrast to the gloom beyond the door and in his head. He approaches a tall, wiry man in a dirty green shirt and stained jeans who appears to be eyeing him up as an intruder rather than a potential customer.

"A mug of tea please."

"Here?"

"I'm sorry!"

"You want drink in here?"

"Oh. Yes. I see. Yes, please. Is that OK?"

"Very OK. Yes," The man beams a smile as unexpected as Nick's request had seemingly been. Perhaps he had just assumed that he was lost, or had merely popped in to check the time of day.

"You sit," he continues, "I bring over."

A few minutes later Nick is pouring sugar into a pint mug of steaming tea, watched carefully by his admiring host who is clearly not going to leave until he has tasted the goods being offered to him. He sips it slowly and, though there is a strange, crusty film along the ridge of the mug, the tea is strong and full of English breakfast flavour.

"It's great. Thanks."

"I pleased you like" beams the Masterchef of the tea-making department if not the sink which, even now, Nick can see is piled up with filthy crockery at an unlikely angle that only Tracey Emin would be truly proud of.

Shaking his hand warmly as Nick leaves, the proprietor of 'Café' wishes him a pleasant day and a speedy return. Nick assumes this means back for another cup of tea and smirks over the idea of a 'Café' loyalty card, given the tiny footfall. Then again, why should Nero hold all the cards and hold the rest of the coffee world to ransom?

He receives a text from Bannister as he steps out onto the street, narrowly avoiding a convoy of prams pushed by large West Indian women, chatting and laughing loudly as they juggle an assortment of shopping bags and small children whose hands they never let go of.

'Finish plebs off quickly and get back here. Blackout issues.'

"Welcome to the Battersea Union!" a small black man, also West Indian, of maybe forty or fifty, dressed in a tatty grey jumper on the point of unravelling, crumpled blue jeans and sporting a woolly hat knitted in an explosion of greens and yellows, lets Nick into what is a tiny rectangular space with a window at either end. It is like a small church hall and yet as secular as the wooden table with a red Formica top that practically fills it, aided and abetted by the six plastic chairs that have it surrounded.

Nick's feet stick to the grey lino in places as he holds out his hand first to a younger white man, thickset and burly with cropped hair and a cropped 'Motorhead' t-shirt, who introduces himself as 'Gaz.'

He then leans across the table, making sure his jacket doesn't knock over the assorted paper cups to shake hands with a rounded, white middle-aged woman in an orange, flowery dress and vastly over-stitched white silk blouse who follows her damp handshake with a fairly intense and unsmiling announcement that all her friends called her 'Cordial.'

"Thanks so much for coming all this way. We had a call from a Mr Timmy ..."

Timothy Goddard-Price is the new business manager at Prindle Massey who prides himself in always talking in the vernacular of his prospects. Unfortunately, this often comes across as some patronising, posh git trying to impersonate the peasants - probably for a prank or a serious bet. Equally, unfortunately, he is Marmaduke's nephew and so his words speak much louder than his actions.

"We didn't understand a lot of what he was saying," the West Indian man (called Lima? Limar? Lemmy?) is keen to get on with the items on his agenda, "but he kept repeating that you could help us to raise awareness of the needs of the people in this community. There are many people here who go unnoticed and many who don't."

Nick tries to ignore Gaz's cold stare (as Marmaduke would say: 'Broadcasting the fact that you are awake doesn't mean to say that you are engaged') but wants to include Cordial, so he moves his chair back deliberately so that both are in his eye line.

"It's a privilege to be asked to join you today. Perhaps it would help if you could first tell me a little more about the work of the Battersea Union and why you think you need help."

"Why haven't you done your homework?" Gaz hasn't blinked or moved any other muscle.

"Perhaps he did and the dog ate it eh?" The West Indian man's teeth are a perfect set and gleam a bright white.

"Ha ha. No. No. We did have a briefing before I came and…"

"Perhaps it was too brief?" Cordial's cheeks wobble as she shrieks with laughter.

The West Indian man nods and smiles, pointing a long but friendly finger in her direction as if to say, 'Nice one, Cordial, we ain't' takin' no shit from this ponce.' Or is this how Timmy would have assumed he would speak?

Nick continues quickly. "As I understand it the Union was set up to bring people together to try and improve their situations. Too many jobs have been lost, thanks mainly to the Labour government and certainly through no fault of the people here; and yet there remains a real spirit of enterprise with lots of projects being set up that people on the ground don't even know about?"

"Sounds like a party political broadcast by the Tory Party!" Those brilliant, white teeth again.

"There are parents of children here," Cordial has her intensely serious face back on, "who work hard outside of the Borough and see how others are doing so much better: the net result is that they then move away for better lives. That's the crux of the problem. They want better starts for their kids than they had and everyone here can totally understand that.

But not everybody has the means to move away. Those people who remain behind often feel trapped and yet that isn't the case at all. There is no cage here that needs to be escaped from. It only becomes a prison at the point when you can no longer see any light."

He senses that Cordial is at a verbal crossroads and isn't sure whether she will now take the route marked social worker cliché (though, after meeting Suky last night, his stereotypical view of what that means has been blown away) or go the other way towards female folk icon - Baez of Battersea, the voice of a generation. But he never gets to find out as Gaz steps forward onto the spartan stage.

"Socially, politically and economically, people feel as if the larger society has let them down. Their collective spirit of enterprise goes unrewarded in their own backyards and yet it has not been extinguished. Through work, people find not only the means to sustain their families and their communities but also develop social skills and an awareness that Battersea could be Lambeth - despite the millions of pounds that haven't been poured into it to prevent riots or buy votes - or even Richmond. Why not?

This isn't about giving us handouts or wringing our hands together and bemoaning the lack of jobs. We have jobs, we have small enterprises and together we can join hands and cause a new chain of events that will make people think about moving in rather than moving out.

We don't need the Labour Party to tell us what we think. We can do that for ourselves. Connecting people through social media - being able to comment and encourage each other - does not require political or economic subservience. Those days are gone and we wish to be up and about with the new dawn."

Before Nick can even begin to regroup in the face of such conviction, the door opens and, astonishingly, the man from 'Café' enters the room. He wonders momentarily if this is some kind of farce, a setup from Bannister to see how he would handle the situation: a role play to try out the execution of the brave new Prindle Massey corporate strategy.

In truth, he is also still reeling from Gaz's measured and articulate assessment of the client situation that no flashy Prindle Massey document could ever have hoped to have competed with. Perhaps 'Café' do the catering here, he considers, gasping for breath. Yes, that has to be it.

"Good morning Martin." Gaz stands up to warmly hug and shake the newcomer's hand which, Nick notices for the first time, is red raw. The caterer smiles and nods in Nick's direction as he sits down at the table.

"Morning rush over now!" he half-whispers.

"Take Martin here," Gaz is glaring at Nick once more, his lecture far from over, "He has lived here for two years. He came over from Poland in search of the better life the EU told his government it would enjoy. Unfortunately, they didn't tell them that it probably wouldn't be in Warsaw.

The free movement across borders for skilled people was largely one-way. That is what is happening in Battersea and yet it needn't be like that. Martin and his lovely wife opened up a café here and business was booming. Unfortunately…"

At this point, he places his smaller hand on top of Martin's much larger one.

"Unfortunately Christina died as a result of complications..."

"She had an ectopic pregnancy and it was diagnosed much too late..." Cordial steps in quietly, but effectively, into the breach while Nick perceives a dampness around Martin's friendly eyes.

"...and Martin had to carry on alone while trying to complete his PhD. He now has a skin condition which Cordial thinks is stress-related..."

"I was a junior consultant at Guy's," she matter-of-factly offers this without any sense of grandeur or Bannister-like desire to dominate the conversation.

Gaz has still more to tell: "The condition flares up in hot water so we all take it in turns to help with his washing up. Martin didn't need to ask for our help and certainly didn't have to pay for it. We're all friends here and we share it around – what needs to be done and how we do it.

Now, there is an Asian guy down the street whose plumbing apprenticeship has been cancelled because his company got into a cash flow crisis. Why? Because its bank had encouraged it to borrow too much money too quickly and has now decided it is too much of a risk after all.

Anyway, Zan has managed to get hold of the parts he needs to build a dishwasher. He's been constructing it in his front room for about three months now and it's nearly finished. We'll all help to install it and then we can re-decorate the café. Hopefully, that will make a real difference and help to get Martin's life back on track again.

And how did we discover Zan? Through the Battersea Union website that Michael over here built in his bedroom. It's like one of the old bulletin boards if you will. Our challenge is to build on this achievement; to broadcast its effectiveness and breed our own success, not to expect and certainly not to ask for it to be parachuted in and just as quickly jettisoned."

\*\*\*

She finds him so easy to talk to; always has. He listens and responds as though he has been concentrating on what she has been pouring out of her heart. It is such a nice change after sound bites and witty asides.

She is lying on the sofa beneath the bay window at the front of the house, the sun pouring in from the furthest right of the three large panes of glass which faces almost exactly south.

"You see my problem though, with it being so close to home?"

"I do and it's impossible to know how he would react if he found out. We have to be very careful as it might throw him right over the edge rather than bringing him back from the brink if you understand my meaning?"

"I do. I do!" Is that purring she hears in her tone of voice? Well, why not; she gets little enough cream at home.

"You don't believe he would be capable of it though, do you? I mean, what we talked about at Seahenge? It happened so long ago. Surely he would have reacted in some way by now if he had the slightest inkling …"

"That's one of the great mysteries though isn't it!"

\*\*\*

James has remained standing by the 'hanging table' (or 'poser table' to the disaffected drinkers who drank there when it was still a traditional pub with certainly spit if not sawdust on the floor). A tall, broad man, his shiny grey *Boss* suit confirms him as every bit the thrusting financial salesman, though his aggressive appearance is tempered somewhat by a natural mass of copper-coloured hair and a face which freckles love to make their summer holiday homes in.

"So, how's the land of death by numbers?" Nick always starts off the game with his 'Best Man' by moving this, or a similar pawn, two spaces forward.

James sees off the hand-crafted harp in the froth of his Guinness and mops his forehead elaborately with a cream handkerchief.

"Very, very busy. You?"

"Yanks want us to use the Facebook and other new 'channels' like Twitter. It's a whole year old now so they've decided that it's 'come of age.'"

"These things are just for the kids aren't they?"

"That's what we thought but apparently we need to be down with them to know what's really going on."

"How's Nora?"

"She's fine; just seems to be permanently worried about Rowena for some reason."

"When do the summer holidays start?"

"Not yet! It's half-term next week."

"Have you planned anything?"

"What for next week or the summer?"

"Either I suppose. Rowena must be looking forward to a holiday away somewhere. At least it will give her somewhere different to transport that mobile library of hers to!"

"Well she hasn't mentioned anything; not to me, anyway."

"How's she doing at school?"

"Well. Very well."

"You mean you haven't any idea."

"No. Really. We had a report just before Easter. Numeracy's coming on and obviously, Literacy is no problem. In fact, they're more concerned that her imagination runs away with her sometimes; want her to reign it in a bit."

"Typical educationalists who can't see beyond league tables themselves. So, if you're not worried about Rowena, why is Nora? You are looking after her I hope?"

"Of course I am." Is he? The open honesty of that morning's event hits him, as it has done regularly since leaving Battersea.

"I met some very kind people this morning."

"You're not developing a conscience, are you? Not sure if I could cope without the cynical, uncaring you ... but, back to Nora, maybe she needs a break too?"

"She hasn't mentioned that to me but, as luck would have it, she's got a new assignment. She's off to Norfolk next week to take part in that History and Mystery thing."

"Not with John Whatsisname?"

"Squires by name, two divorces behind him and a seemingly endless supply of maidens still to ruin. Everyone wants to get into the media these days and he's happy to get into their knickers by way of expert help."

"Now we're getting to it! You're the one with the problem: her being away and spending time with a complete tosser?"

"I have felt a bit unsettled about it since Nora told me she was going up there and I don't know why exactly." There, he's admitted it.

"Do you remember when Nora and Lucy came to stay with us in Exeter for the first time?"

Nick nods sagely, glad of the opportunity to escape into the past.

"I'd never met your sister before or Nora, obviously."

The two of them had arrived by train from Sheffield just before the Christmas of his second year

(James's third). Four of them were living in a tiny house just off Victoria Street which meant that if Lucy slept on a mattress in James's room, the only place where Nora would be able to sleep would be on the floor of Nick's room.

"You two never stopped talking: about anything and everything, only interrupted and then extended by trips to The Waterfront."

"The pub at the bottom of our road? Would have put this place to shame – it didn't even try to fake glamour."

"We'd have been thrown out for wearing clean shoes! The point I'm trying to make is that although it was warm and cosy, you too wouldn't have even noticed if it was freezing. All you wanted to do was sit as close as possible to each other and talk. It's often the simple things, isn't it? If there had been something on Nora's mind in those days she would have told you, wouldn't she? What's changed?"

Nick doesn't speak. He cannot, does not know how to respond

"Anyway, it won't be for long will it?" James cuts short his reverie

"What won't?"

"Nora. Your wife! Leaving for the coast…"

"Seahenge took six weeks - off and on - but no, this is only supposed to last a fortnight."

"And let's be honest: Seahenge was a big deal. This little excavation won't be nearly as interesting to the heavy rock people, will it?"

# FRIDAY 8TH JUNE 2007

"Mothers' Union liked you." Bannister doesn't even look up from his empty desk.

"I assume you mean the Battersea Union?"

"Whatever! Isn't that the vernacular these days? They want you to go back and meet others in the team - sorry, union. Looks like this might work and, hopefully, the God squad and sandals brigades are going to be a bit more down to earth than our usual clients."

Needing to get away from Bannister – at least metaphorically – Nick is soon searching for Waxling on his office PC again. He quickly recognizes a number of the previous search results.

Snuffles the rabbit was involved in a near-fatal accident with a vacuum cleaner but lived to tell the tale or rather listen to the mind-numbing yarn that Amy has shared with the world here about school 'friends' ignoring her. He can't help but shake his head and smile at the line 'I often wonder if there will ever be any point to my life.'

He then finds a much more purposeful sign-off on the BBC site:

"So please tune in this coming Monday, the 11th of June, at seven o'clock for the first of two programmes from Waxling in North Norfolk to launch our 'History and Mystery' fortnight. My name's John Squires and I've got a feeling that this will be our most interesting dig yet."

Nick has a quite different feeling and promptly logs out.

\*\*\*

"Granny is really looking forward to seeing you. She says you'll be a big help with the packing."

"Will Harry be there?"

"I'm not sure. He might be."

"Doesn't he have a house of his own?"

"He does but he's trying to sell it and has been staying with Granny until he finds somewhere new to live."

"So he'll have to find somewhere soon, now that they're moving into that little flat."

"Yes, he will."

"What happens if he can't sell his house? Where will he go?"

"I'm sure he'll find somewhere. He's been a good friend to Granny. She wouldn't just put him out on the street."

"Is Grandad friends with him too?"

"Of course." She remembers what Beryl told her

all those years ago when they first met. She's been thinking about that conversation a lot lately and she too wonders where Harry will go.

"Is Grandad still poorly?"

"I don't think he's any worse than when we went last time..."

"Will he ever get better?"

"He might cough quite a bit but you have to remember that Grandad's quite old now and..."

"Has he got cancer?"

Such a stark word in a sick world should have no place in this snug bedroom, she considers; not where a giant Pocahontas poster covers most of the wall and assorted furry animals are sitting in a half-circle, in readiness for the tea and cakes her daughter plans to serve them from plastic cups and plates.

"Yes, darling; in his tummy. So we need to help Granny with Grandad and try and make him as comfortable as possible. We need to make the most of our time with him."

"Because he's going to die soon?"

At least she hadn't asked when Pocahontas would be starting her periods!

"We all have to die, Rowena. Just make sure you live and love life to the full because you never know when something bad might happen!"

They have skirted around the subject for weeks. She had hoped that Nick would explain all of this to her;

David is his father after all.

"I read about cancer on my laptop. Has Granny got a laptop?"

Nora's neck is feeling warm. It must be the late afternoon sun, still quite high in the sky.

"I don't think so darling."

"Wikipedia has lots of pages about it. There would be a big gap on Wikipedia if they managed to cure cancer wouldn't there?"

"I suppose there would be but lots of other subjects would come along to fill it, I'm sure. Besides, it would be worth it if Grandad got better wouldn't it?"

"But he'll die of old age soon anyway; you just said so."

Thank goodness she deals in historical facts where there is little chance of having her words twisted around. "Are you looking forward to the big school?" It sounds like a pretty straightforward question to her.

"You mean High School! Nobody calls it big school anymore. I'm not a baby, Mummy!"

She pulls her daughter close, loving the familiar smell of her slightly blotchy skin. How smooth it used to be. Even Nick would spend long hours stroking her legs as a baby.

"I'm sorry. Mummy must be getting old too."

A sudden look of panic clouds Rowena's face. "You're not old! You're going to live for years, aren't you?"

She can feel the spasms in her hands as Rowena begins to shake and pulls her even closer, tighter.

"I certainly intend to, darling" she whispers, "I can't miss out on seeing you grow up to become a beautiful woman can I?"

"Perhaps it's sometimes better if we do die early then?" Rowena's voice is sad now, resigned.

"Why ever do you say that?"

"Because then we won't grow up and realize it was all just a dream after all."

"What was?"

"Being a princess. I'll always be ugly – it's true what they all say."

"Who does? Rowena, who says these things?"

"I think it's time for tea; my friends will be getting thirsty." She gets up from the floor abruptly and begins to place cups in front of the toys.

\*\*\*

The front door stands between him and the sounds of riotous laughter beyond. He crosses the boundary to find Nora and Rowena on the stairs. They appear to have collapsed beneath the local furniture salesroom's closing-down supply of pillows and sheets and are laughing so much that neither of them can move.

"Hello, Daddy. We've had a bit of an accident!"

They wait, Rowena a little warily he thinks, for his reaction.

"So I see! I thought you'd be taking sleeping bags?"

Nora picks herself up and begins to gather up the linen trail that leads back to the upstairs bathroom.

"We've been having a bit of fun, that's all. Rowena will be sleeping in the spare bedroom and we're all going to be staying in either the local pub or a Youth Hostel so if I end up in the Hostel I thought these would be better than those sheet sleeping bags they insist on. It's so hot at the moment we'll probably be naked on top anyway."

"Of course, you will," he replies grimly, more out of tiredness than a default to sarcasm.

"I'll do this; you go and finish your packing," Nora, still with her back to Nick, waves Rowena away, "don't forget to pack your diary."

Rowena looks tentatively over her shoulder, reluctant to leave her mother, but Nick has already passed into the kitchen and is filling the kettle.

"I thought we'd get a Chinese tonight?"

So she is trying to avoid a confrontation. Nick considers that sweet and sour is better than just sour and goes with the flow.

"That sounds good. Shall I go and get it?"

"Let's finish our packing first - we're nearly done."

"OK. Coffee?"

"Sounds good too," she edges slightly closer to him.

"I'll be able to email and 'phone you lots," she

senses his unease at being alone. "I'm taking my PC to make notes on. I thought I might try and work up an independent article of my own afterwards, as well as contributing to the BBC material. Sounds like a fascinating project. Anyway, I still have quite a lot to sort out before tomorrow."

"Tomorrow?"

"Never knows?"

# PAST

# SATURDAY 9TH JUNE 2007

"Madeleine's father, Gerry McCann, went on to say 'The emotional time has been in private. We will never give up the search for our daughter.'

Meanwhile, just ahead of his audience with the Pope, Tony Blair has talked about his plans to become a Catholic deacon..."

He snaps the radio off. They have almost made it to Ely without any kind of argument. Rowena has dozed in the back seat for most of the journey and Nora, sitting beside him, may just as well have done for all the conversation she is clearly reserving for her chums on Monday.

Negotiating the ridiculously tight bend from the M11 onto the A14, they head for the A10 turning and are soon north of Cambridge amid the vast flat landscape of its surrounding Fens. Lush, green fields of neatly planted potatoes, wheat and lettuce run away to the horizon with only occasional patches of dark black soil providing space to pause and think.

In his rear-view mirror, he can see that Rowena is stirring. Though ten years old now, she still looks so tiny, so vulnerable and so lonely in the silence that has engulfed the car.

"I bet Granny will be pleased to see us again," Nora seems relieved to be nearing their destination, "I should think she'll be surprised by how much you've grown, darling."

"When was the last time we came here?"

"It must be nearly two years ago…"

The silence hangs in the car as when a CD has offered up its final track but has not yet faced the humiliation of ejection.

"We should see Ely Cathedral in a few minutes," Nick vaguely remembers that his daughter is interested in these ancient relics, though Heaven alone knows why. "We drive very near but you can see it long before then."

"Can you see the sea from the top?"

"I'm not sure but it's a bit like Boston Stump - these tall buildings dominate the area because of the flatness of the Fens."

"Daddy, where is that windmill, we climbed to the very top of - just you and me?"

Nick shivers inwardly and quite unexpectedly. It is warm and stuffy in the car and yet he feels gripped by a coldness whose source he cannot even begin to fathom.

"You know! The one at the top of that hill where you could look back over the village and you pointed out the steam engine in the distance."

He is struggling now, especially with the bit about the steam engine. He always avoids railway memorabilia if he possibly can.

"Could that be it, over there?" Nora has been scanning the horizon and now the faintest of windmill sales appear on the huge white canvas that is the vast, largely featureless sky.

It is the windmill at Haddenham. He recalls it now; but not as a bad memory. There had been an open day and his parents had suggested that Rowena might like to climb up inside a 'real windmill.' There was something else too ... what was it? Something about the top floor?"

"And I remember a black cat that was sleeping in the sunshine, outside on the balcony. You wouldn't let me go out there so I called the cat and it came inside and let me stroke it, and then it followed us all the way down to the bottom again."

That was it. She'd asked for a kitten. That phase has thankfully long since passed. The steam engine she referred to must have been the tall chimney of the old Stretham Engine House over to the east and slightly behind them now. That was a favourite childhood haunt but now it just haunts him.

Nora is keen to keep the conversation going. "You're going to be a big help to Granny, aren't you Rowena? She says you've already arranged to go shopping in the market on Tuesday and feed the ducks afterwards..."

"Did you ask Granny if Harry is going to be

there?"

"He's gone to stay with some friends, I think."

"Juliette Green is going away this week."

"Where is she going?" Again, Nora manages to listen actively even as he is moving the invisible tuning dial to try to find something more interesting to listen to.

"She didn't have time to tell me. We were the first ones into the classroom but then the others arrived, and she didn't want them to know."

"Why ever not?"

It is Rowena's turn to be quiet now. Nora looks across at him but he stares resolutely ahead.

Eventually, Rowena continues to talk, but not about Juliette. "Why does Harry live with Granny?"

"I told you!" Nora is less calm than before. "He is Granny and Grandad's lodger. He has Daddy's old room and pays them money each week to stay there. Granny uses that to buy food and things."

Nick doesn't want to think about Harry; doesn't want to talk about Harry. He doesn't like Harry much and knows that this is – quite irrationally – because his father gets on so well with him despite his legendary and sickening homophobia.

He tries to end the interrogation. "He was in the next hospital bed in Cambridge when Grandad was taken poorly. That's how they first got to know him. He's known for some time that he'd have to move out again one day. He's only really known Grandad as a sick man and must have expected him to get steadily worse."

"Because of the cancer."

"Yes, because of the cancer."

His parents currently live in the far corner of a 'Sixties housing estate and he draws up outside their bungalow, noting the corners of greying net curtains being drawn slightly to one side as he does so.

"Please try not to cause an argument in the first five minutes," Nora whispers her request to him as Rowena collects up her things from the back, before opening the car door and slamming it behind her and in front of them both.

\*\*\*

"She goes out every Saturday morning; thought you'd have known that." David Golding, dressed in a clean, blue-checked shirt over dark trousers with their original flares and held up by ancient brown braces, is pouring tea with the consistency of treacle into three substantial, plain white mugs.

His still-large frame fills the sparse kitchen. As he turns to reach up for the sugar dish he starts to cough. It is like a rattle at first but he is soon bent double, barely able to catch his breath for several minutes.

Rowena looks on in undisguised alarm, clutching her yellow beaker of orange juice. His face grows intermittently red and then a deep shade of purple with the effort of coughing. As Nora pats him methodically on the back, Nick makes his way into the tiny 'front room' which faces the open fields to the rear.

He sits on the worn but comfy sofa by the window, being careful to avoid his father's scuffed leather armchair that dominates what space there is. Rowena soon joins him and sits next to him.

"Some coffee morning or something. Don't know why she bothers at all," his father shuffles in to join them, "never did me any good - all those tree-huggers and whatnot." He sits down heavily and takes his mug from the tray Nora had found by the side of the fridge. He watches her hand Nick his cup then turns to face his granddaughter.

"So, what have you been up to?"

Suddenly shy, Rowena simply replies, "Nothing much, really."

Nick is already irritated by his father's tone and knows full well that he will barely listen to anything she tells him anyway.

Nora comes to her daughter's aid. "You've been using the computer at school, haven't you, darling? You'll have to show Grandad your laptop and the exercises you've been doing. And your drawing - I'm sure you'll both be pleased you brought your colours with you…"

Rowena nods to her mother, gratefully. David Golding shakes his head, as he always does when he isn't convinced about something and coughs his response which is lost in a cascade of phlegm and spray.

"There's lots of packing to do and I'm not a lot of

use."

Nick flinches at the memory of his father always managing to remind Nick that his efforts in school or outside of it were of little consequence to anybody in the real world, least of all his parents.

"She's brought out the wrong glasses case again," he bellows to no one in particular. "How difficult can it be? Blue for reading; black for telly."

"Rowena, can you run into Grandad's room and fetch the blue glasses case please?"

Rowena is happy to obey her mother but returns after substantially more than the thirty seconds it should have taken her, not that Father seems to have noticed.

Nick does notice, though, that her face is slightly flushed and wonders what treasures she has found to poke about in, especially as much of the bungalow is upside down and decorated with piles of junk in transit from one set of drawers to another.

"Who is the little girl in the picture next door?" she eventually asks, as though their lack of questioning has expunged any guilt she felt at touching things she knows she really shouldn't have.

"What girl?" Father snarls, just as Mother comes through the back door and touches Nora lightly on the back by way of welcome.

"About the same age as me but with blonde hair. She's eating an ice cream."

"No idea, I'm afraid." In truth, Nick hasn't

ventured into his parents' bedroom for years and has absolutely no desire to do so now."

"Yes, you do!" Mother jumps in quickly. "That picture's been there for years. It's Denise from next door. You used to play with her: Aunt Cis and Uncle Fred's little girl – not that we were actually related to them. Denise was always at our back door. Surely you remember her?"

Despite Nora willing him to join in the conversation and staring at him again as she did at the recent dinner party, he remains quiet and still.

"Do they still live next door?" Rowena has been back to fetch the picture and he notices how old the frame is; practically coming to pieces in her small hands. She too is examining the picture as a detective might, looking for any visual clues that might tell her more about the subject. "It says 'July 1967' in tiny white letters in the bottom corner."

"They moved to Canada years ago. We don't hear much from them these days."

"I don't think I've seen this one before," Nora is looking over Rowena's shoulder, "I think you'd better give it back to Granny now."

She dutifully hands it over and, gazing at the picture herself, Mother takes it quietly back to the bedroom.

"We don't hear anything from anyone, anymore." Father has decided it is time for him to switch the conversation to a topic he is more interested in, as usual. "Least of all you!"

Mother senses a storm approaching, as they all do; the dark clouds which have followed them from London finally catching up with them, it seems.

"Shall I make some more tea? Rowena, would you like to help me?"

Father grunts his assent, half-turning in her direction as if to honour her with his attention if no more obvious sense of appreciation.

"So you're off to Cromer are you?"

"A bit further round," Nora remains calm and friendly despite the brutal tone of the Inquisition.

Not that it matters as her reply is drowned out by a new bout of coughing.

"What does that mean?"

"She's going to a place called Waxling." Nick recognises the familiar screaming inside his head.

His father stops coughing suddenly, wipes his mouth with his grey-brown handkerchief and then holds it to his face so that his eyes are just visible above it.

"You're not going with her are you?" His cold stare instantly pierces all of the defences Nick may have thought he had constructed over the long years. They are the first words his father has uttered to him beyond the nod and awkward handshake when they arrived.

"No, I have to work. There have been a lot of changes lately."

"What sort of changes?" Father immediately

snaps his false teeth onto this nugget. You're not going to be made redundant, are you? The worst thing that can happen to a man, that is."

Nick chooses his words carefully and keeps up the pretence of a son wanting to tell his father all about his life. "We're going to be working much more with people in need."

"So you're nothing more than a charity now?" is his gruff response.

"Not exactly; we're going to be helping charities and…"

"I can't believe it's come to this; not with all that education. Charity! Should begin at home. Went to Age Concern last week she did - same people as organised that 'creative writing' course for her. Complete waste of time that all was. Anyhow, she walked up there to see if they'd help us with the library books. Told her there was nothing they could do and we'd have to wait for the mobile like everyone else. Charity: Another word for do-gooders who didn't do so well if you ask me. Useless."

\*\*\*

Nora is glad to be out of the house, or at least to have put some distance between Nick and some of the old arguments that would certainly linger at his old home forever.

On the very first occasion of her visiting Nick's parents, David had told her proudly that his father had worked at the Elgood brewery in Wisbech for nearly fifty years. It had only been 'nearly' though as they had sacked him just before his anniversary on some minor detail. David had always assumed it was deliberate to avoid 'forking out for a watch.'

Nick had told her that his grandfather had been far more prosaic about it, and lamented not making it to the Golden Anniversary of his marriage rather more. His wife had died in a car crash near the Mildenhall airbase when they had been married for just the forty-eight years. Nora had never met him and Nick had never really spoken about it but, again, David had swiftly converted this tragic event into a lifelong hatred of 'Yanks.'

She watches her mother-in-law and granddaughter feeding the ducks. Each seems as excited to be there as the other and she notices that they cuddle a lot, holding on to each other for longer than either of them needs to.

"Your mother seems to be bearing up well. I thought she'd be much more tired than she is."

Nick takes a long gulp of beer. The sun is high in the sky and hot now, all mist from the morning journey long gone.

"They never needed me, either of them. What I had to offer was never enough."

"Don't you think you owe it to your mother to…"

"To what? What exactly do I owe my mother? Continue to pretend that I can't smell it on her breath when she's supposed to have been out at some coffee morning?"

"I didn't smell anything. Perhaps you're

imagining it. I mean you've never actually seen her drunk, have you? Last time we were up here you insisted on opening every cupboard door and looking under every bed but you didn't find any bottles did you?"

"You can tell by her face. It's ravaged."

"That could be caused by any number of sad events. It can't have been easy living with your father all these years for one thing."

"Her nose has that drinker's red tinge."

"And you don't think that has anything at all to do with the Fen winds that blast over here directly from the North Sea most of the time?"

"Look. It wasn't my idea for us to drag Rowena up here or for you to leave her here with them for a week, while you go to the seaside. How are you going to explain their behaviour to her?"

"Rowena knows about the cancer and that Beryl is suffering too."

"Not a great advertisement for married life, is it?"

"She's quite used to that!" She lifts her leg over the wooden bench they are sharing outside The Cutter Inn and walks over to the other members of her family.

"Mummy, look at the big brown one - he just won't share…"

"I think we'll have to come back in the week with more bread - I'll save some up."

His mother has said it to Nora but is hoping to include Nick in a discussion that is never going to happen. Dressed in an old pink mac (despite the glorious summer's day) and black slacks, the purple streaks in her straggly hair glint in the sunshine.

She sways a little and almost loses her balance but Nora grabs her arm and walks her back to the bench with Rowena running after them, a concerned look on her small face.

"Are you alright Granny?"

"I'm fine, little one. I'm fine." She sinks down with a thud. Granny's just getting old that's all."

He sees how much thinner she has become, with cheekbones protruding out of a face that is rapidly beginning to sink inwards.

"This is a nice spot." Nora can be relied upon to choose the right words whenever he chooses not to speak at all.

"I thought Rowena would like it. The only other pub I know well is the Minster Inn. Nick's father used to go in there on the way back from the station sometimes. It's right by the cathedral. I believe it's one of the oldest in the city and has its own ghost..."

Nora watches as Rowena's eyes shine and Nick's cloud over.

"A Benedictine monk with a fondness for ale, so they say."

"Coo. Really?"

"Several people have sighted him down the years, little one, and they can't all have been wrong!"

"Oh please." Nick protests, sarcastically. "Stop filling her head with rubbish. Rowena, if you include nonsense like this in your history project I can absolutely guarantee that Mr Lerner will want an explanation."

Nora, though, has already slipped back into the past. "Many Benedictine communities had to leave their monasteries during the Reformation and go abroad..."

"We've been studying that in history, Mummy. Henry got fed up with his first wife but the Pope refused to let him divorce her so he set up the Church of England which isn't so bothered about that kind of thing."

Mother chortles behind them and Nora bites her lip before continuing. "That's right although I think the Church of England is still very keen on marriage. Anyway, it wasn't until the Nineteenth Century really that Benedictine monks came back to this country and settled here again. I did some work at Selby Abbey in Yorkshire, just before you were born. That was one of the places they came back to."

"Because they felt safe again."

"Yes. They felt safe and wouldn't be persecuted for any reason other than history."

"So history should be forgotten if it makes people do bad things."

"History should never be forgotten, Rowena," Mother has interrupted and is suddenly quite animated, "because if you don't know what happened to people you can't ever forgive them."

\*\*\*

Mother has asked him several times since arriving if he'd clear some items out of the loft for them. So, later that afternoon, he finds himself under the eaves of his parents' loft, trying to avoid the dusty, cobwebbed areas and preserve his temper as much as his crisp, hitherto clean jeans.

Father has fallen asleep as usual and Rowena is doing a jigsaw, helped or hindered by Nora and Mother he isn't sure which. He can just make out the songs on the radio which he has left switched on in the kitchen (as he would have done at home), their lilting sounds the only connections with his immediate past.

He can feel the heat below the roof felt: sunshine trying to find a way in and sweat and steam from below trying to find a way out. Lunchtime smells linger, mixing with the damp almost acrid smell of inevitable decay.

To be fair, there isn't much up there to clear. He isn't sure why Mother is making such a fuss about it, but if it wasn't this it would no doubt be something else. The last time he'd put his head up here was when Nora had insisted on him looking for his old story books which Rowena might like to read.

It has taken much longer for her to get round to reading them, but not because he hadn't been able to find them (most of the battered cardboard boxes were fairly clearly marked), more that they haven't visited for months, and the old pages remain piled up neatly in the spare bedroom: waiting in 'departures' with all the other leavers.

Just two cardboard boxes remain, purporting to hold his 'school books' but a pile of what appears to be old newspapers are wedged behind the central heating tank: presumably one of his father's long-ago attempts at lagging the pipes better.

They are preventing him from dragging the first box towards him and he has to prise them out, accidentally tearing the first page with a loud ripping sound. He eases them over his shoulder, the smell of old news lingering for a few seconds, and pulls at the dog-eared carton.

Sure enough, the tatty books – just larger than A5 in size - are soon spread around his feet. Yellow, red and blue are the predominant colours but there are also a few creased pictures on rough grey paper which suggest these date from his primary school days.

He skims through Spelling, Geography, History and Arithmetic until he gets to English. This contains a selection of poems from the teacher, copied down from the board in Nick's neatest writing of the time which makes them marginally more understandable than the 'working out' in their Maths' cousins. Over there his erratic workings seem to just confirm which pieces of his brain weren't working at all at that time.

He cannot picture anything at all about St Anthony's yet the faded name and gold school crest on the books confirm his days of attendance there.

He picks up another 'English' book and starts to read a story, entitled 'My Saturday' by Nicholas Golding, aged eight, and quickly realizes that, unlike the poems, this is an original. The story starts like this:

'My Saturday starts in bed when I read my Thunderbirds Annual before I go to the kitchen and eat boiled eggs and soldiers for breakfast. The soldiers are not real. The soldiers are made of brown bread from the shop. I like the crusty ones best. After breakfast, I go to the train station to meet my Daddy. He works there but stops at dinner time. We look out for trains we have not seen before.

Each train has a number on the front which is called a Head Code. It tells you where it's going. My Daddy has a book that has all the addresses in it. Next week My Daddy is taking me to Peterborough to see the Flying Scotsman. It is the most famous train in the world. It is going from London to Scotland. Scotland is a long way away. So is Peterborough - but not as far as Scotland. I love my Daddy and I love my Saturdays."

In the half-light from the single, dirty naked bulb on the other side of the loft he can just make out a faded star at the foot, a large tick and the words 'Very good effort' - probably in a yellow or light orange ink.

He flicks through the pages and back again to the front of the book which has 'May 1967 -' written on the inner cover. There are no further stories beyond this one, just faint lines and what looks like a pink line forming a left-hand margin.

He leans over and pulls the other, smaller cardboard box over. Part of the side comes away in his hand to reveal an old blue blanket and little bedside light in the shape of a small, brown horse. White flex trails behind it which he pulls gently, soon realising that something is holding it down in the bottom of the box.

With a final tug, he pulls out an old yellow teddy bear which lands with a thud on the floor, sending up a cloud of dust. It has only one ear and the other is covered with what looks like an ancient cobweb. When he holds it up to the light bulb though, he sees that it is a frayed red ribbon which hangs down Teddy's back, invitingly, as if to say, 'pull me and I'll tell you my story.'

# SUNDAY 10TH JUNE 2007

She is woken early by low voices in the toilet on the other side of their wall, though she can't make out what is being said.

His whisper is much louder. "Can't you get to sleep?"

"No," she tries hard not to ascribe any blame to her response."Is it your Dad on the loo do you think?"

"Could be, although he usually likes to make a real fuss – crashing and banging about - just to let everyone know that he's up: it's one of his oldest charms."

They have barely spoken since. Now they are both up and dressed.

She doesn't want to leave Rowena here but she reassures herself that she's only going to be a couple of hours up the road. Besides, Rowena will enjoy the company here and vice versa - at least where Beryl is concerned - and they are unlikely to visit this bungalow again. She thinks that Nick will miss it, and them, one day.

\*\*\*

It is late afternoon when he finally gets home. His

eyes are tired when he finally makes it into the house and all he wants to do is to lie down and sleep. After dozing on the settee for a good half an hour he becomes aware of a flashing red light. He watches it for a few seconds and, in his reverie, imagines that its signal is becoming more urgent the longer he leaves it.

Impatiently, he marches over to the answerphone and clicks on messages that can no longer be kept waiting: voices from the past, all of them.

"Where are you? It's Saturday 9$^{th}$ at nine o'clock. Ring me." Bannister can turn on the charm but only if strictly necessary.

"Hi. It's me. Got here OK and met up with everyone. It's a beautiful day and the beach is really busy. I can see Happisburgh lighthouse from my hostel window. Amazing to think that it was built as long ago as 1791. I might not be quite so enthusiastic if the beam keeps me awake tonight though. Don't forget to 'phone Rowena later."

Good to hear that history quickly became her long-lost best friend as soon as he was out of her sight he thinks, resignedly.

"Hello there. This is a message for Nora. Constance here, Nora. Sunday morning, 10$^{th}$ of June. Unsure of your departure time. Phoning to remind you that 'Hymns of Hope' is live from Waxling church this evening. We're having tea and biscuits afterwards in the Vestry.

We've done a few pieces to VT for the programme and thought it would be a good opportunity to meet members of the community. Hope you can make it. Start time: Eighteen-Thirty Hours. Probably best to be here by Eighteen-Hundred. Have a good journey up. See you later.

So, that's Connie Breeve. Don't have a mobile number I'm afraid. Well, do have a mobile but haven't got it with me. Think I buried it when we were finishing up in Ayrshire last week. Didn't want to phone it for fear of waking the dead. Ha ha. That's it. Bye"

Nick grimaces. What does his wife see in these people? He has met Connie Breeve once before. In her mid-fifties and bedecked in tweeds and facial warts she'd marched up to him and introduced herself to him as Constance Breeve: Senior Archaeologist.

He hadn't been sure if the 'senior' referred to her age or experience but she'd had the capacity to dominate him and everything around her like a grand but crumbling manor house looks down on its lodge keepers' cottages.

He thinks about returning Bannister's call but determines that calling him a day later is almost worse than not phoning him back at all, so he rejects the notion.

\*\*\*

*Even my bad arm didn't stop me. Not today. I kept climbing the dunes, up and up, even though the sand was a bit hot on my feet. The seagulls flew over me as if they were showing me the way to the very top. They looked white against the blue sky - like Apollo space rockets. Then I turned and ran down as fast as I could. Once, I nearly fell* head over heels, but I didn't. Daddy always seemed to know the exact spot to stand. He caught me in his arms every time and swung me around. I clung on to his neck and closed my eyes. I knew he wouldn't drop me. He'd never do that.

\*\*\*

Opening windows to allow in fumes and noise from passing traffic, he walks from the kitchen to the main room and back again, then into the dining room that has miraculously become Nora's study once more. It is unlikely to be used as a dining room again for months now. Last Wednesday had been the first such event they'd hosted for months. He would have preferred years.

As he reflects on the horrific Belinda and (for much longer) the delicious Suky, he notices a strand of red material on the floor below one of the dining chairs. Quickly recognizing it as the red silk worn by the ridiculous Tristan, he bends down and places it on the windowsill behind him.

There are a few books in the single bookcase underneath the window: paperbacks mostly and purple-edged Ordnance survey maps. He brushes his hand over them - presumably to subconsciously assure himself that he is not as far away from her as he knows he actually is.

One of the maps juts out slightly further than the others and he accidentally dislodges it causing it to fall onto the parquet floor with a crash. He retrieves it quickly and is carefully putting it back in exactly the spot it has sprung from when he notices a thin volume of red leather, wedged in at the back. It must have been pushed back too hard and was the cause of the map's subsequent edginess.

He takes the book out and holds it up to the late afternoon light, still flooding through the window, and reads 'Verses from the East: Volume Five' by Jane Standing. He has never heard of the author or come across any of her previous volumes; not that he really knows any poets apart from maybe Tennyson or Shelley.

He assumes that this is a collection of mystical 'discoveries' or perceptions of a previously ordinary life that some drug-induced traveller to India has made in 'finding themselves.' Why Nora would want to read them or keep this particular edition, only she would know. He flicks the book open to find an inscription in bold, blue handwriting:

'To Nick. I hope that these words will help to complete your family. All my love. Nora. Christmas 1998.'

The words 'Christmas' and '1998' stop him like spring-loaded buffers. So this is his book, not hers, and given to him as a Christmas present two years after Rowena was born! Why is it tucked away behind her stuff then?

He flicks through the volume, pausing on a random page and reads:

**'Inside Pain'**

Some say that pain is like clouded window glass;

Indefinite, but watchful all the same.

Bad breath and hot air combine to form the curse

Which starts and ends each sentence with my name.

It builds, grows angry with every broken day

(Old, familiar fingers grasp my nape)

Until it enters, finally to betray –

Bruising proving my failure to escape.'

Certainly not meant for children then and not exactly uplifting for Christmas either! He turns to the back inner sleeve to read about the author, but this reveals little other than the fact that Jane Standing lived and worked in East Anglia and that this was her fifth volume of poetry to be published.

He sits down hard on Nora's chair and tries to remember back to that Christmas but what memories he has of that time blur into endless screaming from a potentially atheist Rowena, spurred on no doubt by teeth trying to make their own breakthroughs.

Unlike the late Rupert Brooke, he has never really seen the point of poetry. He assumes that Nora must have 'rescued' it at some point and stored it among her possessions.

He returns to the kitchen, sits down at the table and powers up the laptop. He trawls through his email box for any messages of interest and quite quickly spots one from Rowena which she had sent earlier that afternoon:

'Miss you, Daddy. Please stay in touch. Look after yourself.'

One other subject headline stands out:

'Nobody defended me'

It is from the Abbots Home blog he subscribed to when researching websites in Norfolk the previous Tuesday. The story continues:

'Rich that they want to build flood defences now. It's more than ten years since the sea swallowed my house and much more that night. Nobody cared then so why now? I don't hear those waves so close in the mornings but I know they're there. They are always there. All I can see from my kitchen window now is the comings and goings at the old mill. Bet that kitchen could tell a few stories from the hearth.'

Nick chuckles inwardly at the futility of such posts. To write for writing's sake is quite beyond him.

"Eternal Father, strong to save,

Whose arm hath bound the restless wave,

Who bidd'st the mighty ocean deep

Its own appointed limits keep;

Oh, hear us when we cry to Thee,

For those in peril on the sea!..."


Elderly gentlemen with red faces and ladies in flowery summer dresses are singing their hearts out, studiously ignoring the roving cameras while earnestly hoping to be noticed.

"...our family shield in danger's hour;

**From rock and tempest, fire and foe...**

\*\*\*

"...as far back as the fourteenth century we know that the Commission of Walls and Ditches for the Sea Coast of Norfolk was set up and suggested the repairs necessary to deal with this kind of coastal flooding..."

Nick cannot remember turning on the television, though does remember thinking that there might be some Sunday cricket on. He vaguely recognizes the tall man with obviously dyed hair, probably mid-forties and with what romance novels might call 'chiselled good looks.'

"...and Henry II set up a lay subsidy where every villager contributed to that effort but, between the mid-fourteenth and late sixteenth centuries, the storms appear to have decreased and the levy was barely charged..."

He recognizes that voice too, but it isn't the man speaking. Its owner comes into the shot, a weathered face above a tweed two-piece suit. It is the same Constance Breeve who had left the message for Nora that morning and, of course, the 'chap' is John (Dear Johnnie) Squires, formerly of the RAF and now seeking his own brand of glory from the skies. This must be 'Hymns of Hope' then?

"...but in 1609 - just two years after the tragedy here and because of increased incidents elsewhere - the Sea Breach Commissioners were set up by

Parliament to restore flood defences and keep them in order. Again, though, there was a lot of variation in how much was actually done and when. Inundations were frequent and unpredictable. In places like Waxling, even after those terrible storms, the locals would have been unimpressed by the apparent lack of resources being made available…"

Thankfully they have cut away to a hymn and shots of the church before Johnnie re-appears, like a veritable vision of the Devil himself.

"So, Connie, as a result of what happened here, this is very much a new church?"

"It is. But we do have the remains of the nearby abbey and one of the key questions for us will be whether it died out after the Dissolution of the Monasteries in the sixteenth century or whether, in beating the waves that swallowed the original village, it also managed to repel the King?"

Nick turns them off, fearing for his survival should they be allowed to live.

# MONDAY 11TH JUNE 2007

"...we're just around the coast from there in the sleepy fishing village of Sea Palling..."

As Nick gradually regains consciousness he manages to pinpoint the digital radio alarm clock from where John Squires is still talking.

"...and we're live on BBC2 as well.

Once a major lifeboat station it was closed in 1940 when a major reorganisation occurred, but you can still see pictures of the old row boats that were used by these saviours of the sea.

Many graves in the churchyard of St Margaret's just behind me are a testament to the devastation experienced on this remote part of the Norfolk coast and, in fact, the bench I'm sitting on is inscribed 'In memory of those villagers drowned in the flood of 31 January 1953.' This was the last serious flood to be witnessed in this area.

Check out our breakfast briefing later for more on this and other threats to this bleak yet beautiful part of Britain from the coast down to the Norfolk Broads."

Nick checks out.

\*\*\*

*It was pouring with rain by the time we got back to the station, and we ran to the waiting room for shelter as the bus back wasn't due for at least an hour. It was nice in there by the fire. I watched the blue and green shadows forming in the flames and then disappearing again. Daddy said they didn't light fires anymore so I suppose railway passengers today must get very cold if they have to wait for long. The engines don't have smoke either. I liked the train journey but the windmill by the sea was the best bit. A pity it didn't have any sails though.*

\*\*\*

He reaches the Bannister floor to find it more chaotic than usual with talk of 'crisis' and 'putting out fires' everywhere.

Bannister is dressed in a lovely, yellow shirt by *Moi* and grey silk trousers he had last worn at the Christmas party. He hands Nick a white card with a picture of a finger on one side and basic contact details of a George Savory on the other.

"George works for DIGit. According to Hank, the group has owned them for six years but nobody here knew. George really knows his stuff on digital, it seems.

Nick makes a mental note to email George and ask if he can track down who the madman writing the blog in North Norfolk under the pseudonym of Abbots_Home really is.

In the meantime, he says, "I think it would be

valuable for me to go up to Waxling on the Norfolk coast. There is a real possibility of serious flooding from the sea and it could provide us with a good return on the ... social pound? They're almost certainly going to need as much coverage as they can get."

"I thought you said the tide was coming in? How much coverage do some people need?"

"I just think it would be worth my exploring. A group there is planning to lobby the EC."

Bannister looks up then, the smirk long gone from his tanned face, "EC as in European Community rather than Eastern Cabbages I presume?"

"Brussels not cabbages."

"Incredible as it sounds, you may be on to something here. Yes, I can see that it might be very useful for us and for them, obviously. Go tomorrow."

"Tomorrow?"

"No time like the present and today will already be the past by then. Go tomorrow and report back soonest."

Nick leaves him to his Christmas cracker wit and despotic style so vital to social media. Maybe he will visit Waxling tomorrow; perhaps take flowers for Nora or would she hate that? Perhaps she has other things on her mind, as he usually does?

***

"Just a background piece to kick us off; you know: we're all at risk of drowning despite our valiant attempts to harness the sea's power, geological changes etc and go easy on the wind farm. A lot of the locals are complaining that Scroby Sands spoils the view, regardless of it providing electricity for thirty thousand homes. I ask you!"

She cradles her empty glass as he directs Connie. He always seems to know what he wants and what he doesn't want. There is no ambiguity, no room for doubt.

"We have to tread a narrow path here because de Criel has got them all wound up about the flood defences. It's great fodder for the masses but we mustn't lose track of the fact that we're here to do our history show. All of us want to be re-commissioned next year, I'm sure."

"All of us?" she asks softly enough to be inquisitive without demanding; resting her case without the need to open it.

"Well, love, that's really up to you isn't it?"

\*\*\*

Nick throws a 'Best of the Best' lasagne into the microwave and, seven minutes later, loads the contents into a pasta bowl, pours himself a glass of red from the Merlot box, and settles down in front of the TV.

"What am I doing?" he ponders, out loud. He thumps the buttons on the zapper as his tongue quickly finds a piece of tomato that is more Margate than Mediterranean. He hadn't intended to watch any of the History and Mystery series that Nora has so carefully programmed in advance but finds himself quite unable to just scroll past the listings.

"Welcome to History and Mystery and two weeks of regular, live updates on BBC2 and Radio 4. You can catch us online, on digital and 92.5 to 96.1 FM.

We're broadcasting to you from Waxling on the North Norfolk Coast and I'm joined by someone who will need no introduction to millions of you: Connie Breeve. Connie, welcome to Norfolk. It's an area you know fairly well, isn't it?

"Thank you, John. Yes, I worked on the Seahenge project eight years ago, which was just around the coast from here."

"This coastline is especially notorious for storms and wrecks. Why is that?"

"Well, for a start, the extensive sandbanks around here have caused many issues with ships running aground. A second reason why this coast suffers is that so much of the rock constituting the North Norfolk cliffs is boulder clay, dumped during the last Ice Age, oh, about ten thousand years ago. It's much more susceptible to the sea and so dramatic events have occurred here throughout history.

Not that it's all bad – there's a chalk reef further around at Cromer which is over twenty miles long (the longest in Europe I think) and gives Cromer crabs their very distinctive taste.

But I digress. The third reason and probably the most devastating one of all is Waxling's geographical position. If you think of this part of the coast as being at the smallest point of a giant funnel where the Atlantic Ocean, posing as the North Sea, sweeps down past Scandinavia towards Holland on the right-hand side and the eastern coastlines of the British Isles on the left, I think that it helps to explain a bit the battering that it receives.

The 'weather window' closes, if you like, with the beginning of autumn and, over the next six months, the North Sea becomes wild and largely unpredictable. Finally, a lethal combination of low air pressure and high tides - as happened in 1953 for example - makes for an immensely strong current below huge waves, sometimes fifteen feet high or more. It's rather like a giant roller coaster only you can't get off the ride, it can't be switched off when it gets too dangerous..."

"And it's no fun!"

"Quite. On those occasions, things can get really tricky."

"And that's what we're here to investigate, of course, the incursion in 1607 and the eighty deaths as a result. But there were plenty of floods and inundations here before that weren't there?"

"Yes, one example being way back in 1287 when Hickling Broad was inundated by a tremendous storm and nearly two hundred people lost their lives. There was a priory there and only two canons survived - by sheltering just under the vaulted roof..."

"Which leads me nicely to the subject of our dig here. To my right, are the remains of an ancient priory which would have stood on higher ground in the early seventeenth century than the rest of Waxling: why didn't the villagers head up there - to higher ground - to escape the hungry waves? And why do we start with no documentary evidence of what went on here?

**Join me at lunchtime when we'll be meeting a local spokesperson, St John de Criel, whose family has lived here since the Norman Conquest. I'm sure he'll have many tales to tell us as we start to attempt to unravel the mystery behind the drowned village of Waxling. Bye for now."**

\*\*\*

He hasn't heard from Nora that evening and supposes they are all 'in conference' at their hostel or the local hostelry. He really ought to let her know his plans for tomorrow or, at the very least, Rowena, so that she will know where he is.

# TUESDAY 12TH JUNE 2007

It's nearly the eighteenth of July! Can't believe I'm going to be eleven. Mum and I went to Wagg's this morning to buy macaroons and an egg custard for Daddy. We passed the beach shop and they're still in there. Wonder if I'll get one for my birthday.

\*\*\*

He hasn't made any calls; neither has he received any. He had gone to bed early but he wasn't alone for long. A throbbing headache had crept in with him and two Paracetamols soon followed from Nora's bedside cabinet.

\*\*\*

'A Whiter Shade of Pale' is definitely my favourite song. I think a little bit of me will always be here. And it's still number one! They're saying it might stay there for the rest of the summer. I'm not sure where they mean exactly but there must be a place called 'the charts.' I expect it's in the sea somewhere because Mrs Rogers brought a chart into school last term and showed us where the Titanic sank. The men on Radio Luxemburg say 'groovy' a lot. I couldn't find the word in my new Collins Pocket Dictionary so I asked what it meant. Mum just said it was because they were missing gravy and meat and vegetables because they lived on a ship. I suppose that's why I can sometimes hear them well but then they get quieter and quieter. Maybe they feel faint? Dad said I'd be better listening to the Home Service, so I'll have to keep hiding the transistor under the pillow. I'm convinced they can hear it in the next room though because I can hear them talking in really loud voices in the middle of the night. Why don't they just come and ask me to turn it down if they can't hear themselves speaking? I think the song will always remind me of today and this beach somehow. I tried to remember the words this morning when it was all misty. If I do get it, I'll be able to play it every day. I'll have to ask Mum if you can still buy songs from shops if they're not number one anymore.

\*\*\*

The radio welcomes him to a brand new day of agency strife - where a problem shared is an individual shafted – but the honeycombed voice of John Squires quickly reminds him that he isn't going into the office today.

"England was in a state of transition. James I had been on the throne for four years but suspicion was everywhere. True, the reign of Bloody Mary was two generations past, though stories of the burnings of Protestant heretics would have been passed down in parlours and taverns up and down the land; so, in that sense, they were very much a living part of people's perceptions of their neighbours.

Of course, the Gunpowder Plot, two years earlier, had re-focused the eyes of the people on the religious divide that was never very far below the surface. Thanks to Guy Fawkes, any citizen could now be required to take an Oath of Allegiance which effectively required them to deny the Pope's authority over the King.

If Catholics could live with their consciences by signing this oath, then they would in all probability survive and perhaps even do rather well during James's reign. But that didn't stop sceptical Protestants from believing that the Roman Mass was being heard in secret locations and a fear that plots were being hatched in quiet corners of every parish - nowhere more so than in priories such as the one we have here in Waxling.

The Augustinian Order was in terminal decline after Henry's Reformation, but it must have been viewed as a potential hotbed of religious fanaticism in a similar way that some might view mosques in England today.

Perhaps history gives us our first clue, then, as to why this wouldn't have been seen by ordinary people as a natural, safe haven in times of flood."

\*\*\*

*Mrs Click Clack told us the 'Miller's Tale' last night. I don't think she really wanted to; not just before bedtime. Said it would give us nightmares. But Daddy was still out and Mum was having a bath so the coast was clear. Sounds funny doesn't it? I mean we're here on the coast. Eventually, she gave in to our pleading and sat us down in front of the electric fire. It was really warm during the day but the wind had got up with the tide. That's what her husband said. It was the first time I'd heard him speak. I* held my mug of hot milk tightly as she began his story that she said had been passed on, like passing the parcel I suppose, for over three hundred and fifty years. I made some notes in my notebook and wrote them up as soon as the sun came through the window this morning. I was too tired last night. I just wanted to pull the sheets over my head and go to sleep. This is what the Miller said: "The winter gales had raged around the coast for days but on that terrible night in the year of our Lord, 1607, under the full moon, they were worse than ever. 'I'd been awoken by the whining noise, low at first but then much higher - like the Devil himself laughing at us all. Being on higher ground I could see the waters rising and then coming in over the harbour wall. Boats that had been tied up there, a few minutes earlier, just disappeared from view. I saw people running from all over the village – bent in double against the wind - towards the old church, then Mistress Elizabeth herself, hurrying down the hill, her skirts quickly becoming wet and heavy in the fast-moving waters. Not John de Criel though. I'd seen him leave much earlier, once darkness had provided him with cover. Heading west he was, as was his usual custom. The waters were rising fast now, deep and ugly, and people were having to wade and then swim when they couldn't remain upright. I had taken shelter up in the cap and already the footings of my mill were under water. I couldn't have helped even if I wanted to. I had no boat you see - had never had need of a boat. Bits of wood, from roofs blown off of houses, were just floating by with articles of clothing and I could see in the moonlight that some were still attached to bodies. Still, the wind kept howling. Then I heard the sound of bells from the church: the call to safety that had been used in these parts since the church was first built - afore even the Frenchies arrived. Solemn it was, *calling people to a safe place in the face of an almost invisible enemy. But it wasn't safe. To my mind it never was. Over eighty people flocked to the church and the last I saw of any of them was when Mistress Elizabeth appeared between those old battlements of the clock tower, her beautiful golden hair flying out behind her in the wind. Shouting and waving her arms she was but I couldn't hear a word she was saying; nobody could have done, only the wind. Then, as if in slow motion, the tower began to move. I couldn't believe my old eyes. But move it did, swaying from side to side until the top part fell over backwards and into the sea, taking everyone with it and removing the only escape route they thought they could rely on. The thing I remember most was how quietly it all happened; not just on account of the noise of the gales and those huge waves crashing over the village, swallowing it whole, but as though I was witnessing the impossible: the only person still alive. But then I did hear them, screams and wailings from out of the darkness, but all around was the sea. Even the big old Manor House lost its front but at least the rest still stood. And when de Criel returned in the early light of morning, just under a week later, it wasn't his own house he stood next to for what seemed like hours - it was the remains of the old church where whole families had perished in his absence."* Mrs Click Clack told us that Elizabeth wasn't originally from around here but had known tragedy in her life before; she was a devout Christian and that's why she had thought the church would be the safest place for everyone to shelter in. Sometimes, she whispered, when the gales are moaning and there is a full moon in the sky, you can see her - the White Lady - way out to sea. She is still shaking her pale fists at the night, trying to save the villagers, but the Devil has cut out her tongue.

*Other people say she has gone over to the Devil's side, in revenge for her husband not being there to help them, and sinks ships, swallowing everyone on board as a dreadful punishment of the living.*

\*\*\*

Nick spots the steel-coloured sea through breaks in the trees as the train flirts with the Suffolk coastline before heading north towards Norwich and the ridiculously tall church towers and spires that appear to grow out of the fertile soil and compete with each other to get closest to the dark clouds above.

As they slow down to readjust to the pace of life offered by Norfolk's capital city, the Norwich City football ground passes him by on his left-hand side, its floodlights proudly blazing in the sunshine, presumably for the club's directors to proactively waste club funds before their manager does?

\*\*\*

*I can't believe we still had to go to church today. I thought we were on holiday from all that. The church was one of those creepy old places with a huge spire. Nobody could ever climb up there to see out of the pointy windows, so what was the point? The floor was made of cold stones and everyone's shoes echoed so that nobody could enter without everyone else knowing about it. They all turned round to stare at us when we got there; they probably thought - 'we don't recognise these people so they must be on holiday; if so, why are they in here instead of outside on the beach, enjoying the sunshine?' Some of the stones had words on - or at least did until everyone's shoes rubbed them out. Mum explained that they were gravestones and that people had been buried underneath them - just like outside, only the stones were lying down like the people they were covering up. I hate the idea of walking on dead bodies. I kept expecting the door in the side wall to open and all of them passing through it slowly and silently to join us in service.*

\*\*\*

"Well let's hope so. We don't want a repeat of yesterday's mess. Overnights are good though: praise the Lord or whoever manages these things …"

She is sitting on the bedside chair in his small room up in the eaves. Reading the evening paper, he remains lying on the bed; unmade but who cares? Clothes are strewn all over the floor; a boot sits forlornly by the door, seeking its partner.

He flips his mobile shut at last. "Sorry about that, babe. The good news is that they've tracked de Criel down and he's on his way back up here but we don't know when we'll get any air time with him."

"Where has he been?"

"London, supposedly. They've been lobbying the local MP who's only really interested in his summer holiday to Tuscany."

"How will we fill in for his lordship?"

"Oh, there are lots of items we can run. A piece up at the priory maybe? We have the divers on standby for the underwater sequence taking in the old church tower so there's lots we can do. Just a case of moving the script around a bit. I'd like to do a piece with you if you'd be up for it?"

Her heart is thundering in her chest, sure to expose her further. "To camera you mean?" She responds far more weakly.

"Why not? It would be good to put this into other marine contexts: Seahenge for one. Are you using your maiden name, as usual?"

"My 'professional name' you mean? Yes, I'm Nora Wright while I'm here."

He beams back. "The real issue we have is that de Criel sees us as the one big chance to make his case. We've rather fallen into his lap as it were."

Without even looking, she can feel his gaze on her, taking in her legs and slowly heading upwards. A damp smell fills the room.

"Maybe it's not a bad thing. Allows us to establish ourselves before involving the local bigwig. Gets the viewers interested in the past, you know, before he yanks them back into the present."

He shifts along the bed until he is practically alongside her. "Look at this as a treat. You don't get treated often enough it seems to me."

She feels his hand on hers, covering it, stroking it gently. "I thought we might pop along to Sheringham later in the week. Perhaps even grab us a sixty-nine?"

"I think you mean a ninety-nine?" she withdraws her hand but not so quickly as to alarm him.

"Perhaps I did?" he smiles and picks up his mobile

once more.

\*\*\*

Norwich station is modern and shiny, unlike a herd of bemused locals in multi-coloured anoraks (you can never trust the English weather in June) who seem bewildered by the Wymondham train leaving from a different platform from the one it has 'always' left from.

He buys a grande latte, pronounced 'grandy' by the toothy cafe attendant who could have walked straight out of a Wallace and Gromit cartoon, and studies the departure screens. Eventually, the Cromer train is announced and he duly takes a seat by the window and, more importantly, under an open window.

A discarded copy of the Norwich Chronicle lies on the seat next to his, folded open at the TV listing page. Turning it over, he sees a headline above an eighth of a page piece in the lower right-hand corner: 'East Anglian Poet – success in volumes' and reads on, casually.

The article makes a reasonably clever play of a local poet who has just released her latest volume of poetry which has won the prestigious international 'Lavender' prize. The intriguing part is that over the last decade, nobody seems to have found out very much about her as she prefers (and, incredibly, has largely succeeded) to remain anonymous, 'like a recluse from the storm' as is quoted from one of her verses.

A further extract from one of her favourite pieces is reproduced at the foot of the article:

**'A light tunnel to despair**

The light sweeps away the darkness; our room

Afloat on old, uncompromising waves.

They've visited before – out of the gloom –

Heard, then seen, salty ghosts from unmarked graves...'

Pretentious claptrap thinks Nick and doesn't bother to read to the end of the column (as Marmaduke would say: 'Discerning readers aim high so never mind the sheep that go into the fold').

He suddenly hears shouting from outside. A tall, wiry man in his mid-to-late 'twenties is being escorted along the platform by two portly policemen in high-vis jackets. One of them is carrying a dark green rucksack – presumably belonging to the prisoner who looks Middle-Eastern in appearance.

"Folk are jumpy these days" a voice nearby states with some degree of sage-like certainty.

He turns to see that an elderly man in a thick black jacket and flat cap has sat down on the seat beside him, despite there being practically an entire carriage of empty seats to choose from. He has large, wild eyes that seem quite unable to remain still.

"Ey a bin here afore bor?" he shouts, eagerly.

"Never by train."

"Ah. Course this be the Bittern Lane. Runs up to Cromer Pier and sometimes on to Sheringham on the far side."

Sheringham is a name he knows, though he has

no idea why. He checks the Wikipedia entry on his mobile 'phone and discovers it was the first place on the British mainland to be bombed by a German Zeppelin during the First World War. Perhaps that's the reason.

"I'm only going as far as North Walsham, then getting a taxi."

"Course there used to be a second station at North Walsham, bor."

Course there did.

"North Walsham Town it were and trains ran in them days from Melton Constable via Aylsham to the west and over to Yarmouth in the other direction. Stopped at Potter Heigham that way them did. Many of us went on day trips in them days, bor. Trains were always packed to burstin'"

Potter Heigham: there is another name that takes Nick away from this modern-day nemesis of Beeching, though that's a connection he somehow also knows that he won't be able to make.

With his travelling companion coughing a cheery goodbye, Nick finds the taxi he has 'phoned ahead for earlier, waiting in the bright sunshine, just outside the tiny station. Huge hanging baskets cling to every available patch of free wall space, conveniently hiding any kind of signage or passenger information.

The burly driver is dressed in the same kind of orange anorak as the Wymondham Rioters back down the line. Nick doesn't see him at first, cleverly disguised as he is by the forest of trailing Geraniums.

"You must be Mr Golding." It is more of a statement than a question, possibly because Nick is the only non-taxi driver or station gardener present.

The driver - either unable or unwilling to speak - eventually finds an unchartered route to escape the North Walsham one-way system and they speed past the almost deserted boat yards at Stalham before turning onto minor roads leading past isolated reddish stone and flint cottages.

Grassy banks forming natural sea defences come into view to Nick's right and the silent white sails of a wind farm way out at sea beyond. More grand, aspiring churches form a loose congregation, observing their journey up towards the coast at Happisburgh.

Nick does his best to focus on the possible meeting ahead, still unsure as to whether this will be a complete waste of a day or not. At least he should get to see his wife.

Google informs him in just 3.44 seconds that St John de Criel is a former coxswain of the lifeboat at Waxling and 'Fundraising Manager' for the North Norfolk RNLI branch. He is the obvious person to approach and have a discussion with over whether Prindle Massey could help him/them to save lives.

Nick figures that, with the TV cameras also present at Waxling, there is every possibility of a short-term gain that will put Prindle Massey firmly on the national, if not international, social marketing map ... and may even do some good.

They pass the lighthouse in Happisburgh, its red

and white hoops partially covered by a banner bearing the words 'Save our Village,' and on into Waxling about two miles further on.

The taxi driver drops him off at what was clearly once a windmill with a few adjacent buildings - tiny houses converted out of the barns' terracotta-coloured stone; others just sheds for old men to hide themselves away in or the things they don't need. One of the houses has a 'Letting Agreed' sign outside.

He shudders in the sunshine as he contemplates a late summer and autumn of Nora trying to persuade him to move out of London to a place like this.

He pays the taxi driver who acknowledges it with a weirdly exaggerated bow and then speeds off. The sky is cloudless and the sea beyond the village reflects the still, endless blue. The odd wave breaks on the surface, revealing a thin white line of spray - like a dangerous animal, still and silent but then suddenly baring its teeth.

He gulps the fresh sea air.

"You wanna be careful of that!"

The voice next to him is tiny and tinny; it could have been voicing a text alert from his mobile 'phone. He looks around but sees nobody, before looking down to find a small but stocky man staring intently back up at him and continuing to intone,

"You could hyperventilate. I've seen folks do it – often. I've seen 'em keel over, so I have. It's too rich you see. We're all rich here 'ent we?"

Nick stares down at the space occupied by the man, half expecting it to be empty now but, no, he is still there. "I'm sorry, I've just had quite a long train journey and..."

"No need to trouble yourself, sir. We're on the edge here true enough. Just like yon' family seat. Stood up and fell over it did."

Though quickly realising that he is witnessing the resulting intellect from generations of isolation – not dissimilar to the sad cases he remembers from the Fens of his youth - he follows the man's gaze to the crumbling remains of an ancient house on the cliff edge.

Great chunks of brown and sandstone-coloured masonry litter the beach immediately below it. Some pieces appear to have been much larger than others but are now covered by the beach and the normal debris of seaweed and shells. He notes also the spiral swirls of old turrets and what looks like the cracked remains of fairly ornate statues. This had once been a substantial residence.

"How are the mighty fallen!" he considers out loud and before he can stop himself.

"That be a fair summary alright! Leslie Pickett at your service."

The man holds out his hand. He could even be a pixie straight out of an Enid Blyton novel, such is the extent of the freckles basking in the sun and his slightly pointed head.

"RNLI. Lived here all my life. I've seen this place –

all of our places - go down in stages. It was always partly ruined of course. North Wing went down in the great storms of 1607: same period that lot up the road have brought all their buckets and spades up here for.

This castle is now well and truly in the sand though, eh! Not that it was ever any more than a Manor House, of course. Would have been the grandest around here for many a mile though! West Wing over there by the lodge house was converted into a library in the 'Sixties. They called it a 'Resources Centre' but that was just a fancy term in my view. Got washed away in the '87 hurricane.

Most of what you can see is the ruin of the old East Wing but it was structurally damaged in the great storms of '53 so he had to move out; lives in the lodge house just over there now. It's small but crammed with all his old stuff, antiques and that. Says he'll go down with his 'ship' eventually and take what remains of his family with it."

"Who is he? The family must have been pretty powerful in its time."

"Still is. This be the de Criel place. Thought you'd have known that; thought everyone knew that!"

"No, it's my first time here. It was actually Mr de Criel I came here to see."

"Well, you might be out of luck then. Mr St John's been down to the big city, although I heard he was supposed to be coming home today. He'll be along to the White Lady if he does. You look as though you could use some shade, not to mention a pick-me-up?"

Nick surveys the cottages that seem to creep away from him down the deserted street towards the whitewashed building with an unmistakable inn sign at right angles to it. As he looks back up the hill to his right he notices that the street appears to stop abruptly and quite unnaturally. Waxling's main street seems to begin or end at a series of black metal railings long before it should.

He bows his head as he enters the tiny pub, in deference to the low beam rather than the brewer - Brancaster Breweries - that he has never heard of. The pub is tiny inside but not as old as he had expected it to be.

A modern bar with a light pine finish and matching stools is empty, apart from an elderly, bald man sitting in a high-backed chair by the fireplace at one end. Despite it being hot and sunny outside, the fire is lit and flames crackle and hiss as they eat their way through huge logs.

A plump, middle-aged woman, with a thinning brown face and dressed in regulation bar room black, eyes him warily from behind the bar. Her eyes are beady and her expression is sour. Satisfied that she is only ever going to provide ice rather than break it, he introduces himself and informs her that he hopes to make contact with St John de Criel, cocking his head subtly in the direction of the man by the fire.

"Oh no sir, that's not St John. Lord love him. That's only Jack. He comes in here to get warm. Says it's the only place he don't feel the cold; well, since he lost his house of course. I expect St John will be along.

Would you like a drink while you're waiting?"

"I'll have a pint of Brancaster Best please." he hears his inner voice come out and say.

"Right you are, sir." The words are the correct ones but there is only correctness: no warmth and definitely no attempt at friendliness.

**"One hundred and forty years ago, twenty-six crew lost their lives on top of the thirteen that were lost the year before."**

He hadn't even seen the TV above the bar when he walked in, yet now it seems to dominate the room.

"Yarmouth and Gorleston Lifeboat!"

The stocky man from the fireplace is standing beside him.

"Bad affair, but not the worst around these parts; not by far. Yarmouth Roads are more unpredictable than any motorway you see."

"Nick Golding" Nick holds out his hand which is grasped firmly by the older man whose hand is burning hot whereas Nick's is just sweating.

"Jack Saunders. You're not from Norfolk."

He wonders what in particular it is that gives him away. Is it the way he is dressed, or the way he drinks his beer?

"No, I've come up from London by train; just for the day. I'm hoping to meet Mr de Criel."

"You'll be enjoying our local ale then? All foreign bilge in London of course. Comes from Brancaster

Staithe along the coast this do. Prime barley country North Norfolk was. Goes back to Roman times.

Nick wonders uncharitably whether all of the local men have taken crash courses in history to front up for the tourists who are bound to turn up in their otherwise forgotten village, now that the TV crews have discovered it.

"Lifeboat business is it?"

"Sort of. I'm from a PR agency in London and want to offer our help to Mr de Criel."

"None finer than St John de Criel. Best coxswain I ever served under, and that includes Henry Blogg for a short time when I first started around the corner in Cromer. Mind you, eight hundred and seventy lives were saved on his watch! Can't see that beaten, can you? Deserved the George Cross right enough."

"How many years did you serve?"

"Fifty-one. Was going to retire after fifty but counting never was my strongest point."

"That's a very long time to put your life on the line."

"Not really. You did it today. Should have driven."

Is this man cutting edge or have all of the sharp tools been taken out of his toolbox? Nick isn't at all sure.

"I did think about coming by car but it would have taken a lot longer." In truth, he had briefly considered stopping off at his parents' house in Ely to break up the journey, but twice in a week was more times than in the previous year.

"Are you still involved with the lifeboats?"

Jack takes an enormous gulp from the glass of beer that has magically appeared via the black hag beyond.

"Ah. I look after their records. Bit of a historian ever since Kennedy. Shook me up good and proper that did. Mr de Criel said it was probably for the best at the time but Lyndon Johnson? Mass murderer if you ask me. More cruel than any sea."

Nick is becoming more certain now that Jack's responses are those of a random madman, fuelled by Brancaster Ale, but he is also aware of the vague yet insistent notes of a melody that is trying to break into his consciousness; rather like the wind that has got up outside and is rattling the windows now, sending smoke from the hissing fire back into the room.

"Tide's changed," he announces, switching seamlessly to shipping forecast mode. "As long as She don't appear we'll be alright though."

"The tide certainly has changed" confirms a deeper and very well-spoken voice from just behind Nick.

Nick turns to face a barrel-chested, red-faced man of medium height, dressed in a sombre grey suit and red, satin cravat. It is as though he has dressed expecting the worst but the cravat offers just a wild chink of optimism.

"St John de Criel," the voice drawls, "how nice to

meet you Mr?"

"Golding. Nick Golding."

The older man gazes at him without speaking, as though expecting more – a middle name perhaps? Then: "Jenny, a pint of Best for Mr Golding here and a chaser for Jack. We'll be in the back room. Send today's specials through would you."

Having expertly dismissed Jack Saunders who all but clicks his heels before leaving them, de Criel takes charge:

"You had a good journey up here I trust?"

"I did, thanks."

"Have you visited this part of the coast before?"

Aware of de Criel's now steely gaze, Nick hides momentarily behind his glass to buy some time if nothing else.

"I don't believe so."

"You believe but you're not sure?"

De Criel waits politely as if to work out whether this is a play on words or, as he would no doubt phrase it: 'jeu de mota.'

Nick continues quickly. "I vaguely remember a church with a very tall spire but I don't know if it was here or not."

"Funny the things that stick out (or up) when we're children, isn't it?" De Criel smiles nicely, as if oblivious to the fact that tall buildings are tall whether the observer is young or old.

"The lighthouse celebrated its bi-centenary a few years ago. There was quite a fuss made I remember. Strange how public buildings become revered posthumously isn't it; a bit like famous writers or composers I suppose? So what would bring a writer like you such a long way?"

Nick quickly fills him in on Prindle Massey's new strategy of social outreach, even as far as the North Norfolk coast. He decides not to mention the link between Nora and History and Mystery.

"My family has lived here for centuries. I learned all about seafaring from my father in his boat: how to read the waves and anticipate tidal changes; navigating by the North Star and, of course, riding out the storms.

Beggars belief doesn't it that money and resources are put in place to defend our island nation against all enemies apart from the oldest enemy of them all: the sea - our greatest threat in Perpetuum?"

It isn't as though those resources haven't visited this region. Norwich itself was once the sixth richest town in England. The great wool churches reflected medieval prosperity, do you see, right round to Yarmouth until the harbour silted up and the Black Death took much of what was left on dry land."

Nick wonders, momentarily, whether de Criel and Saunders are some kind of history double-act. Perhaps there is some kind of North Norfolk Posh Quiz here, every other Thursday?

The sound of an empty glass being placed firmly on the table brings him back to the purpose of their meeting.

"Get another in - there's a good fellow - and I'll commence the briefing."

He is glad of the momentary respite. Even the unsmiling Jenny looks more like a wren than a bat now. He returns to find de Criel with his back to him, pinning what looks like a series of charts and diagrams to the wall.

"Now, see here: how much do you know about this coastline?"

Not another history lecture! He'd spent years at high school trying to spell Boadicea and then discovered that an ancient scribe had already been there. He couldn't even make original spelling mistakes.

"Only a little. Not very much. Please do fill me in."

"Our mission is to see what's right in front of us. Fact is: there's no point in looking for underlying reasons for any of this as the truth is plain to see. We are a leading participant in the joint organising committee that has requested funding from the European Union to build new flood defences from the artificial islands at Sea Palling to the east, right round to Sheringham.

If we do not do this and do it soon, then this area will witness an inundation on a scale not seen since the seventeenth century. We tried to get the Royals interested in it - given the obvious proximity of Sandringham - but the Duke was more interested in shooting birds and the Prince in getting the railway line to Hunstanton working again, in an environmentally friendly way.

We do not wish to see our village suffer the same fate as its predecessor and we need all the help we can get to raise awareness of this potential emergency and in support of our petition."

As de Criel continues his broadcast, Nick is aware of movement in the far corner of the room where Jack Saunders had been perched. He has a restricted view of a studded wooden door which opens slowly and through which a tall figure in a blue crew-neck jumper and light-blue jeans emerges.

With his great shock of lush, dark hair and an elevated nose that could see off de Criel and all of his ancestors, it is unmistakably John Squires. A woman in a white blouse and tight jeans follows. Her face is flushed, possibly by the sudden heat from the fire, as she talks earnestly to Squires' back. As they enter the room though, he can see that she is holding his hand as it trails behind him.

***

Neither Nora nor Squires had seen him and de Criel, he was sure, was none the wiser. He's barely listened to a word since then nor offered many more.

He phoned the taxi company as soon as the meeting had ended; it was going to take half an hour or so to arrive. Nora is nowhere to be seen now and he doesn't feel like tracking her - them – down.

His head throbs as he descends the seemingly endless stairs of a black, wrought-iron staircase before finally jumping onto the concrete sea defence structure.

The grey, featureless wall stretches far away from

him in both directions, offering a flat walking surface without walkers having to get their feet wet or sandy. An elderly couple promenades along it with their panting dog, enjoying the late afternoon sunshine. Other than them there is no one else in sight in either direction for what seems like miles.

The rhythm of the nearby waves does not soothe him. The elderly pair pass him slowly and the man shouts a cheery 'hello' while his wife ignores them both. Perhaps they too are having a secret affair and she wants to play it low-key?

He feels the heat of the late afternoon sea on his neck and the sea spray on his cheeks. He can smell its strange otherworldliness. Occasional seagulls cling to waves, bobbing up and down with the tide, as though anchored there by something below the surface.

More examples of erosion greet him as he progresses along the sea wall. One chunk of masonry looks as though it had started life as a shed before tumbling over the cliff and now lying embedded in the sand at a ridiculous and useless angle.

Reluctantly but strangely drawn from the safety of the sea wall, he slips off his shoes and socks and jumps down onto the beach itself. As he is bending over to examine some old pieces of blackened driftwood he spots two pairs of bare feet, standing right beside him.

He straightens up immediately to see a young woman and presumably her daughter. He is momentarily taken aback, almost embarrassed, as he hasn't heard their approach and, only moments earlier, wrongly assumed he had the beach to himself. They must have run like the wind to get here, he thinks, or been hiding in the dunes somewhere?

The woman is, frankly, stunning. Probably in her early thirties, with fairly short, blond hair, she is dressed in a long, plain white dress with what looks like a more formal collar. It probably had a belt as well, he thinks, as the dress billows out in the onshore breeze, but she's probably taken it off for her walk along the beach.

She simply radiates beauty: a pale, natural purity, as opposed to the unnatural purgatory the young girls in the office often find themselves in on their inevitable paths to the hell of scarred and damaged skin.

The woman's eyes are a striking greeny-blue and the fact that she looks past rather than at him only adds to that primeval male desire to capture her attention. The small girl wears a red swimsuit and has a blonde ponytail – a slightly lighter colour than her mother's - which she wears to one side rather than straight down her back.

"Good afternoon" he ventures.

The girl, probably eight or nine, just stares back, her dull, grey eyes never once leaving his face and saying nothing.

The woman appears to notice her daughter's mute gaze and sees the need to apologize, "she has seen many terrible things that a child should never see, and has been silent ever since."

He feels enchanted by her voice and yet strangely uncomfortable in her presence. He hadn't asked the woman to explain and yet she had felt compelled to do so. Had he been staring back?

"Do you live around here?" he asks, weakly.

"I used to but then I was forced to leave." Her voice is level, almost monotone, without any real variation to it. "But I am unable to prevent myself returning to a place I once loved, as you will understand yourself."

What does she mean and how could she possibly attempt to know what he does and doesn't understand?

"You would do well to leave this place," the woman continues her monologue, "the tide is not yet high and a storm is brewing. The lanterns on the end of the breakwaters over there warn fishermen when they are getting too close. At high tide, the ends of breakwaters could not be seen otherwise.

Seagulls like to perch there. This is their first or last piece of dry land, depending on which direction they were flying from. They can sense when the wind is building beyond the horizon - that none of you can see - and they seek higher ground. How many do you observe on the breakwaters today?"

He turns and, though he sees no obvious sign of heightening waves beyond, it is true that the birds that appeared to be nesting on the ancient lanterns that morning - when he was being lectured by Leslie Pickett - have all fled.

He turns back to face her but she is already halfway down the beach, the young girl an appendage at her side. Neither of them looks back to see if he is still there.

# WEDNESDAY 13TH JUNE 2007

He is sitting in a train carriage but he knows it is much older than the one he travelled home in last night. An engine in full steam chugs past them and Father slides the two halves of the window together so that the huge belches of grey-black steam do not fill their space.

'That only arrived about a month ago' he hears Father announce in a booming voice.

Nick is much smaller than usual – or the carriage has become very big - but he can read the legend below the window panes: 'To prevent draughts, do not open windows beyond arrows.'

His father has always wanted to be an engine driver and never wanted to do anything else, even as his contemporaries moved on to the steady careers that would see them remain in the sidings forever.

Father has taken the exams three times but has unfortunately never passed them all at the same time, so he is and will always be a platform announcer on Ely station.

A small girl is there. She is jumping up and down on the big bench seat which is covered in blue cloth and pointing over to the coast but he can see only the relic of a building on the horizon.

He knows who the girl is but can't remember her name. He asks Father what it is that the girl is so excited about but he just frowns back at him. Father never really takes the time to explain things, especially when struggling with the anger and frustration from within.

\*\*\*

He wakes up with a jump. The vivid scene he has just experienced is quickly replaced by the description of another:

**"Now, I'm very lucky to be joined by someone who is once again working with us here on History and Mystery and was also part of the historic dig a little further around this coast at Seahenge: Nora Wright. Hello, Nora."**

"Hello, John."

Nick sits up and re-arranges the crumpled pillows.

"Thank you. It's good to be back here."

"Seahenge must have been an amazing experience for you?"

"I think, on a professional level, the dig there was equal to anything I'd ever been involved with before - or since. Although the top sand had shifted quite considerably, as Tim said in your intro. piece, we are blessed with a very high peat layer which effectively cushions the effect of the surface weather and keeps artefacts intact for much longer than would otherwise be the case."

"And what was your reaction when you saw the wooden circle for the first time? Weren't there around fifty posts?"

"There were fifty-five oak timber posts encircling a single upturned oak tree which has since been dated to 2050 BC and the other oaks a year later, so we knew that there was a deliberate process at work there. Another timber ring had been discovered about twenty years earlier, half a mile from Seahenge, and we found various other timber posts between the two sites - seemingly arranged in a line - which could have marked out a primitive causeway between them."

Nick gazes at his wife, gazing into the dancing eyes of Squires. He had felt uneasy when Nora had returned from Seahenge and even more so now.

"Fascinating stuff, isn't it Nora? We're almost out of time but just a comment on what you hope to find on this Norfolk beach?"

"I suppose that, as at Seahenge, archaeology is very much about peeling back the layers and understanding what went on before. Very often layers act to preserve the truth but, in doing so, they render it secret.

I think the priory buildings themselves will yield a good deal of knowledge about the village that once existed here and which has been under the sea for some three hundred years. I can't wait!"

"Nor me. Thanks very much, Nora. Nora Wright there and I'm looking forward very much to working

**again with her and, indeed, all of the History and Mystery team as we seek to find out what happened here at Waxling and what lasting effect it has had on innocent people's lives. Join us again later."**

\*\*\*

Thankfully Bannister is out on a 'golf day' which, along with tennis and shooting, occupies the majority of his 'client liaison time.'

Nick 'phones James and finds himself punching the numbers into the handset to finally make the connection.

James listens patiently to Nick's tirade against John Squires (which doesn't, at this stage, include his suspicions about Nora) before responding, evenly:

"History and Mystery is just a vehicle for him to be number one. You know this. It hasn't suddenly changed, any more than the clowns you work with."

"He's just so seedy!"

"And successful at what he does. Can't have been easy after leaving the Forces?"

"Maybe. The thing is I need the job here. Rowena has years of studying ahead yet."

"What does she want to do; you know, does she have any profession in mind?"

"Nothing professional as far as I know."

"Because that would involve talking to her and listening to what she has to say …"

Nick can feel his face reddening.

"The point is: I'm not sure I want to carry on, you know, pretending."

"Pretending?"

"That I am a committed PR man and that I believe in all of the garbage that gets re-packaged every five minutes."

"So why not try something new?"

"At my age? I don't know how to do anything else. I don't technically have any skills you know."

"You should take some time off before they give you more time off than you bargained for."

\*\*\*

Nick heads home just after three o'clock and immediately lies down on the settee below the main window which the sunshine is pouring through. A few moments later he is aware of a red light flashing up the need for answers.

"Haven't heard from you and neither has Rowena."

Nick dials Nora's mobile number, resting his arm on the sofa's arm to avoid having to admit that his hands are shaking slightly. She does not answer. It just goes to voicemail. He does not leave a message but 'phones his parents' number instead.

He listens patiently to the news bulletin from his daughter, filed online in worried tones:

"He hasn't stopped coughing for ages. When we were in the park this afternoon I thought he was going to choke."

"What did Granny say?"

"She said that he was worried about moving house and didn't want to go. Apparently, he never did want to move away. Why do they have to move, Daddy?"

He's never heard her use words like 'apparently' before. She must be reading a lot.

"Because they just do. OK!"

He realizes much too late that he has snapped at her and feels bad. She had been so happy when Mother had handed the receiver over after the barest of cursory pleasantries. He knows he is thinking about what Nora might be doing instead of answering her mobile but it is unforgivable to take it out on his daughter - their daughter.

He continues much more gently: "We talked about this, remember?"

"Not really, no."

"Granny needs a bit of a hand with Grandad these days. I know she tries hard but one day she might wake up in the night and need to get urgent help…"

"Like calling for an ambulance?"

"Could be, yes. Or just people around her who can come quickly to help her."

"Or a fire engine?"

"If Grandad had set the place on fire, yes. It's called sheltered accommodation and means neither Granny nor Grandad would have to go into a home."

"I thought this was their home? What's the new house going to be called if it isn't a home?"

"I meant a nursing home, where old people go when …"

"Nobody wants them?"

"Exactly. Well. No, not exactly. They go there when doctors and nurses talk with their families and think it's for the best."

"And then they sit around all day asking the same questions over and over again before weeing on the carpets?"

"Who told you that?"

"Julie Walker. Her Gran's in a 'home.' It's in Enfield. Julie has to go and visit her every other Sunday. She hates it. Says the smell is terrible and the old women keep taking their teeth out and dipping them in tea."

He smiles unkindly at the scene she is describing but tries not to let it show in his voice. " Not all places are like that and anyway, as I said, Granny and Grandad are years away from …"

"Grandad says you already don't care though."

"What do you mean? When did he say that?"

"This afternoon. Before he had the coughing fit he showed me some photographs. Some of them were of you as a little boy eating an ice cream on the beach somewhere. Grandad said you were a lovely little boy then but you didn't care about anyone now."

"That's not true is it - you know how much I care."

"I suppose."

"Of course I do."

His hand is gripping the 'phone even more tightly than during 'conversations' with Bannister. Why does his father do this? Why has he always done this?

"We have our own photo album to prove what good times we have all enjoyed."

In truth, he isn't in many of the family pictures with the regulation beaming smile to prove that everything has always been rosy in the Golding garden. He comforts himself with the knowledge that he had been the one behind, rather than in front of the camera. That isn't entirely true either though; they were usually taken when Nora and Rowena were spending days out together while he worked weekends on the nonsense his clients threw at him.

"History doesn't count though, does it? My project isn't going very well so I asked Grandad about it. He said that history is for those who can't face the future."

Later that same evening Nick is lying in bed, a paperback open about a third of the way through. Why do jacket details make them sound so interesting and different when there is very little difference between so many of the 'new and important voices.'

He should try Nora again before another haranguing voicemail but picks up the zapper for the portable TV instead and idly skips through the channels eventually settling on BBC 2 where a caption shows that the late-night update from History and Mystery is about to begin.

"Welcome back to Waxling on the North Norfolk coast. My name is John Squires and we're almost at the end of day three of our two-week investigation here. This evening I was able to catch up with one of the 'village elders,' if you like, a Mr St John de Criel, and I'm sure he won't mind me describing him in that way because his family are one of the oldest landed families in the area.

I started by asking him first about the infamous year of 1953. To some viewers, it will instantly take them back to iconic events such as the Queen's Coronation, Hillary's conquering of Everest or even the Matthews Cup Final but for people living on the East Anglian coast, it means only one thing: the worst natural disaster to ever occur in the United Kingdom.

"St John de Criel. A warm welcome to History and Mystery on a warm evening, I'm pleased to be able to report."

"Indeed. Welcome to Waxling."

"Thank you. 1953: I imagine that date is firmly etched in the memory of any person living along the coastline from parts of Lincolnshire right round to Suffolk and Essex but particularly in Norfolk?"

"It is. But then we are rather used to this kind of thing you see, though I must make one tiny correction to Ms Breeve's analysis."

"Please."

"Well, she described the Atlantic as forcing its

way into the North Sea from the tip of Scotland and down through the North Sea. Of course, that's perfectly true but it's really where the North Sea surge hits the fierce Atlantic waters heading up through the English Channel that you have such a dramatic impact: it is sea meeting sea as much as sea hitting land, though obviously the impact spreads a long way inland.

It slams into the dead end of The Wash for example and up the Great Ouse for miles, causing damage all along its banks, because the water can't get away, it just keeps on coming upstream. The coastline itself is decimated. We lost the sea wall for over one and a half miles - it simply collapsed under the pressure of the waves."

"And that's what happened in 1953?"

"I remember it being a full moon - The Waxing Moon - which always indicates a higher than average spring tide in January and February - and that was certainly the case on January 31$^{st,}$ 1953 - but perhaps the defining factor was the hurricane-force winds that had been blowing on the surface of the water throughout the day.

Due to the low-pressure conditions, as Ms Breeve alluded to in your previous broadcast, a wall of water had built up and was heading down towards us from the north-east of Scotland. We call it the North Sea Surge. Due also to the rotation of the earth, the surge is deflected to the right as it heads south so the effect on our coast is rather higher than say on the Netherlands over to the east of us."

"Though there was terrible damage and loss of life there also."

"There was."

"And why in particular was the 1953 flood so bad?"

"A lot of it was to do with the lack of flood warnings. You have to remember that there were far fewer local radio stations then and none of them broadcast at night. Weather stations had reported the surge earlier in the day but it takes about twelve hours for it to travel from Scotland down to the mouth of the Thames. The meteorologists had long since called it a day by the time it hit us here."

"So many people all along the coast here went to bed as normal that night, completely unaware that this huge bank of water was heading towards them?"

"Indeed so. Here in Waxling, we in the RNLI did what we could to try and persuade people to move away inland for the night but people aren't always persuaded of danger until they see it or witness it for themselves. Some thought we were just being officious."

"And some 307 people in the UK were thought to have been killed as a direct result of this disaster?"

"On land, yes; many people clung to rooftops and others made for their local churches where they assumed they would be safe."

"Was that because of their elevated positions along the coast or purely faith?"

"Whatever it may have been, the churches offered little protection and rescuers often rowed straight into the buildings and down the aisles to save people. Churches along the coast do represent safety in many people's minds though, especially for older people. They have a healthy fear of the sea, you see, borne out of generations of respect for it but also so many examples of how dangerous it can be, living on an island."

"Was it just a belief in God do you think or other 'powers?' There is a legend around here that survives to this day ..."

"I wouldn't read too much into hearsay. People around here, when they meet you, might still present you with flint stones to ward off witches but it doesn't mean to say that any dark powers existed in the first place. Only the stones are real. If you are here to find out the truth over the next two weeks, I suspect you'll find it in the examination of the facts. Isn't that what your programme normally concentrates on?"

"Of course. Well, it just remains for me to say thank you very much, St John de Criel, for colouring in some of the sketches of storms and flooding and, sadly, drownings, that we came to Waxling with.

It's always insightful for our listeners and viewers to have a personal perspective and we will call on you again if that's OK - especially as your family history stretches right back to the Conquest, I think you told me?"

"It will be my pleasure."

# THURSDAY 14TH JUNE 2007

"So, what precisely does this Mr de Criel want us to do for them?" Bannister sports an air of mild disinterest while plucking invisible specks of fluff from his lovely cream jacket. "And, much more importantly, is it going to cost us a fortune? Do share."

"I don't see why it should. There's a move to build new sea defences just off the coast but they're enormously expensive and the government has made it clear that it cannot and will not guarantee any kind of flood defence system or even warning systems in the future.

They call it a 'managed retreat' but there's not much management involved. Waxling sits on a nine-mile stretch of coastline that's been under threat for many years now. Environmental scientists have advised the powers that be that there's no point in just building more concrete sea barriers for the tides to pick holes in and eventually destroy.

Their advice now is that they should just manage the retreat from the sea instead, knowing that several villages like Waxling and Happisburgh will disappear within a generation."

"Rather like Canute in spectacular reverse!"

"So, the residents led by the esteemed Mr de Criel are, instead, going for EU funding for the programme. At Cromer, just round the coast from Waxling," he ignores Bannister's melodramatic stifled yawn, "they got money from Brussels previously for a major regeneration programme. That included a new lifeboat museum which is where de Criel first became aware of the rest of Europe -and he's been involved ever since.

Any publicity we can give to them would be easy and cheap enough to implement."

Nick's mind begins to drift back to the strange, pale lady on the beach and is only saved by an urgent call from Bannister's 'dentist' which he hurries away to take in the privacy of his office.

A short time later Nick finds the BBC website page devoted to the live History and Mystery project and, headphones on, clicks through to the live audio stream:

"**And Sam and Nathan have been busy since very early this morning putting in two trenches, one north-south and the other more north-east to south-west, both leading away from our Priory remains. Sam, can you tell us your reasoning here?**"

"Yes, I can, John. We're trying to date the last occupation of the priory. Unlike most priories of this period, we haven't been able to find an inventory…"

"And that in itself is unusual isn't it?"

"It is. When these places were finally dissolved, the King's men would instruct the village authority to list everything in a fair bit of detail. For archaeologists, these are significant clues for us to date activity and occupation."

"So why do you think ours is missing here at Waxling?"

"That's one of the mysteries we're going to have to solve over the next few days I'm afraid. It's unlikely that the Augustinians would have moved out quickly but we do know that they did eventually move away from this coastal area altogether."

"And Nathan, I believe you're already quite pleased with what you've found already?"

A younger voice fills Nick's head, altogether more dynamic and almost breathless in its desire to seize its moment on the airwaves.

"Yes, I am. We've turned up some herringbone masonry just down there by the cliff edge. As you can see the pieces seem to form part of a yellowish, glazed floor tile which might date from the 1100's. We'd need to check it out of course. But, if so, it would make sense to us as this would have been made during Henry I's reign when he is known to have given a good deal of land over to the Augustinians for building."

"So although it doesn't help us with our investigation of when they left it perhaps does help to confirm when they might have first occupied this area?"

"Indeed so."

***

*Daddy went to see the man about the fishing trip today. I think Barney is such a nice name. I'm going to wear my new red pullover with the lighthouse on it if I can persuade him to let me go with them. I do like wearing matching colours and I might try a ponytail if Mummy will let me. Daddy was gone for ages though and Mum was cross with him when he got back to our chalet so I didn't mention it. She wanted to know why it had taken him so long. She was hoping he'd drive us into Stalham this morning to get some food for our lunch so that we could get a good place on the beach before the sun went in. But it's already gone in because the clouds are rolling in from the sea. I wrote a poem for her – to cheer her up. She said it was nice but I could see that it had made her cry.*

\*\*\*

"I am so pleased we followed your advice!"

Squires is glaring at her. They haven't moved for more than twenty minutes and the air conditioning fan fills the ensuing silence as it manfully attempts to cool things down.

"I'm not sure how much of this is holiday traffic and how many people are just coming up to see the set?" she ventures, hoping the latter possibility will make him feel better or at least calm him down. "It should have cleared by tonight."

"Assuming we come back tonight ... always assuming we ever get there!"

"What do you mean, exactly?" she can feel her heart pumping below her soaked blouse. "We have to get back for the briefing later."

He grins back at her. "I just thought, you know, if it's as bad as this we might have to stay over in Sheringham."

She feels like a parcel that has been handled but not unwrapped and then promptly placed back on the shelf for later. They eventually reach the small holiday town to the west of Cromer whereupon Squires yanks the handbrake aggressively up into its upright position and turns off the engine.

"I'm sorry. I didn't bargain on quite that amount of holidaymakers. It was springtime when I was up at Seahenge and the A149 from Blakeney was much clearer then."

"Quite the little geographer aren't we? Did you do much colouring at school?"

She ignores his goading, relieved as she is just to be able to open the car door at last and feel the gentle breeze playing on her damp face. "I loved map reading. I'd have thought it was a pretty key part of your training in the RAF too?"

"That was then. This is now." He snaps back and begins to walk ahead of her, out of the car park, inconveniently situated along the cliffs from the old fishing station of Lower Sheringham.

As she watches him stalk off, she recalls a poem:

**'Flying, unable to flee**

He never seems to notice anyone

But, then again, he doesn't miss so much:

The sweet voice of a yet unsoured child –

Sunny thoughts described through the softest touch.

He cannot feel and does not hear the sounds

Beyond the darkness and the dead of night

That wake me and to which I am still bound:

Invisible tails from a soaring kite.

She catches up with him as they reach the station. He is reading an information board about the coming of the Midland and Great Northern Line to Sheringham in the late Eighteen Hundreds and how this, the North Norfolk Railway has been preserved to take passengers by steam to the inland town of Holt.

They had travelled along that line, her, Rowena, Nick and Nick's father: a day trip, one crisp autumn day, when their daughter was little more than four years old. 'The Poppy Line' it was called and, though David Golding had been obsessed with original carriage features such as the wall-mounted lights, Rowena had been transfixed by the windmill over by the sea at Weybourne.

She has made initial enquiries about them spending Nick's fiftieth birthday at another nearby windmill – Cley - whose owners offer bed and breakfast in specially converted rooms. It would be a special place to celebrate a special birthday and Rowena would love it.

Of course, there was the risk of it being too close

to Waxling and that had prevented her from making even a provisional booking. Besides, it was still a couple of years off yet. A lot could happen in her world in a couple of hours!

They head down towards the beach and are routed alongside a long sea wall, similar to the one in Waxling itself. She looks behind her at the stark, orange-brown rocks, their jagged edges pointing up at the blue sky above. They are more like rock formations out of the dusty Wyoming scrub, rather than a damp English fishing village.

"There's an interesting historical reference we can use here!"

She turns back to read the inscription, edged in black lettering.

It tells the story of one Anna Gurney who had lived in the town and funded its first lifeboat. Despite suffering polio as a child and being wheelchair-bound, she had supervised the first firing of a 'Manby Mortar' which was used to fire a line to a ship in difficulties and could help to secure a lifeboatman's passage whilst trying to save the lives of those on board.

"I know about Anna Gurney," she responds, "I visited her grave at Overstrand which is just outside Cromer. I'd read about her because she was something of a scholar and the first woman member of the British Archaeological Association – hence my interest."

"Great. We can use that to add some academic flavour and tie you in as well. This is going well. Sounds as though she was a real local hero; unlike that 'White

Lady' or whatever they call her back in Waxling - you know, the one who is supposed to be responsible for all the drowning?"

"I think some might argue that she gives out warnings to sailors about trouble ahead, but it is the fact that they pay no heed to her which results in accidents happening."

"Not such a good story though, is it? We can't ever let fact - or even a debate about the truth - get in the way of a good legend, can we? I mean this is television."

She shudders inwardly as a cloud passes over the burning sun, only just past its daily zenith, and recalls the other reason for remembering Anna Gurney.

"Anna Gurney was also an inspiration to a close acquaintance of mine. Her determination in the face of adversity and desire to do the right thing was the driving factor for much of her early poetry, in fact."

"Poetry and fact should never be mentioned in the same sentence, I'm afraid." He pats her gently on the shoulder and leads her gently but purposefully towards a scruffy white building, bedecked with flags and bunting, announcing itself imaginatively as 'Sea View Café.'

Poetic, she considers, sadly.

\*\*\*

"I still can't believe that you didn't call her!"

Nora sounds genuinely surprised. Is this all part of an elaborate cover-up – to divert her guilt onto him in a 'perfectly reasonable' hospital pass?

"She's your only daughter for goodness sake!"

"I have been pretty busy at the agency and assumed they would 'phone me if there was a problem!"

It sounds faint-hearted and indeed it is.

"She's worried about her grandfather; about both of them getting old and, one day, not being there anymore. Can't you see that she just wants to ask all of her questions and hear their stories before it's too late?"

He is hot and tired and has a headache. As usual, he tries to change the subject and move to safer ground.

"How is dear John?"

"He's very well. Not that you're at all interested."

"Oh, but I am..."

"He was with Nathan earlier when they discovered the first signs of a revetement near the priory and next to some old timber remains from Trench One."

"Which is?" The combination of heat and stress is causing his heart to pound. He's not sure how long he can keep this up before needing to discuss the elephant in the room that appears to be standing between them.

She responds coldly. "It's from the French - revetment - a kind of stone structure that was built as a defence to protect dwellings. It offers further proof that this part of the coast was of such strategic importance that they needed to do all they could to protect their houses and farms from attack."

"Unless the attacker was the sea, in which case,

according to bigwig de Criel, there isn't much anyone can do."

"How do you know that? Our interview with him doesn't go out until later?"

"I think I read about some campaign he is involved with – it came through on one of our European Union wires; he's seeking funding for sea defences or something like that?"

This is going wrong, so wrong. Her apparent deception has been festering in his mind and now the lies trip off his tongue like the light fandango …

She is back in work mode though. "We recorded it earlier: he and a lady called Audrey. She used to be married to the vicar. They're talking to Connie about the committee they've formed to try and get the EC to pay for new flood defences, as you say."

"I'll check it out."

"Or are you checking up on me again? You're behaving very strangely. What exactly have you been doing since I've been safely out of the way?"

"Watching the TV; listening to the radio … there's not much else to do in the evenings."

"You usually find plenty to do when we're all at home." She isn't convinced but neither has she pursued her line of enquiry.

He just has to pray that she doesn't get into a conversation with de Criel.

"So you will 'phone Rowena this evening then?"

"Yes. Yes, of course, I will."

"And be gentle with her. She doesn't need to know about all the bad things in the world yet awhile."

"You don't have to be an archaeologist to discover them."

"No, Nick, but burying them in the first place doesn't mean they no longer exist either." The sudden click in his ear does not do justice to the force with which he imagines her throwing her mobile down onto a chair or maybe even a bed.

\*\*\*

She gathers up the glossy Estate Agent property sheets. She had picked them up in Sheringham, leaving false contact details of course. She had called into three separate offices on a whim; a kind of private adventure, though John may have seen it as something more concrete than that.

She flicks through the 'beautifully presented,' 'flexible accommodation' and 'affording glorious sea views' clichés but does find some possible properties: a hit-list of new homes – new starts for them.

The sea frightens her, but she is more frightened still of her and her daughter being swallowed up in London if he doesn't or even if (especially, if) he does come to his senses.

\*\*\*

The introductory shots are as contrived as ever. De Criel, stiffly upright as a soldier on the parade ground is all but marching towards the camera to a steady but silent beat while the voiceover introduces him to new viewers. He is wearing a crisp, white shirt with a purple, acrylic tie featuring a coat of arms, and smooth beige chinos.

He greets an excessively-painted woman, affectionately. Bedecked in a white, linen trouser suit, her lush, grey hair is forced into a bun with a blue ribbon that clashes violently with his tie. Her blue stilettos (to match the hair ribbon?) make a loud clack on the concrete pavement.

For a brief moment Nick is reminded of Rowena when she was very young (he must remember to call her after this). They were on holiday by the sea somewhere as he had been giving her 'horsey rides' on the beach, her shrieking with laughter and singing along tunelessly at the top of her tiny voice urging her feet to go - what was it…'clippety clop?'

De Criel kisses the woman on both cheeks and Nick is sure that not only does she blush and become duly deferential in his presence, but she is positively skittish. These are, after all, her fifteen minutes of fame.

De Criel takes her arm gently and leads her into what looks like a small boat museum where they are both, in turn, almost suffocated by the welcoming embrace of the ultimate museum piece: Constance Breeve.

**"Thank you both for joining us this evening. For the benefit of our viewers and listeners, I'd just like to introduce St. John de Criel, whose family has lived here since the days of the Norman Conquest and Audrey Bracken, who was born here too and**

married the local vicar. Both are on the local action group seeking funding for more comprehensive flood defences.

As we all know by now, the original Waxling village disappeared beneath the waves some four hundred years ago precisely because the flood defences were so lacking. I assume your husband's prayers and those of his congregation have gone unanswered, Audrey?"

"Unsurprising in his case, given that he died in 1970."

"Oh. I'm so sorry, I ..."

"Hadn't done your homework eh!"

De Criel collapses into a fit of worthy giggles. Audrey Bracken's face is unmoved; fixed and uncompromising.

"But the reefs at Sea Palling must have had some beneficial effect against tidal erosion!"

Constance 'Connie' Breeve, red-faced and flustered is trying to get this back on track as quickly as possible, while Audrey is loving the camera - even if that sentiment isn't reciprocated,

"A few boulders aren't the answer, with respect. You'll know, I hope, that as long ago as 1309 'The Commission of Walls and Ditches' made it very clear that new defences would be necessary to protect the Norfolk coast from inundation and, over the many intervening years, they've been proved absolutely right. All we are doing is picking up the argument and taking it to the EU and saying 'Look, we don't have much time left!'"

"The authorities here weren't prepared to help any further?"

"The Environment Agency which has what it calls a 'Strategic Overview' of the whole of the British coastline doesn't have us on their radar. North Norfolk District Council are responsible for maintaining the coastal defences as far down as Cart Gap but seizing on the Environment Agency's own blind spot, it has now washed its hands of Waxling altogether.

"So finance is more important here than flood defences?"

De Criel can be heard chuckling approvingly out of shot. Audrey, meanwhile, replies testily as her cheeks begin to melt under the arc lights above.

"People do form much more benign views of the sea when they don't live with it each day: views normally formed from day trips and childhood holidays? I expect your being here will bring in even more voyeurs. In a few years, there might be nothing left for you or them to see and we may well go the same way as the original Waxling village that you referred to in your preamble."

Constance has clearly been listening to voices in her head and very obviously attempts to re-focus.

"And what do you consider your chances to be? With the EU application, I mean?"

"We had our first visit from the Commissioner's

department last week - funny how the names they use haven't changed over the years, isn't it? They were very polite of course and asked lots of questions in a Belgian kind of way, but there's no mystery here apart from the made-for-television contrivance you've come up with regarding the priory.

We've also been talking to a PR agency from London,"

Nick freezes, his throat tight and his heart thumping in his chest.

"to try and raise our profile - isn't that how they describe it? So, hopefully, more and more people will become aware of our sheds and back gardens and even homes slipping into the sea whilst our own councillors tend to their roses and mow their lawns, safe in the knowledge that they won't wake up one morning to find that their land has disappeared!"

The BBC producer, ever mindful of the cost of the License Fee, has had enough and the camera switches to de Criel while Constance can be heard asking him:

"And St John; thank you again for joining us this evening. It must seem like old times being back in this former RNLI shed?"

They're not going to ask any questions about Prindle Massey's (his) involvement. He relaxes a little but knows that Nora will follow up on it as it is so close to home.

"Yes indeed. I had many happy years here, though, of course, it wasn't happiness we sought, but rather the saving of people's lives."

Cut to an admiring glance from Audrey whose watery mascara certainly needs rescuing.

"Of course. We've been hearing a lot already this week about the perils and dangers of this coastline. Can you tell us about the worst disaster you were personally involved in?"

"Oh, any lifeboatman will tell you, Constance, that each rescue is as important as the previous one and those yet to be required. But sadly they will continue to happen. That's the point here, and I should remind viewers that all of our funding comes from donations and our operations rely entirely on volunteers - the authorities can't cut the grants in our case because they've never existed."

Constance has been instructed not to let him off the hook.

"I visited St Mary's church in Happisburgh this morning and saw a gravestone in the churchyard referring to HMC Invincible?"

"Ah yes. Tragic, tragic case. That was back in 1801 – even before my time here – when it hit the Hammonds Knoll sandbank just east of Happisburgh Sands. The guns were fired because they'd lost their rudder you see - sheared right off - the first moment people on the mainland would have even known about it. Must have been very alarming for people here as well as those on board. I imagine a few homeowners could even have believed that they were under attack by the French.

Lifeboats were launched from here and further

along the coast but they were quickly overwhelmed. Over four hundred people lost their lives and their bodies were washed up on the beaches for days afterwards. The locals loaded them up onto carts and buried many of them in the communal grave on the north side of the churchyard - which you will have seen earlier."

"Absolutely. The de Criel family is one of those long-standing families isn't it; I believe your ancestors came over with the Conqueror originally, didn't they St John?"

"They did. Our family has its origins in Criel-sur-mer, northeast of Dieppe, at the mouth of the River Yeres. Its first known mention was as Criolium in 1059 - seven years before the invasion."

"And the family has had a protective role over this community pretty much ever since?"

"Indeed. My ancestors in the Navy were involved in active engagements against the Spanish and we were part of the lookout deputed to watch for straggling Armada ships limping around this coast. We also played a key strategic role here in monitoring the invasion plans of the French and then the Germans of course.

Through changing times I can tell you that we have never let the people down, not once, and never lost the trust of our tenants and neighbours."

"And yet the de Criels seem to have been found wanting at the beginning of the seventeenth century when the original Waxling Village was inundated in such a horrific fashion. History suggests that the incumbent squire abandoned his wife and village leaving them quite alone to do what they could."

"I'm surprised at you referring to 'historical fact' that you haven't yet proven, Ms Breeve! After all, I thought that was the mystery part of the history programme you were so anxious to investigate. The sanctity of life is everything to us - a bon droit. It forms the central motif on our coat of arms as I assume you have discovered?"

"We are not here to judge anyone, Mr de Criel; merely to discover – to unearth."

Nick notes the change to a rather frosty 'Mr de Criel' from 'St John.' Audrey and now de Criel must have got under her skin but he isn't sure what point Constance Breeve is trying to make. Perhaps they have already discovered something off-camera that Squires and his followers are waiting to reveal in a History & Mystery episode with a much bigger audience than this late-night summary.

# FRIDAY 15TH JUNE 2007

He reads another dreary post from the Amy girl, noticing that she is using longer words than usual and it is more essay than quick note:

'I told you not to fret. All will be well if we truly believe that bad people get found out in the end. History tells us that this usually happens and we just have to put up with things for now. At least we have our stories and most of them have happy endings. If something bad had happened we'd have heard by now.'

There has obviously been some sort of upset at home and the poor, deluded child is trying to big things up for her rabbit. He knows he is being cynical but, really!

'We're very lucky, you and I. We can hold on to each other like a brother and sister. I can't imagine an existence without you.'

Nick can hear the bees buzzing outside Bannister's open window but refuses to be lured into his honey trap. Moments later, however, His Greatness stands, framed in the doorway, like a modern god in an ancient fresco.

"You'll never guess who I've been conversing with, Golding."

"I really can't imagine."

"That I can understand. Your lack of imagination is legendary in the creative industries ... a Mr de Criel. He doesn't want you to work on the account, should we even agree to proceed. He doesn't think you're up to it - wants someone with a bit more ... presence."

"I've only met him once, and that was little more than a fact-finding mission."

"Well, these are the facts. He wants someone else on the account so I'll probably slot Petra in. Usually works with men of a certain age, I find."

Nick finds that he is angry, really angry. The unsettling sense of insecurity he has experienced over the last few days, coupled with broken sleep is a surprisingly potent combination. Last night he'd heard the Christ Church bell strike every hour and only when he was in the shower had he remembered that it didn't have a belfry or a working set of bells.

Bannister inadvertently letting him off the hook concerning his involvement at Waxling - and Nora not needing to know about it after all - is suddenly secondary. In fact, it is no longer important to him at all.

The look of mild amusement on Bannister's pretty face only serves to provoke him even further.

"Petra knows nothing about Waxling and they deserve much more from us than an average account executive with practically no experience."

"Don't flatter yourself. Age is irrelevant in our business; it's what you know that counts."

"Some of these people may be bigots and delude themselves as to their local and social importance but they are still people after all. Their community has been drowned once already. My wife's up there at the moment, trying to throw some light on what happened all those years ago."

"How touching: a family affair."

"Don't you care at all about the general population?"

"What a ridiculous question. Of course, I care. This whole agency cares. Any demographic change is potentially a cause for concern and …"

"Very Malthusian of you!"

"I'm sorry?"

"Malthus. He was concerned that population growth would outstrip supplies of food while those in authority would just sit idly by and let it happen."

"Well then," Bannister claps his hands as if he has singlehandedly made one of the great discoveries, "the solution is within our grasp, as you quite correctly point out. A major flood along the Norfolk coast would help to alleviate the problem. You see, it's not just about supply but demand too; isn't that right?"

He laughs out loud: a long, lingering laugh that inevitably results in a lovely mauve, silk handkerchief being used to dab imaginary tears.

"Oh dear. Oh dear. This just gets better and better."

"I'm off."

"Good plan. Take a few days away but do stay in touch."

Nick is dismissed with a flourish of Bannister's hand but the process isn't quite complete. "Oh, and Golding ... we wouldn't want to unnecessarily muddy any waters, would we? Don't go anywhere near Waxling again. That's an order. I'm sure it won't be too difficult to obey if your wife's already up there."

\*\*\*

"But you'd have expected this, Sam?"

"Yes. Grimston Ware is found all over East Anglia. It's very similar to Thetford Ware - which is made from a similar sandy clay - and has the same kind of sandpaper texture. This piece may have been a fragment of a simple jug as used in their refectory and I'm thinking that Trench One probably runs underneath that original part of the Priory. Further on, we've found remnants of what at first sight look like plates or bowls."

Nick is still in the office, with his headphones on, logged in to a live radio feed from the History and Mystery site. He watches and he listens but doesn't see or hear anything. His mind is racing to keep up with two of the Four Horsemen of the Golding Apocalypse: potentially losing his job at Prindle Massey, and explaining to Nora about his one and only visit to Waxling before the spiteful Petra lets it slip (if de Criel hasn't done so already).

The only realistic possibility he has of talking properly with Nora is to go back to Waxling but Bannister has made his thoughts perfectly clear on that expedition. A third Horseman is also approaching this self-destructive outlook: he hadn't phoned Rowena as he had promised to do and has to face both her and his parents again in two days when he drives back up to Ely to fetch her.

**"Thanks, Sam. Now, Constance, the rain's really sheeting down outside so we may not get much more digging done this afternoon but a question does come to mind: why would there have been a priory and a church in such a remote part of North Norfolk; I mean the original village of Waxling was even smaller than this one wasn't it?"**

"Yes, it was, Johnnie ..."

Johnnie?

"... but, overall, East Anglia was one of the most densely populated areas in Medieval England so, relatively speaking, these villages would have been pretty significant and, as we have been learning this week, their place in the strategic defence system would have been considered to be vital."

"Alright, well we're going to catch up with the others to see what else they've managed to turn up about both Waxling and also the nearby seaside town of Cromer which has suffered very similar marine attacks to those experienced here. We're back at 7.00; join us then."

Nick smiles enigmatically, even as he turns his back on Prindle Massey and departs.

\*\*\*

The holidays have been really good so far. Much better than last year when Mum and Dad were sad because of the rain. We finally got the kite flying yesterday too but I got worried that its tails would drop off. The wind was so strong. Dad said it could blow as hard as it liked but kites could never lose their tails and would lead me back here again when I have children of my own. Yuk! Never. I wouldn't mind being an Auntie though. I think I'd be good at looking after other people's children. I wish Mrs Click Clack hadn't told us that story about the White Lady. She knows I don't like the dark. At least the beam from the lighthouse means it isn't dark for long and nobody would be able to find me under the eiderdown anyway. I wonder if she's out there like Mrs Click Clack says. It was very windy last night and that means she usually pays a visit. It's not just Mrs Click Clack saying so; I read the same story under the painting at the big house so I know it must be true.

\*\*\*

It seems appropriate that he is preparing a fish dish: his version of haddock kedgeree. He wonders what Nora will be eating and, perhaps more pertinently, where and who with.

Is this how it starts then, he reflects, grimly, slicing the white flesh of a once living creature into the pan. All of those signs from your partner that you didn't stop to consider previously should be the very things you should focus on and, as for the 'important' matters occupying your mind most of the time, well maybe they have no real case to make.

He checks the rice which is about five minutes from being ready so he lights the gas under the adjacent pan. The kitchen is very quickly full of a delicious aroma of gently frying fish, garlic and herbs. Some people like to cook to take their mind off of other things, but Nick finds that just the act of slowing down a little enables them to catch up in his time rather than theirs. He can't stop time or the things that the clock faces see.

He considers whether he is morphing into some kind of fatalistic character like Tess of the d'Urbevilles. Is everything he touches – everything he previously believed to be true – going to be woven into a new narrative that describes a broken, fruitless existence? Is Martin in Battersea drawing the same conclusions? Some help Nick or the agency has been to any of them!

# SATURDAY 16TH JUNE 2007

"... where the most popular boy's name is now Muhammad and not even in the occupied Arab zones of the country. Israel has long cited atomic weaponry – most notably from Iran – as well as suicide bombers as the major threats to its security but, perhaps, the real enemy is from within. Quite simply, Israel is less Jewish than it used to be."

"And there will be more from David Weissgold this evening at eight, as we continue our series of special programmes from the Middle East, forty years on from the 'Six Day War.'

But now we return to Waxling in North Norfolk for the first of today's updates from the History and Mystery Team. Over to John Squires."

"Thanks very much indeed, Geoffrey. Well, not a great deal to report from yesterday as we had torrential rain sweeping across from Denmark and the northern parts of the Netherlands so we were unable to dig much deeper - not through any fear of getting wet of course!"

Why does he always have to patronise his audience in sound or vision? Nick rolls over toward the sunlight streaming through the window but, strangely, it does not warm him.

"... more to do with the fear that we might damage any artefacts that we do find because of the water in the ditches. So, we sent Bill off to nearby Cromer, or 'Crow mere' to get another perspective on this troubled part of the English coast and he sent us this report. You can also download this podcast from the usual place online:

'We first hear about Cromer during Richard II's reign when the first pier or 'pere' appears, possibly from the Norman French word meaning 'support' and which could equally apply to 'father.' It is the earliest-known mention of pier and more specifically the pier here at Cromer, which was probably little more than a wooden jetty.

There is still a pier here. This one was built in 1901 and has managed to survive for over a hundred years, including the major storms of 1953 and 1987. In Richard's time, however, Cromer or Crow Mere – literally 'lake of crows' - was itself inland and the coastal hamlet which grew into what we now know as Cromer was called Shipden or, to give it its full title: Shipden Juxta Mere.

The reason we mention it now is that Shipden has a very similar history to that of Waxling. The storms of 1790 raged around the coast here with the same lethal combination of high tides and low pressure that we heard about earlier in the week.

Shipden was overwhelmed by the inundation and was drowned, all but disappearing overnight. It's still out there, under the water, just as old Waxling is.

The new village of Cromer was born out of the wreckage of that disaster, and it eventually prospered and grew, despite many of its buildings that were less than fifty years old being washed away in the great storms of 1836.

But - and it has been a familiar theme this week of human resilience against natural disaster - it withstood the ferocious weather and people lived to tell the tale. More importantly for us historians, those tales were passed down through the parlours and taverns, where storytelling around stove or fire would have been one of the few collective comforts against gathering storms outside.

However, whereas the remains of the old Waxling church could still be seen for many years after the former bell tower caved in, all that was left of old Shipden was a giant mound, known locally as Shipden Rock. It stayed that way until 1888 when a paddle steamer called 'The Victoria' from Great Yarmouth - further around this coast to the east - was wrecked on it.

In truth, Shipden Rock had been a danger to shipping for generations, along with the treacherous sandbanks and, of course, the terrible weather that can blow up here. After this dreadful episode, Shipden Rock was itself blown up and nothing at all now remains of Shipden.

Cromer is a popular seaside resort and probably had its heydey in the 1880s. A poet and theatre critic – Clement Scott – visited the town in 1883. Like so many others during that period of great expansion, he first ventured up here via the new railway line from Norwich to Cromer.

He yearned to escape the great Victorian metropolis and found peace here, walking through the fields of poppies which adorn this part of the coastline from Overstrand right round to Mundesley. It's still known as Poppy Land today.

Twitchers head over here from Blakeney Point to see Sandwich Terns with their little black caps (the birds, not the bird watchers!) and, of course, Cromer crab is famous the world over.

But, unlike with our priory at Waxling, there are no remains of the settlement that once existed here: where babies were born in seaside cottages, played games on the beach and up in the dunes, grew up, got married and had children of their own - all against the background of a hungry sea and assuming that they weren't consumed by its insatiable appetite first."

The 'phone rings: shrill and urgent from the place where it otherwise rested all day on the hall table. Nick snaps off the radio.

"It's me. I assume you remember who I am?"

"How could I forget?" Calm. He has to remain calm or he will never get through this.

"Well, that's reassuring I suppose," Nora sounds as though someone has just woken her up – as her team effectively did him via the radio waves – and she is distinctly not amused, especially on a Saturday morning.

"Do you also recall that you have a daughter?"

"The one I shall be fetching home from Ely tomorrow, yes."

"Except that you might not ... things have changed."

He feels colder than ever. If people talk about others walking across their graves, his wife has just dug his up and exposed all of his failings; it is what she does, after all.

"What's changed? What do you mean exactly?"

"What do I mean exactly? Let me see: if you had bothered to contact either of us during the week, as I asked you to do, you would know, wouldn't you? Thankfully each of us has been in safe hands; caring hands I might say. It's nice to be spoiled a little."

He has to let her have her rant but recoils at the 'safe' and 'caring' hands references.

"Is Rowena all right? Has something happened in Ely?"

"She appears to have gone down with flu."

"Flu! In the middle of summer?"

"There are lots of different strains and she has been quite run down lately – not that you will have noticed anything out of the ordinary. This has made her vulnerable according to the doctor."

He senses that she is softening now; that she has had her say and imparted what she knows. Wrong.

"Thanks so much for asking. Your mother and

father are fine. It seems that Beryl took her straight to the Princess of Wales on Wednesday afternoon."

"Not sure how she could have helped, after all …"

"In Ely. The children's unit at the hospital. Honestly, Nick, I don't know how you can make such jokes when your only daughter is feeling poorly and you haven't even contacted her to hear how she is."

He says nothing. Of the two of them, he knows that he should at least have contacted Rowena and his red face describes guilt over his selfishness rather than rage over his wife's guilt.

"I'll be up there nice and early tomorrow and bring her home with me."

"Well that's probably not going to work, is it? She can barely move as it is! Besides, what were you aiming to do with her all day while you head merrily off to work?"

"I don't head merrily off to work as it happens." He has recovered his poise – has remembered that he is not the one entirely at fault here. "You carry on with your precious dig. I'll look after Rowena somehow."

"That's hardly fair, Nick. I haven't been on site for many months, as you know very well."

"Ah yes and how is Mr Squires?"

"He's fine as far as I know. We don't see that much of each other. I'm trying to discover what happened here and he is trying to increase his personal ratings. The two don't always go together."

Ah but sometimes they do, he thinks, unhappily.

She is on the more comfortable ground though. "Did you hear the summary piece about Cromer?"

"Yes, I've just switched it off. Nora, I ..."

"I wasn't sure if you remembered or not?"

"Remembered?"

"Cromer pier?"

"Why would I remember the pier?"

"Oh, Nick. Come on. Do try."

"I'm trying."

"No funny word games. The night we first went out together. We went back to your room and watched that film – 'Seascape' - on your sofa. Our legs were rammed close together. We often laughed about it."

"I remember when we used to laugh."

She either hasn't heard him properly or the lack of visual clues gives her no indication of his state of mind. "There was the scene on the pier which he runs along at the end. You remember! He was running for what seemed like ages and then, after all that, she wasn't sitting there waiting for him as he'd hoped."

"I cried."

"Yes, you were inconsolable and then upset because you thought I would go away too and not come back."

"It was our first proper date and a pretty weird impression I was giving."

"I'd give anything to see the real you again."

"What! Unhappy?"

"Just you, without the layers you've covered yourself up with. Do you remember the main reason you were so sad?"

"I suppose I thought you would leave?"

"Maybe but you told me that it was because you recognised the pier."

"I couldn't have done. I've never been there before." He feels sweat under his armpits and a vague taste of fish on his tongue. Not a nice taste. Not a taste from the present.

"That's what you said at the time but you've never mentioned it since and neither have I. I just thought you might have remembered our first date ..."

"Nora ..."

She is hurt and it isn't just the irony of his lack of communication. He wishes he could catch hold of her hand right now but she is already much too far away from him.

"No matter. We have skeletons of our own to deal with now."

He can hear her voice but it is as though someone else is speaking the words for her, interpreting them for him and yet he is still unable to comprehend what is being said.

"What do you mean?"

"The storms we've been having here got a lot

worse yesterday and kept most of us awake throughout the night. The rain was incredible and the wind has been howling around the buildings since early dawn."

"Sounds awful," he is trying to be sympathetic but the thought of 'us' being awake at night is clouding his mind - everything.

"Part of the church wall has been washed away."

The clouds begin to clear. "Sorry. I, I still don't understand what you're saying."

"The cemetery was packed. Part of it was only consecrated after the 1607 flood because there were so many unidentified bodies to deal with. They built a mass grave and surrounded it with stones and family vaults for those whose names they did know. Then they built a new church next to the cemetery they'd already created.

'Needs must,' I suppose. Many newer graves have been dug since then, all around the new church, but it's the original wall next to the oldest chamber that has been breached. That chamber is the original de Criel family vault but it's been locked up since John de Criel himself died and has never been used since. The family have another, grander version on display nearer to the church entrance.

The church records are missing for some reason, and St John seems unusually reluctant to talk about it, but local legend has it that John de Criel's wife - Elizabeth - was the first to be buried there: a sort of foundation stone if you will.

John de Criel never got over her death and only

survived her by a few years. The trouble is: there are three skeletons and one of them is very different to the other two. It's that of a young girl. We don't know much yet but she most certainly did not walk this earth in the eighteenth century."

\*\*\*

She hadn't meant to sound so blunt. She wasn't sure - even as the news came through - whether or not she would 'phone and tell him. This skeleton is not old. She has a very strong suspicion as to who these remains belong to. Because of this, she knows to tread very gently indeed and wait for the team to properly research its origins.

"Tremendous excitement here this morning with the discovery of not one but three skeletons. They appear to have been washed out of the vault adjacent to the 'new' church wall. I said earlier that we had been experiencing terrific rain and gale-force winds, with the result that part of that wall has simply disappeared into the waves. Connie, this was unexpected, to say the least.

"Well, it was, John. Aristocratic families were often worried – some might say obsessed - about purgatory, especially in the Twelfth and Thirteenth Centuries. That's why they looked to establish places like monasteries and priories so that they would have somewhere to be buried and hope their holy works would see them through to the next stage. The monks themselves, on the other hand, were usually buried outside of the consecrated ground, often at the feet of boundary walls?"

"So where does that leave us?"

"Well, clearly the child must have belonged to one of those aristocratic families …"

"I guess monks fathering children wasn't common?"

"Ha. Ha. No, and if it did happen the church certainly wouldn't have taken any risks by allowing them to be buried so close to the wall. Guilt by association was rife during this time. As we heard earlier in the week, religious suspicions were heightened in this period and simmered for much longer than that.

No, I think we can be pretty sure that this child belonged to a later branch of the de Criel family, though we can't find any records as yet which point to the death of a female infant and/or possible names for the little girl."

"Is this a cover-up, if I can put it so crudely? Could this be the kind of indiscretion or mistake that great families such as the de Criels would have been keen to hide, which is why the tomb would have been opened? This sort of thing wasn't unusual one, two centuries on from then was it?"

"I think you're being a bit presumptuous there, John. We shall have to see what the experts come up with as to a much more precise date of birth. It may make for great broadcast drama but we mustn't lose sight of the historical facts."

"Indeed not, Connie; perish the thought."

If Squires had felt put down by the 'expert's rebuke, his ego wouldn't have allowed him to show it, thinks Nick – or is that the essential skill of a good anchorman: that they ask the questions the audience want them to ask – however controversial or insensitive – and take the facts on the chin if strictly necessary?

Whatever; the viewing or listening public would always rather see or hear the questioner rather than the expert responder. Job done.

**"Thanks, Connie. Well, we've brought you up to date with this most unusual turn of events and we'll let you have more news as it comes in. At the moment we're waiting for the coroner to tell us when we can go back on-site but, officially, this is now a potential crime scene. More later ..."**

\*\*\*

"Hi. Nora. I know you're not there - I've sent you a text as well but know you often don't reply to them so ..."

"Hello. It's me!" She has snatched up the 'phone, genuinely excited to have intercepted his message in time.

"I'm taking a few days off."

"What's happened?"

"Why should anything have happened? We're all entitled to a break now and again." He pushes that familiar sense of irritation back down inside him and away from his vocal cords.

"But you never have time out from the agency

and, even when you do, you still spend most of it doing their business for them rather than your own."

"I know. I know. Any more news?"

"Nick, what's wrong?" She is worried that he sounds so worried. You've never shown the slightest interest in any of my work and, to be honest, I'm a bit surprised to hear that you've been following it on the TV and the radio." Is it Blackout - are they putting pressure on you?"

"Blackout relieves stress, not the other way round!" he waits for some response to this witty aside but it doesn't arrive. "It's nothing to do with the agency, honestly."

There is a long silence, broken only by background voices at her end before she speaks again.

"John's here. We're going to see de Criel again, to see if he can throw any light on how a much younger skeleton could have been buried in the family vault. Connie tried to get hold of him earlier but he wasn't answering his 'phone. Some of the locals in the pub are saying he's taken the find very badly."

"Possible collateral damage to the family reputation I suppose?" He is biting his lip. He hasn't done that for years – not since he was young.

"Exactly! His family have lorded it over this area for centuries."

"He still does!" He hesitates, acknowledging his slip and hoping she hasn't noticed.

"He's even worse in real life. Believe me."

She hasn't. He breathes out again.

"The TV doesn't do him justice! I think many of the villagers are secretly afraid of him, which is just how he likes it."

"Intriguing to see how he plays this then."

"What is with this sudden interest? Are you checking up on me – us - again? Just like you did at Seahenge?"

"No. No. Why would I want to do that?

"You sound so different; it's as though you've done a five-day crash course in the Arts or something."

"Are you disappointed in me, Nora?"

"Not if your interest is genuine."

\*\*\*

*It was raining again this morning. We walked over the dunes but it was misty on the beach. Daddy said it would lift later and we'd be able to play on the beach but it didn't. We went to the old windmill instead. I thought at first there would be lots of other people in there because it was raining. When we went to Hunstanton last year the café and the storm shelters with their funny, pointed roofs, were always full of other people on holiday. They were all trying to get dry. The windmill was nearly empty though.*

*The posh man from the lifeboat shed was there again. He said hello to Daddy but ignored us. He had been talking to a much younger man called Barry. Barry was the man who owned the windmill but he told Daddy that he couldn't afford to run all the machines any longer so was going to make it into an art gallery. He said this would be the last chance to look around so we went up lots of old ladders until we got to the top floor at last. Daddy said it was called a cap but I think he must have been teasing me.*

*There was a little door next to a huge pipe that was going round in the middle of the floor. I popped my head through the gap. It was a very long way up. I could see that there was a white fence running around the edge of the building. I thought it was a funny place to put a fence. The garden was a long way down. The sails were going round but in the gaps in between, I could clearly see the red and white lighthouse and some ruins next to a big house nearby.*

*'That's part of my house' said the posh man, 'or was.' He gave me a bit of a jump because I hadn't heard him climbing up behind us. 'There are lots of nice books in there. You should come and visit.' He looked at my little brother for a long time but didn't say much.*

*Daddy suggested we go down again. Barry stopped him though. He talked in quite a high voice and waved his arms around a lot as he showed us where the corn went into a giant chute. It went through lots of wheels and then came out at the bottom. It looked a lot like the talcum powder Mummy puts on us but the posh man said it was flour. He said the windmill had been making flour for a very, very long time.*

*Barry showed us some pictures he'd been drawing. He called them sketches but I knew that they were pictures really. They were of people I didn't know. Barry said there were more pictures in the posh man's library that he would be bringing over to the windmill instead. Daddy said they were really good and Barry was so pleased that he gave him a big hug. The posh man seemed happy and he hugged Daddy as well. I didn't think Daddy liked being hugged – that's what he always says to me. I might try again tomorrow, though, when he's not looking. Like a surprise. It was nice to see him smiling for a change.*

*Barry told us to come back next year but that it wouldn't be a windmill anymore. The sails would still be there but they wouldn't be able to turn, whether it was windy or still. It was still raining when we left and we spent the rest of the day inside, playing Monopoly.*

\*\*\*

Realizing that he can stay at home for the whole day, Nick feels more unsettled than ever. He takes his laptop into Nora's study.

Scrolling past all of the latest results concerning History and Mystery, especially sensational news reports about the skeleton finds which have, remarkably, already been found and indexed on Google, he finds a link to the Mill Gallery. On the site of a former corn mill, it had been in the Thurlong family since the 1500s and a working mill until 1968 when it had been converted into a studio and art gallery.

Another search result just below this one catches Nick's eye. It is a blog entry from Abbots_Home which he quickly scans. The entry is brief and merely pointing out that:

**'another skeleton has been found to add to the body of evidence. The guilty will be squirming under their silk sheets now – make no mistake.'**

He looks up the author's profile page but it

states only that they have lived in Waxling for many years during which they did volunteer work for the RNLI where they 'first came to learn computers' and, much more intriguingly, describing themselves as an 'island for lost souls.' A bit poetic for Jack Saunders he considers, though no door remains closed for the unhinged.

He leaves the page and switches the radio on:

"So I'm afraid there's not much more to report from Waxling today but what a day it's been. We don't yet have any updates for you on the skeletons that were revealed yesterday when the graveyard wall collapsed in storms which, I'm very pleased to say, have moved away now. All we do know for certain is that one of the skeletons is much younger than the other two.

Years ago, as Nora Wright and I discovered in Sheringham earlier in the week, drowned fishermen could be identified by the kind of 'gansey' they wore. These were knitted by the fishermen's wives and featured vertical patterns. Each coastal village had its own particular pattern which meant that the victims' places of residence could be crudely determined and they would be sent back there for burial.

In this case, because of the similar preservative qualities of peat to those mentioned by Nora when digging at Seahenge eight years ago, our latter skeleton does have tiny fragments of red material attached to it but, as I speak, it could be some time before we get the results of tests currently being carried out on the fibres.

Much more on this story when we come back on the air tomorrow. It's approaching two o'clock and you're listening to BBC Radio 4 online, on digital and on 92.5 to 96.1 FM."

# FUTURE

# SUNDAY 17TH JUNE 2007

At just after eight, the hot shower has cleaned the outside but deep down inside he still feels quite unpurged. He runs the damp towel once again over a scalp that used to provide more resistance. He knows that he is just putting off the moment when he has to leave for East Anglia. Perhaps St Edmund had once thought the same?

\*\*\*

"And finally, the local squire at the centre of the sensational skeleton find in Waxling, North Norfolk, Mr St John de Criel, has vigorously denied reports that his family has anything to hide. He issued this rebuttal after the BBC's History and Mystery team confirmed that one of the skeletons from the de Criel family vault was of a young girl and provisionally dated much later than Mr de Criel's ancestors:

'I know a lot of people will be sniffing out some kind of a scandal over this find but I can assure you now that I am as keen as everybody else to identify the young child first and then worry later about her tragic death and why her body was hidden in our family vault in the first place. This is a deeply unsettling time and I would hope and pray for understanding rather than supposition.'

**BBC Radio News. It's three minutes past nine."**

\*\*\*

*"We went swimming today but Mummy wouldn't let us go very far out. She said the currents were much too strong and she didn't want us to be in the water too long as Daddy wasn't there to help us if we got into any trouble. I didn't understand this because Daddy usually told us off if we got into trouble. He didn't usually help us. Perhaps he thought that shouting at us would stop us from doing it again so I suppose it was helping, in a funny kind of way.*

\*\*\*

"Yes, I'll be there about eleven o'clock. If the traffic's bad on the M11 I might be a bit later but I should be ahead of it so I'll see you then. Mum says you've not been feeling well; how is it today?"

He had pounced on the ringing 'phone, hoping it might be Nora. He hadn't heard from her since yesterday morning and was anxious to know whether she had been feeling anxious about him; then he had heard his daughter's voice instead.

"It's not too bad really. I just feel ever so hot and my head hurts quite a bit."

"Have you been up to much this week – before you started feeling poorly I mean?"

"Not really. We couldn't leave Grandad for long. Besides, I had my books – and I've still got one to go. Thanks for getting them for me. Anne Frank was very brave wasn't she?"

There had been a new book out about Anne Frank just after Easter and he'd bought it for her from Amazon as she was doing a 'heroes' project at school. She'd proudly presented him with the brown envelope when he'd got home one evening: empty of course.

"She never gave up hope of seeing her family again even when she was in the camp. Granny told me that we should never give up hope of finding people who have been lost or who have lost their way."

He shuffles uneasily at the thought of the Mother Evangelist but allows Rowena to continue without interruption.

"I had a lovely chat with her when we came back from the hospital but she started to cry a bit. I think she'd been worried about me. 'Even if we try and forgive and can't do it,' she said, 'we should at least remember people and places that once meant so much to us.'

I found some other old books; Granny says they were yours when you were little. The covers are all bent and a bit dirty and some of the pages have been written on, but mainly in pencil, so I hope you don't mind but I've rubbed most of it out. I hope it wasn't a secret code that you were keeping …"

'She is trying so hard' thinks Nick, as she proceeds to give him chapter and verse on the various characters who get into scrapes at their 'Fifties boarding school.

"Were the Mallory Towers books your favourites too or did you prefer the Nancy Drew Mysteries?"

He can tell that she knows he hasn't been listening. She has developed a technique lately – probably sponsored by her mother – of slipping a question into a 'conversation' when he isn't concentrating. It catches him out every time and there is no point in pretending otherwise.

"I'm sorry darling I was thinking about something at work." Thankfully she can't yet tell that it is still a lie of sorts.

"The books? Which ones did you like best?"

"I can't honestly remember. I suppose I must have enjoyed all of them. I remember the Hardy Boys mysteries mostly. The books were published by the same company though."

"Really? They must have been so clever to understand what characters and plots boys and girls wanted then!"

He considers how wise she sounds – like a budding author's agent, without the superior attitude.

"Granny said you always had your nose in a book when you were little."

He genuinely cannot remember this either but supposes it must be true. He certainly remembers reading 'War and Peace' at college which gave him plenty of time to escape from 'De-industrialisation: the Thatcher years' which he should have been revising.

"I'm sorry I haven't 'phoned more often."

"That's alright," she responds generously, "Mum said you've been working much too hard lately."

"Did she? When did you speak to her last?"

"Yesterday. She phoned quite late last night. It must have been after eight o'clock because I was in bed and had already finished my milk."

"Was she OK?"

"She sounded very excited."

"Do you know why? Did she give you any clues?"

"Now you do sound like Nancy Drew!" He hears her laughing above that racking, coughing sound in the background. "She said something about a skeleton: that they'd found a 'brace'?"

\*\*\*

"It does indeed look like a robber trench doesn't it, Nathan?"

"Yes it does, but I think it was more likely to have formed part of a stone wall foundation. Geophys reckon there was a structure of some kind which headed in a north-easterly direction from here."

"The difficulty we have, I suppose, is that the walls we are talking about would have long been under the sea and subject to the power of the tides?"

"Indeed. We can, though, establish parts of buildings that would have been under water now for around four hundred years with the old church tower being our main point of reference - and have an idea of the street plan through the original Waxling village – but it's difficult to make all of the joins and state with any degree of confidence that this is how our jigsaw fitted together as a whole."

"OK. Well thanks for that, Nathan. We'll come back to you later to see if you've made any more progress. In the meantime, let's look deeper – if you'll forgive the pun – at what happened on that night in 1607, and we're going to try to look at it through the eyes of Elizabeth de Criel, once of Dunwich in Suffolk.

To tell us more about it I'm delighted to introduce you to Mr Jack Saunders, who served on the lifeboat here for over thirty years?"

"Ahh. Be nearer forty though."

"Wow. Well, that's hugely impressive in itself, Jack, and thanks again for stepping in for St John de Criel who is unable to be with us this morning. Having said that, you do have a reputation in these parts as something of a historian I believe?"

"Ahh. That and butchering."

"I'm sorry ..."

"I was the village butcher here for even longer than that: cutting up meat and disposing of bones."

"I see! So tell us about Elizabeth if you will."

"Old Elizabeth as we call her wasn't from around these parts. She was a stranger you see. Came from down Suffolk way ... a place called Dunwich. Another drowned village - swallowed up about sixty years afore this one here. Church fell off the cliff and into the sea. It's said three other churches are entertaining the fishes there too. No bells though. You'd never know any of them had ever existed now."

"They reckon Dunwich was the tenth largest town in England back in the Conqueror's day and some say it was the capital of all East Anglia. This is where Elizabeth Harrison came from. She was born into a Navy family - her father was an Admiral.

When Elizabeth was a little girl she first heard the story of how her family had to move inland, years before she was born. Many villagers had drowned in violent storms and the church caving in and falling into the sea was the last straw. Port silted up after that and, with less food grown, the place never recovered.

Elizabeth was terrified of the waves, because of those stories she grew up with, but also because her father would be away at sea for long periods himself. Something of a hero he was: part of the English fleet that drove over a hundred Spanish ships up into this part of the North Sea in 1588 – all the way from the Flemish coast."

"The Spanish Armada?"

"That be it. Anyhow, he retired and the family moved up here about two years later but not before old Elizabeth had given birth to a daughter. She was also called Elizabeth.

Well, despite the sea not swallowing her father up, old Elizabeth's prayers turned into premonitions. Hers was a plain, some might say 'harsh' upbringing, with her father away so often and having little time for home comforts when on land leave.

She gradually re-interpreted the Dunwich drowning as a sign from God that the trappings of life were not really needed and against His Will. For this same reason she was anti-Catholic for the whole of her life – not helped by the Spanish War I suppose."

"And she had these 'visions' or out-of-body experiences didn't she?"

"She will have spent long periods on her own and no doubt made up stories of pretend to pass the time; only in her case they ceased to be a game and became 'real' to her mind. She saw figures in the waves, by all accounts, that nobody else could see and she put it down to some kind of religious vision."

"And so, putting all of these things together, she would have been deeply suspicious at the time we find her in Norfolk, wouldn't she, Jack, with people imagining plots everywhere? It sounds like Elizabeth was pretty highly-strung so she would have fed off all of that."

"As I said, she was a deeply religious woman and never let her daughter forget that God controlled the seas as well as the land. When she started seeing those ghosts – or thought she did – she immediately connected them with what her family had always called Papist enemies, from nursery to wedding chamber."

"And her daughter is key here, isn't she?"

"You mean to the story? Oh yes. She was a leading character. She married John de Criel of this parish and they too had a child – also christened John, though everyone knew him as Jack.

It was Elizabeth the younger who rang the

church bells that night in 1607 when the storms came and took Waxling away from the land. Old Elizabeth would have seen the church as a safe haven you see. Eyewitness reports tell us that she was up there on the tower with her daughter when it crashed into the waves."

"And John de Criel?"

"Which one?"

"Well, both: Elizabeth's husband and their child?"

"Both survived but nobody knows how or where they were at the time of the inundation. Jack simply disappears after that."

"And the old church bell can still be heard at certain times – when the wind blows in a certain direction I suppose?"

"It could be that or maybe it's a warning of danger. Some around here will tell you that they have seen a White Lady appear out there in the darkness, just before the bell tolls. Some say it is young Elizabeth and some her mother: warning of danger."

"And do the timings of these sightings coincide with any major disasters around here – we've heard this week that there have been plenty of those?"

"Ahh. They do. In 1692 there was another night of terrible storms. Colliers on their way from London to Newcastle were wrecked off Winterton Ness. That same night, ships from Lynn and Wells – just along from here – were carrying grain to Holland and were all sunk.

More than two hundred ships went down and some say more than a thousand people perished."

"And there had been visions beforehand."

"Oh yes. Several days before the storm folks reported they'd seen a strange white light sort of shimmering over the old church tower; some say it was an actual figure. The bell sounded for more than a week before that.

Then there was 'The Peggy' around 80 years later. She was passing here to join up with the main fleet raised to head off to The Falklands after the Spanish had invaded it.

She went aground near Town Gap in Happisburgh, just down there. It wasn't until noon on the following day that people from the village could even reach her. Thirty-two people died that night and are buried in the churchyard near the graves of those who died on the Invincible. I heard you mention that incident on the radio the other day.

The same thing happened. The bell rang from beneath the waves and the very few that survived talked of a bright light out there on the sea. I suppose you'd call it one of them near-death experiences these days but more than one talked about the figure of a woman with hair streaming about behind her, high up in the rigging frantically waving her hands, urging them to turn back."

"So Jack. All of this is the stuff of tragedy, isn't it? Do you believe any of it?"

"In my opinion, Mr Squires, it would be a fool as would dismiss that which he don't properly understand. Water has always been a source of life and death and is particularly associated with women, though they may be weak in life and strong in death.

I spent my whole life trying to rescue people at sea and I think Elizabeth is trying to do the same. I do believe that she thought she was doing the right thing by ringing that bell all those years ago and still does."

\*\*\*

Nick has been unable to relax or settle into anything since speaking with his daughter earlier that morning. How could one of the skeletons – one of the once-human, beings – have been wearing a brace? When did braces first appear on teeth – certainly not in the seventeenth century? Nora had been right in saying that this was much more recent. But how had the remains got into the de Criel family vault, and whose were they?

Another seemingly quite unconnected post has been loaded from Abbots_Home – the blog of tales from the Norfolk Coast – yet it is dated August of the previous year:

'Shock horror in the village! A naked torso has now appeared in the window of Mill Gallery. The WI has written to the paper to complain about it. To be fair, the artist could have chosen a better model than one with a port wine stain across his fat bum. But I've spoken to the head.'

'Spoken to the head?' What does that mean?' Nick

cannot even begin to work it out. If it is Jack Saunders writing these posts how would he know who it was from that private part of the anatomy?

The 'phone rings – his mobile this time – urgent and certain.

"Golding? Bannister. We need you in. Now."

Nick holds the handset away from his ear, just far enough to hear the 'talking telegram' issuing its instructions.

"Golding? Speak!"

"I am on leave. Remember. My daughter has flu and I am about to travel up to Cambridgeshire to look after her."

"No, Golding. That is quite out of the question. It's Blackout. They've called a pitch, as I quite correctly predicted that they would. Be in the office by midday and cancel all plans for tomorrow as well – if you have any that is. I have no doubt your daughter will survive another absence from her father."

"I don't think so." Nick disconnects.

The 'phone rings again almost immediately and, hoping it will be Nora but anticipating Bannister again, he half runs to pick it up.

"Nick?"

Not the female voice he has been hoping for. Not at all.

"Of course it is. Who did you expect to answer?" His hackles obey an ancient call to rise.

If the caller is flustered by his curt response she doesn't show any sign of it. "I thought you should know that Rowena is quite poorly. What time do you think you'll be here?"

"I know. Nora told me and, as I said earlier, it all depends on the M11 traffic."

"She was sneezing a lot yesterday and I heard her coughing in the night. She feels very hot to me this morning."

"Have you spoken to Nora about it – today I mean?"

"I tried to call her mobile 'phone this morning but there's no reply. I did try several times but thought I'd better let you know instead. Your father said I should 'phone you in case you wanted to bring some extra clothes."

"Why would I want to do that?" The memory of his father issuing instructions only worsens his mood and Nora not answering her 'phone doesn't help matters.

"I was just thinking that she may need to stay a few more days. You could stay too if you wanted to; you know you're always welcome. I could make up the bed in your old room."

'Two beds, one on each side of a small, damp room: the window open to let in the sea breeze.'

"Your father says he wouldn't mind that."

"I have work to do. I can't drop everything just like that."

"I'm sorry. Silly of me."

He detects no sign of sarcasm in his mother's voice. Why is he lying to her? He has no intention of returning to the Prindle Massey office and could quite easily stay and help look after his child.

"I think Rowena would like you to be with her until she's feeling better though; she's so pale and certainly won't be able to travel for a couple of days, I wouldn't have thought."

"Have you called the doctor?" his question sounds more like an interrogation.

"They only come out for emergencies on Sundays and that can sometimes take all day. Your father had an attack a few weeks ago – just after Easter – and they didn't get here until gone four. Said I could go to the Casualty department in Cambridge, but how was I supposed to get him there and how long would we have had to wait then?"

He hadn't known about this, any of it. Nora might have mentioned it to him but he must have blanked her if she did.

"I'll be there at eleven." He slams the 'phone down, relieved as ever to terminate the connection.

He has just passed the Stansted services when Nora's voice comes through on the hands-free.

"I presume you've spoken with your mother?"

"I have and that's why I'm driving as fast as I can to get there." He glances down to see that his speed is still the steady fifty it has been since he exchanged the 'free parking' of the M25 for the equally monotonous M11, some fifteen miles back.

"You were aiming to go this morning anyway weren't you?"

"I was and I'll stay with her until she's better. It's fine."

"I can come and stay there if you like; you can then get back to work."

He knows that she is trying to keep the conversation light but her hypocrisy goes straight to his accelerator foot and the car lurches forward.

"You can't commute from Ely to Waxling each day and you're only there for another week! No, I'll stay with her. I may even come up to see you for the day."

There is a very definite pause at her end while an uncontrollable and overwhelming sense of sadness and loss rises inside him as tears begin to pour out of his eyes, such that he almost collides with a small white van that has slowed down to leave the motorway for the delights of Royston instead.

"I'll see if I can get away tomorrow. It only takes about an hour I think and I'd like to see her."

Her. Not him of course.

"OK." His voice is shaky and he pauses again before continuing. "I think she'd love that. Any developments up there in the meantime?"

"We've found some pottery in one of the Priory trenches. Could be English Delft but we're waiting to have it confirmed. Anyway, I have to go. I may see you tomorrow."

She hangs up abruptly and he feels bereft.

As he pulls onto the A10 just north of Cambridge he turns the radio on to catch her colleagues' update from the dig.

"And now we go over to the History and Mystery team for the latest update from the Norfolk Coast:

Thanks, James. You're listening to John Squires in Waxling on the North Norfolk Coast. The exciting news from here is that since we were last on the air we've had it confirmed that the pottery we found late yesterday in Trench 3 at the Priory is indeed English Delft.

For those of you who tuned in yesterday, you'll recall my conversation with Sam in which he described the beginnings of 'delftware' in this country when potters left Antwerp and other parts of the Low Countries in response to their persecution by the Spanish in the mid-sixteenth century.

The earliest known immigrants settled in nearby Norwich and it is thought that this was due to the quality of Norfolk clay for the production of this particular kind of tin-glazed earthenware.

The two pieces we discovered yesterday are thought to be fragments of drinking vessels and bear the wording 'Elizabeth our Queene,' which means that not only could they be amongst the earliest examples of their kind ever discovered in all of England, but also that our site was occupied on or before 1603 when

**Elizabeth the First died.**

**It could lend weight to the argument that the Priory was indeed still a going concern at the time of the Great Flood of Waxling, four years later..."**

His mother attempts to kiss his cheek as he enters the bungalow but he quickly ducks down to undo his shoelaces and escapes to the spare room, ignoring his father's attention-seeking coughs from the living room.

"Thanks for coming all this way, Daddy."

He is momentarily taken aback by the sight of his daughter. She is propped up on several pillows, a plethora of cups and glasses on her bedside table. Her eyes have sunk much too far into her small face and he sees instantly how pale and pinched it is. Her lovely golden hair is now lank and matted to her face.

She looks as though she barely has the strength to stay awake or that she has used all of the remaining energy she had to be conscious when he finally arrived.

Nick feels ashamed, a deep and undeniable wave of guilt over his lack of care or caring. He hangs his head and simultaneously bends to whisper in her ear, "It's alright. Daddy's here at last."

She holds his head gently in her tiny hands and he feels both the heat pouring out of her body and the earnest reassurance he tries in vain to pump back into her by way of its replacement. He lets her keep him there for what seems like an age, making no attempt to try to break her hold or, remarkably for him, to run away.

At last, her gentle snoring breaks the spell and he very gently lifts his head and folds her arms back on top of the sheets.

As he does so he notices what looks like red crayon marks on her right-hand wrist. On closer examination, he finds that they are cuts which are healing over now and are dry and crusty to touch. He carefully lifts her other arm and notices a similar pattern of very faint scars.

He has no idea what has caused these injuries and, assuming she must have fallen over at some point and grazed herself, leaves her once more, closing the door softly behind him.

"Your father says it's the flu?" his mother peers enquiringly at him for a second opinion as she hands him the ubiquitous cup of tea in a delicate china cup.

"We need to get the doctor out tomorrow to give us his professional opinion." They each hear the pomposity in his voice and then the usual put-down of his father who reacts first.

"No need. He won't be out 'til dinner time as it is; can't do it earlier because she's not registered here so they won't see her as a regular patient. We have to book up to be ill for weeks in advance as it is. She has all the signs of flu and regular fluids is what she needs, not some jumped-up dimwit doctor, just out of medical school."

As his voice collapses in a particularly vicious bout of coughing, his wife takes up the slack.

"I remember when you were children, you had flu

one winter time – proper nasty it was but all we could do was wait for it to pass. Frightened me half to death it did."

"I don't remember."

"You don't remember anything about it?"

Before he can answer her, his father, quite animated now, butts in.

"What were you doing up there? You've no business going up there; it will just end in tears!"

Nick is as mystified as if he had declared he was heading for the North Pole.

"It is just business; nothing more. We're doing some work with a local group who are trying to get money to build up their flood defences."

His father just snorts, as has been his knee-jerk reaction to most of the things his son has tried to tell him over the years, especially when related to work - mentally and often physically removing himself from the conversation altogether.

"Is it something to do with the body they've found?" Mother isn't letting this go easily. She is quite alarming now. Her eyes are wide and dark and something is menacing about the way she moves.

"Leave it Beryl!" his father commands in his breathless voice. I told you not to bring it up, but you wouldn't listen, would you?"

"Bring what up? Tell me, Mother. Mum ..."

But he is too late. As usual, Mother does as she

is told and won't be drawn any further. He leaves the two of them to fight over the silence and heads back into Rowena's room where she has woken and propped herself up again, book in hand as usual.

"Is everything alright?" she whispers shyly. "You didn't mind coming to fetch me, did you? Mum says you're busy."

"I bet she's always saying that isn't she?"

Rowena considers her response before opting for transparency over evasion. "Quite often, but not always."

"I will have a bit more time now. Even if I didn't, it wouldn't have been a problem coming here to see you – Mum and I had already planned it that way - but I don't think we'll be going back to London yet awhile. We'll see what the doctor says tomorrow. I'll 'phone him in the morning."

"It might be a she!"

"Yes. It could well be. A bit like Doctor Levy. Do you remember her?"

"The one with the bad breath who came when I fell out of the tree?"

"I'd forgotten about the bad breath but yes that's the one. You haven't fallen recently have you?"

"No, why?" she is just a little defensive and her eyes are fixed on his.

"Oh, no reason. I just thought, you know, you can often feel a bit off balance with the flu; if it is flu."

Rowena tries to clear her throat and coughs as she pulls herself into an even more upright position. He lifts and puffs up the top pillow for her, noticing little hairs and sweat marks from her hot scalp.

"Granny's the one who's been jumpy. She's been dropping things and then bursting into tears. She always dries her face before I can see it but you can usually tell, can't you?"

He nods his agreement and for the first time wonders if there might be something else on his mother's mind or, Heaven forbid, in it.

"I heard her talking with Grandad one night after the news had finished. She said she couldn't believe that it would be Mummy who was digging up the past. Grandad seemed very upset then as well."

"But that's Mummy's job!"

"I know. That's what I thought. She said something to Grandad about a body and he got very cross with her. I couldn't hear what he said as they started whispering and I fell asleep anyway. I've been having very long sleeps this week."

Why would his parents be discussing the body of a little girl found miles away on the coast? Nora would no doubt have phoned Rowena during the week and mentioned it, and you could hardly escape the coverage on radio or television, but his Mother did seem to have a real thing about it.

"You don't mind if I sit with you for a while do you?"

It is nice to spend some time with Rowena for a change and he has to admit that it is good to have her all to himself. He certainly won't be encouraging anyone from his previous life to come crashing in on them, like a wave destroying a newly-constructed sandcastle before they'd had a chance to put the flag on top...

*'before we'd had the chance to put a flag on top?'*

He shivers though the room is baking and full of decongestant oil fumes from her pillow. Where did those words come from and why do they remind him of a time and place he knows to be from many years ago if only he could picture it?

As Rowena snoozes once more, he gets out his laptop and opens the blog reader, finding yet another post from Abbots_Home:

**'We used to have a vicar here called Jonas. He wasn't from these parts originally. Something bad happened to him – tipped him over the edge, so it did. Perhaps his wife can tell us all about it?'**

That is the sum total of the message. Maybe the writer is experiencing sudden flashbacks in the same way that he almost is, and trying to make sense of them by writing them down. Or maybe these are just the jottings of someone unhinged by the past?

He hears a little gasp from behind and turns quickly to see if Rowena is alright, only to find Mother staring at the screen. He hadn't seen or heard her come into the room. Had she crept in thinking Rowena might be asleep?

"What's the matter? What is it?"

"Nothing," she is wiping her eye with a brown handkerchief, "it's nothing at all. I've been doing the Yorkshires and the fat was spitting from the tray. I came in to ask if you'd like two or three. I've made plenty."

\*\*\*

Later, he has just brought Rowena's lunch tray back into the kitchen when the 'phone rings. Mother answers it.

"Hello. Oh hello. Yes, he's here. Late morning; not sure of the exact time, but all fine. We've just finished lunch. Have you? Right. Sounds lovely. She's much better, thanks; do you want to speak to her or Nick? Right you are. I'll pass you over. No other news I suppose?"

After a few seconds, she passes the receiver to him without so much as even looking in his direction.

"Hello. Nora?"

"Who else would be interested to know if you'd arrived safely?"

Her tone is much more abrupt than earlier but he is resolved not to respond in the same tone as he almost certainly would have done just a few days beforehand.

"It's still nice to know that you care."

"Forgive me while I puke up my rather nice seafood platter."

She is either slightly drunk or trying to impress someone listening in on her conversation or, most likely, both.

"A group lunch?" he asks, harmlessly.

"No. A tete a tete in a secluded sand dune. That's what you want me to say isn't it?"

"Not at all. Look…"

"How is Rowena?"

"She's very hot but she says she feels cold. The doctor is coming out to see her tomorrow - in the morning I think - but it looks like she'll be here for a few days yet. I'll 'phone the school in the morning."

"You don't have the number!"

There is definitely a slur in her voice and a slur in the words she is using as well.

"I'll find it online." He feels sad and can't even summon up the energy to be sarcastic.

"You do that. I'll try and get down tomorrow. I can't come today as I have to talk with the local police force; they've now parked their tanks on our lawn."

"Do they have any leads?"

"Can I have a quick word with Rowena, please?"

# MONDAY 18TH JUNE 2007

"She looks tired this morning. Doesn't look as though she's been sleeping much. Do you think she could be sickening for something else?"

Mother has been rattling off these kinds of statements since he'd sat down at the breakfast table that morning. She has seemingly used every available half-empty cereal packet to build a barricade between him and the rest of the kitchen while reaching up to pluck individual jars of marmalade and jam from still-cluttered cupboards.

He finds himself sneaking a look at sell-by dates on the bases of the jars and can find nothing younger than January 1999 which confirms his suspicion that none of these has seen the light of day since his father departed Ely station for the last time.

The 'phone rings; Mother springs from her chair opposite him and is soon talking animatedly to her daughter-in-law.

"Yes, we've just had our breakfast. I took Rowena's on a tray and she's managed to eat most of it."

He can just about make out Nora's voice above the

domestic bulletin telling her that she had hers at about seven.

"They must rise early up there?"

"Oh, they do." Nora continues in her tinny voice, "It's because the owner used to be a fisherman and some of his old colleagues pop by for breakfast as they used to do when they were fishing full-time. They don't stay here, just show up for breakfast sometimes."

"Must be nice for them!"

Mother silently holds the receiver out to him but he shakes his head and gestures for her to proceed.

"Have the police found anything out yet?"

He perceives a small sigh before Nora speaks again.

"Not yet. The skeleton was taken away as soon as they found it and forensics are on the case. I guess they then have to send samples back to their labs before they can feed back with any degree of certainty."

He isn't sure how much of this his mother has taken in because her next question is bizarre:

"I assume they'll be looking at dental records as a priority."

Nora doesn't quite catch this so he does now take the receiver and broadcasts the question to her in full. She is quite slow, almost guarded, in her reply.

"I would think so, yes. But that will also depend on the quality or state of the teeth they've been able to examine. Don't let your Mum read too much into TV detective programmes. It can often take quite a while to identify bodies such as these, even though this one was in a remarkably good state."

"But you're sure that it's not ancient?" Rowena mentioned a brace, so it can't be one of the children who drowned in that terrible flood they were telling us about on the radio last week?"

"No. Even the mid-Nineteenth Century versions were pretty basic but this one isn't. I can assure you that it's much more recent than that and definitely from the modern era but, as I say, we just have to be patient until we know more."

Mother hangs around for a few minutes and then leaves the kitchen with a disappointed look on her face.

"Connie is pretty certain that the skeleton is no more than fifty years old, perhaps not even that. It's only a guesstimate at this stage though."

"She's not usually far out though is she?"

"Not usually, but there's such a pressure on us now that it's been found. For a series of quite specialist summer programmes, the ratings were already good but since we found the skeleton they've gone through the roof. Not sure that this is exactly how the Controller anticipated us bringing history to the masses."

"Any other news from the dig?"

"Not much. We're certain about the altar position and so we're now concentrating our efforts on the gap between that and the edge of the east wall. We're hoping to find some kind of reliquary."

"A what?"

"It's a kind of container (the French call it a Chasse) containing bones or pieces of clothing worn by saints. It would tell us a lot more about the Priory and whether it really did survive the Reformation, though that in itself isn't proof of course."

"Because it could have been buried by this wall before the monks were forced out?"

"You're getting quite good at this, aren't you? Many reliquaries were melted down during Henry's purge or forced open because they were known to also contain gemstones. 'Medieval grave robbing' you could call it. That wall is in quite good shape so we may find something reasonably intact."

Nick decides to switch the conversation back to the present. "I got through to the doctor. He's going to pop in to see Rowena on his way to the surgery because he won't have time after. They're a bit short down there so he already has a lot of calls to make today. The woman on the switchboard mentioned something about 'summer flu'?"

"Let's hope she hasn't got that! You'll be able to get back either way, won't you? I could always pop down and check on her and she'll be fine with your Mum."

The thought of not seeing Nora is too disappointing to contemplate. Even if his worst fears are confirmed, he knows that he has to see her: talking is not enough.

As he is washing up his cup and plate in the old white sink, the 'phone rings again. Wiping his hands on

Mother's pristine tea cloth, he rushes to the other side of the kitchen to answer it.

"Could I speak with Mr Nick Golding please?"

"Yes, speaking." He doesn't recognize the voice though detects a formality behind a quite clumsy attempt at friendliness.

"This is Chief Inspector Derek Hudson of Norfolk CID. I wonder if you might be able to pop up to see us at some point today? I'm based in North Walsham in Norfolk and I understand you're staying with your parents in Ely?"

"How did you know that?"

He has no idea what a policeman could be calling about and yet it seems inconceivable, given that Nora is currently based just a few miles from there, that it wouldn't concern her or the dig in some way. He remembers seeing a little blue police lamp on one of the buildings they had passed in the taxi.

"A Mr Julian Bannister – your employer I believe – thought that you were staying at your parents' house down there in Ely."

"Is this about the History and Mystery dig at Waxling?"

"I'd rather not discuss it on the 'phone if you don't mind sir. We could come down to you if you prefer but I thought it might be less worrying for your parents if you could get up here. I believe the train connections aren't too bad at this time of day."

He speaks in a quite broad Norfolk accent which

is at once disarming and not at all unfriendly, yet with an undeniable sense of requirement behind the request for him to go 'down to the station' or whatever they used to say on Z-Cars.

"I have to wait for the doctor to come and examine my daughter but could leave straight after that?" he is gripping the 'phone tightly so that his hand, still sweaty, now aches.

"That would be splendid sir. I'll be here all day. Just ask for my name when you get here."

He replaces the receiver but is left with the detective's words still ringing in his ears: 'I thought it might be less worrying for your parents'

\*\*\*

The doctor finally arrives at about eleven fifteen, looking harassed. Dr Hugh Barling is a tall, reedy man replete in a brown, tweed suit and yellow waistcoat, with a smoker's breath and no sense of irony. Nick opens the door just wide enough to let him in and instantly spies the new, white, open-top BMW resting grandly beyond the tired, old gate. The doc. is mopping his largely bald head with a brownish handkerchief. Heat rather than stress, Nick assumes, naughtily.

Of course, Mother immediately offers him tea as though she desires to open up those pores even further. Like most doctors Nick has ever experienced, he formally declines, citing important further calls after theirs and so little time in which to make them, as though Rowena has already diverted him from his rounds.

His bedside manner amounts to a fairly brisk checking of Rowena's pulse and temperature, ignoring her diligent feedback on symptoms she has experienced, and airily pronouncing it as a 'summer cold' which would 'pass soon enough' but prescribing Paracetamol to keep the temperature down, 'especially at bedtime.'

Having worked on the Blackout account for the previous five years Nick knows that the medical profession loves immensely detailed data when licensing drugs and equally vague information when it comes to dispensing them.

He has no idea how long interviews with the police normally last or, indeed, whether there is any such thing as a normal police interview. He tells Rowena that there is nothing to worry about and that he expects to be back later that day.

"Granny says we might go for a walk this afternoon or maybe tomorrow; would you like to come with us?"

In order to assuage his guilt over leaving his daughter so soon again after arriving, and silently cursing the Norfolk Police for getting their wires well and truly crossed, he promises her that he would love to do so but not to wait for him.

He is on the road just before midday and soon heading towards Norwich on the A47. He has Horsham St Faith as a place name in his head which is ridiculous and quite without explanation as he knows Horsham to be a town in West Sussex where they had once visited a tinned pears client: 'try a pear of these for size' had been the direct and rather crass headline approach to their press releases at the time.

He puzzles over this for a while but is much more concerned that something bad has happened to Nora. He has tried her mobile 'phone five or six times since the call from Hudson and sent several texts but there has been no response so far. In truth, she had told him last week that mobile reception on the coast was distinctly unreliable. Or is it she who is being unreliable?

He reaches North Walsham, turns off Happisburgh Road and rolls up outside the Yarmouth Road police station just over two hours later.

Chief Inspector Derek Hudson is a fairly short, squat man with a middle-aged spread having set in a bit too early. Despite his thinning hair and pudgy face, Nick guesses he isn't much past his mid-forties.

They sit opposite each other on chrome chairs in a dark, utilitarian room with only a small window on one side and, perversely, a Picasso print on the opposite wall. He feels suddenly nervous and sits with his hands clasped firmly in his lap.

Hudson is patiently watching Nick watching him and, quite ridiculously, Elvis Costello leaps into his brain with that familiar 'Watching the detectives' refrain before the real detective switches the radio signal in his brain off with an abrupt opening line:

"Didn't you consider it odd that you would be contacted directly by a Chief Inspector?"

Nick's heart lurches. He hadn't even considered it that morning but, yes, it is strange that such a high-ranking officer would request the pleasure of his company.

"No. I suppose I was just so worried about Nora."

"Your wife?"

"Yes."

"When did you last see her?"

"Last Sunday. I saw her last Sunday at my parents' house.

"And she travelled from Ely directly to Waxling, is that correct, sir?"

"As far as I know, yes."

Hudson's bottom lip shakes, almost imperceptibly, but it shakes all the same. "When you say 'as far as you know' what do you mean? You have spoken to her since?"

His tone is not unfriendly but neither is it one that engenders too friendly a response.

"Yes: that night. She contacted both Rowena - our daughter - and me to say she'd got there (Waxling, that is) safely. I was back in London by then. Rowena has been staying in Ely during half-term. She has a chest infection now – or summer cold and …"

"I see. And when was the last time you spoke to your wife on the telephone?"

It sounds so old-fashioned – 'the telephone.' Nick tries hard not to show any sense of metropolitan superiority as he quickly replies.

"Just this morning, before I came here; she was definitely alive then!" he blurts this out to the amazement of both of them.

"Did you have any particular reason to suspect that she might not be alive now?"

Hudson's pupils have dilated as a result of Nick's outburst and he has subtly shifted his bulk forward so that his head is at least two feet closer to his suspect's than before.

"No, no reason at all, but something's obviously happened to her hasn't it?"

"Why is it obvious?"

"Because you've called me up here and, as you said, surely you're a pretty senior detective to be working on a missing person case. It must be more serious than that."

"What would make you think she or anyone else has gone missing? You seem fairly certain about this. Is there something you need to tell me?"

"I don't. I mean, I just get anxious sometimes."

"About your wife?"

"Yes. No. Probably not in the way you think I do."

"And what way would that be Mr Golding?"

His use of Nick's surname instantly cautions him that he is sitting in a police station. This is not verbal sparring with Bannister; this is serious. Senior police officers do not waste their time on summer afternoon chats.

"You are involved in several affairs I understand?" Hudson continues.

"Sorry?"

"Your line of work; I thought it was managing corporate affairs? Do correct me if I'm wrong, sir."

That 'sir' word again. Such a small word but big enough to get under anyone's skin.

"For a London firm called Prindle Massey?"

"Yes. For many years now."

"Indeed. As I indicated earlier, we have had a little chat on the telephone with a Mr Julian Bannister – your superior I understand?"

"He's the Group Account Head, yes." How pompous that sounds here in rural Norfolk.

"It seems that you've been under some stress. You're taking some time away from your work …"

"It isn't so unusual. People need a break sometimes and I needed some mind space." He immediately regrets the feeling of sliding into an abyss of New Age cliché and London-centric mumbo jumbo.

"Do you think that your current state of mind, coupled with your wife being away, is making you especially nervous?"

"My wife has been away before and I've been perfectly fine. It must be all the changes going on at work I guess."

"Changes?"

"We're looking to use some new media techniques on behalf of our clients. One of them is the flood defence action group up at Waxling."

"I didn't know about your connection with the Waxling people. What does your wife think about this?"

He feels suddenly chilled as, awkwardly, he informs Hudson that she doesn't know anything about it.

"Doesn't know? Isn't that rather strange behaviour sir?" he has raised his voice very slightly.

"Would you describe yourself as having a good marriage?"

"It's fine, thank you."

"Nothing you need to tell us?"

"No, it's fine, it really is. We do have some communication issues but ..."

"A little ironic in your line of work wouldn't you say?" Hudson does not smile. If anything his lips have narrowed a little. "Or do you just have secrets from each other? Guilty secrets perhaps?"

"We don't have secrets from each other and ..."

"Oh, but you do. You've just admitted that your wife knows nothing of your connection with Waxling?"

"Yes but," he feels his face reddening. "Look, please just tell me why I'm here. Have I done something wrong?"

"Had you visited Waxling previously to Tuesday 12$^{th}$ June 2007 sir?"

How does he know about that and, much more importantly, why? The softly, softly phase seems to be over.

"No. Never. That was the first time."

"Are you quite sure about that?"

"Of course I'm sure." I was thinking about a place called Horsham this afternoon though. I don't know why because I know it's down south but ..."

Hudson stops him in his tracks. "There is a Horsham in Norfolk too, sir. Horsham St Faith was the name of a site near here. It was owned previously by the RAF and then the USAF during the last war. It came back into the civilian domain in 1967 – March time I think it was. I wonder why you would think of that place today, sir, or indeed if it was that place - that time – that you were recollecting."

Why do the police always talk in such peculiar prose? They are worse than train announcers and their insistence on customers taking extra care during 'inclement weather.'

"I have no idea and even less about what this has got to do with Nora or me?"

He stands up – far too quickly as he immediately feels faint. Hardly the pose of a man in control.

Hudson is just as calm as when the friendly interrogation began.

"Very little to do with your wife, sir, but very much to do with you. As I'm sure you are aware, two days ago a skeleton was discovered close to Waxling

Beach. The skeleton is of a little girl who had been wearing a brace at the point of her burial – or incarceration - and, thanks to that, we have been able to trace dental records to a dental practice in Ely, Cambridgeshire. Your home town I believe, sir?"

Nick sways again. His mind is having real difficulty in processing this new information; He hears the sounds of Hudson continuing but it is as though he is speaking from either a different room or a different age.

"... an incident there in 1967. The body was never discovered and, of course, even if it had it turned up, there was no possibility of DNA analysis at that time. Mercifully, now that we do have a skeleton to work with and, because of the scientific progress we've been able to make since then, forensics have been able to take DNA from hair strands that were preserved.

It was buried in a cool, dark place as opposed to the many poor souls who died there after the big flood your wife is investigating, so we were lucky, even if the little girl was not. Does any of what I'm saying make any kind of sense to you?"

"I ... I just don't understand what it is that you are telling me."

Hudson does not even draw breath: "In 1967 a ten-year-old girl drowned off of Waxling Beach while on holiday there. Her body was never found – up until now, that is. We believe we've finally discovered the body of your sister, Mr Golding"

\*\*\*

He barely hears the lead news story on the Labour Party spending two billion pounds each year on Whitehall advisors, nor the subsequent update from the History and Mystery team, other than to register that the police are now carrying out their own investigation there as well.

He has no idea what Hudson or Leigh are talking about but his lack of understanding goes much further than that, much deeper. How can they be asking questions about a sister or a family holiday from so long ago when he is an only child and, frankly, has no recollection whatsoever of ever being at Waxling?

His gut reaction had been to return to Ely immediately and bring his line of questioning to his parents – or at least Mother – about this incredible story, to see if they could help to explain such an obvious case of mistaken identity.

He doubts that his father possesses the brain power to adequately cover anything up or keep it from him for so many years. Mother, on the other hand, has acted increasingly strangely on the few occasions he still sees her, as though she has become semi-detached from reality. He has always blamed drink for her descent into madness.

He 'phones Nora instead but the call goes straight to voicemail. He asks her to 'phone him back as soon as possible and then examines his texts. There is just the one, inevitably from Bannister.

His words of persuasion are as eloquent as ever: 'Get yourself on a plane to Geneva tonight. Meeting at Blackout: 1.00 PM their time tomorrow. Be there.' He deletes it with a single, hefty press of the delete key.

A situation is unravelling before him – all around him, in fact, over which, unerringly, he seems to be able to exercise no control. And yet, he is always in control. It's what PR people are there for.

He winds the car windows down. Even though the birdsong laments the cooling of the day it still feels humid to him and he requires the late afternoon breeze to cool both him and the car down. As he leaves the car park he recalls Hudson's parting comment, with just the slightest hint of menace. 'Please do let us know if you intend to leave the area.'

Being just a few miles from Waxling he quickly finds the coast road and heads north. He must see Nora – to talk it through with her first; has to talk to her like he hasn't talked to her for years. She will know which questions to ask Mother. She is still his wife in name after all.

About five minutes after leaving North Walsham he notices the red light on his mobile begin to flash on the adjacent seat where he has thrown it after leaving his voicemail for Nora. He eventually finds the rutted entrance to a dusty farm track and pulls over, pleased that she has replied so quickly. He opens the text and sees that the sender is not Nora but someone called 'Lionel-Goater.'

He scans the message, disappointed as he is that it isn't from Nora:

"Hi, Nick. Got a fix on that Abbots_Home blog site you mentioned. It is being written from an IP address at Waxling in Norfolk and from a private rather than an organisation's address. You might also want to know that your daughter, Rowena, is writing a blog.

Her latest observations were updated today. Her post was sent from Littleport in Cambridgeshire, and almost certainly from a desktop PC located in the public library. I'm not sure what she would be doing there. Best. George."

Nick has quite forgotten about his email to George Savory, the digital guru. How on earth did he know that Rowena was writing stuff online when Nick – her own father – didn't? If George is right then the Abbots_Home blog must be being written by Jack Saunders.

As for Rowena's blog, he really must find time to read it. She must have walked up the road to Littleport – or taken the bus? And yet, when he'd left her that afternoon, a trip to the kitchen looked like being a trip too far for her.

Just as he closes this text another one arrives. To his absolute astonishment, it is from a 'Beryl Standing' which was his Mother's maiden name. He had forgotten that he had her in his contacts list and clearly hadn't felt able to list her as 'Mum' like any normal person would have done.

"Please come home quickly. The police have been on the 'phone. Mum."

Less than twenty minutes later he approaches the sea once again. He has heard on the radio that traffic on the coast road from Sheringham on the other side of Waxling is still heavy with holidaymakers and 'day trippers' (though it is now mid-afternoon) being drawn to the tiny village by the sea – presumably by the power of television – and the police are allegedly considering restrictions on the number of cars being allowed to enter the village itself.

He doesn't encounter any kind of roadblock, though, as he enters from the southeast. Cars are parked (a loose term) at a variety of angles on the side of the narrow road from what must have been a couple of miles out from the village - as though they've been dumped there by a giant wave - but he manages to find a space in the car park of what seems to have been an old windmill.

No cap or sails remain but the building shape gives it away. The lower windows are boarded up but, with no obvious way to climb up the circular wall, the owners have not bothered to do the same with those on the higher levels, of which he estimates there are at least four. It looks unused and unloved but he reasons that it would have a fair few stories to tell if it could speak, being placed in such a commanding position.

He has left yet another voicemail on Nora's 'phone suggesting that they meet at the pub and finds himself walking quickly into the village, thinking he might surprise her, despite his apprehension over what further secrets might yet be waiting in store for him.

As the street bends to meet the sea wall he becomes aware of movement on the beach just beyond. It is the beautiful young woman and girl whom he had addressed on his only other visit to this remote and lonely place. The woman is wearing the same white dress and the girl is wearing her red bathing suit with a red bow in her hair to match, still pulled down to one side.

As on that Tuesday afternoon previously, they walk remarkably quickly and yet, looking at the backs of their legs, it appears that they are not walking very fast at all – just ambling along really. He spots the break in the wall where he had left the main street before but they walk past it and he feels compelled to follow.

He wants to ask the woman about the History and Mystery find and what they, as fellow visitors, think about it all, but is almost jogging after them just to keep up until, quite suddenly, they stop by the wall of the church, the square tower looming up behind them.

So, this must be near to where the body was found, he thinks. He can see the blue and white police tape, fluttering in the breeze on one side, and an unexpectedly large group of people just beyond. They just seemed to be standing there, as though waiting to be witnesses to whatever event was due to happen next.

He looks back toward the woman and child but assumes they have continued with their walk, leaving him quite alone there in the afternoon shade.

He spots a wooden door to one side of the church. The image of Martin in Battersea floats suddenly into his mind. Had he married his beautiful but doomed Christina in a church? Nick feels unreasonably certain that he would have done so and brushes away an unexpected tear just as the small door opens outwards.

A woman with lustrous grey hair and dressed in cream trousers and an expensive, blue, silk blouse exits the church and immediately turns to his right. She is quite stocky and her clothes are just that little bit too tight on her curves and folds to be classy rather than trashy. She is carrying an armful of dead flowers which she promptly hurls over a short brick wall in the corner of the churchyard.

As she turns to come back he recognizes her face. She is the lady in red stilettos who had attended Connie Breeve's boathouse interview with de Criel.

"Hello," she waves cheerily, "Audrey Bracken. Can I help you?"

He feels unreasonably self-conscious now and more than a little foolish. What exactly is he doing there and does he need her help?

"I was just visiting, thanks. My wife is part of the History and Mystery team and I've come up to see her for a few hours."

"And you thought you'd pop into the church? Well, come on in; as long as you're not from the red tops, looking for some kind of inside scoop."

The Woodentops would have formed more likely starting points, such is the gaucheness he still feels in the company of powerful or knowledgeable people. His father had for some reason been determined to mentally batter all semblance of self-worth out of him and so other figures of supposed or assumed authority such as Bannister, de Criel and now Audrey Bracken still manage to do the same without really having to try.

He hears his stilted reply of "Marvellous, thanks; if it's not too much trouble ..."

He always expects churches to be dark inside, as though reflecting his doubts. This one, though, is quite refreshingly light due to the preponderance of windows which aren't made of stained glass. Audrey Bracken is finishing a flower arrangement of what looks like large daisies just below the pulpit but he knows that she is monitoring his every step into the unknown, even with her face turned away from him.

"It's very peaceful I think you'll agree?" without waiting for an answer she proceeds to broadcast her knowledge about the tower here being square, like that at Sea Palling, but quite different to the much younger St Andrew's at nearby Hempstead.

"Many Saxon towers were round, especially in areas like this when the only real stone available was flint. Flint isn't easy to deal with as it's quite small and usually available as individual stones rather than slabs which you can cut into building blocks. Square flint towers need stone to strengthen the corners and that can be pretty expensive if there isn't any nearby – the curse of East Anglia I suppose!

By the time you've brought in stone and dressed it, it would be beyond the reach of most village communities – especially little coastal ones like Waxling. So, it was much cheaper to build flint towers without corners and the original church here was almost certainly round, as was its replacement out there under the sea. This church was to be a kind of monument to the already dead as well as those yet to perish, I suppose.

There are some etchings in the library in Norwich I believe that also confirm this. You won't find much though – a lot of the really old manuscripts from the late eleventh century were in the vault of the Reference Library when it caught fire, what, twelve or thirteen years ago?

Terrible that was, especially as they'd just spent a lot of money on refurbishing it! You could see the smoke from as far away as Wroxham. Some buildings aren't meant to last, are they? God's will of course."

Nick – a mere mortal - becomes suddenly aware of a different voice then, way off in the distance. It is the voice of a man who is repeating the same words over and over again: 'I'm afraid that there is nothing more we can do for you' but so quietly that they are intoned in little more than a whisper – an incantation.

Audrey appears not to have heard anything and, mercifully, it quickly fades away again as the sound of the sea can be heard beyond this 'safe house.' The waves seem to be crashing over the beach outside, as he remembers the occasional sea birds nestling in the foam from his previous visit.

"You ought to ask St John about it," Audrey brings him abruptly back to the past, "he's something of an expert on church architecture around these parts, as was his father, Barnabus, before him I believe. Have you met St John? I've no doubt your wife has!"

"Yes. Yes, I did meet him. Our PR agency is planning to run a campaign for you in support of the EC lobbying you're doing ..."

"For the flood defence fund? Between you and me I think that lobbying the Good Lord might prove more beneficial – but, if anyone can pull it off, St John can. Let's hope so at least. He's lost so much already but I'm afraid we're all in the same metaphorical boat now."

"Lost? You mean family, friends?"

"His house! He lives in what was the lodge house now. The last bit of the de Criel mansion fell into the sea during the hurricane. Not that there was much left by then. He lived in the South wing next to the Centre."

"You mean the Resource Centre?" He remembers the previous lecture from Leslie Pickett.

"Big white elephant if you ask me! Someone – probably St John's late father - had the brilliant idea that schoolchildren and the like would come up here to learn about Waxling's sad and undistinguished history. I suspect it was more likely an ego trip to show off what was left of the family fortune and to channel funds into the lifeboat station from grateful teachers and their parents who got some respite care as a result!"

"And it's no longer here?"

"You don't need to be part of the History & Mystery team to work that one out. The building and ground it was built on have long since disappeared, much like the vicarage where I used to live. So much for the power of prayer!" She bends her head slightly at this sudden outburst, as if in silent apology.

"I take it that you and Mr de Criel go back a long

way?"

She rounds on him unexpectedly and he quickly sees that the smile has departed from both her face and tone of voice. "What exactly do you mean?"

"Only that you seem to know him well enough to be able to speak so highly of him."

Her reply is a little more relaxed though the guard is still there – much like the giant arch which continues to frame their 'conversation.'

"I have come to know him quite well over the years and admire him very much. His lifeboat reputation precedes him of course but there is much more to him than simply a brave commander of men."

Nick finds the military analogy somewhat inappropriate but her scrutinizing stare prevents him from voicing his dissent out loud.

"Almost legendary status I'd say," he creeps instead, "He certainly seems to have preserved the family reputation."

"Indeed so, if not enhanced it. A remarkable achievement if you think about it, given that the ancestral home was literally falling into the sea throughout his lifetime. He had to take on and try to arrest the decline in his own family as well as the community it is so proud to serve. Without people like St John de Criel, communities like ours would have died out long before the sea's waves washed over them.

It's all very well helping each other and forming defence committees and so on but people need direction and inspiration. That is what sets people on and keeps them on the right path. St John brings those attributes to us. We are lucky and we are grateful for them."

She is still staring at him and he can more clearly see that she is considerably older than she tries to look, the heavy layer of makeup and expensive clothes notwithstanding.

"Is your family well established here too?"

"Who are you? You sound like a journalist but look like an estate agent."

"I'm not a journalist. Take my word for it. I'm just interested in this whole project that's all: so that I can talk intelligently about it with my wife rather than just at a distance via the TV."

"Well then," she bends down again to tidy the loose stems and other horticultural paraphernalia together, "if you'd done any research at all you'd know that I've lived here for most of my life. My husband was the vicar here and it was our first married posting."

There is that war-like analogy again. He gets the distinct impression that Audrey Bracken never takes prisoners, just goes for the kill each time.

"And was he a local man?"

"His name was Jonas Thomasson."

"Swedish?"

"No, but they were originally from Sweden. Jonas's family moved to Riga in medieval times. That's the capital of Latvia if you'd care to look it up. They were cloth traders and first came here when the Hanseatic League was at its height in the late 1300s. They decided to stay and settled in Bishop's Lynn, which became King's Lynn."

"I imagine you wish the EC were as strong now as a trading bloc that protects its own as the Hansa was in its day?"

"No man-made institution and no amount of money can keep us from the sea, Mr?"

"Golding. Nick Golding."

"Yes. I do know your wife: pretty, dark-haired lady." Her voice remains monotone, lifeless amid death; she could have been reading about Nora from an inscription on the faded kneeler she is rigorously brushing.

He thinks back to the woman and child on the beach. If anyone knows who they are, Audrey Bracken would no doubt be that person.

"I saw a woman walking on the beach today with a little girl. She was quite tall, with short dark hair and wearing a white dress: plain but quite classic in a strange kind of way – like something you might buy from Laura Ashley..."

Audrey Bracken is upright in seconds, a fixed stare on her pale face, and appears to be examining his own eyes and face as if for clues.

"Who are you really?" she whispers so softly that he has to lean in towards her to hear her properly, "you're investigating something or someone aren't you?

Is it her?"

He leans back again, not wanting to be at all intimidating and holds out his hands in that age-old gesture of apparent innocence, rather like the misunderstood figure on the cross above them.

"I assure you I'm not trying to find out about anybody, though I'm interested in the body they've just found, like everyone else, and the flood itself of course."

"Oh, I think you are. Maybe you're trying to find something out about yourself ... from your past perhaps?"

Even in the fast-moving world of PR, he finds this a bit of a leap but she is hurdling with ease the barriers he has hastily thrown up.

"You've been here before I think?"

"A few days ago, yes, I met Mr de Criel here but, before that, I'd never even heard of Waxling."

"Are you quite sure about that? St John got the impression that you knew a good deal about the area and its history."

So she does know who he is and was aware of his connection with the defence lobby all along! What is she playing at? Again, he feels as if the metaphorical rugs have been pulled from underneath him, revealing only stone – hard and uncompromising.

"Anything I do know about the area has been gleaned from Jack Saunders and ..."

"Man's mad."

Nick isn't sure if she is referring to just Jack or all men. He waits for her to elaborate, which she quickly does - almost too quickly.

"Oh he's loyal – devoted to St John of course - and means well no doubt, but you'd think we were about to be captured by Samoan pirates to hear him talk. He does love a drama, does Jack."

"Do you know if he keeps a diary, perhaps on his computer?"

"A blog you mean?"

The Prindle Massey school of going round the houses to find the estate strikes again, he concedes. "Yes, well, possibly. I've been reading something called Abbots_Home but I thought that might just be a pen name."

"Like a handle? Oh, don't look so surprised. We used CB for years around here until the licensing louts got on to it. The web's really just today's version of that, isn't it? You have a Facebook account I assume?"

As with de Criel previously, he feels as much in control of the conversation as he does the tide beyond these ancient walls. How could the agency ever hope to manage this process – not that he really expects to be part of the attempt now?

"We're looking into that at the moment for our clients."

"You should look at yourselves first; talk to each other. You won't find Jack Saunders online unless he's fishing off of the harbour wall – that's the only form of networking he knows about, Mr Golding. As for his opinions – well, let's just say that they are amplified in direct correlation with the amount of beer he's consumed in 'The Lady.'

The only Abbots Home I've heard of was a guesthouse run by the village gossip, Gladys Pickett. I'd be surprised if she was especially computer-savvy either but she did do all the admin for the RNLI when St John was in command so it's possible I suppose. She lives up by the old mill with her husband, Leslie. Quaint old bird but he's just an empty nest."

"They live alone?"

Audrey gives a horsey kind of snort before replying, in an impatient voice, "Ever since the Good Lord failed to bless them with children. Perhaps that was why he sent the flood here in the first place: to deal with people like Leslie Pickett who don't help themselves.

If you try and talk to him about any of the lifeboat rescues he was involved with, he'll tell you he can't remember anything about them."

"Isn't that called dementia? It happens."

"Doctor Marr prefers amnesia, I believe, apparently brought on by trauma – perhaps this unforgiving sea has something to do with it? By all accounts, he just sits at home, day in and day out, asking Gladys the same questions and ignoring the same answers. I doubt very much you'd get much sense out of either of them: a shopping list for the Spa store is likely to be the peak of their joint writing abilities."

"And your husband," he enquires more out of politeness than any great thirst for knowledge and realizing that his question about the woman and child on the beach had been either neatly side-stepped or conveniently forgotten by this formidable woman, "was his death in any way connected with the sea?"

"He was spared that indignity," she isn't upset, more cross about it all if anything, "no doubt you were still playing with your Chopper at the time?"

\*\*\*

*Today we went to see the sauce centre. It wasn't like our library at school at all. All the shelves there are full of scripture books about the Holy Land or science books about how the car works or what's inside a camera. Daddy took a picture of me yesterday but I can't look at it until we get home, he said. It needs developing or something. There weren't many books there at all but there were quite a few charts showing the sea and maps like the ones Mrs Bell draws for us in class. There were quite a few old pictures on the wall with big, dark picture frames around them. My brother sat and stared at one of them for ages. It was of a woman called the 'White Lady.' I knew who it was not just because it said so underneath but because Mrs Click Clack had described Mistress Elizabeth. She had long golden hair and this woman had the same colour hair which must be pretty wet now if she spends so much time under the sea. I could just make out Daddy's voice and went to look for him. He was with the man in the office. The door had a glass window in it that made the shapes inside a bit blurry and it said 'Private' on the outside but I knew Daddy was in there because I recognized his voice so I knew it was OK to go in. The posh man had his back to me and Daddy was kneeling* down in front of him so I was very quiet as I thought he was praying. Then I realized that he wasn't praying. He was helping the posh man to mop up the Ribena stain on his bottom with tissues. The posh man turned round. I don't know why he was so cross to see me. He wasn't cross at all yesterday when everyone was happy and hugging each other.

\*\*\*

She has been pacing up and down the empty beach since mid-afternoon. De Criel – as insufferably grand as ever - has installed himself in the pub having called all of his cronies to a 'war cabinet.' In they'd come, one by one, wiping their feet dutifully before entering the sacred back room.

John Squires was amongst them, subpoenaed to give whatever evidence he had access to which would undoubtedly prove that the instability of the rock formation led to the ground below the church wall collapsing.

The huge number of unexpected viewers - both remote and now local (sometimes both) - has given the flood defence volunteers their finest hour in which to make their case to both the nation at large and the narrow-minded observers from the European Community who rarely left Flanders - like so many who had once fought to save them.

To be honest she's grateful to be away from Squires; mercifully, since the visit to Sheringham, he seems to have targeted his attentions to poor Hayley instead. Nick would have been so self-righteous about it all if he had been here. She doesn't need him to tell her about the roving microphone, clasped in roving hands. She knew this long ago; before Seahenge even. She just wanted someone to talk to - properly talk to - but men like Squires love to put words into her mouth and always want to follow them up with something else.

Words leading to sentences. Tears prick the edges of eyes as she remembers the words of a little girl with everything to live for, and yet, seemingly also a reason to die. She heard the story long before their wedding day; she never truly believed him capable of it but there were times when he was left alone with Rowena that he seemed so lost, and rarely showed much love or devotion to his own daughter.

Neither, though, had he ever done anything to suggest that he would hurt her, from when she was little until now. As an archaeologist, her aim has always been to learn from the past and let it help those in the present to move forward. Will this be the case here? Whatever the truth proves to be – and his being able to come to terms with it after so many years - frightens her. How can they even begin to justify keeping such a secret for so long?

She misses Nick, really misses him and wants to protect him from what is about to happen. Or maybe it already has? What have the police already told him? Have they confirmed the identity of the body yet? How has he reacted and why hasn't he contacted her?

She must try to be patient with him. It will come as an enormous shock and Rowena's struggles would only compound it. They may yet prove to be unfounded, though how she longs to share them, discuss them with him too. Maybe he will fold his strong arms around her and just hold her close, not speaking at all. Perhaps he will just cry: perhaps all three of them will.

\*\*\*

St John de Criel is in full flow when Nick walks into the White Lady later that afternoon.

"The harvests were really bad in the years leading up to the 1590's but, thankfully, my ancestor had turned much of the land around here over to sheep farming. Wool was the Norfolk Gold in those times... " de Criel is seated on a wooden stool in the main bar area and Nick notices several people from the History and Mystery production team sitting dutifully in a semi-circle around him.

"Of course, this had been mainstream Catholic territory for centuries. The Bigod Earls were very a very important, established family in East Anglia, indeed England itself, being present at the signing of the Magna Carta in 1215 by King John, so they went back almost as far as my own good family line.

From our own 'amateur' research we can say that they definitely played a part in establishing the priory here as well as a monastery in Thetford but, of course, after the dissolution this would have been a tricky alliance to defend publicly and may have put both their wealth and their position in society at risk.

Thomas Howard – the fourth Duke of Norfolk – wanted to put Mary Queen of Scots on the throne. Do you remember the Ridolfi Plot with Philip of Spain? No, well it didn't work ... "

Much laughter from the disciples.

"He was executed for treason in 1572 and all of his lands and titles were forfeited. The Duke of Norfolk title wasn't fully restored for some four generations but some of the titles and estates were restored to Thomas Howard's namesake – known officially as the Earl of Arundel (the Collector Earl as it happens) – after James I came to the throne. We believe the de Criel estate was one of them."

He sits back, beaming at his audience, a man at peace with his ego, and swallows the remains of half a glass of beer in front of him. On cue, several fellow drinkers head for the bar, each wanting to be the one to buy the next round for Waxling's 'Celebrity Squire.'

The same plump woman who had served Nick on his previous visit is not beaming at anyone. She is glaring at him from behind the bar, making it very obvious that he should be ordering a drink as payment for free use of the bar space.

She is dressed all in black as usual. Following his encounter with the all-in-white beach lady again today he considers that this part of Norfolk has given up colour altogether. Perhaps they just want clarity and everything to be in either black or white? Strangely though, things here do not seem any more straightforward than in the metropolitan world of Prindle Massey.

Thankfully, he sees Nora enter the pub before she is even aware of him. She is wearing a tight pair of blue jeans that hug her shapely legs, and thin, white blouse. He knows this is much more to do with it being worn and washed so often than any desire for provocation which Petra at the agency, for one, would have wholeheartedly approved of. He notices also that her long, curly hair has lightened a little as it always does during the summer months. She looks positively glowing.

Unfortunately, someone else seems to think so too. John Squires arrives at her side out of seemingly nowhere, dressed casually in grubby blue tee shirt over nearly-white shorts. He seems to be in something of a hurry.

Disregarding the unwelcome presence of his rival, Nick is thrilled to see her; relieved that she is there at last and that he is not having to deal with all of this on his own anymore. He is trying so hard not to rush over to her and hug her that - in his much more restrained and deliberate walk across the bar space - he sends a low, wooden table flying, then almost trips over it.

"We meet again!" Squires, an amused smile playing on his sunburned and cracked lips, is holding out a beautifully-manicured hand. "How have you been?"

Nick points to Squires's hands. "I see you haven't been doing much of the digging!"

He tries to feign friendliness but his eyes harden and his reply is a closing statement: "It's a team effort and I wouldn't want to get in the way of the experts any more than you would. Now, I'm afraid I have to dash. Lovely to see you again."

With that and a 'hail fellow' wave in de Criel's general direction he strides out of the pub and they watch his bony knees pass the tiny windows which look out on to the street.

Nick turns to face his wife. Her eyes seemed to light up with delight when she first saw him, though she is now strangely shy and rather gauche; most unlike the strident woman he last saw a week ago.

"Hello," she says, "I've been waiting for you."

"For far too long," he gushes. "Nora, I have so much that I want to say to you. I've been to the police in North Walsham this afternoon and…"

"I know."

"You do. How so?"

"Beryl told me about the call."

"Oh. Oh, I see. Did she have anything else to say … how's Rowena?" His voice is steady though the dryness in his mouth stands at the point of an inner betrayal.

"She's fine. They're both fine."

"Where is Squires rushing off to?"

"As I think I may have told you, the police are here too. They've set up an incident room at the Village Hall. They don't like to be kept waiting: looks suspicious."

"And you don't think there's any connection at all with the dig?"

She shakes her head slowly, her eyes never once leaving his. "What happened here belongs to a distant past, which is part of its charm for viewers: watching someone else's secrets revealed from long ago.

That's why they've enjoyed 'Who do you think you are?' for these past three years. What they forget is that the past is a continuum right up to the present and can have a profound effect on the future security of everyone concerned, even those who don't yet realize they are part of it."

She frowns, deep in thought as she always is when she is in the middle of a dig: on the brink of discovery or, more likely, just affirmation of what they already knew. He loves the concentration she brings to her work but then it has a purpose, unlike his which has always seemed fairly pointless.

She is continuing. "There must be a reason why John de Criel left his village at the worst possible moment, leaving his wife and fellow parishioners to perish. It was just so out of character. From the accounts which we do have, he was a benevolent man - more Father than Squire to the people here."

"What accounts have you read? I mean what are you basing this on?"

"Hayley went to Norwich Central Library – you know, the big new one - and found a journal of one of the residents here at the time who was full of praise for de Criel. Unfortunately, she became ill and had to leave."

"The resident or Hayley"

Nora laughs - naturally not nastily. "Possibly both but definitely Hayley. We had a fish pie in here last night and Sam was a bit queasy this morning as well."

"Did she find out anything else?"

"Only trading records from the old Mill which has stood here since Elizabethan times. She found that corn was still being milled and much of the flour being distributed to the Priory in 1600, but never on Fridays."

"And the significance of that is?"

"Fridays are traditionally fasting days for Catholics. You remember that project Rowena did about fish and why many people only eat it on Fridays? No, well it suggests here that the Austin Friars – as the Augustinians were known by then – must have survived as a religious order much longer than most after the Reformation. We don't have records of any that survived for longer in England or Scotland though some did in Ireland I think. They didn't re-appear as an Order in this country until the mid-Nineteenth Century."

"So that could also reinforce the History and Mystery argument that the villagers wouldn't have sought sanctuary there because they, the Friars, were viewed with suspicion: religious belief first, practical help second?"

"Or the Friars could just have been unwilling to engage with the villagers in practical matters at all. They were effectively hermits."

"I know the mill you mean. I'm parked next to it. It's boarded up now – well the ground-floor windows are - and it has no sails on it."

"It was turned into an art gallery in the 'Sixties. Usual psychedelic stuff from local artists I expect. The owner moved away at the end of last year apparently. Nobody knows if or when the mill will go up for sale. I was speaking with Gladys Pickett – she lives next door to it – and he had it really nice inside, she said."

"I could go back to the library and do some more research if you like. Like I said, I'm taking some time off this week."

"Yeah right!"

He doesn't blame her cynical response. She won't believe that he has left Prindle Massey; he doesn't entirely believe it himself."

"No really. I'd be happy to."

"Aren't you going back to Ely tonight?" she isn't alarmed by his offer of help - a little surprised perhaps, but pleasantly so.

"I could do if you want me to, but I'm not sure there's much I can do. I told Rowena that I might not be back until either late tonight – well after she's gone to bed – or tomorrow. I can always ring later to check she's OK. She'd fret less if she thought I was with you anyway."

Nora is reassuringly happy about this outcome. She visibly relaxes and even blushes slightly.

"Actually that would be really nice. But where would you stay?"

"I'm sure I could find somewhere but it might be a bit tight."

"No doubt about that! Nick, we have a lot to catch

up on – Rowena is feeling very lonely at school and has started imagining things. I think it's probably down to all those books she reads but there are so many other things I need to talk to you about as well. I should have got some of this off my chest years ago but ... well, you're just going to have to trust me. Can you still do that?"

Before he can speak another word, de Criel is looming up behind his wife, arm around the shoulders of Audrey Bracken who sports a smug grin on her unnaturally full lips.

"Look at the two of you!" de Criel slurs slightly and, a little more pompously, "A lovely evening for getting away from it all, I'm sure."

"Indeed it is" he hears Nora respond without even a hint of irony as they both nod in Audrey's direction and bow their heads (due to the low level of the arched door they are now walking swiftly towards, and that alone).

"I hadn't expected to see you again, Mr Golding," the voice of doom booms behind them for the whole village to hear, "or at least not so soon. You had to see for yourself that your pretty little wife wasn't up to mischief I presume?"

# TUESDAY 19TH JUNE 2007

It is a seagull that has awoken him. He tries to straighten up on the back seat of the car and realizes that his knees and feet have gone to sleep along with the rest of him and need more time to wake up, especially as it is only just after four o'clock. There is a mist out at sea, lit by and reflecting the first rays of the new day's sunshine.

He instantly recalls the previous evening's final scene before a dark, impenetrable curtain came down. Yet again he replays Nora's shocked face which quickly changes to a knowing disappointment as de Criel and Audrey Bracken smile their sickly good nights. She heads (alone now) to the door in the far corner of the room, opens it purposefully and slams it behind her. How long ago it now seems since she came through it, accompanied by Squires.

There had been things she wanted to tell him yesterday; had seemed so keen to do. In return, he had kept his own movements a secret from her. He is the one who had travelled up to Waxling without telling Nora. Whatever was he thinking? What logic could possibly have justified it in this cold light of day? What other conclusion could she reasonably have drawn other than that he was so insecure, so pathetic as to be spying on his wife?

He had thought about driving back to Ely immediately but, after ten minutes of just sitting, motionless in the car, he'd leaned back on the headrest and that was the last piece of a sad and confusing day he could remember.

His reverie comes to a shuddering halt as her face fills the back window of the car: so pale in the unravelling gloom. It is the woman from the beach. He sits up straight to see if her daughter is also there but, of course, it would have been much too early for a child to be up and about. He wraps his jacket tightly around his shoulders as he opens the driver's door.

She is dressed in the same white dress – a beach dress he supposes - and is looking up at the old mill building.

"Good morning" he whispers softly but she offers up no response, just begins to walk towards the beach.

He locks the car and follows her, noting again how quickly she walks, especially barefooted. His old trainers sound like a drill sergeant's boots as they echo around the small courtyard car park formed by the old mill building and two other cottages opposite.

Descending to the sand through the gap in the concrete sea wall he becomes immediately aware of the fierce sea breeze on his face and the much louder sound of the waves just a few feet away. He can no longer see the woman and, laughably thinks at first that she might have taken her dress off and dived in but, just like yesterday afternoon, she has simply disappeared.

He looks around disbelievingly but she is nowhere to be seen. He heads towards a rusting, rotting breakwater and marvels again at how fast she must have travelled, his own footsteps being held back by the hidden pull of the sand below. He glances out to the sea and notices, through the thick sea fog, a white light, way off in the distance; and yet he cannot make out any sign or shape of a boat.

Jack Saunders had talked about 'sandbanks crisscrossing Yarmouth Roads' and he supposes that fishermen might know safe routes to follow when wading out to the relative safety of higher points from which to fish with lines before the waves have a chance to encircle them. But, again, he can make out no figures and listens carefully for the lilt of voices that would come in on the breeze.

Nothing disturbs the stillness. He shivers and then he feels it: a lingering chill which rises behind him and grips the back of his neck, holding him there and making him strangely frightened of turning around because of what he might see.

He expects to hear her voice at any second. The silence grows deafening and he edges round, inch by inch, until he is facing up the beach again, over the breakwater and towards the lighthouse at Happisburgh.

Icy fingers are grabbing at his heart as though trying to rip it out and halt the beating noise in his ears. He no longer sees the sea nor hears the waves. Looking straight ahead he observes the exact position of a scene from the past – whether it is from his own past he isn't sure - but he does know beyond any doubt who had appeared in that shot.

It is the girl in the photo that Rowena had found in the piles of stuff in his mother's bedroom. She had been sitting on the breakwater with the lighthouse behind her. Why, though, does such an innocuous discovery frighten him so much that he is shaking uncontrollably and his teeth are now chattering against each other in his head as though tapping out some distress signal in an ancient code?

He holds on to one of the breakwater's decaying poles for support until the primaeval fear has passed over; his mind and body calmed sufficiently for him to walk or half run back towards the car, not wanting to be out there on his own and suddenly craving human company.

The tiny flint cottages provide a border to the car park on the western side. Each of them has seen better days he thinks as he takes in the peeling red paint of their doors. At least the one right in front of him has had its old metal windows replaced with shiny white UPVC double-glazing. The assorted hanging baskets of deep red geraniums and trailing blue lobelia either side of the door do at least give it a sense of being loved and cared for.

He is aware of a sudden movement and he quickly realizes that there is a figure at the window. The sun is shining directly on his or her face so he can't make it out clearly but he doesn't need to because, just a few seconds later, the door creaks open and an elderly woman steps out.

She is quite portly, of medium height and boasts a mane of grey hair that tries its best to escape her round head on the morning breeze.

"Going to be nice today," she announces to him and anyone else who might be insane enough to be up that early, wiping her mouth as she does so with a blue and white, checked tea towel, "once that mist clears off."

She reminds him of his Gran – his mother's mother - who he hasn't thought about, literally, for years. The layers of his childhood seem to be peeling away in front of him and he knows now that the catalyst for it is here somehow.

Her own cottage had been crammed full of brasses, particularly horse brasses from her family's farming past. She used to talk endlessly about those days, telling him stories of planting and harvesting around Spalding and marshes round about.

Nick later learned that Gran had a nervous breakdown in the late 'Forties and attended a clinic at a place called Rauceby near Sleaford. The experts there had decided that electric shock therapy was required to expel the worrisome electrons that orbited her mind.

Sadly, this 'treatment' had left her physically incapacitated for long periods and mentally segmented such that she could target the ancient past in her mind with a great deal of clarity but the present or recent past was seemingly un-indexed and inaccessible, even though it was all there in similar detail. Perhaps he'd had an illness when he was young and his mind had been messed up in some similar way?

The old woman is leaning forward slightly, obviously waiting for him to say something about the weather.

"The mist is quite thick down on the beach" he hears himself murmur in response.

"Rolls in and out, so it does; sometimes she hang around, twirling those wisps round the breakwater till mid-morning but she normally gone by dinner time."

Gran had spoken in this way too: more semi-colons than commas.

"Have you lived here long?" he ventures, sounding like Prince Philip on his best behaviour for once, feigning interest in one of his more eccentric subjects.

"Just over ten years." She looks at him mischievously.

"And where did you move from?"

"Over there." She points a finger behind her. "Back down the cliff: when there was a cliff."

"I'm just up here for a visit," he intervenes quickly, "with my wife."

"With her or visiting her?" She glances behind her as if trying to impress a hidden jury with her penetrating interrogation.

"With her! She's part of the History and Mystery dig."

"So what went wrong?"

"Wrong? Oh, you mean the body." He thinks back to the conversation with Hudson for the first time that day and hopes he has sorted out his mistake now. Perhaps that was why he had telephoned Mother – to explain and apologise?

"It's you and your wife I'm worried about."

Nick begins to imagine her emerging from a cave to deliver some great homily or life-changing prediction; like an old sage.

"Why do you say that?"

"Because I sees you here, alone; sleeping in your car outside my window."

It could have been a line from a Genesis song. Relief and a little bit of reality must have come back into his face because she continues without waiting for an explanation.

"Doesn't happen often in our car park, though strange goings on some nights there are. Why aren't you staying with her down the road?"

He is partly right. If she isn't an oracle of the future, she certainly doesn't miss much that lies behind.

"It's a long story."

"You'd better come in then. Leslie loves stories and his kippers won't wait much longer. I'm Gladys by the way. Gladys Pickett."

She leads him into a cosy back room which serves as kitchen, dining room and quite possibly a lounge too.

At any rate, this is clearly where the family spends their time when they are in residence.

Nick remembers Leslie as his willing guide to the remains of the de Criel residence when he had first arrived in Waxling by taxi. Looking much less pixie-like today, he is dressed in an enormous brown cardigan, buttoned up to his thin neck, over dark trousers eventually revealing brown socks and blue zippered slippers.

Voices come from the far side of the room, like so many whispers which suddenly break into song.

Gladys, seeing his bewilderment, pipes up: "That'll be the laptop you can hear; there, sitting on the bureau. I stream radio online these days. FM's no good to us here. The signal's hopeless and coastguard interferes with it. Good for Hilversum, surprisingly, but AM generally just drifts in and out with the sea."

Nick has the sense of a recollection flash before him but it doesn't linger long enough for him to understand it.

"Digital's the future and it keeps Leslie connected. Now, make yourself at home" Gladys seems quite oblivious to the fact that there is only one other chair, which is piled up with a mass of wool comprising clothes about to be washed or awaiting ironing, on top of which is perched a huge, black cat.

Nick is aware of a sudden thump from upstairs and looks towards the ceiling's cobwebs and faded yellow paint, but there is no further sound. He stands beside Leslie and waits for the scene's denouement.

"Leslie's been praying for Susan Hampshire, haven't you Les?"

The old man's unshaven face moves to one side, just to prove that he is alive and willing but, when he doesn't reply, Nick jumps in:

"I didn't know she was ill?"

"Who?"

"Susan Hampshire?"

"Is she?"

"I don't… you said he was praying for her?"

"Been praying for her for years; don't mean she's going to come here anytime soon do it? I expect she's too busy. So, what lies buried in your world?" Gladys fills a gypsy-style kettle as she continues her interrogation.

"I'm sure we all have skeletons we could talk about."

"Do we now! Do we Les?" Her false teeth hiss and click together loudly as she barks out another question.

Leslie blinks his eyes twice as if transmitting a signal the two of them have agreed many years before and which only they can decipher.

"The problem is that skeletons don't talk back do they; not in a natural way? Ghosts do and you looked as though you'd seen one down there by the waters."

"I didn't see anyone. Well, apart from the lady I've seen a few times here on Waxling Beach. She usually has a child with her but she was on her own this morning – too early for the child to be up and about I expect."

"Or she'd already left." Gladys crashes bottles around in the fridge and momentarily disappears behind the kitchen wall from where much puffing and panting can be heard while an old rope washing line simultaneously sways over the sink.

Eventually, she reappears with two large black fish and he now understands that the wall masks a small pantry. She must have hung the kippers on the line like bats and had struggled to reach up to un-peg them. The fish are duly tossed into a large silver pan which dwarfs a tiny cooker, as the cat leaps off the chair and proceeds to brush itself up against her legs.

Gladys fails to notice this and stands on the poor creature's tail three times before it skulks behind Leslie, all the time keeping a keen eye on the frying fish.

What sounds like an urgent news bulletin suddenly fills the room:

**"It's softer ground here and the earth falls away quickly behind it. We've only managed a small hole so far but there's no doubt from the Geo Phys which came in overnight that there is a substantial hollow some way below ground."**

**"Could it be a sort of cave?"**

**"I knew you'd ask me that. Well, Sam's working on it as we speak and we should know more fairly soon. Come back to us in an hour"**

That must have been recorded the day before, he considers; nobody else in their right mind would be up at this hour. He wonders if Nora is up and about yet.

"So the White Lady's entertaining your wife?" Gladys is bending over the stove, sweat leaping from her brow and joining its liquid cousin below with hiss of snake and splash of magic.

"I'm sorry, I don't… "

"She stays at the pub don't she?"

"Yes, she's there for the duration of the dig."

"They're digging up the pub?" She throws him a look of mock surprise as she continues to stir. "You'll have met Lynne then?"

"Lynne?"

"Works behind the bar most nights; keeps her away from home anyhow."

He realizes that this is almost certainly the sister witch, dressed in black.

Gladys continues in a sage-like, much less playful voice.

"Lost her husband just over a year ago."

"At sea?"

"Sort of … went out to his shed late one night and she never saw him again."

Nick has this unreasonable urge to ask if she has checked whether he is still in the shed but Gladys is still talking at him.

"She never saw the shed again either - or most of her back garden: slipped away quietly in the dead of night. The whole village is drowning once more; just bit by man-made bit this time."

He begins to appreciate the full horror of what she is saying: "You mean the cliff collapsed, taking her husband and the shed with it?"

"Just like our own dwelling. Leslie knew we were about to be eaten but they didn't want to believe it, any of them. Looked down their long noses at us they did but we have equally long memories, Leslie and I. We don't forget easily nor forgive either. Neither do our own White Lady who's still digging, still searching for a way out perhaps?"

"Who is she?" every time he gets close he finds himself further away than when he started.

"Who indeed? Folks around here have their pretty theories."

"Is it connected to Waxling's past – the drowning of the village?"

"In 1607? Could be: 'Water's high, the clanging leaps. When spring's away her silence neaps' goes the saying and that old bell usually sounds danger. It's the drowning since then that occupies most folks' minds."

He still isn't entirely sure if Gladys is actually addressing him or her husband or anybody at all. He hears the familiar ping of a text. To his absolute amazement, Gladys leaps forward to retrieve a Nokia mobile 'phone from the pocket of a green Barbour jacket that hangs from a gigantic hook on the wall behind her husband.

She frowns and thrusts it back dismissively. Nick

takes his own 'phone out of his pocket, still a little damp from his walk on the beach. There is a message from Nora: "I'm awake." That's it. He isn't sure if brevity is a good thing here or not but is relieved to read that he hasn't been frozen out altogether thanks to the previous night's events.

Gladys meanwhile has barely drawn breath. "Drownings will always be part of this coast until the entire village has disappeared again. People are afraid of the sea's appetite. Every time we hear the bell out there and see the white light we know it's her. Still trying to raise us from our slumbers she is, and still looking for that escape route."

"Is this someone who lived here at one time? Do you think it is her ghost come back to try and save the rest of you?"

"Save us!" Gladys turns to face him and he sees that there is a scowl on her face. Les notices it too and turns his head away from her as if trying to avoid an inevitable slap, the morning sunshine glinting on his grey whiskers. "She couldn't save us then so how could she possibly achieve that now? Nothing's changed you know."

"Who was she?" Nick tries again to make the breakthrough.

"Her name was Elizabeth: Elizabeth de Criel. She thought she could save the village. Rang the bells like she does now and they all filed into the church like rats after the piper. She'd heard about a tunnel you see: a tunnel to lead them to safety on higher ground - that'll be the one they're talking about on the web no doubt -

but the sea had found it first and there they were, cut off at the top of the tower and then the ceiling flew away. What use were those bells to her then? What use are they to us now?"

Nora had warned him that they were having difficulty finding an actual tunnel or evidence of its route and yet here was Gladys Pickett verifying its existence as though she and Les had been down there with their shovels, digging it out themselves.

"You think the current village will be inundated too."

"Most people do." She sniffs, disdainfully. "Our house toppled into the sea it did; one weekend we were sitting in our front room looking down on the waves, the next we were swimming with the fishes. Helpless and homeless we were and Abbots Home was gone forever just like all those other houses that sit under the sand and the sea."

"Do you think that's why the villagers gathered in the church rather than going directly to the Priory? They thought God would help them … save them through Elizabeth who they trusted and looked up to, rather than the Friars along the coast who they viewed with suspicion?"

"Excepting John de Criel that is. Abandoned his flock didn't he, including his own wife! The miller saw him leave the village and when he came back there was no wife, nor villagers nor village left: seems like there's a male gene in that family that's come right down the line."

She is staring at him now. Even as an old penny finally drops.

"Abbots_Home is the name of the blog you write. So it is you, not Jack."

"Jack. Don't make me laugh. Oh, he likes to talk but couldn't commit much more to paper than poor Les here. They weren't book-learned. All they really know is the sea."

"But you blame the modern day St John de Criel for your house falling into the sea?"

"You obviously didn't read the posts properly did you, master?"

Nick feels very small and lost once more.

"I don't blame him for what happened; that'll be more down to her out at sea. What Lord 'High and Mighty' didn't do was offer any shelter or other kind of help. Some kind of patriarch eh! Turned his back on us. All of them did. Just lucky we managed to get this cottage. It was cramped when we first moved in but plenty room for the old bugger and me now."

Nick remembers the blog post about an accident in 1997; also the one about the vicar. His wife, Audrey Bracken, obviously doesn't want to talk about it and he is hoping that Gladys might.

"Why do you write these pieces?" it seems like as good a place as any to start.

"I don't write often; just enough to let Lord Muck know I'm still here."

"You mentioned an accident in 1997 and I remember a post about the vicar – another accident?"

"Was it though?" she smiles at him benignly. "I was hoping you might find out for us."

"Why me?"

"You were sent to help us weren't you?"

"To raise funds for…"

"And you might learn something to your benefit along the way."

"I'm sorry, I … I guess your husband never got over losing his home?" he ventures more softly now.

"Oh he got over that alright; he heard the bell two nights earlier and knew what was coming, especially when he saw her out there on the waves. He wasn't in denial like the rest of them were. No, his problems really began the following year: a betrayal much closer to home. Like I say, you should take a trip to the library and read between the lines. When was the last time you talked with your mother?"

"My mother?" he feels the sweat pouring down his back though it couldn't have been much past six o'clock. "Yesterday. I spoke to her yesterday. I was at her house yesterday morning"

"Ah but that's not what I asked, is it? I asked when was the last time you talked with her. Barely tolerating someone is not at all the same as communing with them is it?"

Not for the first time, he wonders whether Gladys

might be on some kind of medication and forgotten to take it that day - or for several weeks. Her next comment does not provide any answers, only more questions:

"We all have our stories to tell, you know, but Beryl is better with words than I ever was; should have run in the family, so it should. Ask her to show you what I found."

How does she know Mother's first name? Her retrieving the kippers for Leslie's breakfast is a useful cue for him to leave but her parting comment is a strangely knowing "we'll see you again very soon," before slamming her front door shut (or perhaps the wind caught it).

Gladys and Leslie and all of the tales with no proper endings are temporarily thrown into a box in his mind as he walks into the freshening breeze, but nothing and nobody seem able to keep the lid on it now.

He checks his mobile for messages. There is just one: 'Blackout is moving. So are you. B.'

Bannister usually loves ambiguity far more than clarity as he feels it gives him many more options: buys much needed time and space. Today, the sentiment could not be clearer: if Nick's flagship client is leaving the agency, there is little point in them keeping him on any longer.

He is considering whether to dignify it with a response or not when the 'phone starts to ring. It is Nora.

"I sent you a text."

"I got it. I was talking to Gladys and Leslie Pickett - well, Gladys."

"I'm very happy for you." Her voice has the coldness and sharpness of a sheet of ice, incongruous in the rising heat, and from a different time and place, it seems.

Nick presses on. "She has it in for de Criel big time and I think I will go to the library to see what else I can find out."

After a measured silence she replies. "So you're still avoiding the truth by pretending to be seeking it out."

"Why would you say that?"

She knows he is exasperated but her tone melts only very slightly. "Only that Julian Bannister rang me at some unearthly hour this morning to tell me that you've been fired; St John de Criel said you'd actually spent a whole day here last week, oh, and the police have apparently identified the girl's body as being your sister.

Good that there aren't any secrets to hide between us, eh! Well here's another unearthed fact from the past and the present: I'm not sure whether or not we have a future together…I've tried to reach you. Over and over again I have tried to make you face up to your demons, whatever they might be, and tried to help you to deal with them. But you just shut me out.

You switched off from your only daughter too, pretending that all is well and that you're happy – with us, with your job, with your life. But you're not. I don't think that you ever have been. I've tried not to intrude:

your mother told me to tread carefully right from the beginning and that's what I've done."

"Nora! Please!" his head is pounding.

"No! Enough. If you don't want us in your life, then fine. If you can't confide in me now, you never will."

As he perceives her form - his memory of her very being - fading behind the thickening fog he longs to reach out and hold on to her; to pull her back into his world. But he can't. She has all but gone.

"But I do love you, Nora, and Rowena, too. I cannot imagine what life would be like without you."

"I'm sure even non-fiction writers have some imagination."

Her jibes sting in the same way that the sand is now beginning to sting his cheeks in the stiffening breeze but he must not let go; must not let her leave him.

"Nora. I didn't tell you about the agency because I wasn't sure about it myself – any of it – and didn't want to worry you. The same with my trip up here. If I'd told you about it, you'd just have assumed I was somehow stalking you. As for this thing with the police: it's a huge mistake but I don't understand where it's come from."

"I thought you understood everything." Her voice has softened a little. "I am sorry about your job – I know it meant pretty much everything to you."

He recognises that this time she isn't sparring and means it.

"That's just the point though, isn't it? I didn't care about it at all, any of it. I never have done. It was just something I could do; the only thing to stop me from facing up to fear and failure..."

"What fear and why would you ever be frightened of failure? You are not your father, Nick."

"I know. I know that."

"Let me help you! Don't shut me out. We're supposed to be a partnership, not double agents. I can't bear secrecy. You know that. Why do you think I became an archaeologist in the first place?"

"I'll come and meet you."

"No."

"But you said you wanted me to talk to you. I want that too. More than anything, honestly. I can't make sense of this on my own."

"No. I mean, I know you can't. I think you should go back to Ely and talk with Beryl."

"But..."

"No buts and no ifs." She is much calmer now, and less wound up. He silently thanks whichever the God is that manages these things, grasping as he has been for any encouragement he could find.

"What good will talking to her do?" How can she possibly know anything about it?"

"She is not the person you think she is, Nick. She once told me that she has had to find an inner strength for the longest time. You're going to need a lot of that today, trust me."

"Please explain, Nora, I just need to know…"

"Like I say, trust me. Listen to what she has to say about this body we've found. It all starts and ends with her. Call me when you can."

The 'phone clicks off. This is the full stop at the end of her sentence.

He walks slowly back to the car, not aware of anyone or anything else apart from the curtains of Gladys Pickett's cottage being opened wide.

\*\*\*

She barely realizes that she is walking towards him until she sees the old mill ahead of her. She wants to see him, wants to throw her arms around him and hug him tightly. His whole world appears to be caving in as did the pasts, presents and futures of so many villagers on this very spot.

They must find out why the inundation took so many lives here; why the villagers didn't flee to higher ground and why they were led astray. She is determined about this, if not in the remaining time they have on location then through further detailed research of her own. Squires will probably sponsor her to write it up and then take out chunks of it to fill one of his history paperbacks. Such is the price to pay for digging up the past.

But she mustn't see Nick, not quite yet. She turns and walks slowly back towards the White Lady. It isn't for her to reveal the truth to him about his own past.

Though it precedes her time with him, he and therefore she is inextricably linked to it - as they all are to their individual and collective family histories. No, Beryl has been waiting for this opportunity for so long. No more riddles now.

\*\*\*

As he prepares to leave Waxling once more his 'phone rings.

"Mr Golding?"

It is Hudson, who already knows the answer to his pointless question or he would have dialled somebody else.

"Yes." There is little point in not going with the conversation flow.

"I wonder if you could come and see us this morning? I understand that you are here in Waxling at present and..."

"Who told you that?"

Hudson asks the questions and doesn't answer those from other people.

"So, if it would be convenient..."

"I'm afraid it isn't. I am already on my way back to Ely. My daughter is unwell."

"I am sorry to hear that, sir. Is she seriously ill?"

"They're not sure at the moment but I do need to be with her."

"And yet you told us yesterday that it was just a

chest infection and that she was quite well enough to leave – when you kindly came over to the station and then came up here last night, rather than rushing back to her bedside?"

Hudson's voice is friendly but utterly uncompromising.

"The doctor told her she needed rest but I'm just anxious to see her – as a concerned parent, you know."

"Must have been a wrench to lose both your wife and daughter at the same time?"

"I'm sorry. I don't…"

"For half-term. You'd already said 'goodbye' to your wife for two weeks and then the daughter, who you are so close to, for a week as well. Being away from your loved ones must have made you feel very lonely."

"I have my work."

"Which you are taking a break from, yes? Do you think we don't know where your car is, right at this very moment? Is lying to the police something you do often – as you did when you were just a small boy?"

"I have never broken the law in my life."

"Oh come on, Mr Golding. Thirty-seven miles an hour in a thirty-mile limit; a few units over the limit, the odd insurance claim where you've added a couple of items the loss adjuster couldn't possibly check up against! It's a bit loose for a PR professional to say they've never covered anything up or, shall we say, re-interpreted a story to improve it isn't it?"

"What is it you want from me?"

"Just another little chat that's all."

"OK. Well, I do have to get back to Ely but I'll be coming back up here as soon as I have some answers."

"Be sure to do that, sir. I need you back here tomorrow at the latest please."

With that end line, Hudson terminates the call, though his words continue to ring in Nick's ears.

As Nora has taken the Sat Nav in her car, he searches for the OS maps in the glove compartment. He'd never worn nor chauffeured anyone grand enough to wear gloves so hadn't been in there for literally years. A slightly yellowed piece of folded white paper falls out. It is a crayon picture with Lowry-type figures of a man, woman and baby. Underneath and in large spidery writing at an increasing angle across the page is scrawled 'Me and my family' in thick red crayon and the initials R.G.

He doesn't remember her doing it or showing it to him or Nora and, in any case, wouldn't have spared more than a second to show his pride and appreciation for her little gift, which would have meant so much to his daughter.

He rummages around for the battered collection of pink-covered maps and, piecing four of them together via the grid guide on the back, works out a route that will avoid Norwich altogether and join the A10 just south of Downham Market. From there it is just a twenty to thirty-minute drive back to Ely and, handily, the road will take him very close to the village of Littleport.

He turns on the radio and catches the beginning of the History and Mystery update which follows the ten o'clock news bulletin:

"...so Paul McCartney is sixty-five years old today – I guess he found that people did still need him when he was sixty-four and so he decided to carry on! Welcome everyone to another beautiful day up here on the Norfolk Coast and I can report that one mystery has been solved this morning,"

John Squires sounds none the worse from his police interrogation yesterday. Nick had rather hoped he might have been roughed up a bit, as in a good left-wing anti-establishment drama the BBC specializes in.

"the tunnel that we thought might be heading towards the old de Criel mansion is, in fact, leading us out to sea. Of course, back in the early seventeenth century, it would have had a destination on land and, from new scans of the sea bed we've received this morning, there is no doubt that it led out to the original Waxling church, now some mile and a half out there under the waves."

Gladys Pickett has already broken that news to some of us, he thinks; so much for John Birt's rolling news revolution.

"We know this now because a hole we were excavating this morning does indeed have a passage leading back to the Priory and then to the church. It could be that it was some kind of escape route during those dark days of religious persecution.

The second bit of news I have to give you is that the hole itself was, we think, some kind of underground cavern – a meeting place if you will. We've found the remains of an arch and buttresses. The size of these suggests a fairly substantial roof was supported and it might well have been a stopping place for those coming up or down the tunnel.

A metal cross has been discovered, suggesting there may even have been an altar. If this all sounds as though it's coming from the dark side, I should remind you that houses up and down the country had priest holes and other, ingenious escape routes where Catholics could hide and pray to God until the danger to their lives was over.

In our case, the danger to lives came from the other direction – from the sea itself and it's pretty likely that the younger Elizabeth de Criel led villagers to the Church, not just because of her simple faith in what this building represented to her. She couldn't have led them to the Priory directly and publicly as everyone would have seen it as a closed order - even assuming it was still occupied by monks at the time.

The elder Elizabeth would never have gone near to it and she would have had a great bearing on her daughter's decision-making – even at a moment of crisis such as this. No, the more practical reason would have been that she did know that there was an underground tunnel leading directly from the old church to the Priory.

Even if she had defied her mother and been prepared to compromise her own religious beliefs, it would have given them a better chance of escape than trying to get to the Priory along the coast directly, such was the speed at which the sea was coming in.

It's even possible that John de Criel had entered the tunnel from the other end with the aim of leading them to safety on higher ground, knowing they would not have trusted the Friars themselves to do so.

Perhaps the meeting point was this chamber. If this was the case, it proved not to be successful because while soil samples suggest that neither it nor that part of the tunnel leading back to the Priory was itself filled with water, the ground to the north of it gives us a quite different water analysis. Though still part of the land today, this part of the tunnel must have either flooded at the time or the water table has sprung through at some point since.

It could be that the villagers discovered this when they got to the church or very shortly after entering the tunnel from that end. If so, they would have had little choice but to turn and rush back. They could only go upwards from there: up the tiny spiral staircase until they came out onto the tower's narrow ramparts, before being caught and carried out to sea by the waves.

So the de Criel family could have been good eggs after all! Plenty for the modern-day version to cluck about.

"We have also discovered a lead-lined casket which we hope will give us further clues. Constance Breeve is with me and this is a really exciting find isn't it, Connie?"

"Yes, Johnnie it is. We believe that it has been here since the actual inundation and, incredibly, no water or air appears to have penetrated it which means that whatever is inside it – if there is anything – will hopefully be in a good state. We'll tread carefully and let you know."

"Thanks, Connie. We'll have more, later; so don't forget to tune in."

'Tread carefully.' Nora had used the same words that morning. What was it that she had said? His mother had told her to tread carefully from the beginning. What could she have meant by that?

He listens to the radio for a little but the truth is far from plain to see. As he passes some cars towing caravans in the opposite direction, he ponders that it has never seemed to him to be more complicated.

As he passes the Marham airfield to his right he remembers the huge and noisy Vulcan bombers that used to fly overhead when he was a small boy. His father had once told him that they were heading out for bombing practice at a remote place called Gedney Drove End on the Wash.

He hasn't thought about them or him for years but it feels now as though some kind of cork has been released; like a ship trapped in a bottle suddenly being given the unexpected opportunity to sail again.

The square tower of Littleport's St George's church soon appears on the skyline with the towers of Ely Cathedral looming up beyond it in the summer's haze. Just past an avenue of trees he spots a 'Library' sign and takes a left turn down Victoria Street, at the end of which stands what looks like an ancient Parish Hall and a modern, glass-fronted library building.

He parks the car in a small car park beyond 'The Barn' - some kind of council building - and walks back to the library where he is soon directed to a tall, bearded man in a yellow checked shirt and light blue jeans. He turns out to be Kev, the IT Support Officer. Nick asks him about locals using the PCs and whether anyone has asked recently about accessing blogs, in particular, one called Abbots_Home.

The man begins to talk about the East Cambridgeshire District Council Privacy Policy and that he would have to apply to them (online, ironically) for answers to these kinds of questions, and that there would have to be a very good reason to justify such an invasion of privacy.

Nick tells him – almost wholly truthfully – that he is with the History and Mystery television programme up in Norfolk. Rather than being impressed, Kev scowls when he mentions the neighbouring county, as though he would have preferred a concrete wall by way of a more visible boundary, but Nick can tell that he now has his attention and the small print has got smaller still.

"We have lots of occasional users who take advantage of this community facility," he begins, still going through the motions of covering his tracks, "but now you come to mention it a fairly elderly lady came in here yesterday, with a young girl. They sat at separate terminals. I've seen the woman many times: reddish hair and a thin face. Wore a faded red mac. She didn't need much guidance from me, to be honest, though most do of course…"

"I'm sure they do." Nick massages his ego even further before he has time to consider whether his expertise or their ignorance is the main reason for their using this public electronic gateway to the outside world.

"She had a username and password to hand. I just needed to remove some old Blogger files first and then she got the login screen and Bingo."

"Did she look at anything else?"

He pretends to be mildly affronted. "I don't stand over our customers when they're browsing so I really couldn't tell you. As to our offline media, no she didn't…"

"Read any books?"

He nods a silent assent.

"And the young girl?"

"Looked very pale to be truthful."

Nick thanks him and leaves before he can ask how all of this can possibly be connected to the most intriguing media story to hit East Anglia since the Soham Murders which had taken place just down the road. On the few occasions since Nick has come back since then, Mother has never failed to mention that terrible event which hurt so many more people beyond the immediate victims and their families.

\*\*\*

"He's not speaking to me at all now. They're all cross with me, except Mummy, who sits in her fold-up chair on the beach for hours. She is scribbling on a pad but won't let me read any of it. I don't know why grown-ups have secrets – we are always being told that we must tell the truth and not ever try to hide anything from them. He won't even look at me. Something in his eyes has changed, though. I saw it when he was whispering to Mum behind the windbreak. He didn't know I'd finished paddling. I couldn't hear what he was saying because the seagulls were making such a noise. The look on his face frightened me though. I've never seen him look like that before – at anybody."

\*\*\*

It is just after one when he gets back to Ely. Mother is out, but his father is hunched up in the sitting room, reading the Ely Standard for probably the sixth or seventh time that day. Father grunts in his general direction before returning to the local news which is clearly of more local interest than his own family.

Rowena is cuddling her favourite toy bunny whilst sitting up in bed, reading. Her hand covers part of the title but he can still make out Girl Detective. She immediately puts the book down on the duvet as he enters her room, a weak smile on her still pasty face.

"I was hoping it was you?"

"Not Granny?"

"Well her too."

She looks a little abashed and he feels a stab of guilt.

"Granny went out just after lunch but said she'd be back soon."

There is something about the way she looks up at him – genuinely pleased to see him and not feigning it or putting on a show for her father's benefit. How real she is. He tucks her in more snugly and sits beside her on the edge of the bed.

After half an hour or so, they hear his father fumble and wheeze his way past the bedroom door and then the faint sound of a key in the front door lock. Nick supposes that she has spent years stealing furtively back into the house (the sort of thing Nancy Drew might legitimately do to avoid being seen or heard).

The sound of a plug being rammed into the wall is rapidly followed by the familiar click of the kettle switch. His father wouldn't dream of making tea for either of them so he knows it is Mother; knows also that now is the moment he needs and simultaneously dreads.

"I need to have a word with Granny if that's OK?" he stands and bends down to kiss her on her forehead. She still feels quite hot to the touch.

"No problem. Nancy and I have made good progress this morning and will have this case solved by tea time I think!"

He returns her grin and gently closes the bedroom door behind him as he leaves her. He holds on to the doorknob before moving away though. He realizes that he doesn't want to leave her there alone. He is horrified to feel tears on his cheeks and quickly wipes them away before composing himself and walking back along the corridor to the kitchen.

Mother turns to face him as he enters. She looks tired, wasted even, but he can't smell anything on her breath.

"Oh, so you've bothered to come back then?" Great dark sacks hang below her eyes which are alive and blazing.

"I'm sorry." He lies. "I did try to 'phone you yesterday." He lies again.

"Tried? You mean your brain had forgotten how to tell your fingers how to press telephone buttons in a simple sequence?"

"What did the police want?"

"You don't know?"

He feels like a small child all over again. He had once been chastised for damming up one of the many streams that divided the nearby fields and causing a small flood. He had been proud of his small feat of engineering but the farmer was decidedly unimpressed, wanting to give him a smack rather than a plaque.

"Bumptious Bamber Gascoigne said he had lots of questions I might be able to help him answer. He said he'd already spoken to you and Nora. Pompous little man – told me he once served Her Majesty at Sandringham. As though that was going to make any difference to me! He's had delusions of grandeur ever since, or just assumed I was some stupid old woman like most men do."

"He didn't say anything else?"

"No. He didn't. But I've got plenty to say to him; to both of you and not before time."

"Rowena still feels a bit warm to me," he ventures by way of moving the first pawn on the board.

"It's not easy to keep her cool in this weather. I bought her an ice cream when we were out yesterday but most of it had melted down her front before she could eat it... "

He grasps the nettle, fully aware that it is going to sting.

"The police called me in for a meeting yesterday, up in Norfolk."

"Has something happened to Nora?"

"No, nothing like that. I wondered the same thing myself, to be honest, but no, it was about the skeleton they found at the weekend. You remember that they thought it was contemporary: much more recent than the ancient remains the dig team expected to discover... "

"I do know what contemporary means; there's no need to patronize me now that you have decided I'm worthy of a conversation." Her face is impassive but paler than when they'd started whereas he'd have expected anger to colour her cheeks, not drain them.

"I'm sorry."

"No, you're not. You're not really sorry at all." The voice belongs to his father who shuffles into the room, his frayed brown dressing gown slightly open to reveal sweaty yellow pyjamas and a cluster of dark, protruding hairs.

"David!" Mum springs up and ushers him out of the tiny kitchen but he continues to stare at Nick over her shoulder, muttering through moist lips.

Mother shuts the door and sits down again. He can see now that her eyelids are red and quite swollen.

"What did Dad mean?" he asks gently.

"He doesn't know what he means half the time; don't mind him."

There is an uneasy silence before she continues, a little too quietly and much too quickly.

"I'm just a lush to you, aren't I? An embarrassing old woman, living out her boring, unfulfilling days with a cantankerous old man!" Her words are harsh but whispering them tones down the impact of their delivery.

How articulate she sounds.

"Mother – Mum - I don't want to get into all that right now."

"All that? All what? You're supposed to be so good at reading people and writing it down and yet you can't see what's right in front of you, can you? You can only see what others see. I thought you were cleverer than that."

He begins to seriously wonder if she has had a lunchtime tipple after all or hasn't quite recovered from the previous binge, and yet he still can't smell any alcohol – nor does any other aspect of her body language spell intoxication.

'They're clever though,' Bannister's voice arrives, uninvited and unwanted, at the back of his mind, 'remember Jocelyn - the Children's Librarian from Stockwell who dropped acid in the afternoons while the kids were doing their 'private reading?' They only found her out when she mistook that little girl for a Bonsai plant and tried to water her one day, just as her mother arrived ...'

As with the Librarian, he dismisses him instantly and forces himself back to a kitchen in Ely in Cambridgeshire in mid-June. "What's the matter, Mum?"

"Why should anything be the matter?"

"You just seem so, so angry and defensive all of a sudden."

"Well you're right about my feeling cross – though that is a bit of an understatement - but completely wrong about it being all of a sudden. I've waited for this moment for more than forty years but now, instead of being afraid, I do feel angry; perhaps that's just my way of dealing with it, your father and you."

"Me. What have I done?"

"Sometimes," she is barely even whispering now and he draws closer to hear her properly, "you need to stop being so self-important. Not everything in this world revolves around you. There are some things that you are not responsible for and cannot change, no matter how hard you might try. What I'm about to tell you is something that did happen to you – to all of us – a long time ago and we are the way we are now because of it."

"Is this to do with the police thinking I had a sister?" he blurts it out and she visibly flinches. "I don't understand how they could have got their records mixed up so badly."

She shifts slightly in her chair. When she does speak again it is in a much more resigned, almost despairing tone. That earlier bravado has exhausted her, it seems.

"When you went up in the loft last Saturday did you read any of those newspapers?"

Now she sounds like a wounded Gestapo agent, eyeing him intently and asking him trick questions about papers.

"I don't know what you mean. There was hardly anything left up there, apart from the school stuff I brought down."

"I wouldn't mind if you had looked at them – just the front page maybe."

He feels uneasy now and not a little confused. He opens the window and they are instantly aware of the traffic hum from the main road.

"There weren't any papers up there so how could I have read any of them!"

"Not even a pile over in the corner wrapped up

with string."

A memory stirs. He has forgotten about the pack of old newspapers behind the tank. He might have torn one of the pages but isn't sure.

"I do vaguely remember something now," he responds cautiously and swallows as her stare never wavers, "but if anything I just threw a parcel of them to one side. It was the books I was interested in. I certainly didn't read anything."

"Well then. Perhaps it would be best if you went back up there and brought them down so that they saw the light of day once more. It's been far too long as it is."

About ten minutes later he returns to the kitchen with the torn, yellowing pile, wiping cobweb remnants from his hair and trying to rub yet more of them off of his shirt.

"Put them on the table." Mother is immovable.

He turns the package over so that the front page is face up and, finding a battered pair of scissors in one of the kitchen drawers, carefully snips the fraying string. Still, she stares at him, seemingly waiting for any change in his facial expression, however slight.

He lifts the top paper from the pack. Dated Saturday 15$^{th}$ July 1967, it is a copy of the *North Norfolk Gazette* - a weekly title, published every Friday. The front page article is written by a Paul Neaverson. Nick carefully places together the old and yellowed pieces of the page which he had inadvertently torn on the previous occasion that he had handled it.

The headline reads:

'Boating trip ends in tragedy for Cambridgeshire holidaymakers.'

He reads the rest for himself:

'A ten-year-old girl was reported as missing yesterday after a boating trip went tragically wrong. Details are still sketchy at this stage but the police have named the victim as Jane Golding. It appears that she was being rowed offshore with her eight-year-old brother, Nick, by their father David, 31.

It is thought that they were looking for the remains of the old Waxling Church, which collapsed in the early part of the Seventeenth Century (parts of the old tower can sometimes be seen at low tide). It is not yet clear exactly what happened but Jane appears to have fallen overboard and, despite her father's best attempts to save her, she quickly disappeared below the surface.

Search and Rescue helicopters from both Cromer and Yarmouth were scrambled but the search was called off earlier today. Police and coastguards believe now that the body of the little girl could have been washed out to sea. The family - thought to be from Ely in Cambridgeshire - was enjoying a week's holiday in Waxling and staying at a Guest House on the seafront. The children's mother – Beryl Golding, 29 – was being comforted by locals as she and her husband tried to come to terms with their loss.'

Nick looks up at his mother whose eyes are moist. She is looking through and way beyond him, seeing a younger version of herself as well as him perhaps …

"So the police didn't make a mistake?" he doesn't know whether he is incredulous or angry or just very, very unsure. It seems in that moment that a previously unknown event from history has changed the entire basis of his being.

His parents didn't just know about this, they had endured it and kept it a secret. The police were aware of it at the time, as would anyone who had witnessed it, written about it or read the report about it in the Gazette or anywhere else. And he had not been an only child; only afterwards. He feels nauseous and hotter than he has ever felt before.

"So I did have a sister? How could you never have told me this?"

Her reply is mechanical. "You were just a child and, once the police had finished with you, we were advised not to talk about it."

"But how come I don't remember any of this; don't recall a single detail about her?"

"You were so upset, crying all the time – we all were. We left that place as soon as we could but still had to go back up there several times while the enquiries continued. You and your father were key witnesses and it brought everything back to us each time we tried to forget it." She stops abruptly and he appreciates that she is seeing things he cannot.

"What happened Mum; did they find out?"

She doesn't reply for several moments so he peels

away more chronicles from the past. He reads the report from the Coroner's office a few weeks later that declared the case would officially remain on file for up to seven years, but that, because of the nature of the incident and the absence of a body, the event was being treated as a tragic accident with no other person adjudged to be culpable.

"So it was an accident!" he looks up and automatically places his warm hand over hers. She returns his gaze but is drowning slowly behind her eyes.

"That's not what they thought at the time."

"What do you mean?"

"It was a relatively calm day which is why your father agreed to row you out there. Gladys – the lady who ran the guest house – said you'd have a good chance of seeing the top of the church tower."

"I've met Gladys."

"Did she tell you anything about this?"

"I got the impression that she knew more than she was saying but she just seemed to speak in riddles much of the time."

"It's how a lot of people cope. She had to deal with her loss to the sea."

"But if it was a calm day and there were only three of us in the boat, how could she – Jane – have fallen overboard?"

"Your father was completely traumatized and you were much too upset to describe what happened.

The police visits just made it far worse. It was obvious that you were not going to be able to help them; wetting the bed and screaming in the night, most nights. We went to see a specialist at the hospital in Peterborough in the end. Your father insisted on it.

Endless journeys they were, especially getting held up at Thorney each time. Your father refused to say a single word all the way there and all the way back again. They did lots of tests but eventually gave up."

'... *there's nothing more we can do for you ...*'

"The only good thing to come out of that was that they advised the police to leave you alone, that you were in denial about the whole thing which was the brain's way of giving you the space you needed to face up to the trauma. It was as though you were unconscious most of the time while your mind repaired itself. At least that's what they told us and the police too. Eventually, they could see that it was useless trying to question you and they put their notebooks away. You were only eight years old after all."

"And school; friends?"

"You never really had a lot of friends to begin with and the teachers never really paid you much attention, which suited you down to the ground as you preferred to be invisible.

You'd bike off on your own across the Fens, sometimes for the whole day. You'd always be back in time for tea, mind, but never would tell us anything about where you'd been or what you'd done. Three years later you went to Ely College and that chapter in your life was closed."

"Except that it wasn't, was it?"

Anger suddenly surges through his veins as a reaction to the incredible knowledge that he hadn't known his own back story. Here he is today – a PR professional, a storyteller who doesn't know the full history of his own life. He is forty-eight and must have read about Janet and John but never Jane.

"We did what we thought was best for you, that's what the specialist suggested: that only time would heal."

"But it didn't, hasn't! Father never has a kind word about anyone or anything. He shows no interest in his own child."

He stops suddenly, playing back in his mind what he has just declared out loud.

Mother continues on his behalf, calmer now. "Your father had many other disappointments in his life to contend with. It wasn't just this."

"What disappointments? What things?" Nick feels as though if he were to scratch the surface almost anything new and unexpected might be revealed now.

"Just to say he was unhappy with you, me: with everything."

"And her? Did he blame himself? Did you blame him for what happened?"

"We never knew what happened, as I've just said. None of us did – least of all him."

"But he was there. In the boat!"

"People deal with grief in very different ways."

"Oh spare me the clichés Mum. Why would you protect him now after all the years of Hell he's put you through - put all of us through? No wonder you turned to drink."

She visibly flinches but does not raise her voice. "Would it have been such a surprise if I had?" She turns towards him but he cannot face her. The heat he can feel in his head is too intense, burning into the memory he had thought was real, not virtual. He has to leave the room, get some air.

He leaves the bungalow without another word, marches past the hospital on his left and on into the City Centre. He walks down the High Street that runs alongside the great cathedral walls, past the Market Square and on down the hill leading to the medieval 'Maltings,' joining the riverbank near to the Cutter Inn. Is it really just a few days since they'd sat there with their drinks and their packets of crisps?

An older memory stirs but he forces it to the back of his mind. He isn't ready to face any more of this; not now ... not yet. From the towpath, he watches as a small cabin cruiser heads under the road bridge: Daddy at the wheel and Mummy holding on to two tiny children in orange life jackets, each bigger than either of them.

He hasn't even asked his mother what Jane looked like, what she liked to do; whether they had been similar in any way. He walks on, willing himself forward while becoming aware of his clenched fists and jaw set so tightly it is beginning to make the rest of his face ache. Although his eyes are wide open, they might just as well have been closed.

He proceeds along the uneven but dry and muddy path along the river's eastern bank, leaving Ely and its revised origin of species behind. If he is insanely uncomfortable with his beginnings, he simultaneously has absolutely no idea where he is going to.

At length, the path, having left the bank momentarily to cross the Wicken road, arrives at a rotting wooden fence which runs down to the river itself and features a small stile: big enough for humans to cross but not the cows it seeks to contain. As Nick clambers over it with little thought or appreciation of the drop on the other side, he stumbles and slides down the bank head first until he comes to a painful halt in a clump of dark green nettles.

Either the throbbing of his bent ankle or the multiple stings cause him to scream out loud. He yells and yells but knows that this outpouring of grief has not been caused by physical accident alone.

How can this be – any of it? How can his parents have deceived him so while turning to drink and prolonged anger at the world to make his childhood so miserable that he has all but blocked it out?

They had lost a daughter and gained a darkness that separated them from him and the world beyond their bungalow. A holiday trip that should have been all about having carefree fun had turned into a dark veil that nobody had dared to lift.

Had the set of circumstances over the last two weeks not arrived in the way it had, that summer of 1967 – hot and steamy like this one – might have been permanently blocked out: thrown away to be replaced by a new calendar for each new year.

He is not an only child; never has been. He shouts out this confirmation as the skylarks' chattering overhead confirms that they've received the message, loud and clear. He once had a sister – a playmate – who he must have gone for walks or bicycle rides with – almost certainly down to the Stretham steam engine; helped to build dens in the nearby spinneys, played endless games with.

Would it have been better if he hadn't remembered; hadn't been conscious of any of it, rather than having to face up to it now in middle age? Is this truly what Mum meant; what the doctors had believed all those years ago? Perhaps it really was more of a protective shield than a plot? Or is he merely calming down, rid of the rage that had all but consumed him?

He manages to hobble back up to the top of the bank. His ankle protests vehemently but he is at least able to put weight on it so he continues his forward rather than return journey.

A long boat driven by a darkly tanned man with flowing grey hair passes by, chugging back towards Ely, seemingly with no particular deadline. He raises his hand in greeting and Nick does the same, becoming aware of the tell-tale white blotches from the nettle stings as he does so.

A persistent memory from earlier pounces on his

unguarded consciousness. They had hired a different boat for the day. It was inland, not on the coast - possibly on one of the Norfolk Broads? He remembers passing a disused windmill by the river. Jane had loved windmills just as Rowena does now.

He remembers this clearly and with no doubt at all in his mind, though he still cannot make out her shape or picture her face in his minds' eye that is gradually learning to see all over again. They had gone on to moor up near a bridge that they couldn't have got under as it was too low. He can just make out the sign: Potter something.

In a trice, he realizes that it was Potter Heigham – the place where the trains used to stop, according to his travelling companion in the flat cap on what he had thought was his first journey up to Waxling last week.

They had sat on benches at a wooden table outside a pub, with bottles of lemonade and very long green and white straws. Dad had presented them with a bag of crisps each. He was smiling and so was Mum. They were drinking glasses of Brown Ale.

'Watneys Brown, drink it down.'

Dad looked to each of them in turn before bursting out laughing. Then ... nothing. The picture fades as quickly as it arrived or, rather, after Nick had given it permission to arrive. It must have been towards the start of their holiday week in Waxling.

He shudders in the bright sunshine as he passes a village sign proclaiming 'Upware,' turns a corner and immediately sees a pub from the present, directly in front of him: 'The Five miles from Anywhere No Hurry Inn.' It almost certainly won't be serving Watney's Brown but he is aware of how very thirsty he now is and enters the busy bar.

An unusually tall, rather gaunt man greets him as he makes his way past his more rounded, sweatier clientele – many of whom he guesses by their appearances to be local farmers.

"Good afternoon sir, what can I get you on this bootiful day?'

His accent is more Norfolk than Cambridgeshire but he is friendly enough. Nick orders a Guinness (that stout he had just remembered his parents drinking still looked really cool and inviting in his new memory bank). As he hands over the money the barman remarks on his hand.

"Looks like a nasty stain you got there, matey? Dock leaves are best for that. Joe, where's the best place for 'em?"

Joe turns out to be a burly, sunburned man in a fading tweed jacket. He is a little older than Nick, he thinks, though the effects of wind and sun on his skin probably give him a weathered look beyond his years.

"Ah! Come along the bank, did you? Well if you turn right out of here you'll come to a spot where the river divides. You can't go no further. Just behind you, right there, there's a whole feast of them. Sort you out in no time they will."

Nick thanks them both and heads over to a small alcove away from the noise of the bar, very friendly though it all is and quite different to the toxic atmosphere in the White Lady at Waxling. It is also one of those pubs that tries to imitate your own front room, with logs stacked up by the side of a broad stone fireplace and books on shelves, snaking round the back of comfortable armchairs.

He imagines it to be a really snug place to be in the harsh, winter months, quite alone out here in the watery expanse of the Fens. For generations of nearby residents and boatsmen and slodgers, it would have represented journey's end or at least a break in the lives of those working hard in the bitter winds to make sure this reclaimed land remained that way.

He glances at the books. There are the usual olde worlde editions of Dickens and Defoe, their bottle green and sepia spines adding to their authenticity. Another slim, brown, leather-bound volume stands out and he reaches up for it before sitting back in his chair and nonchalantly turning the leaves.

The author's name shocks him out of his comfortable repose: Jane Standing. It is another volume of poems by the same author he had found in their dining room at home, just after Nora had left for Waxling.

This one is entitled 'Verses from the East: Volume One.' He opens the book and quickly finds that it was first published just over twenty years ago in June 1987. The author is described as living in East Anglia, married with one grown-up son. There are no pictures of her and only a brief foreword:

'I have learned to understand forgiveness

through words, where actions have let me down so cruelly. This is my first attempt at re-interpretation and through it, I hope, peace.'

It sounds just like the kind of arty farty review one might read in a 'quality' newspaper's 'Weekend Review of Books...' What is the matter with him? Is it delayed shock from his throbbing hand or the stress of discovering a secret that has been kept from him for so many years?

He has to re-write his own truth but hasn't a clue where to start; how to start. He rewrites other people's stories for a living and this has, in turn, helped to forge the narrow-minded bigot who sits here now, trying to trash someone else's literary output before he has even read any of it.

Involuntarily and quite by surprise, he bursts into tears for the second time that afternoon. Being in an English public situation, most of the clientele move gradually away from his corner of the room, and absolutely nobody looks over in his direction. He supposes that this is the point: if you can't see pain or admit that it exists then you don't have to share it.

Joe, his erstwhile homeopathic adviser appears silently at his side and, without waiting to be invited, sits down, taking Nick's hand and holding it firmly.

"Good aren't they? Make you remember things or, at least, think about them differently! I've always loved poetry, me. She lives locally, you know. Though I've never met her myself, she has been in here sometimes. Arthur will tell you. Sits in the corner here with a glass of orange apparently.

Sometimes she feels obliged to buy a sherry or a shandy but only ever one, mind – tells him she can't afford to have her thoughts clouded. Typical poet eh? A nice lady though, so Arthur says. She's written a lot more since this and I think her later work is less frantic, more assured somehow. This is desperately sad; uncontrolled in places isn't it? 'Shame' is one of my own personal favourites.

He squeezes Nick's shoulder as he stands up again and leaves him quite alone with the volume: this man who Nick had instantly taken for a poor, ignorant farmer who could only have felt at home in one of the bastions of male superiority.

**'Shame**

Shame comes over me in warm waves of salty spray;

Crashing in as I try to push my past away.

A pale, unlined face which no sunlight will now mark,

As she floats out of place in the cold and the dark.

What had I been thinking to let go of her hand

That held mine so tightly as we ran on the sand?

Wanting to return, she has instead been preserved:

Her words and her images are all I deserve.'

Nick can barely see as he half-walks, half-stumbles back along the riverbank – except that he is not blinded by drink, more by a realization – a new understanding - that it has taken just a simple poem to unlock.

His parents had had to live through the trauma of losing their only daughter. How on earth did any parent begin to deal with that? Bad enough if it was at the end of a long and drawn-out illness but at least then the resolution and their means of dealing with it would have had an element of planning.

His sister (he still has to say those two words out loud to try to make them somehow more real) had died in an accident at sea while on holiday when, unlike the other fifty-one weeks of the year, her only mission was to enjoy herself, unconditionally.

Nick has a daughter too. What if something unexpected, something tragic, happened to Rowena? How would he react? How would Nora and he react to each other? Had the interruption in that certainty and assumed sanctity of life destroyed his parents' marriage?

Had his mother, in her desperation to make sense of what had happened, sought out the only other person in her life - her own husband - whose response was to reject not only her but also their one remaining child?

Is Nick the third victim of all this, with neither of them being prepared to ever tell him again how much they loved him, for fear that he might be unexpectedly taken from them too? Is this why Nick can never say those words to Rowena in case the little person he loves – adores – is also removed from his life? Is this the scar that he carries with him in spite of the doctor's advice all those years ago that by not revisiting the details of childhood trauma he would be more likely to get over it in time - and heal?

Perhaps, after the accident, he believed that he didn't deserve another chance at love and so tried to avoid ever expressing it. That would also account for why he always feels so screwed up inside whenever Nora is away for any length of time and yet does his level best to avoid both her and Rowena when they are at home.

He can hear Rowena stirring in the bedroom beyond as he closes the front door behind him and practically runs down the short corridor.

"Is everything alright, Daddy?"

That single word; that most childlike assertion and understanding of possession for a little girl resonates with him as he throws open the metal windows to let fresh air pour into the tiny, stuffy room. He feels a little like Pip at the end of Great Expectations, except that Jane had never grown old enough to be disappointed with life.

He sits down beside Rowena – his Rowena - and she shifts her little body across happily and deliberately, putting down her book in her lap without even thinking about bookmarking the story.

"Everything's fine," he hears his voice waver again, "Granny and I were just talking about something earlier from a long time ago, that's all."

"What thing? You look sad. Have you been crying, Daddy?"

How perceptive we are as children! He understands implicitly that he had been like that once - before bad things had stopped him seeing things for what they were, only what he had wanted them to be - and long before he learned how to do it as a graduate trainee with Prindle Massey?

"I'm not sad. You mustn't worry. He puts his arm round her neck which feels hot to touch but so, so rewarding as she snuggles into him. "Stories from the past can sometimes make you think about things differently."

"Is it Mummy's work you were talking about ... the body they've found?"

"Partly, yes. Mummy has spent a lot of her life finding out about things from the past and making sense of them so that we can change our understanding of them if necessary and move on."

"So history does come first then? It allows us to make our own history but we have to understand the past to make sense of the present."

He had forgotten about her school project and was simultaneously humbled by how quickly young minds could grasp concepts that they spent millions of pounds on in research exercises and focus groups.

"That's how it should work, yes." He is stroking her hair now. Dry and tangled it feels like the nicest thing he has ever touched, sitting there in that hot little room, just the two of them.

"Sometimes unexpected things happen to us when we're very young, but we're taught at school that those who live unusual or exciting lives are the exceptions to the rule aren't we? But – and it's a big but – there is no such thing as a normal life or even a boring one.

"Mine would be quite boring if it weren't for my books."

"And your friends at school!"

"I don't really have any friends at school, Daddy. I know lots of people – especially the ones in my class. I know some of their Mummies and Daddies and they seem really nice but I don't get invited round to play like the others do. If I go to a sleepover it's usually because Mummy has to go out or you're going to be back late from work, not because I'm really part of anything.

He takes two tissues from the box on the cluttered bedside cabinet: one for her and one for him. He has tried to be so clever about explaining things to her and to himself that, once again, his own voyage of discovery has failed to see the rocks right in front of him that cause such pain and distress to others.

Nora had been about to talk to him about Rowena's school issues when de Criel had muscled in on their conversation and their happiness. He wonders if it has anything to do with the cuts on her arms. They sit quietly for a few minutes, both reflecting on history.

"We'll sort something out, I promise you." He

carefully gives one of those tiny, thin arms a squeeze.

"And you'll find a solution to your problem too, Daddy. I know that because you're the cleverest person I know – even including Mummy, but don't tell her I said so!"

She looks up at him, a hint of a smile – perhaps even a suppressed giggle - on that pale face now. He smiles back: a broad, uncomplicated and entirely unforced smile.

He leaves her then, promising to return quickly and finds Mum – his own Mum – sitting where he'd left her, holding the newspaper and knowing that she'd read the article over and over again while he was out.

She glances up at him, as though he had only popped out for five minutes or so and offers "more tea?"

As she directs the supporting cast of teabags, tea cosy and sugar bowl, he observes that these processes are essentially just to give people some time out from the real world around them.

"Tell me something else about Jane ... please."

Mum sits the newly-laid tea tray on the table between them. A little smile plays on her face, as though she welcomes the prospect of telling her tale, as much as Nick is looking forward to hearing it.

"Jane? She was a lot like your Rowena. A tomboy really; her hair tied up in bunches but always wearing dungarees. She loved reading: always had her nose in books.

She never really wanted to go very far from home.

Whereas you always wanted to be up and out, she was content to sit in the garden and read until the sun went down. She liked writing stories too and kept a diary. Did Gladys mention that to you?"

"No. As I said she didn't make a lot of sense but just kept hinting at things. I know that Gladys writes the Abbots_Home blog though."

Mum looks up at him, genuinely surprised, he thinks; not that he is any judge of truth or lies anymore.

"When Nora first told me she was going up to Waxling I was really worried in case it brought memories back to you. Your father always felt that all of it should be left, buried," her voice tails off and he instinctively places his arm on her bony shoulder and rubs it gently.

"Except we didn't know that she was buried. We'd never known what really happened to her."

He starts to cry again for about the hundredth time that afternoon: great uncontrollable sobs. Mum gently wipes away his tears with the tea towel until the flow diminishes and finally comes to an end.

"This is why I was worried. But Nora was set on going and there seemed no likelihood of your joining her."

"Nora hinted that you had things to tell me. Has she always known the truth – the whole truth?"

"I had to tell her when you first started getting more serious. I told her that Christmas before you finished in Exeter - when she came up on the Boxing

Day. It was mild for the season and you went off for one of your walks down the bank while she and I sat by the river. It was a crisp day if you remember, cold but sunny. We just talked and talked. I thought she deserved to know - needed to know. I'd had to keep it from the one person I loved most in the world and I wasn't going to have secrets from the one person he loved."

He hugs her then, holding her tightly and taking in the vaguest hint of the same perfume from that day and all of the days in the past.

"I loved you too, Mum."

She does not relax his grip but clings to him even more tightly.

"No. No, you didn't but I always saw that as my penance for not telling you about Jane. It was like losing a child all over again but who were we to challenge what the doctors had told us? I suppose we were lazy really and didn't ever look for a moment when we might have felt strong enough to tell you.

Your father never, ever spoke about it to me, the police or the doctors so I was quite alone with it. It was actually a relief to be able to talk to someone and your Nora is a very good listener."

"Did you not worry it might put her off me?" he continues to snuggle his face in her old, grey hair.

"I did at first but I thought it would be far worse if she found out later on and, besides, if you were to discover the truth one day, you and she were going to need all the help you could get. One of you was going to need to be strong and I assumed you'd continue to blame your father and me for everything, just as you always had done."

"You've always been close, haven't you? You and Nora? Maybe if you'd confided in me too we might not have lost so many years."

"Some tales are hard to begin, especially when they lead you back in time."

"I'm sorry. I'm so sorry."

"It was my decision. It's something bad that happened in the past, changed us; I could see no reason why you'd find out now ... or ever. Then Gladys 'phoned me to say that she'd heard you'd been in the village. She'd had it from that Bracken woman."

"Audrey Bracken? De Criel must have told her."

"I let Nora know. I wanted to warn her as soon as I could. Likewise with the police. She knew before either of us."

"So Nora knew I'd been there before and about my visit to North Walsham!"

"We did it with the best intentions Nick, we... "

"No. It's alright. Really it is. She doesn't hate me then and she doesn't want to leave?"

"Of course she doesn't. She adores you – they both do, her and Rowena. She's been trying to reach you for years but, at the same time, scared of doing so. When you carry a secret like that around with you for so long it begins to weigh heavily and you don't know if or how you'll ever be able to lift it. She couldn't have known how you'd react. I guess she finally saw an opportunity to shock you back into life – like a car battery that's not broken, just gone flat."

A part of the pressure he has felt for the last twenty hours, let alone twenty years, has lifted. He is beginning to feel energized to deal with this, whereas he had previously been flattened by it: like a headache that lifts and leaves you feeling alright once more and wondering why you'd ever doubted your ability to ever function properly again.

Beryl is continuing in the background.

"You were so afraid to show any kind of emotion and God knows we didn't do much to help as parents. I could live with your rejecting us but it nearly broke what was left of my heart to witness you excluding your own daughter from your life. We only have the one chance of life and how quickly that can be taken away from us again."

He pauses for a few moments before replying.

"I'm pleased you told Nora when you did and I'm pleased she knows the story – has known all along. I don't want there to be any more secrets. I suppose it's comforting for Gladys too that I know. She seemed to be trying to nudge me towards something but I just thought she was a little mad, to be honest."

"If the truth be told, and no, I'm not trying to be ironic here, Gladys is a little crazy but losing her house in the way she did and then the incident with Leslie ... "

"She talked about that. A rescue that went

wrong?"

"I don't really know the details but she's had it in for John de Criel ever since. That man has a dark side. I saw it for myself when she … when Jane drowned. He was in the church that evening: on the day they assumed that Jane was lost. Your father was far too upset to say or do anything so I left him with Gladys for a little while. I just needed some space I suppose; isn't that how you young people phrase it these days?

I hadn't set out to go to the church, just found myself in there, by the main cross. Then I saw St John de Criel in the shadows to the right, in that dark part of the church with no windows. He was with that priest, what was his name, Jonas something … I don't think they were expecting anyone else to be in there or at least the priest didn't. He fair jumped out of his skin when he saw me.

I suppose it was late and had been a traumatic day for him and all of the villagers too. De Criel came up to me immediately and took my hands in his. I remember how hot they felt or perhaps I was just cold (I had very little feeling in them at all for months after it all happened). I remember thinking that he was being too helpful, too eager to please us after that. We'd only met him a few days earlier and there he was trying to act like our new best friend all the time.

I do know that being the village bigwig was really important to him and so was the RNLI. Whatever happened a year after Gladys and Leslie lost the house stood to destroy both."

"But you don't know what it was?"

"I think you'd have to look it up."

"I'm planning to go to the library in Norwich tomorrow; I'll see what I can find."

"Gladys won't find peace until she knows one way or another. Her blog idea was a way of being a kind of online thorn in de Criel's side. I think she thought he might come clean in some way and tell us what really happened.

Leslie never recovered from whatever it was and none of the others on the crew would talk about it, so Gladys thought she'd try and tease it out of him. She learned about Blogger when she was working in the RNLI office there. She may be strange but not at all incapable and, if you've got the motivation you do learn rather more quickly."

"Is this why you go the library in Littleport: to write to Gladys?"

"I don't possess a laptop for a start and, yes, it's just too difficult to talk here. I have to take the 'phone into the bedroom whenever Gladys calls and your father just follows me in. He knows of course and gets agitated about it. It brings back far too many bad memories for him too. He doesn't want to face up to it – them – he just wants to pretend that none of it ever happened.

So, I write to her up there and Rowena's then used the same machine while I go off and read. I usually clear the cache from whatever device I am using. I must have forgotten to do so that one time. I suppose your agency knows all about third-party cookies which is how you found out?"

Nick considers yet again how unsophisticated the experts at Prindle Massey really are when dealing with self-serving commercial concepts rather than the media realities of real people. For all of the little homilies and missives from Marmaduke, the agency isn't up-to-speed at all with the digital world that George Savory inhabits, much less so with the online existence of ordinary folk that they so lazily allow themselves to think of as merely consumers of paid-for products and services.

"I wanted to help Gladys and secure your help at the same time. I know how clever you are at searching, turning stones over. All along the line, it seems that the de Criel family is involved in some way with tragedies that befall Waxling. I'm hoping Nora's team might help to solve the early part; perhaps you could help to bring closure to the rest of it?"

"I'll start the search tomorrow" he promises, dutifully and delightedly.

"Keep on looking until you find the right answers!" she replies with an urgency that suggests this isn't just about the exhibits in front of them but beyond that: way beyond.

"There were no computers, least not like now, when this happened so, a bit like the diggers up on the coast, the authorities will only have access to old newspaper reports and paper witness statements at the time."

"At the time of what? A statement is still a statement, Mum."

"You haven't heard of the Birmingham Six then?"

She is always assured; now she is clearly reassured. He drains his tea and nods deliberately, urging her to continue.

"Things were just not very sophisticated in those days, compared with now. Norfolk in the late 'Sixties was largely unchanged from what it must have been like when those poor people drowned centuries before.

You had the landed squire and his followers and then you had the ordinary folk who were expected to do just that: to follow meekly, never questioning their betters. Of course, the police were on the side of the rich and didn't want to rock their boats any more than their owners did."

"I didn't like de Criel much when I was up there." He fleetingly recalls Prindle Massey and the unofficial, unsolicited 'pitch' to handle the PR for EC funding. "He obviously didn't like me either because he didn't want me on the account."

"He said that?"

"A few days later. He 'phoned my boss at the agency. Well, former boss now. I should be in Geneva at the moment."

Nick's future – their future – is clearly still of concern to Mum.

"You can't just give your job up though can you? I mean you have a family to support. I know Nora's busy at the moment but she hasn't been able to get work for months; not through the lack of trying though, I grant you."

To his shame, he hasn't been aware that Nora has been applying for work or looking for new projects but then again she's not the kind of person to just sit around and wait for things to come to her. She is certainly no daydreamer. Which brings him back to the sister he must once have known.

"What did she look like: Jane I mean?"

"You already know."

"No, I mean I can't remember, not yet anyway... "

"That picture of 'Denise' you saw in my pile of stuff. You never had a cousin. I was an only child, just like your father."

He shivers and keeps on shivering as he recalls that sense of déjà vu by the breakwater at Waxling that very morning, though it feels like years ago now.

# WEDNESDAY 20TH JUNE 2007

Their 'Breckland Line' train to Norwich is delayed due to a signal failure. Nick shuffles in his seat; far from relaxed. Though he longs to get nearer to the truth he knows that Hudson is on a similar mission, though for quite different reasons. He can't help feeling like a fugitive on the run. He half expects men in uniform to board the train at any moment, asking to see his papers and listening carefully to discern if he is from their part of the world or not.

" ...see all tickets please?"

He nearly falls over in fright. The ticket inspector smiles pleasantly as the trains begin to move forward at last.

"Can I ask you a quick question?" Nick hears himself ask.

"Of course but only if I can answer it correctly!"

He sees that the smile has become a broad grin and relaxes a little.

"Is there a railway line at Sheringham?"

"Well there is but it's private – the North Norfolk Railway – some steam enthusiasts about forty years ago must have thumbed their opposition to Beeching's lot. 'The Poppy Line' they call it these days. Pleasant journey it is. I took my grandson up there last year; travelled up from Holt to Sheringham on it, we did. Mind you he was more taken with the view of the windmill by the sea, to be honest..."

Nick thanks him and puts the ticket back in his wallet. Images of windmills are flooding into his mind but some of these memories are from much further back and it is as though he is even now recalling them in black and white. He imagines that this is what it feels like when someone is suddenly cured of amnesia or when some kind of cerebral blockage of the past is no longer there.

He still cannot see Jane in his mind's eye but had gone to bed the previous evening clutching the picture frame that Mum had given to him and knows it is only a matter of time before light and shade will give way to detailed lines from the past.

What he dreads the most is events coming into focus from what happened to her - to both of them - while out in that boat with Father. He isn't prepared for them yet. It is exhausting enough as it is.

It had been late when Nora had 'phoned to see how they all were and, when she had finally hung up, he had recalled her words, over and again throughout the long night that followed:

'I always want people to know the truth. It's my job. But I was also afraid of being the messenger and, anyway, still thought this mystery might go with all of us to our graves - even after the incredible coincidences of us both being called to Waxling and at the same time as your sister's body being discovered. Perhaps it was fate, but I don't believe in that.'

\*\*\*

They are traversing a black peat landscape, though cabbages and potatoes make it more eco-friendly on the eye. The white domes of the Feltwell air base fall behind the window to his left as the train rattles through the remnants of Thetford Forest that the army hasn't done its level best to level.

Another memory stirs within him. He and Father are watching a steam train hurtling towards them. They must have been on some kind of footbridge looking down on to the tracks. The carriages are a brown colour with white roofs, snaking back behind the engine, all steam and whistles. The engine is green and has LNER painted on the side in bright red letters.

Nick closes his eyes and concentrates, really focusing hard now. Something keeps telling him that he is about seven or eight years old and, gripping hold tightly of his father's hand: Daddy's hand. He is exhilarated but also terrified by the noise at the same time. Then everything is engulfed in steam. When it finally clears he is looking down at an empty railway line. The warm hand no longer encases his and he knows that he is quite alone again.

They arrive in Norwich at last and he walks briskly away from the station and down Rose Lane, towards the looming stone towers of the castle on the hill. As he passes an ancient war memorial to 'Our Glorious Dead' a sudden thought stops him in his tracks.

When St John de Criel dies, there will be no remaining members of the de Criel family in Waxling. The line ends there. Has the beguiling St John never 'met the right person?' Surely there will have been offers or prey in the offing? His closeness to Audrey Bracken could surely not have been expected to result in progeny? The family line had faced termination before, of course, through the inundation that Nora's team is now investigating. Given the death of Elizabeth, did that de Criel re-marry or was there another child?

With these questions ringing in his brain he passes through the huge glass panels of Norwich's Reference Library where he is swiftly but politely directed up the stairs to the Norfolk Heritage Centre by a receptionist who is simultaneously telling another first-time visitor in a broad Norfolk accent that the fire and burning down of the previous library was a blessing in disguise because they wouldn't have had such a space otherwise.

Nick tries not to dwell on her logic and is soon watching history pass by rather more rapidly as he scrolls through the microfiche editions of the *North Norfolk Gazette* from the mid-sixties onwards.

He isn't entirely sure what he is looking for apart from digging up some background information on Audrey Bracken's late husband, Jonas and stories of wrecks or other accidents off of the Waxling coast around 1997, which Gladys Pickett is so obsessed with.

He supposes he could have asked George Savory for search engine help but the library had seemed the obvious place to look first. Perhaps he'll contact George afterwards, depending on what he does or doesn't find? He knows that he will come across the articles about Jane from July 1967 and resolves not to dwell on them but, equally, knows that this is another resolution he will break.

After just a few minutes he finds a piece, written by a local journalist called Ian Pape that refers to an investigation into the activities of the local Church Youth Club at St Andrew's Church in Waxling on 17$^{th}$ August 1966:

' ... the group is drawn from other churches in the shared parish of Waxling, Lessingham and Hempstead and it isn't clear exactly where the substances came from or who brought them in. All we know for certain is that they were found locked in the communion cupboard at St Andrew's in Waxling by police acting on an anonymous tip-off.

Parish vicar, Jonas Thomasson, originally from the Akershus region of Norway, denies all knowledge of their existence and could offer no clues as to how they came to be found on church property.'

A later follow-up article at the start of September by the same journalist features the infamous Audrey Bracken, then wife of Thomasson:

'Mrs Thomasson, President of the Waxling Horticultural Society, presented the Gold Award for class 144: 'onions with the most original shape' to local gardener, Leslie Pickett. This is the second year running that Mr Pickett has won the trophy.

With the presentations at an end, Mrs Thomasson thanked the organizing committee and everyone for attending, before finishing with a heartfelt and very public defence of her husband – the village vicar – Jonas.

She said, "These have been a difficult few weeks for my husband but I would like to thank him for all the help he has given me personally to ensure that the Show has gone ahead as planned; we now look forward to next Sunday's Harvest Festival and hope as many of you will attend as possible."

Chairman of the Parish Council, Mr St. John de Criel, added that Mr Thomasson had the 'full support' of everyone in the village and praised the work of all volunteers who served the local community, as he had done for so many rewarding years.'

Nick can find no further articles or reports from 1967, apart from a summary piece from Paul Neaverson whose reporting Nick had first encountered the day before. It didn't add much to the story, only that the same St John de Criel was 'horrified' at events that had taken place and never, in all his years as a mariner, had he experienced such a calamity in calm waters and in broad daylight.

There is little further information other than the community being in shock as voiced by one, Gladys Pickett, whose guest house was where the family had been staying: 'Lovely family they are. We've known each other for years now. The little girl had been hankering after a fishing trip all week but the mists had lingered on most days. Today was as calm a mill pond so Lord knows why the little boy got so upset out there.'

And that little boy was Nick. He tries to think back, to zoom in on any detail that might now be emerging after so many years; but there are none. Had he got upset and, if so, over what, or whom? Does what went on out there explain why his father has been so distant and difficult with him for all these years? Does he blame Nick for the death of his only (one assumes) daughter?

A further thought suddenly assaults his troubles senses. Did de Criel recognize his name last week? Is that why he wanted Nick to have no involvement with the PR campaign for new flood defences? Is Nick a liability, not one to be trusted? Has Nora had similar doubts all these years?

A young library assistant called 'Monica, gangly and slim with a pinched, unremarkable face, approaches him quietly before asking, in little more than a whisper:

"Have you found what you were looking for?"

"Sort of; but I think there is a lot more still to discover."

She smiles benignly and knowingly.

"That's the beauty of historical research, isn't it? We can't bring back the past but its stories live on. We are all products of events that precede us and remain linked to them even as we make our own journeys through life!"

With that note of triumphalism, she creeps away

again, her black plimsolls barely making a sound.

About an hour and three years later Nick is taken aback to find another article concerning Thomasson under the headline 'Vicar found hanged in coastal village.' Written by Ian Pape again, it describes the moment when Jack Saunders discovered the late Jonas Thomasson, hanging from a makeshift noose made out of steel rope and slung over the flag pole in the playground of St Andrew's C of E school.

"I couldn't believe my eyes. Apparently, I was the first person on the scene and my only thought was to get him down. I cut into the rope but that fights back: too strong for the likes of me and my knife. So I mounted the pole, managed to undo one of the knots and the whole thing loosened enough for me to get the poor chap to the ground. It was too late though: there was no pulse. We always knew when someone was already gone and couldn't be rescued."

There was no apparent reason for his suicide, though his wife did hint at a recent instability of mind 'brought on by devotion to duty.' A later report on his funeral service reported only that his sister had flown over from Norway to attend and, of course, Audrey Bracken was pictured prominently as the quite inconsolable widow in black.

As to any reported incidents in Waxling during 1997, there was just the one report he could find from November of that year and written by a 'Coastwatch' reporter called Graham Black. It seemed that an already high tide had been whipped up by a depression that had hung over the North Sea for days and caused a

Spanish freighter to get into difficulties in the blackness of night.

Flares had been fired and the lifeboat had been ready to launch but there had been an unexplained delay in the boathouse and, during that time, the ship had listed on to its side and gone down almost immediately.

By the time the lifeboat had arrived at its last reported location there was no trace of it, though unconfirmed reports spoke of a glow over the sea – most likely caused by the last of the flares fired in desperation by the doomed ship's crew. Eleven lives were lost. The coxswain in charge of the lifeboat - a Mr Leslie Pickett -, would not be drawn on the reason for the delay, blaming only 'operational difficulties.'

Why was Leslie in charge and not de Criel and what could possibly have gone wrong that prevented a lifeboat being launched as quickly as possible? Nick knows little of the RNLI but does know how critical timing is to any kind of accident attended by the emergency services either on land or out at sea.

Concluding, somewhat disappointedly, that his time there has led to far more questions than answers, he leaves the microfiche film at the presently-unmanned reception desk and is turning to leave when he notices a painting on the wall to the left of the entrance.

It is a portrait of a woman, dressed all in white, staring straight into the camera with a self-confidence that befits her station in life. The caption below reads: 'Elizabeth de Criel, foreteller of tragedy at sea: the original White Lady.'

"Ah, I see you've met one of our benefactor's ancestors!" Monica is back at her desk. "The present Mr de Criel presented that to us about ten years ago after he lost part of his home in the storms. I suppose he wanted to keep her safe! She would have been in her mid-thirties at the time it was painted, I believe."

Nick cannot take his eyes off of the beguiling face. He has seen the painting somewhere before. It must have been as a child but, like so many memories now pouring into the cavities of his mind, it isn't clear. He does remember it also being in a library of sorts.

However, the cause of the sweat on his forehead and under his armpits is because he has seen this face much more recently than that. This is the lady he first met on Waxling Beach a week ago.

\*\*\*

As Nick races through the cathedral precincts, he cannot help thinking about that pale face. He has an uncanny and yet irresistible sense that the current St John de Criel was present when he saw it before, though this is completely illogical of course and no doubt due to his mind playing tricks as a result of the shock he has just had.

Had de Criel been having an affair with Audrey back then and is that what led to Jonas killing himself? Had Audrey seen de Criel as far more of a trophy partner than the poor immigrant cleric she had married? That could explain why she had been so spiky when he met her in the church two days ago, especially as she suspected he was some kind of reporter. Well, perhaps he is.

He needs to head north again and, as he takes his seat in the near-empty railway carriage, George Savory's voice comes into his head. He takes out his mobile 'phone and rings the office number he had saved in its 'address book.'

"Afternoon Nick. How are you?"

"I'm fine," he knows that he lies far too easily and resolves to do something about it – soon, but not today. "I'm visiting my wife up on the Norfolk coast. She is part of the History and Mystery programme."

"Wow. Small world eh! We've been hooked on it here: the tunnel leading from that old Priory to the church under the sea – fabulously romantic."

"Yes, isn't it? Look, George, you're an expert in online searching. There's someone I'd like to track down but she's based in Norway or at least the last reference I have for her is there… "

"Norway, New York, makes no difference on the World Wide Web; the techniques are much the same. You say you have a reference?"

"Just from what I could glean from the local newspaper archives from 1970; I did wonder whether I should have come to you first."

"Not at all but I'm pleased you've contacted me now. We're still going to be relying on hard-copy texts and micrographics for years to come yet. What is it you are looking to find out about this lady?"

"Just contact details really and an e-mail address would be great. I don't know her exact name but she was the sister of a Jonas Thomasson, who was a vicar at Waxling and who died there in January 1970."

He disconnects and switches to his FM radio, plugging the ubiquitous white headphones into each ear several times before they agree to remain there, much to the amusement of the rotund woman in a homemade scarlet tent opposite him and her rotund-in-training daughter who insists on slurping a white chocolate Magnum at the same time as dripping it down her grubby grey vest top.

He tunes into BBC Radio 4 and picks up the end of a History and Mystery bulletin:

"... **the diary came into our hands a few days ago and is believed to have been passed down through the family. Our experts have authenticated it and it gives us a real insight into Robert the Miller's life. He would have seen most things from his elevated position above the village and central role within this tiny community by the sea.**

**We learn that his wife was the lady-in-waiting to Elizabeth the younger so there is also an exciting and direct connection to the de Criel family there too. All of this is fascinating of course."**

He waits for Squires to interrupt Connie Breeve but he doesn't. This must be a podcast then, rather than an interactive piece.

"**From an entry in early January 1607, we learn that Elizabeth is sitting for a portrait painter,** up from London at de Criel's behest, to celebrate their 'ten glorious years of marriage next year.' That anniversary was never celebrated and Robert writes, much later in the year, that 'every time there's a storm hereabouts, I am haunted by the sight of her, dressed all in white with her dark hair covering her face, swaying on that church tower, like a ghost...'

Robert's wife insisted on staying with her mistress and was drowned along with her but, though doubtless, he was heartbroken and never re-married, Robert stayed on in Waxling as did generations of his family after him as the village was gradually rebuilt on the same higher ground as the mill."

\*\*\*

The taxi driver – Will – (from North Walsham this time) is much more informative than his colleague had previously felt the need to be. With just the hint of a Merseyside accent, he chats away apparently without a care, in between breaking off and eating giant chunks of chocolate from the slab on the front seat beside him.

Nick asks him about the death of Jonas and whether he can remember anything at all of the events from thirty-seven years ago.

"Oh most certainly, yeah; I worked as a barman in the 'Lady' on occasion. Course I was a young man then – making my way you might say."

"Did Jonas drink in there?"

"God no."

"He was too holy for public drinking?"

"Not really but I did hear that his father had some kind of drink problem when he was growing up which is why he came over here in the first place: would put you off the stuff for life wouldn't it?"

Nick nods knowingly but says nothing.

"He was good with the young kids though, Jonas. I remember him being into all that flower power stuff and weird music. I think he may have walked around the village in some kind of long skirt at one time… "

"Sounds a bit risqué for Waxling. I'm surprised his wife stood for it."

"Audrey? That's one stuck-up woman if ever there was one. Always hanging over de Criel even before the vicar hung himself. After something better you might say!"

"The drug bust must have been a difficult time!"

"Oh, you've read about that, have you? Well, I wouldn't read too much into it, to be honest. Nothing was ever proved and not everything was locked up in those days – definitely not like it is today. Audrey was dutifully on her knees with her husband, at least in public."

"It was a curious match though wasn't it – her and a Norwegian vicar."

"She wasn't always so snooty. Quite the opposite as I recall. We used to go to dances in those days - in the villages around here, you know - and she often used to turn up on her bike with various 'friends'.

Wasn't afraid of flashing her knickers in those

days either. Hems on those girls' skirts were up and down like a yard of tripe, as my dear mother would have said. There was talk that Jonas got her in the family way and he wanted to do the right thing by her. It was scandalous of course but the baby wasn't showing when they got married and it never did – show, I mean.

She told everyone that she'd miscarried but the big rumour was that she'd got rid of it. A child would have been far too much for Audrey Bracken to take on, wouldn't it? I mean, how could she have remained the centre of attention? In any case, she became even holier than thou (and certainly than the vicar) once she got married and was really keen to forget her slutty past rather than be reminded of it every day."

"But Audrey and de Criel? Is that just a social status thing?"

"Certainly on her part but I think St John de Criel definitely saw it as a means of continuing the family line. He wouldn't have wanted Audrey as she had behaved in the past but at the same time he must have supposed that she'd be more than willing to open her legs again to one so refined."

He practically spits out the last word in open disgust.

"Once the fuss had died down I reckon he'd have taken her on: properly, you know, with all the trimmings."

"You don't like him?"

"Who does?"

"Did Jonas?"

"Jonas was paid to like everyone, wasn't he?"

"Do you think he knew of the affair? Is that why he hanged himself?"

"Possibly but it's a bit extreme isn't it? Why not just look for a different parish to preach in – get right away from here and make a new start - you know what I mean? He'd already travelled all the way from Norway, hadn't he? Even Suffolk would have been a small step for him, though it's the other side of the world to many of them round here."

"I haven't met the new vicar yet; I assume Audrey approves?"

"It's a shared parish now and the new vic is based over in Lessingham. He's an old fellah I believe. I don't go for much of that stuff I'm afraid. I like the old bible stories, mind; who doesn't love a good story that's been passed down by so many for so long? People who talk about religion though: I reckon they've forgotten how to listen to their hearts."

They arrive at Waxling just after one o'clock. Nick is excited - longing - to see his wife again but the conversation in the cab about unrequited love and infidelity reminds him of his own suspicions over Squires.

The White Lady is not overshadowed by the 'Lady in Black' today and the young girl behind the bar is altogether sweeter and more approachable. She tells him that Nora came into the pub about an hour ago but went out again almost immediately. It seems that some important letters had been found and she was going to walk along the cliffs to 'clear her head.'

He walks away from Waxling in the opposite direction to the church and is soon out of the village and following the old cliff path with the sea now on his left. Will had mentioned (in between character assassinations) that the sea fog had hung around for much of the morning, but it has almost completely gone now, just leaving a slight haze over the sea.

His mind wanders to the woman in white on the beach and whether she is really part of some elaborate hoax. A seagull screams overhead as it soars away from him, no doubt disappointed at the lack of sustenance he brings. He watches it float on the breeze adjacent to the cliff, defiantly, as if egging mere humans on to give it a try without ropes or other more sophisticated safety nets.

He can see the funnels of tankers way out on the horizon. The whirring blades of a helicopter mingle with the steady hum of bees buzzing in the gorse bushes and clumps of purple heather. He guesses it is a supply craft heading out from nearby Bacton to service the crew of one of the many gas rigs off of the coast and just out of sight to the naked eye. Maybe it is taking personnel out to relieve the existing team?

It seems odd, he considers, to think of a small group of human beings being ferried over the very water which has covered so many other people for more than three centuries: to think that the rig's borehole could penetrate deposits that have lain below the sea bed before Waxling was first discovered and settled, let alone developed, drowned, re-developed and now drowning once again.

The modern, brick-built lifeboat station comes into view ahead of him as the ground falls away steeply. This is Ingle Gap, constructed solely to enable the lifeboat to be launched along its concrete causeway which stretches out into the sea. At one time the rescue vessel would have been a large, wooden boat, launched with the help of horses. Wells-next-the-Sea, just along the coast from here, was the last lifeboat station in Britain to use horses for launch and then powered by several pairs of rowers.

He reads all of this on a large information plaque attached to the smooth, yellow walls of the shed and learns also that de Criel had been coxswain until 1998. The latest incumbent is a Sandy Jackson of Palling Way.

He moves inside, out of the wind, and immediately hears voices from the far end. An elderly woman in blue headscarf above green Barbour jacket is talking earnestly to a younger, tanned and very well-built man who is bent over the reception desk, partly obscured by the blue and white lifeboat vessel itself.

On seeing Nick he comes straight over and stretches out his hand.

"Peter Jackson. I'm a helmsman here"

Nick shakes it warmly. Peter has a strong grip and his palm feels slightly crushed as he withdraws it. "Any relation to the coxswain?"

"My brother! Sandy and I joined up on the same day."

He makes it sound like conscription; as though they had made a family vow to defend any invasion plans the sea may have had and to fight back with selfless bravery.

"Was that after St John de Criel or did you serve under him too?"

There is just the slightest pause before he responds in the affirmative. "Just the two years before he retired. We passed ten years of service last summer."

"I imagine you've had some really bad nights here."

"We do our bit, Mr... "

"Golding. Nick Golding." He holds out his hand to the woman and is momentarily taken aback by the vice-like grip she produces. When he finally gets to withdraw his hand he finds that she has left a tiny piece of flint which he now clutches in his fingers.

"Be careful of the company you keep, Mr Golding," she is still staring, unblinkingly, at Nick, "and carry this in your pocket at all times."

He is suddenly aware of Peter Jackson watching him closely too. He must have heard everything she has said.

"I'm sorry, I don't understand," Nick smiles benignly.

"None of us do." She smiles back, equally sweetly, "but all are exposed by the tide eventually."

"Coffee, Mum?"

It is Peter, obviously preparing a diversion and beckoning him into a small anteroom where a red kettle and various half-open bags of sugar occupy a low, wooden table.

"You mustn't mind my mother; she means well but comes from a different time."

"Sorry, I… "

"People around here: they're simple folks like my brother and me. Sometimes things happen out at sea that they can't find the meaning of so they look into the past for clues. That's when they hear the stories again that have been retold down through the years. Read more into them than perhaps they should"

"You mean the White Lady?"

"Closer to home I'd say. There's some queer folk here in Waxling and people use that don't they?"

"Because they're different - harder to understand, you mean?"

Peter carries on as though he would have done anyway, whether Nick had asked the question or not.

"It's more than being different. We're all different, aren't we? If people make a mistake out on those waves or just hit bad luck we don't sit here and decide whether they deserve to be helped or not; we don't save the poor people and leave the posh ones to drown or make a risk assessment that the people were too fat and the boat would have capsized anyway."

Nick's mind flashes back to Battersea, not for the first time, as he considers how badly he had misjudged the integrity and sheer determination of people like Martin, struggling on his own against almost impossible odds and quite unresolvable memories.

"You're talking about Gladys Piper here? I assume her and Leslie are ostracized because they're a bit eccentric?"

He nods as if relieved at not having to say her name first. "It's not really their fault you see. They lost their house and nobody really wanted to help them. Leslie was liked well enough but even then they kept themselves much to themselves. With the guests and everything, I don't suppose they had much spare time.

We live on the edge here right enough, Mr Golding, but, for a lot of us, that only serves to remind us of how beautiful life itself is. Unfortunately, Gladys sees Waxling as a thin dividing line between the living and the dead, and those waves never stop coming in, do they?

She would keep going on about the ghost of the White Lady though; as if she was to blame for the drowning and accidents all the way along the coast. 'The Devil's Revenge' she calls it. People staying with them would tell us all this when they came down to the pub in the evenings, asking us all about it and so on.

We've all heard the bell and some of us have seen a strange light out there more than once, but people don't want to keep hearing about it. What happened here took place centuries ago. If those people from London want to dig up their remains then that's one thing but scaring people with supernatural tales is something different isn't it?

"You don't think there's anything in it?"

His mood visibly darkens.

"I didn't say that and neither would anyone in their right mind. There are many things that are unexplained out there. We've been out on many a shout to find sailors terrified out of their skins but not because of the waves. They've pointed to the spot where a wild figure of a woman is supposed to have risen out of the water and, yes, it's nearly always near the old bell tower or thereabouts.

The trouble is, the more Gladys reminds everyone and tells every newcomer that comes to our little village about it, the more people who perhaps haven't had the best education begin to think she may be part of it.

'How does she know so much?' they whisper to themselves, behind her back, 'how come she's always around when something bad happens?'

It don't take much for this to spread like wild fire and each new incident just reinforces those daft thoughts."

"So the villagers think she's some kind of witch?" He puts into words what Peter would have just left as a note in the margin.

"Keep your voice down," he hisses, "I don't want Mum to hear any of this. Some do. Just think how it looks to those people we're trying to influence in Brussels, you know, the campaign for new flood barriers or whatever. It's not going to look very good for us if Gladys portrays each and every one of us as being frightened to death by legends and folklore is it?

I mean: they're hardly likely to exchange French farmers' cash for a mad woman and a bunch of weirdos from the Dark Ages that believe in witches and ghosts are they? That Audrey Bracken's been trying to tell her this but she won't listen; never did."

"I met her at the church yesterday – Audrey Bracken. If anything she was more peculiar than Gladys."

"Don't you cross her. There's a lot of history between her and de Criel!"

"De Criel's family has been here for generations hasn't it? He seems to command a respect which belies his real status these days."

"I don't know too many that do respect him - not after what happened to poor Leslie. Gladys certainly never forgave him; that's for sure."

"What do you mean?"

A deafening ringing noise suddenly starts up in the lifeboat shed which is so loud that Nick can't process it for several seconds until he realizes it is a telephone ring tone, presumably amplified so that nobody present could ever miss it.

Peter Jackson half-walks, half-runs to the traditional black handset on the opposite wall from the kitchenette. Nick hears the urgency in his voice but then his shoulders visibly relax. He appears to be making some arrangement or fixing a time.

Finally, he replaces the receiver and shouts across the shed,

"Mum! Paint's coming tomorrow at about eleven."

He starts back towards Nick but is halted mid-stride and he hears him say, in a much more gentle and hesitant voice,

"Hello. Can I help?"

The new arrival is Nora, dressed in a white cotton jumper and tight-fitting red jeans which Peter probably noticed first.

"Shall we go, Nick?"

It isn't a request. He shakes Peter's hand again and assures him that they will continue their chat at another time but, even as he utters the words, there is a knowing sense of finality within him that this will never happen.

\*\*\*

"How are things?"

She avoids answering his real question, rather playing for time, which is especially nerve-wracking for him as he has no idea how much time they have left.

"John is worried about the effect of this child's body on the programme – doesn't want the original thrust to be softened by the modern-day angle."

He ventures, "De Criel isn't all he seems to be, though, is he? Some of the villagers also seem to think that Gladys Pickett is involved in some alarming way."

They step down on to the beach itself and she removes her sandals.

"And you're not just using this as a convenient PR

opportunity to shaft St John de Criel to put yourself in a better light?"

"I don't need to shaft anybody."

"Don't let Julian Bannister hear you say those words."

"I won't but I don't care what Bannister thinks anymore."

"Oh please!" she walks a little more quickly as if to emphasise the physical as well as the mental gap between them. They kick the soft sand before them. At least they are walking in the same direction, back towards the village.

"It's true. Nora!"

She stops and turns, hostility openly consuming her as she places her beautiful hands on her hips. He hasn't thought about her hands for so long - those long, slender fingers that had once sensuously wrapped themselves around his.

"I've left the agency. Something's happened. I can't really explain it but I do know I'm not going back."

"So what exactly will you do instead?" her voice is still harsh - sarcastic even - but where there was previously just outright rejection, now there is a tiny element of interest.

"I don't know exactly but perhaps I'll finally do something worthwhile. I was talking to Peter in there about accepting – allowing - people to be different. Well, maybe I've always just tried to fit in and hide from that. Maybe that's why I'm bored and disillusioned with it all."

"It took you long enough."

"The one thing I am certain about is that I have never wanted to be in the limelight - ever. I dread being in the forefront of anything. Shine a light on me and I run for the shadows. I want to be normal, not special."

"Just as Rowena does."

"I'm sorry?" She really has taken him by surprise. The breeze blows her dark, silky hair in front of her face and she draws it back again, slowly and deliberately. Once again he wills her to touch him, to hold him and stop him from breaking.

"Rowena likes to be all alone too. She would rather read a book than go to a party or even a friend's house. I had to really push her to go that sleepover before I came away but all of her class friends were going and if she'd come up with some excuse – as they were all expecting her to – she'd have been more alone than ever.

Can you not imagine what it's like to be a young girl who doesn't fit in? Rowena is a very unhappy little girl, with spots and puppy fat and a father who doesn't seem to notice."

"I did notice that she always seemed to be in her bedroom, even at weekends."

"On her computer, usually. She's been trying to tell us how lonely she's feeling for months now and the thought of going to 'big school' is terrifying her. It's too big, Nick, everything is. She's feeling hemmed in – we both are."

Tears fill his eyes and flecks of sand blown in by the sea breeze make them sting all the more.

"I didn't notice. You're right. I didn't but I should have done. I did come up to Waxling to visit St John de Criel. I thought the agency could help with the local flood defence effort and to try to secure EC funding. There was nothing secretive about it. There was no reason not to tell you, Nora, I just didn't. I am so sorry you had to find out in such a cheap and vulgar way."

She resists the urge to run over and hug him, needing to discard all of the baggage that has piled up first.

"I was beginning to wonder if something had happened to Rowena; whether she had been traumatised by something ... or someone."

"You didn't think that because of what happened when I was little? I could... "

"I didn't want to but... "

"That I was responsible in some way – that I could hurt a child? Another member of my own family?"

"No. I honestly didn't believe that but I went to talk to her teacher and, although he was pretty useless and loved himself to bits, he did say that children tend to write honestly: that they haven't yet learned not to unless there has been some kind of trauma.

Then, when Mike talked that evening about PTSD, I didn't know what to think anymore. If we could have talked about it then it would have been so much easier, but, well, we just couldn't. I've sometimes wondered if you were planning to move out altogether, away from us."

"Leave you? I could never do that – you're the only family I have."

"No Nick, you have a mother and father too and I saw how you treated them: so cold and ... events change people – sometimes forever – and, yes, they can make mistakes as a result. We all do. That's what being human is all about isn't it?"

"I guess I just lost my way."

"But you are the lucky one here. You can begin again if you're sure you want to; starting with Rowena. She needs a new start, Nick, with people around her who care enough to guide her through what remains of her childhood. Jane never had that chance but Rowena does. Waxling does not need to be the end of our story."

She watches the tide roll in across his anguished face but still, she waits.

"Nick, I hope you can at least try to understand why I never mentioned her name. I – we – both thought... "

"Mum, you mean?"

"Beryl, yes! I haven't heard you call her that for a very long time; not since our earliest days together."

"You thought it would plunge me into some kind of nightmare from the past?"

" You didn't seem to have any memory of any of

it when I first met you and I certainly wasn't the person to bring it up. I genuinely worried about how you might react if I did."

"You must get this often – on digs I mean: history being revealed and those in the present having to rewrite their personal and collective stories sometimes?"

"Except I never expected it to happen to you, to us. Even when I first mentioned the History and Mystery gig in Waxling there wasn't a flicker of recognition from you. Beryl was more anxious about it than I was but none of us could have expected the storms to reveal… "

He can see that she is also close to tears now and reaches out to her. She snuggles into his arms and makes no apparent move to leave them anytime soon.

"It must have been a shock for you too. I can see that it was," his voice is soothing and he feels a peace returning, "especially knowing what you did and making that connection."

"I have been dreading your finding out about Jane all of my married life but then, when the worst thing did happen, I thought the best thing was for you to know. I offered to tell you myself before that officious Hudson did but I couldn't do it on the 'phone. Besides, Beryl has been waiting for this moment for far longer than I have and it seemed the right thing for her to tell you face-to-face. I admire her bravery and think it might help her too – in the long run of course."

"Much more so than a bottle at least."

"Nick, there's a message in that bottle."

"Which is?"

"That Beryl did not and does not drink the contents."

"But the visits to the pub ... you can't pretend they don't and didn't happen?"

"Or that she might go there for other reasons altogether!"

"To get away from him you mean?"

"Partly and maybe also to get away from her past: a coping strategy. You might be remembering it happening much more often than it really did."

Nora is looking at him anxiously as if probing his face for what: answers or assurances? She has always tended to defend his mother, no matter what the situation or background.

"You were always able to talk to her! I remember the long telephone conversations - on Sunday afternoons."

"She used the 'phone in the pub more often than not; saved up coins during the week. She couldn't talk to me while your father was around. You couldn't honestly have blamed her if she had turned to drink; not in the circumstances. But she didn't."

He sits down on what he had thought was a nearby rock, before realising it is actually part of a red brick wall, once mounted on the clifftop, the cement still glueing the bricks together in spite of the trauma that has befallen it.

"There are many loose ends leading away from this beach aren't there? What happened here affected so many people: then and now."

She gently pulls him upright and they walk as they talk, approaching one of the old breakwaters. Most of it is buried under the sand but the iron pole which marks the end of it still stands as proudly as it can, facing up to the waves below what looks like a triangular hat. Old and forlorn it has rusted through age and the exposed timbers it is perched on are largely peeling or rotting away.

"Nora, I think I may have seen a ghost"

She doesn't flinch. "Connie thinks we may have disturbed many spirits here who are calling, reaching out to us. She's been having terrible nightmares for the last week or so. Nothing seems to stop them. We had her tanked up on gin last night but they still visited her in the night; made her hangover even worse this morning I expect."

"Connie can't believe in all that stuff, surely," he is truly sceptical of her if not of himself, "all that knowledge based on scientific discovery and so on. There can't be any room for ghosts can there?"

"There is always room for the unexplained, Nick. That's what keeps all of us going. Life would be very dull without death to contemplate wouldn't it?"

"What do you make of Gladys Pickett? The lifeboat people seem to think she needs rescuing or at least reining in?"

"Gladys is a tortured soul and has been good friends with your mother for some years. She blames de Criel for pretty much everything bad that has happened to her or, if not him directly, the sea. We can't do much about the latter, as generations of people who live here have found out, but de Criel's ancestors at least do look to be in the clear.

We've found some letters in the casket they discovered yesterday. As we thought, they were in remarkably good condition and Nathan's been translating them into modern English for us. It seems that old John de Criel was trying to save his community after all. I'll show you when we get back to my room."

To her room? He feels a sudden warmth inside that no amount of gin or other spirits could have provided.

"I did believe that Mum saw the world through the bottom of a glass you know."

"I know you did and you were always wrong. For her, it has been about having space to think and make sense of the world. The drink might have been no more than a glass of orange or a shandy that she made last a whole evening…"

He considers her last sentence. A recent memory stirs but he can't wait for it to catch up with them; can't afford to perhaps?

"But she never denied it or told me any of this."

"Would you have listened if she had?"

"Probably not but I do wish I could remember

things more clearly than I do - as they were. I suppose I've put a personal spin on everything."

"Which is almost certainly what the doctors and your parents would have wanted you to do – a form of protecting yourself? The police did have a strong suspicion at the time that you could have been involved in Jane's death… "

"In her death? My own sister? How could they possibly have thought that?"

"Apparently, you were very angry before getting into the boat…"

"We'd probably had an argument over something stupid, but Dad was with us wasn't he? That's what the newspaper report said."

"He was but he would never speak about it afterwards – still won't."

"I can't make sense of that at all. You'd have thought he would have wanted to tell them everything he knew; maybe not straight away, but if the police were giving them a hard time… " he hears the words drift away on the stiffening breeze, "unless he was protecting someone?"

"Which doesn't mean that you were guilty in any way," she steps in quickly, decisively. "He may just have been far too upset by the whole thing and was worried that the police would have, you know, taken anything he did say out of context or twisted it around, with you being an easy target. Perhaps he genuinely thought it better to say nothing at all. You were only a child!"

"It would make sense though, wouldn't it? I mean he's barely ever had a good word to say to me – or about me? What if he has always known that I was guilty of killing my sister – his beloved daughter?"

"Beloved? Do you have any evidence of that or are you trying to dress up an inscription somewhere? Remember, there's never been a grave?"

"But he must have loved her. All fathers love their daughters don't they?"

"Yes, Nick. They all do in their heart of hearts."

\*\*\*

After a long bath and several cups of tea, they make love in Nora's little room in the eaves of the pub, gently and tenderly. Neither of them has forgotten how good it feels or how much they have missed this, the most important connection of all.

Later, they lie back on the pillows, resolutely refusing to separate their bodies, as once had been the case in Exeter and then London. Now it is true again in Waxling and, they both consider happily and maybe even at the same time, hopefully beyond: definitely beyond.

"You mentioned that Nathan had been translating the letters you found in the casket?" he inches up the pillow gradually, not wanting to disentangle her lovely, naked body from around his legs.

"Must you always bring your work home with you?" she laughs and he joins in. It isn't a hollow laugh any longer, it is wholesome. His life is being joined-up again and it feels so good.

She eventually slides her head up and rests it in the warm crook of his neck, "Yes, he's made a lot of progress in a short time." She glances up at Nick expectantly and they burst into laughter once more.

"The first thing to report is that the papers were literally thrown into the container, not neatly folded in an orderly way. This actually does suggest a sudden need for flight, which is unusual and could be either as a response to the inundation or some other external threat. Remember, these were dangerous times for Catholics or anyone seen or known to condone their ancient rites to worship as Papists.

It does contain an inventory of plates and jugs and sheepskins which we were unable to find at the outset of the dig and must have been made in their final days here. It's dated January 31$^{st}$, 1607 and I can still remember the exact words: 'all is in place as we take our leave. We arrived with no earthly goods and so it is as we make our departure from the greedy mouth of the sea.' It doesn't prove that the drowning caused them to leave but it does prove that the Priory was inhabited at the time of the storm."

"Do we know where they went to?"

"No trace and almost impossible to find out as none of the monks' names are listed … although one family name does come up, time and again."

"One of the monks?"

"No, not one of the monks. A regular visitor

though."

"Not John de Criel?" He feels a wave of excitement and turns to face her.

"The same. He was a regular correspondent with the monks and we have discovered a series of letters from the autumn of 1601 onwards to prove it."

"Was he a closet Catholic?" Nick can feel his heart racing, as can his wife.

"Hey, not so fast." She sits up too and holds his hand tightly. We can't have you leaving us again; not now we've just reclaimed you!"

She climbs out of bed on his side so that he can once again feel the full extent of her warm, silky skin. She heads over to the tiny wooden shelf, built into the dark recess of the wall, and plugs in the kettle adjacent to the television which she switches on, quickly swapping channels until John Squires comes into a focus which is far too sharp, even on the portable screen. She falls back into bed, zapper in hand and kisses Nick on the cheek. "I'll make us some more tea shortly."

Squires is confirming what Nora has just explained.

How nice that he looks and sounds so second-hand, thinks Nick. Nora too is surprisingly pleased with how old he looks. The sun has not been kind to his skin and no amount of stage makeup can hide the rents in his burnt skin.

**"And we know now from these same letters**

that John de Criel was also concerned about his wife, Elizabeth, being sympathetic to the 'Fen Slodgers': women who lived off of the land by snaring, fishing and cutting reeds – a way of life that would have been ruined by the planned draining of the Fens.

Capitalists wanted to cultivate this area because of the high price of agricultural produce – an argument entirely opposed by de Criel's wife who saw the land and its progeny as God's gift to his people and not to be artificially manipulated. Sounds a bit like one of the arguments against genetic crops today doesn't it?

They were swimming against the tides of change though and the women of Deeping Fen were punished for starting a riot over this issue in 1603. The Fens were eventually drained, of course, with not a little help from Dutch engineers who crossed over the sea from just east of where we are now, here in Waxling."

They recognize Connie Breeve's voice just off-screen and it is clear that Squires has asked her a question. Nora turns up the volume and is also assisted by the kettle in the corner switching itself off, but not before it has contributed a small cloud of steam to the bedroom's already steamy atmosphere.

"Not really that surprising as it happens, John. We know from the trading records, which we also found in the casket, that Robert the Miller of Waxling visited the Priory regularly and undoubtedly also delivered letters from Squire de Criel at the same time. In that way, de Criel would not lose face or bring his community or own family into disrepute by visiting the Priory himself.

Robert would have traded flour for wool which he could then exchange in Norwich for food or cash. After the dissolution of the monasteries in the previous century vast tracts of land were put out to pasture and of course, the enclosure movement led to what were effectively small prairies here and elsewhere. Sheep farming was booming and the wool churches around here are a testament to that.

However, this letter from 1601, written by de Criel to the monks when he was just twenty-five years old is quite revealing I think. The modern translation shows us that de Criel was in great distress because he too had spent most of the family savings on a sizeable flock of sheep. The monks farmed the land on his behalf and paid him a monthly duty for the wool and meat they sold at market or traded with the likes of Robert for flour.

Sadly, in the spring of that year, he describes how 'lambs, both black and white, were beginning to dance across the land for as far as the eye can see before they fell: all of them. None were saved.'

We wondered if the fencing along the cliff edge had been damaged in one of many storms and the sheep had somehow got through a gap but he goes on to talk about them having convulsions and 'wide, bulging eyes' as they slowly died. It must have been terrible for both him and the monks to stand by – quite helpless to help.

Some of these early years of the seventeenth

century saw drought conditions during the summer months and we think that, aided by the dry weather, the saltwater couch grass, which spreads underground from the dunes, might have accumulated either prussic acid – hydrogen cyanide – or a much higher level of nitrate toxicity.

We don't know which it was for certain but our agricultural advisors are pretty sure that the sheep eating that couch grass would have precipitated yet another tragedy here, given the symptoms observed.

De Criel was clearly a broken man and felt responsible not only for effectively squandering his family inheritance by being caught up in the race for profit from wool at that time but also because he feared for the prospects of the poor in his own community. He writes to the Priory's Abbot:

'I have been a foolish man in so very many ways. I should have paid more heed to my wife and her terror of the waves – how they consumed her family's home and community and knowing that they would not reside there alone. Always restless, always waiting for an opportunity by day or by night, the sea's appetite can never be satisfied.

I thought Elizabeth unstable but perhaps that person was me: to even imagine that I could help to clothe and feed this poor fishing community when it is God's responsibility, not mine. To think that I could assume that role was true madness indeed.'

We learn that de Criel had also been buying flour directly from Robert the Miller, with the monies received from the monks, and passing it to the village baker to bake bread for the people. Records show that almost a third of the families left the village in the years 1602 and 1603 and we have to suggest that one of the key reasons for this migration away from the sea was not because of fear of inundation but because they sought food inland once the de Criel bread subsidy effectively ended.

All of this goes some way to explain de Criel's state of mind at the time of the flood but one further letter that he writes to the Priory monks is perhaps the most telling of all... "

They both sit up, simultaneously perceiving the change in Connie's tone of voice and sense of anticipation she has conveyed in her words. Nick places his hand over Nora's.

"It is written just the day before the tragic events of 24$^{th}$ January 1607 and addressed to the Abbot. It reads: 'My dear old friend, I shall be away for a few days now but am sending this via Robert who will watch over my dear wife while I am gone. I pray that all will be well but should any danger arrive in any form she knows the secret of the tunnel from St Andrew's to your good home and I pray that you would welcome her there as you have always welcomed me. I shall be taking John the Younger to Eton and then residing in London for a few days before my return.'"

They look at each other as if, quite miraculously, they have found 'x' in a seemingly impossible equation.

Connie is reaching her own conclusion:

"We know that John the Younger – Jack - later

went on to King's College, Cambridge, obtaining a First in History and then concentrated his efforts on Land Economy. Certainly, this is how the de Criel family line survived. The male de Criels did not drown along with Elizabeth and her mother at Waxling; John de Criel did not betray his village and neither was he found wanting at the community's greatest hour of need because he was simply not there at the time of the disaster."

Half an hour later they are dressed and walking down the narrow staircase, Nick just in front of Nora. At the bottom, she asks him to take her hand.

"It's a bit tight and I tripped up on my first day here. I always asked John to wait for me after that, especially after we'd all met in his room for team meetings."

Nick smiles as another mystery unravels and his faith in human nature is restored.

"I was jealous of him you know!"

"John Squires. Whatever could you have been jealous about?"

"I think it is because he is more or less my age but he has done something with his life. I know he left the armed forces under a bit of a cloud but he still has a service record to gloat about. Then he left all of that behind and did something completely different: and is really good at it."

"So you envy him his success?"

"No, I envy his bravery – not in the air – though

that too, I suppose, but right here on the ground. It takes courage to do what he did. I want to make a difference too. I owe that to you and Rowena - and to Mum."

"And maybe also to Jane."

He looks at her with pure love watering his eyes before softly replying: "Yes, especially her. I think she might have made quite a difference to the world."

She strokes his face but in a soothing, comforting way this time.

"I know that she would have done."

"I guess this is what it's like for you," he doesn't open his eyes, doesn't need to. "Revelation upon revelation?"

"You could describe it like that," she flushes, happily, "but I don't think we've quite come to the end of this particular Bible story yet."

\*\*\*

An hour or so later they are sitting in the bar, an empty coffee cup in front of Nick and an empty teapot, milk jug and teacup in front of Nora, when Nick's 'phone pings. It is a short text from George Savory and simply says: 'Hope you got my e-mail. Illuminating stuff eh! Told you it wouldn't take long.'

Nick checks his email but there is nothing from Savory or his agency. He is about to reply when the device rings. For a split second, he forgets how to answer incoming telephone calls until Nora gently hits the screen for him.

They both stiffen as the clearly distressed voice of his mother comes over loud and clear: "Nick, Nora. I'm so sorry to disturb you but ... it's David. He's been rushed into Addenbrookes. He just couldn't get his breath and they put an oxygen mask over his face. I've never seen him so pale.

I didn't want him to go in the ambulance alone but was worried about Rowena so I stayed behind. Thankfully Mrs Wright from next door offered to sit and do her knitting with her. She's ever so good you know! I'm following them in a taxi now. I hope you didn't mind my leaving Rowena – I think she's over the worst of her cold now."

\*\*\*

Just under an hour and a half later they have passed Ely and are now on the same stretch of road that Beryl 'phoned from earlier. Nick had assured her that they would leave immediately and, though she had argued the case, they had both heard the sense of relief in her voice. It wasn't fair that she should face this alone – no matter the history between Nick and his father – and neither should she have to cope with the additional responsibility for their daughter.

They have chatted on and off but Nora has been mainly focused on making the journey as quickly as possible within the confines of narrow Norfolk bends and narrow-minded road traffic officers. Nick reflects on the last time he took this road, just a day and what seems like a lifetime ago, so much has happened since then.

"Say if you want me to take over," he offers for the

umpteenth time.

Initially irritated as if it were a slight on her driving prowess, Nora recognises that it is just nerves on his part and that now, possibly more than ever, Nick really needs to speak with his father – to hear his story directly rather than second-hand or from a newspaper report, or e-mail message.

"It's fine. I'm fine. We'll be there in twenty minutes or so. Which side of Cambridge is the hospital on?"

"It's the far side from here but there's a ring road that should speed things up. We'll take the A14 then head down through Fen Ditton."

He peers out into the summer dusk. It's just after nine thirty and shapes are becoming less distinct by the minute now that the sun has finally set on another summer's day. He has been quietly reviewing the life-changing events of the last couple of days and knows that it will be hard, if not impossible, to make-up for lost time with his mother but the more immediate and really nagging doubt in the back of his tired mind is whether they will get to the hospital in time for him to properly say hello to his father for the first time in years, let alone goodbye.

Just after Stretham, they pass a car towing a boat trailer. As Nora speeds past, Nick notices the boat's name: 'Fjord.' He says nothing but opens a new internal enquiry. Nobody – not witness nor journalist – has ever mentioned whose boat it was that he and his sister and father had boarded. Why is that?

Could it be that this is somehow connected to the suicide of Jonas, the vicar of Waxling? How would that work though? Vicars were generally poor and unlikely to have their own little fishing side-line, any more than more than a bakery producing five loaves for the entire village.

Fifty minutes later they arrive at the entrance to Addenbrooke's Hospital and are soon half-walking, half-running down endless perfectly straight and brightly-lit corridors that must have been built on the same grid as New York City.

Eventually, they find the Accident & Emergency department and Nick asks the Receptionist about his father. He hasn't spoken the name, David Golding, for so many years that it sounds now like it belongs to a stranger with no connection to him at all. Except of course, it does and always has done.

Told that he has been admitted, they are re-directed to a ward at what seems to be the other end of this vast site. A nurse greets them as soon as they enter it, presumably so that they won't make too much noise and wake the other patients.

"Mr and Mrs Golding?"

Nick nods a silent assent.

"Would you like to take a seat in here please; the doctor will be in to see you shortly." With this, she leads them into a small ante room with three functional chairs and a matching wooden side table adorned with cheerful leaflets on erectile dysfunction.

"I don't think we need to worry about that just

yet," announces Nora with a forced smile but gleaming eyes.

He loves her for it. He knows she is trying to lighten the tension but at the same time not make light of why they are there in this strange, unworldly place.

A very tall, sinewy man enters the room almost immediately, as though he has been awaiting their arrival. His white coat signifies that he is a member of staff, which he confirms by introducing himself as, indeed, 'Dr White.'

"How is my father?" Nick hears himself ask and they all note the slight tremor in his voice.

"I'm afraid I have some bad news, Mr Golding."

Nora takes his hand and gently squeezes it as Nick begins to sweat more in that air-conditioned room than he has all day in the blazing sunshine.

The doctor sits down next to them and Nick notices how far into the room his spindly legs extend: anything to distract his mind from what he fears is coming next.

"I'm afraid we were pretty busy when your father arrived in A&E earlier this evening…"

"I imagine it's always busy here!" Nora suggests politely.

"Well, yes, and we're trying to plan our move to a new lung function unit next year; so much paperwork, you wouldn't believe."

He throws his hands up in the air to support his

case but it only has the effect of making them both think he could almost touch the ceiling from a seated position if he put his mind to it. He collects himself and continues, gently, "But we did treat it as something of a priority and he got the very best respiratory care: I can assure you of that."

Nick immediately notices the change in tone from coldly businesslike to softly sympathetic.

"May I see him, please? I, we, really need to talk with both him and my mother too. Could you take us to them?"

"I'm afraid that's not going to be possible; you see your father died about five minutes ago. There was really little more that we could do."

"But artificial respiration – some kind of life support?" it is Nora who replies first but without letting go of Nick's hand. "Surely you could have kept him going while you undertook further tests?"

"I'm afraid not. His entire pulmonary system had collapsed. We discussed it with Mrs Golding and she made it very clear to us that she did not want us to do anything that would prolong his suffering. I realize that this has come as a terrible shock to you both – as indeed it was to her – and may I say how very sorry I am to have to break such sad news to you after a long and ultimately fruitless journey."

"A waste." This is all that Nick can say. Nora knows that he is not referring to their failed bid to see Nick's dying father in time, rather the time they might have had together but which was squandered thanks to the events of forty years earlier.

She puts her arm around her lovely, lost husband who was so recently found again.

"Where is Beryl - Nick's mother?" she asks, ignoring the tears that have formed in her eyes, like unwanted raindrops at precisely the point of a major find on a dig.

Dr White leaps to his feet. "One of my nurses took her down to the café for a cup of tea. I could take you down there if you like or page my colleague to tell them that you are here?"

"I think we'll find our own way. Thank you, doctor."

They stand and she takes Nick's arm, feeling the slight shake and noting his stumble as they leave the ward and all of its darkness behind.

"I am so sorry, Nick." She holds him ever more tightly as they shuffle back down the same corridor they had practically run along only minutes earlier – minutes too late. "We so nearly made it. At least you did your best."

"Did I though?" he murmurs, glad of her supporting arm. "Did he even know I was trying? After all these years of nothingness, why would one more day have made any difference?"

They find Beryl at the far end of the café which, according to the cardboard sign, is run by volunteers throughout the day and night. It is, mercifully, less brightly lit but not so dim as to hide the tell-tale lines of Beryl's own grief. They relieve the nurse, politely sending her on her way, and sit either side of her.

How small and insignificant she looks, thinks Nick, in this vast and sophisticated environment where even the molecules have letters after their names such as MRSA...

"I'm so sorry we didn't quite make it, Beryl." Nora holds out her hand and Beryl grasps it without looking up, her tea cooling in front of her, soon to be stone cold like her late husband.

"You tried." She turns to Nick. "Thank you for trying."

He hugs her fiercely. "I'm here now, Mum, it will be alright."

"I don't know what I'm going to do about the new place – I won't need it now will I? There'll be folks who'll get far more benefit from it than I ever will. But the bungalow is sold; the new people are due to move in next Friday!"

"Don't worry about any of that now. We'll sort it out for you." He hasn't even considered what would happen to his parents in the event of illness or death. In truth, he hasn't really considered his parents at all until the last few days.

"There's a delay with the undertakers apparently: too many deaths to cope with. The nurse said sunstroke has brought a lot of it on - well, in older people anyway. It's alright though because they'll keep his body here. They don't have much choice do they?"

"Come on Mum, let's get you home."

"I don't rightly know where that is anymore."

"Well let's go and find your granddaughter and relieve Mrs Wright at least."

"I think it will be the other way round. Poor Rowena's probably been talked at all evening - told the same old stories over and over again; either that or she'll be covered in a giant, woollen eiderdown."

"In this heat?" he takes her by the hand and slowly draws her upright. She gives him a nervous smile and he returns it reassuringly as only a son can to the mother he now cares for.

# THURSDAY 21ST JUNE 2007

Nick wakes suddenly, relieved to find that he is in the familiar bedroom. He has needed, longed to fall into sleep's cushion of oblivion for the last two days. Small holes, in the ancient bedroom curtains he remembers so well, filter the early morning light into yellow beams and project them against the once white wall beside his bed.

He watches as the whole expanse gradually turns a golden yellow. Sunshine had always offered the promise of new beginnings when he was a small boy. There are picture hooks above the bed head but he knows for certain that he never hung any pictures there. Perhaps Harry, the lodger, did so when he rented this room some years afterwards?

Hearing voices from the kitchen, he finds Nora and Mum sitting closely together at the table and separated only by a teapot.

They look up as he approaches.

"I was going to bring you a cup of tea," Nora says, "but you looked so peaceful in there."

"It must be something to do with being in your

old room again." Mum looks tired but her eyes are bright or wired if Nora's rate of tea consumption is to be taken into consideration.

He laughs and takes a seat opposite them both.

"Rowena's still asleep," Nora tells him after watching him silently count the cups on the table, "she was really tired last night, what with all the upset and I'm not sure she's really over the chill yet."

"She could do with some sea air. Why don't you take her back with you for a couple of days?"

"And leave you here, Mum, at a time like this? No chance."

"What do you mean 'at a time like this?' There's no time like the present – isn't that what they say? I'll be fine. I've got all the arrangements to make and that will keep me busy enough; take my mind off things."

"There won't be anything to do until after the weekend I shouldn't think," Nora gives Nick's shoulder a squeeze as she passes by him to refill the kettle, "the death certificate was signed and they said the undertaker would be in touch when this…" she hesitates, not sure of how to describe the reason for the delay.

"Backlog?" Beryl grins.

"Yes, I suppose that's what it is, isn't it?" Nora is clearly relieved. "Once this backlog has cleared."

"In any case, we're not leaving you here on your own." Nick smiles back at both of them. "Why don't you both come up to the coast; that is if you wouldn't find it too upsetting, Mum?"

"Well I haven't been back there for so many years and I may need a bit of quiet time but, if you're sure – completely sure – I would rather be quiet up there, knowing that you were nearby than all on my own here."

"Great. Shall we tell Rowena or let her sleep for a bit longer?"

"I think we should let her wake up naturally, darling, I don't have to be back there until this afternoon. They have pretty much got everything wrapped up now and just have the final piece to shoot giving their conclusions and so on. Mind you, Connie did send me a text this morning to say that Hudson is planning on having some kind of Press Conference in Waxling tomorrow."

"Press Conference? Why on earth would he want to do that?" Beryl is unsure again now, the prospect of being outside of her comfort zone striking home mercilessly. Nick has to acknowledge, shamefully, that if the sudden revelation of him having a sister who then died is almost too much to bear, how much more corrosive must the long, slow process have been for his mother; and now her husband has left her behind too.

"Heaven knows! I do know there have been calls to the police station from people coming forward who were also on holiday at the same time that you were there."

"Why would they want to dig all that up now?" Beryl looks years older, all of a sudden. "They allowed bad news to be buried at the time. Nobody will ever really know what happened. Why can't they just let us give her a gravestone at last and leave us all in peace?"

"I suppose some people want their fifteen minutes of fame, Mum!" Nick offers, glumly.

"It's celebrity this, celebrity that these days. Andy Warhol painted thirty-two Campbell's soup cans; you tell me how many of the people who work at their canning factory up in Lynn have any real variety in their lives?"

"Not like real artists, eh Beryl?" Nora has a glint in her eye and Beryl smiles her assent.

"I'm sorry. Lecture over. Your father hated all the falsity, that's all. I suppose it stems from him having to watch those 'very important' people heading off to the capital, day in and day out and abusing him over the price of the tickets that he could never have afforded."

Nick marvels once again at how articulate his mother is. He recalls now his father's barbed comments over this - at teatimes usually - when she had phrased something better than him or become 'too la di da for her own good.'

Beryl is talking again – it is helping her to do so. Her words fill the room as if she is performing a reading:

"David always wanted to be an engine driver. I know that many young boys want to do this or play football for England or something equally heroic that they soon grow out of but, for him, it was always the trains. I think his father used to take him trainspotting as a boy and he fell in love with them.

It broke his heart when he couldn't pass his driver's exams. Three times he tried and then they wrote to him and said it really wasn't worth applying again but that they could offer him a job in the ticket office in Whittlesford. You were only little and ... Jane was about to start school and needed new shoes – you know, it soon mounts up. So, he took the job and got a transfer back to Ely about six years later."

"He took me to see the trains didn't he?"

"He did. Yes. You went to see the Flying Scotsman once on its run up to Scotland and we always seemed to find a steam train wherever we went on holiday, or a disused railway line to walk along. I think he liked to imagine what it would have been like to be at the throttle..."

"I vaguely remember wanting to talk to him about Uni but the first weekend that I came back he said something about it all being a complete waste of time and I might just as well have gone out and got a proper job."

"I don't think he meant that; he was so proud when you got in at Exeter – though he couldn't tell you that to your face - but it made him feel even more useless about his own life."

The Star FM DJ – who sounds about twelve years old – is addressing them from the radio on the sideboard: "The Beatles for you there with a song that went to Number One in July of 1967 after it was broadcast on the world's first live television link when one hundred and fifty million people in twenty-six countries tuned in simultaneously. Sounds a bit tame now doesn't it? It replaced the debut single from Procul Harum which had itself been on top of the charts for six weeks... "

"Jane loved that song," his mum whispers.

"'All You Need Is Love?'"

"No. Not that one. 'A Whiter Shade of Pale.' Some say that it defined a generation.'

"I like that song too!" it is Rowena who plods into the kitchen, tiredness filling the cracks in her pale face. She gives her grandmother's shoulders a squeeze and sits between Nora and Nick.

"How are you this morning?" Nora fills an empty cup with milk and tea.

She yawns "I'm alright. How are you Granny?"

"Better for seeing you again, little one, that's for sure."

"We thought we might take you and Granny up to the seaside for a couple of days." Nick is eager to see her reaction and it doesn't disappoint.

"Really! Oh, that would be lovely. But don't we need to organize the funeral first?" her voice trails off as she recalls the events of the previous evening once more.

"We can do that after the weekend," Nora reassures her, but there is something else. Something much more urgent. Nick sees it in his daughter's face immediately before she rushes out of the room.

Nora half-rises but Beryl catches her arm and

gently pulls her back on to the chair beside her. "Leave her for now, Nora; we all react to death in very different ways. It may take her some time."

Just moments later, though, Rowena arrives back in the kitchen, slightly red-faced or at least with more colour than usual. She is carrying a brown envelope which she hands to Nick.

"I forgot to give you this last night, Daddy; I'm really sorry but I was just so tired. Grandad gave it to me yesterday morning and told me to give it to you if ever, if ever… " she bursts into tears and flings her arms around Nora's neck, sobbing uncontrollably now.

He gently takes the envelope from her.

"Read it next door if you like?" Nora offers kindly, also observing Beryl's eyes, round and expectant.

"It's fine. I have no secrets anymore," he smiles at them but cannot quite hide the nervousness with which he slits open the envelope and draws out a single piece of white paper, immediately recognizing his father's handwriting, even though it has been so long since he has exchanged words with him. He reads it through once to himself and then, a mixture of surprise and anger forming on his face, out loud to his family:

'Dear Nick

I have asked Rowena to pass this to you when I am gone. She is a good girl and reminds me so much of your sister when she was your age – always with her head in books and full of interest in the world. I suppose we were all like that once! I could never speak to you about Jane, or to Beryl either. It wasn't just what the doctors advised us; there's more to it than that. I wanted to be sure that you really couldn't remember any of it because I knew then that you would be alright; that he wouldn't come after you. There were times when I came close to telling you though – that day when we went to the nature reserve up at Sutton Bridge together for one; it was so quiet and peaceful that day, watching the seals out on the flats. Hard to believe then that anything bad could ever happen out at sea. But I couldn't do it I'm afraid. I wrote it down a number of times and tore the paper up again each time. I'm not clever like you and writing's not really my thing - this is turning into a bit of a ramble isn't it? But knowing that you now know about her makes it a little bit easier for me. You did nothing wrong at all on that day in the boat, and Jane's death was in no way connected to your being out there. You did panic when it happened and stood up, trying to reach her, which caused the boat to rock a good deal, but she had already gone by then. He did it. It was his boat you see and he had offered to take us out fishing. Jane had been babbling on about it all week until I finally gave in. It was a calm, sunny day and she asked if we could head over towards the old church tower first. She was always on about it, thanks to that Gladys, and wanted to take a closer look - though what she expected to find there I couldn't tell you. Just as we got close and could quite easily see the white rock below the waves he lifted her up and held her over the edge of the boat to get a closer look. Then, without saying a single word, he just dropped her into the sea. After splashing hard and screaming out to us, she disappeared. None of us ever saw her again. I couldn't tell you this because I could never come to terms with what I had done. I was as guilty as he was. I should have stopped him or at least dived in after her – tried to rescue her if I could - but I didn't. I was terrified of what he might do to you if I did. You saw it all and he knew that. I have heard those screams every single day since then and tried to comfort myself that I have saved you from them at least. I am so sorry that I have otherwise been such a terrible father to you, selfish and absent from you and your mother when you have needed me most. I was trying to shut out the memory of what happened that day. I failed and failed all of you. I hope that you may one day be able to forgive me but, if you can't find it in your heart to do so, please care for and care about your own wife and daughter in the way I wish I could once have done. These are my last words and they are all yours. Dad.'

The crowd called out for more. None of them knew who 'he' was but each remarked in their own way how absolutely certain David had been about the person responsible for Jane's death. There was no ambiguity and no absolution.

"If the police couldn't work it out at the time – and they wouldn't have needed to pester you if they had – I think it's extremely unlikely that we will ever learn the identity of the 'killer.' I'm sorry." Nora strokes his arm once again as she has done almost continuously since Nick had revealed the contents of the letter.

They say little on the journey back up to Waxling, arriving there by mid-afternoon. Rowena had snuggled up to her grandmother practically the whole way since crossing the Norfolk border and has been snoozing since then.

Beryl has said little apart from the odd question about Waxling. She is alarmed to hear that both the local butcher and baker have long since gone but then so has the street on which they both once stood.

They have been unable to book an extra room at The White Lady, such has been the interest in the dig and now the prospect of tomorrow's press conference which Hudson must have deftly leaked through PR 'spokesmen' close to the Norfolk Constabulary. The two remaining rooms have been taken by journalists 'up from London' that very morning, apparently.

Beryl comes to their unexpected rescue by 'phoning her old friend, Gladys Pickett. Gladys has a spare room that she and Rowena can use as the previous occupier has now 'moved up the road.' Beryl seems to understand what this means and relays the good news to all, including a special message for Rowena: "Mrs Pickett says she hopes you like kippers!"

They leave Nora at the pub as she wants to freshen up after the journey, before heading down to the BBC team who are wrapping everything up this afternoon with a final broadcast. Squires is keen to stay an extra day 'if the budget will stretch' so that they too can take in the press conference that he sees as having 'more impact on TV than any press rag.' Nora reports this back to Nick as they embrace and hold each other closely before he takes his leave from her room.

"Hard to think we were here just a day ago, isn't it?" he offers.

"Are you alright?" she surveys him anxiously. "Be aware that delayed shock might set in at any time and a lot of <u>shock</u> has been delayed in your case for a very long time. Keep a close eye on your Mum too as she is even more vulnerable to it, what with coming back up here and everything."

"I will. You can count on it," he assures her.

Rowena has made a last minute appeal to stay with Nora for the afternoon and see the broadcast team in action. They all agree – through a combination of barely discernible nods and knowing glances – that this would be a good thing given that Nick and almost certainly Beryl are probably going to need a little time and space of their own.

They agree to meet back there at six o'clock but not before Nick has hugged his daughter tightly and kissed her warm cheek farewell. He and Beryl then walk slowly, him tucking her old arm under his, towards the old mill and Gladys's cottage. She stops after just a few paces and he worries she might be feeling faint.

"Not faint, no. Don't go worrying. I am just trying to take it all in."

"The changes since you were last here you mean?"

"Yes, although quite a lot is still the same; much closer to the sea's edge than I remember. No, I was thinking about your father's letter."

They lean on a low wall and look out to the sea, blue under an unbroken sky.

"Did you have any idea of what happened that day, Mum?"

"None. All I remember is you and your father running back to Abbots Home. He looked as though he'd seen a ghost – pale and shaking. You were hot and sweaty from the running but it was Gladys who saw that it wasn't sweat at all and that you'd been crying; still were.

I asked them where Jane was but all you could do was point back out to sea. Leslie seemed to understand better than all of us and got us organized with cups of tea and blankets. I suppose he'd seen people in shock before. The police arrived shortly afterwards and then Mr de Criel of course: to find out what had happened I suppose."

"But Dad never said anything about it?"

"He never said much about anything – nothing that made any sense anyway – for a few days but, no, he was never able to talk about it; not even after the Coroner's verdict.

At least this makes it absolutely clear that you had nothing to do with her death. We'll need to send that letter through to the police, won't we? Not that they ever really believed you had anything to do with Jane's drowning, and certainly not a scrap of evidence if they did.

They didn't have much of an idea about anything really. They might have been frustrated by the doctors' insisting that they stop asking you questions about it all but trying to lead a flimsy investigation against a minor who was in shock would have been really difficult.

People actually read newspapers from front to

back in those days and talked them over with their neighbours, on train journeys, in pubs - more time and fewer distractions I suppose. The story would have spread quickly but you were certainly no Ian Brady or Mary Bell or remotely like any of those troubled souls. You weren't even disobedient let alone naughty as a child."

"And Dad just felt incredibly guilty about it all. No wonder he didn't argue when the doctors advised a blanket of silence."

"He lived in a silent world after that but not a peaceful one. I always felt he needed a grave to go and visit but we had no body you see. He won't be visiting any grave now will he?"

He catches her as she begins to sway and holds her while she drowns out the seagulls with her wails. All of her anguish over losses, past and present, is allowed to flood out with nothing held back.

He wipes her face with his handkerchief, and they find themselves on the Picketts' doorstep shortly afterwards.

"Bless me, it's been far too long" Gladys hugs Beryl long and hard before, to his complete surprise, she then embraces Nick fiercely, as though greeting a long lost son, home finally from his voyage to the other side of the world.

"Welcome, once again; come in."

He notices that there is a lightness to her step that wasn't there before; she even looks younger somehow – the worry lines below the white hairline are less pronounced and she has on a clean blue dress - which her ample frame has filled but not yet creased - and simple, white cardigan.

She has been looking forward so much to seeing her old friend again, he considers, and has made a real effort. The poky room they had sat in just a couple of days ago is transformed. The washing line and assorted hangers-on have gone and the clutter of books and papers tidied away. As has Leslie been it seems.

Gladys answers the unspoken question. "Leslie's just popped down to the shop for some extra milk – I told him we had plenty but you can never have enough milk can you? He won't be long."

Beryl sits back in the old, worn armchair, as directed by Gladys, who sits directly opposite her. Nick perches on the aged settee between the two of them, trying not to notice the assorted stains and cat hairs that have stubbornly evaded Gladys's late spring clean.

"I was so sorry to hear about David, my dear," Gladys is holding Beryl's hand as she speaks in a low, soothing voice, "I remember him before ... when he was so full of life and ambition. I was thinking this morning about those evenings when we used to play cards, once the children had gone to bed."

"Gin rummy!" there is a slightly pinkish tinge to Mum's face now. A welcome tinge that he would so recently have misinterpreted.

"What was he like when he lost?"

"Oh, my goodness, don't." Gladys throws back her head and laughs.

They all know that this is a release valve and are so grateful to her for turning it.

"He got that mad, didn't he? And yet he was a quiet man, on the whole."

"He was a disappointed man; that's the truth of it. He could never escape from the tragedy of the past and the future seemed to hold no hope of better things to come. People say that you become stuck in the past but he was stuck in the present; like a no-man's land. But still, we both of us could have fared so much worse. How is Leslie?"

Gladys hesitates before replying. "I doubt you'll notice much difference in how he looks but he's changed. He never quite got over losing the house and then…" she stares at the wall opposite but he knows she is seeing something way beyond it.

"It must have been truly terrible for both of you."

She jumps back into her sitting room. "Yes. Well, we know all about loss up here, don't we? That television programme has brought death by drowning down to a whole new level. Oh, I'm so sorry I… "

Beryl holds up her hand and he sees that she is not in the slightest bit offended by Gladys's faux pas. "It's fine. I kept all of your letters. They were a great comfort to me. They still are."

"And yours to me. But the tide has turned. I put a blog piece online this morning … ah, that will be Leslie now."

They hear the front door bang shut and wait

for the newcomer to join them, which he does shortly afterwards; only, it isn't Leslie.

A short, stocky, quite elderly man in a faded grey suit over a bright yellow shirt and highly-polished tan brogues enters the room, removing his cap as he does so. He has a ruddy, baby face and his hair *is* bristling with sweat but Nick recognizes him immediately as the man who lodged with his parents for years.

"Beryl!" Harry approaches her immediately and places his hand on top of hers, "Sad business about David. It must have been really dreadful for you, darling, what with being all on your own and everything."

His voice has a higher pitch than Nick would have expected, given his gait and age.

"Thank you, Barry." Mum is relaxed with him, easy in his company as you'd expect from so many years sharing that small bungalow together – just the three of them.

"Luckily Nick and my daughter-in-law were there to look after me afterwards so I was in good hands."

He spots immediately that she has got his name wrong and moves to correct her but stops himself in time. The last thing he wants to do is to embarrass her in front of old friends, though they would surely forgive her in such a time of distress.

For the second time that afternoon, Gladys wades in and saves him.

"I think you probably knew him all these years

as Harry?" she is asking the question of Nick, not his mother.

"Yes. Well, we all did." He feels his own face reddening now.

"Just as I said earlier, the tide has turned, and how!" Gladys stands and then heads for the kitchen where she can bang and crash crockery around to her heart's content. He quickly realizes that she has left the way clear for Mum to explain:

"I think it was the on the second occasion that your father had to go into the hospital that we met Barry. To be honest we both misheard him and thought he had said Harry but he did nothing to correct it at the time.

He had been transferred from Norwich because he had been hit on the head and they wanted a trauma specialist in Cambridge to monitor him. He had almost died but they managed to keep him alive while they were able to establish that the brain was at least still functioning."

"Beryl and David looked after me when the hospital stopped doing so," Barry chips in, sitting down in the chair so recently vacated by Gladys. "The doctors told me I could go home but Beryl and David both knew that I could not."

"I'm sorry, I don't... "

Barry shakes his head. "Please don't worry. No need to worry anymore. I think you've had a lot to take in just lately, haven't you?"

Nick says nothing; how can he contribute to a conversation between people whose meaning he does not fully appreciate - this is not PR, after all, this is (very) real life?

"My real name is Barry Thirling." Again he looks closely at Nick to see if this information disclosure has any effect, dramatic or otherwise. "My father owned the mill here for many years. I remember you and your sister and father visiting us just before the conversion?"

"Conversion?" To what, Nick wonders inwardly, some kind of flour shrine?

"I am an artist, not a craftsman. The upkeep was becoming huge and the family money was dwindling. We were here at the time of Nora's dig and even before that. We may not quite go back to the days of Magna Carta but then neither do we go back to the days of greed and self-advancement that led to its need in the first place."

Again Nick is humbled by the power of words, spoken with conviction and no plates of expensive biscuits, or freshly-ground tea or bowls of exotic fruit in sight. That agency life seems as vacuous now as it does distant.

Gladys re-appears with a tea tray and plates of freshly-made crab sandwiches.

"Leslie went off on the bus to Cromer yesterday. He always brings fresh fish back; keeps us going for a couple of days it do. Course it's not the same without the fish van. Lovely that used to be. Do you remember Mr Pridmore, Beryl?"

"I remember there being a fresh fish van – Wednesday's wasn't it?"

"Ah, and chip van every Friday. Your Jane loved that one more!"

"She did." Beryl's eyes are shining for the first time since they'd left Ely but a happy recollection this time, a memory that neither man nor nature could destroy. "And we always used to have to go and find an inn afterwards to wash them down with lemonade."

"She was a lovely, little girl," Barry shakes his head slightly, "if things had been different – if I had been different."

Gladys pours him a cup of tea and her eyes linger on <u>his</u> as she passes it to him. "It's time to share, duck." She half-whispers.

Barry nods and continues, at first not taking his eyes off of Gladys, as if for courage, but then back to Nick. "I was not – am not – 'normal.' In the 'Sixties, this was akin to a crime. To some people, I imagine it still is. Being … unconventional usually means hiding from everything, everyone, but mainly yourself.

In a tightly-knit community like Waxling, that is almost impossible and I always knew that. I think people must have suspected it anyway. My dear father probably went to his grave knowing it but never said anything. I don't suppose he had the words.

So, I had the choice of forever living a lie or letting folks make their own minds up about me. I converted the mill into a gallery – an art gallery – and held exhibitions, some of which were not to everyone's taste

– Audrey Bracken's for one."

"I heard she wasn't always so strait-laced?"

"She wasn't. No. Quite the opposite. One of my sketches left little to the imagination."

"A nude?"

"I called it 'unwrapped' actually."

"Of her?"

"Suggestive ... only the twitch grass came from my own, direct experience" he smiles at the memory. A strangely sad smile.

"She must have gone mad! Not to mention de Criel?"

"Oh, he continually fought to have me closed down but for other, quite different, reasons."

"May I ask what they were?" Nick realizes that he is sitting, literally, on the edge of his seat now. "No doubt they were couched in terms of decency and the public good?"

"But that's just it, you see." Barry's voice is no longer faltering. "I did a sketch of him too, in an even more compromising position – but I didn't have to imagine it."

\*\*\*

She examines her daughter's face, waiting for a reaction. They are sitting in the unbroken sunshine behind the vast mobile studio which had made its temporary home here just two weeks ago, along with corporate logo, uniformed crew and the very latest technology that license fees can buy.

"I know it's a lot to take in but I'm sure Grandad would have wanted you to know the whole story, just as Daddy does."

"But it couldn't have been a very happy childhood if he can't remember any of it now – not even that he had a sister? I mean what's the point of having a childhood if you can't look back on it and sometimes wish you were back there?"

"Is that what you wish?" she puts her arm around her small shoulders. "Do you wish it wasn't time to move on: to <u>big</u> school I mean?"

"I like school, Mum; well not the Maths but I love the reading and the writing and I might even be good at netball one day! It's not school, just that it's all so big and I am still so small.

"We all have to grow up."

"Auntie Jane didn't. She wasn't given the chance was she?"

She has never really considered her as Auntie, or as the sister-in-law she never had.

"Bad things happen I'm afraid." She hugs her even tighter, though both are sweltering from their shared body heat. "We have to be strong now for Daddy and Granny too."

"If I had an Auntie I'd want her to live by the sea so that I could come and visit and tell her what I'm worried about. She'd take me for walks up and down the beach and the wind would flow through the ribbons in our hair as she would tell me what to do, while I listened, quietly, not needing to say anything..."

A few minutes later, John Squires beckons them both back inside the studio. If the outside world was hot, the 'pretend world,' as Rowena always refers to it, is positively baking.

"We're just about to record the final piece – should go out tonight but there's been a big thing about 'Healing through Remembering' in Northern Ireland. It's a day of private reflection today, apparently, and they're expecting some kind of trouble; ironic that it's the longest day today isn't it?"

A few minutes later Connie Breeve is summing up the findings of the History and Mystery visit to Waxling:

"**...and far from being a closet Catholic with plenty to hide, John de Criel was actually a straightforward, family man of the people. He felt the same noble pressure to feed his family as he did the wider community which his family had served for centuries.**

**Similarly, his wife was not some kind of witch, leading innocent people, Pied Piper-like, to their watery graves. She did what she felt was right – what both her husband and her God had told her was the right thing to do – by leading them to an ancient church and its tunnel, giving safe passage below.**

**Even if she had wanted to head straight for the Priory herself, it is unlikely that the men, women and the children of the village would have gone with her.**

Neither would she have told them where the tunnel led.

The villagers were fearful of the unknown and viewed the monks as fanatics - worshipping the same God in a way which was different to theirs and to be shunned every bit as much as the witchcraft that they saw in every deviance from normality in their lives.

But they didn't make it from the church tower to the tunnel or the monks waiting, expectantly, at the other end. The sea got there first as it almost always has done in this part of the world... "

As the director cuts at the end of her piece, and while waiting for Squires' microphone volume to be tested, Rowena creeps out of the side door, signalling wordlessly to Nora that it is just too hot for her in there.

Squires delivers his usual sensational conclusion which has a vague historical bearing but the real mystery is that they haven't found someone better by now. Nora shudders at the memory of his clumsy, drunken advances towards both her and Hayley.

She remembers once more the email from yesterday and smiles at the deliverance that tomorrow will bring to the people she cares about the most.

***

Nick cannot believe what he has just heard. Barry Thurling is munching a sandwich noisily while Beryl and Gladys hide their faces behind the teacups.

"St John de Criel is gay?" he half-shouts, incredulously.

"I didn't take you as a homophobic sort of person, Mr Golding." Barry looks less sure now, fearful even.

"I'm not. Please don't think that at all. I just cannot believe that sanctimonious, self-righteous know-all should hide behind, behind…"

Beryl jumps in as Barry still looks anxiously from his empty plate to the empty expression on her son's face.

"Let him finish, Nick, there's much more to come yet."

Barry continues, uncertainly at first but soon getting into his stride again. "We had an affair on and off for years. It only ended when that ship from Holland went down ten years ago."

"When Leslie took the blame for the delay in getting the lifeboat launched?" Nick turns to stare at Gladys but she gives nothing away, not even a flicker, so he quickly turns back to Barry.

"That would be the one. St John was delayed and nobody knew why apart from me. He was in the mill with me you see. Nobody knew how to get hold of him. There were no mobile 'phones in those days. It was only when the flare went up that St John realized he was needed."

"Leslie never said anything of course," Gladys does speak now, slowly but assuredly. "He wouldn't have broken the code you see; would never have gone against one of his colleagues – especially not de Criel who was the coxswain, after all.

They waited and waited but de Criel didn't get there in time. Leslie took the blame and never said a word. He didn't even know the full truth of where de Criel had been until Barry told him this morning. Barry didn't forget it though. He offered us this cottage a year later when we lost our own home and we still only pay him a peppercorn rent. I don't know what we'd have done without him."

"But de Criel did know." Nick is still struggling with this. "He wouldn't have forgotten that, would he? I mean losing face in the eyes of the community his family took so much pride in dominating? Just changing your name wouldn't have made much difference?"

"He did remember and I didn't change my name." Barry again, much less warm. "He was always urging me to move away from Waxling. Said I should make a new start where people like me would be welcome."

Again, Nick thinks back to the false worlds that Prindle Massey creates and grimaces. "But you held on; you weren't prepared to be intimidated?"

"Oh I was intimidated alright; often couldn't sleep at nights but this had happened before you see - when I did my sketch of him. He couldn't risk that happening again so he marched up here one evening, just over a year ago, once it had got dark. It was an ugly night – the wind was howling around the mill – and we had a furious row which ended with him hitting hit me over the head with his stick. Thankfully Gladys had seen him arrive and 'phoned for an ambulance or I would not have lived to tell my tale."

"After all you'd done for us, it was the least I could do. Worried sick we were. Then, a few days later, I get a call from Beryl here. Took over for me didn't you dear?"

"Barry was very poorly and needed nursing back to life." Beryl takes up the story. "That was the upshot of it. He was also terrified of moving back to his own home so we agreed to take him in. It was pure fluke that he should occupy a hospital bed next to your father - all those miles away from home and after nearly forty years.

We stuck with 'Harry' as part of the subterfuge, not that we expected de Criel to go looking for him as far away as Ely - he wouldn't have taken the risk of being found out himself. Once Barry had told me his story I contacted Gladys to let her know he was safe and recovering nicely, and he stayed with us from then on. Your father enjoyed the company too."

Nick notices the two old women exchanging glances. "So why did you come back now? What's changed? I mean de Criel is still as much a threat to you as you are to him? I know you had to leave Ely because of Mum & Dad moving but..."

Before Barry can answer there is an urgent knocking at the door. Gladys deftly lifts the corner of her net curtain and, relieved, declares that Nora is outside. Nick joins her at the front door but quickly realises why she hadn't simply knocked just the once.

"Is Rowena here - with you? I haven't seen for at least an hour."

\*\*\*

Pausing momentarily by the sea wall, they are hoarse with calling out her name. The seagulls overhead have twisted their words and turned them into their own cries of anguish which the breeze from the outgoing tide has all but blown out to sea.

With Barry wanting to remain out of sight, they agreed that he would stay at Gladys's house in case Rowena should turn up there. Gladys and Beryl took the path towards the lighthouse while Nick and Nora headed back towards the main village and the church beyond.

That was two hours ago and lights, flickering in the collection of houses so used to missing persons, are becoming more prominent as the natural pinks and oranges high above the sunset to the west are being slowly swallowed by darkness.

"We have to find her. I cannot rest until we do." Nick hears his voice, torn by endless calls that haven't been returned.

"We will. She won't have gone far; can't have. Anyway, the police are encamped here." Nora's words are more reassuring than the voice which says them and yet, no sooner has she spoken than Nick's 'phone rings – metallic and insistent. With incredible timing it is Hudson.

"Mr Golding? If you recall, I did ask you to attend for interview yesterday."

His voice is, like the 'phone, mechanical.

"I'm sorry. I had things to sort out."

"Things?"

"At home. My father passed away yesterday."

"Yes, I was sorry to hear that, sir."

"You knew?"

Again Hudson avoids answering easy questions.

"I believe you have returned to Waxling and therefore I must ask you to come down to the Parish Hall where we have set up a temporary incident room."

"I can't. You see Rowena – our daughter - has disappeared?"

"I thought she was ill and being attended to by your parents; forgive me, your mother now I assume?"

"Well, your assumptions are wrong. Quite wrong." Nick needs to let off steam He has needed to do so for several days now, and especially today.

"And what assumptions would they be, sir?"

Hudson remains perfectly calm as Nick shouts into the strengthening wind.

"About me. I am just an innocent man looking for his daughter."

"You say she has disappeared. I find that hard to believe."

"Look, I need your help. The local police say they can't act on a missing person's case until twenty-four hours after the person is reported missing."

"Unless an actual event has been known to have occurred, sir – such as an accident at sea – that is quite correct."

"Can you not tell: we are frantic here! My wife and I don't know where to look for her. She is just a little girl; she is missing and we need her to come home."

"Not the first time this has happened to you then, sir. There must be something about this place for history to keep repeating itself."

Hudson says this with no sense of irony but Nick can tell that he is noting, logging everything and, given that he has already lied to the police and failed to turn up when requested (ordered) to do so, his own character is looking flaky at best. The police deal with coincidences like opposite poles of a magnet.

"So you won't help us?"

"I can't interfere with local police matters I'm afraid but do expect you to come here right now to answer some further questions."

"All my life I seem to have deferred to authority figures – male authority figures. I know now beyond any doubt that this was due to my father's utter domination when I was a little boy. I also know that he had his reasons for the way in which he behaved towards me. I couldn't do anything about Jane drowning but I can do something about finding my own daughter, even if you won't help us."

"Once again, sir, I am very sorry for your loss."

The line goes dead but Nick knows the light will be flashing again soon enough.

"He won't help us?"

Nora's reply is more enigmatic than he was expecting.

"I'm sure he is nearing the end of his investigation and wants to do everything by the book this time."

Before Nick can ask her questions of his own, he spots two figures along the beach and moves towards them hoping that one of them, smaller than the other, will be Rowena; his daughter, his present and his future. But it isn't. The smaller person is his mother and the other is Gladys.

He embraces them both but their faces alert him to the fact that there is nothing to be alerted to.

"I'm so sorry, Nick." Gladys has clearly been crying, while Beryl just looks anxious, glassy-eyed through seeing no sign of her beloved granddaughter.

"We'll find her, Mum." He knows that this is not just about the search for one little girl.

"We were just about to go into the pub to ask around." Nora adds as they turn and head towards the White Lady.

"I put a Facebook alert out earlier," Gladys surprises them both. "Might as well have put one out for my husband too, seeing as he's also disappeared without trace."

Nick opens the main door to the Lounge just as Audrey Bracken steps through it. She hasn't seen Rowena and doesn't seem to share their concern, disappearing quickly and without speaking but not before looking Gladys up and down, as though inspecting a slab of dead meat.

Lynne does speak to Gladys, through a shroud of dark eyeliner, makeup and tyre tracks of lip gloss. "Your Leslie was in here earlier; caused a right stir he did."

"What happened?" Gladys is clearly relieved that there has been at least one sighting.

"Came in here demanding to know if Mr de Criel was in. I presume he visited his house first? Anyway, St John was in the back room so he just barges in without as much as a by-your-leave. I heard voices. Shouting they were. I'm not paid to listen in to other people's conversations but there was something about a girl."

"Rowena? Could the girl's name have been Rowena?" Nora is desperate, her resolve to be calm blown away as the storm inside her finally breaks.

"It could have been I suppose but, like I say, I'm not one to eavesdrop. This is a public bar, not a church. Now, what can I get you?"

"When did he leave?" Nick is fighting back his own assault from within.

"I don't spend my time monitoring other people's…"

"When?" Nick growls at her and the collective hum of assorted bar conversations is silenced.

"If you mean Mr de Criel," she answers, testily and in her own time, "he left just over an hour ago. Mr Pickett must have gone shortly after that but I don't remember seeing him leave."

"I did." Jack Saunders sidles over to them. "Leslie left fifty-five minutes ago. I asked him how he and his good lady wife were." He bows to Gladys theatrically. "He seemed quite pleased with himself but then we all are today aren't we?"

"Today?" Nora asks.

"Yes, of course. You of all people must know what I'm talking about."

They turn to face Nora but her face is a puzzle. Saunders quickly supplies the answer: "You and your History chums. Proved de Criel's innocence beyond any reasonable doubt. St John's family honour was vindicated as we all knew it would be. He's been in here most of the afternoon, celebrating, though he hasn't had to buy many of his own drinks!" He breaks into a strange, braying laugh.

"You haven't seen a young girl in here have you?" Nora is neither flattered nor flattened by his comments

"A young girl, you say? Saunders can barely speak for laughing but eventually manages to address Nick and the audience that has gathered around them all anyway, "we don't see many young girls around here I'm afraid or, at least, not for long!"

# FRIDAY 22ND JUNE, 2007

It is a few minutes after midnight. Nick leaves Gladys's cottage once again. They had all returned there for more sandwiches and tea and now, accompanied by Barry, he has taken the early shift of searching for Rowena while Nora, Beryl and Gladys get some much-needed rest.

Nora protested long and hard about this, of course, her pinched face displaying tell-tale dark rings around her eyes and confirming her exhaustion through sheer worry.

Beryl and Gladys had both remained quiet and Nick understands implicitly that both are 'seeing' this as another episode in a continuum of tragedies from the past.

He shakes himself as if to make sure that he is intact. His head is banging but also serves to dull his imagination of what they might or might not find.

They have agreed to return in a couple of hours if there is nothing to report but Nick already knows that he will pay no heed to the shift system and will stay out there, on patrol, long after the police have reluctantly agreed to get involved.

He had 'phoned Hudson's direct number again earlier, only to have it confirmed that the force would do nothing until daybreak at the earliest. Children went missing all the time around here it seemed and unless they were actually spotted in the sea - whereupon the Air Sea helicopter would be scrambled and, of course, the Lifeboat launched - there was little they could (or would) do before then.

"That's more about money than people." Barry offers, reading Nick's dark mood. "Bean counters seem to run the world these days, don't they? Perhaps that's also why they're not as good at counting as they used to be – too much ambition? That's why I'm going to be renting one of my own cottages rather than staying in the mill: more tax efficient apparently."

"I'm sorry to hear that; everyone around here seems to lose their homes in one way or another and there's us living in a big, pretentious house that none of us particularly likes and in a place we none of us really wants to be, mixing with people we don't really like."

It is as if Nick is just mouthing the words which are in any case instantly lost in the wind, but he is glad of the older man's company.

In truth, he has run out of platitudes for Nora, Beryl and even himself. He is genuinely worried about where Rowena may have gone. It is so unlike her to go off anywhere without telling either of them and his skin crawls as he slowly begins to accept that she wouldn't have done so voluntarily here either.

"We will find her, Nick. Then the three of you - and your mother too - can begin to build new lives together. Start again as it were."

"I would give anything to be able to do that, Barry." The conviction in his voice surprises him at first but he knows that this really is what he wants.

As he mentally resolves not to give in, he notices a white light out at sea. It seems to dance on the waves and he takes a noticeable intake of breath.

"No need to worry." Barry seeks to quickly reassure him. "It's just the moon lighting up the white brick of the old church tower below the surface. It only happens at certain times when the tide is low and the wind is blowing in a particular direction, slightly away from us here on land. It also requires a good-sized moon and no real cloud cover." He looks above them. "You'll see it in a moment."

Sure enough, the moon emerges from its temporary captivity behind a long, black cloud and, as it does so, the effect out at sea is quite startling. It is as though a twinkling image is floating over the sea."

"The White Lady!" Nick hears himself exclaim.

"I wouldn't read too much into that. Don't believe everything Gladys tells you."

As Barry says this they both spot a small boat, gradually bathed in the same light and just above the remains of the old tower.

"I can make out one figure but it isn't moving at all, just seems to be sitting there." Nick is on his feet and shouting "Rowena! Rowena, up here… "

But there is no acknowledgement, no movement

in the boat at all.

"I can only see one person as well but it's too dark to be sure." Barry has his fingers curled around his eyes as if to enable a pair of digital binoculars. The boat drifts into the darkness again.

"If they're not careful, whoever it is, they'll need to start steering away from those rocks pretty quickly," Barry still speaks from behind his hands, a chunky silver ring glinting in the moonlight.

At that moment they hear another voice, to their left. At first, it is unclear but then there can be no mistake, no mistake at all.

"Daddy! Daddy! Over here…"

Nick sprints towards it, down the path along the sea wall and jumps onto the beach itself. He feels rather than sees the uneven surface of hard stones and soft shells and the occasional finger of seaweed but still, he plunges forward until he almost collides with a small figure similarly running towards him.

"Rowena?" he shouts, then much louder, hysterically, "Rowena. Is it you?"

"Yes, it is. Yes, it's me, Daddy."

They meet and hug and Nick thinks he will never again be able to let her go, not as the sun rises and sets again nor the waves creep in and steal away. They shall not take her from him.

He smells the salt in her hair and feels the dampness of her clothes.

"Where have you been?" he asks as gently as he can, not wanting to frighten her, not now that his fear is a thing of the past.

"I went for a walk on the beach and met a lady. She had a young girl with her but it was only the lady who spoke to me. The girl wasn't her daughter. She'd only ever had a son, she said, but she'd had to go away and never saw him grow up. She said she knew you, Daddy, and the pain you were going through."

"What did she look like, darling?" He holds her away from him at last but doesn't let go of her hands. He wants to see her, even in the half-light; to see her face, see her mouth speaking words to him.

"The lady was dressed in a white dress; a long white dress which went right down to her ankles. We talked for ages but then she said she had to go and they left. It was only then that I realized how dark it was and heard you calling my name. They walked really fast, but Daddy!"

"Yes. What is it, Rowena?" He is so overjoyed at finding her that he can barely take any more in but knows that he must.

"You know the old Teddy Bear that Granny let me bring with me – the one that had been living upstairs in the loft?"

"I know it – him – yes. What about him?"

"Well, you know he has a red ribbon attached to his head? The little girl was wearing an identical one in her hair. Before she left, the woman told me that you would understand."

Nick feels hot tears cascading down his tired cheeks. He does understand and knows that neither he nor Rowena will ever see the woman or the little girl again. Elizabeth's message has been delivered at last and their family line is once again complete.

\*\*\*

Suddenly, Barry is there behind them both, pointing to the ancient breakwater, mostly exposed now by the retreating tide.

"Someone is sitting down there – right at the end, look!"

Urging his daughter to stay on the sand and not move a muscle he leaps after Barry who is already on the first section of the structure, walking gingerly so as not to miss his step on the damp boards.

They inch further and further along until the figure turns to face them. Although they still cannot make out his face there is no mistaking the Norfolk drawl: "You're here then! I s'pose you had other people to look out for first. Was always the case for me too and yet nobody looked out for me, did they? I know that for certain now."

Shortly afterwards they are back in the warmth and relative comfort of Gladys's tiny kitchen, Leslie bedecked in a huge red shawl, sipping hot chocolate from ancient, bluish-green mugs that could conceivably have been found in Nora's dig.

Beryl had insisted on taking Rowena straight to bed and Nick finds them cuddled up tightly just a few minutes later, snoring amid the relief that has thrown its own special blanket over them. Nora is sitting in the tiny chair by their bedside and simply smiles an indication that she will stay there for a while longer yet.

As he enters the kitchen once more, Gladys is interrogating her husband who remains elusive, either refusing or unable to answer her questions.

"And how long were you sitting down there; you were soaked through when they found you?"

"I just needed some time to think."

"About what? About him? Did you have it out with him?"

Finally, either through world-weariness or just the desire to leave it all behind, Leslie admits that after Barry had told him exactly why de Criel had been delayed all those years ago he felt a 'final nail had gone in.'

"He was so superior in every way - made us all feel second-best what with his breeding and the way he talked down to us. Yet it was all a sham, wasn't it? I wanted him to know what I knew and what I was going to tell everyone else; wanted the satisfaction of seeing that smirk wiped off of his smooth, spotless face."

They are unable to extract any further confessions and soon everyone drifts off to bed. It transpires that Barry had been staying in the spare room now occupied by Beryl and Rowena so Gladys makes him a bed up on the sofa.

She returns to Nick who has stood, ready to head back to the pub, Nora now by his side. Gladys has what looks like a small school, pink exercise book under her arm which she hands to Nick.

"I found this down the side of my old armchair when we moved here. I reckon it must have been stuck down there for thirty years and it's high time it was read."

\*\*\*

Back in their tiny room in the pub's ancient eaves, he opens the first page to read:

'My story by Jane Golding, aged ten'

The pages that follow are written in neat handwriting, often in different coloured inks but always with the same slant – a steady reference to the life of a young girl growing up in rural East Anglia.

She talks about the blackbirds that *'chased away the starlings who wanted to eat all of the breadcrumbs instead of sharing with all of the other starving birds'* on snowy winter mornings and the joy of seeing huge swarms of them in summer *'spread across the sky in a 'v' on their way home from school.'*

There are lots of snippets of poetry but it is the mentions of Nick that cause his fingers to shake as he turns the faded pages:

*'...he already writes better stories than I do but they're much too flowery for my liking. I like to get to the end more quickly but I think words themselves are the best bits for him...'*

Later, she talks about their latest school reports: "*...Mrs Bell says I ask too many questions but it's just that

*I'm really interested in what happened in the past. She says that Nick needs to speak up more! I know he likes Mrs Rogers the best because she's happy for him to just sit and write his stories. I suppose you could say that he's 'English' and I'm 'History.'*

In almost her last entry she notes that: *'Nick notices things about other people that I don't. He just seems to know what will make people happy or sad. I only know when they actually laugh or cry.'*

"Did I lose all of that?" he whispers to Nora who has been reading the diary with him. "After the accident, I mean – not that it really was an accident of course."

"You've never lost any of it, but it hasn't made you happy!"

"I haven't spoken to you about any of this but I'd like to start again: with work I mean. I'd like to write stories about real people and what they need to make better lives for themselves."

"You're talking about those people in Battersea: real social PR?"

"Or the people here who really do need better flood defences but with someone who really cares about them and yet still has the skills to help them, maybe. I know it sounds idealistic but I don't know that it's ever made more sense to me than it does now: my own consultancy without the need to follow any Prindle Massey corporate line."

"What would Marmaduke say?" she asks levelly.

"Who cares? He doesn't; he never really did!"

"How much money would you need to set that kind of thing up?" she is much calmer than he thought she would be.

"I haven't really thought it through but my startup costs would be low – just me, a laptop, a 'phone and access to the web."

"So you could do it from almost anywhere?"

"Pretty much. Let's finish this and then talk about it some more?"

They return to Jane's diary and are soon on the final entry. She is about to go on a fishing trip but it isn't going to be in Barney – which she thinks is such a nice name – it is in *The Barnabus* which is actually the name of the boat.

He has seen it moored up outside de Criel's house. But this isn't the only revelation in these days of revelations and the pages of history being turned and altered. He reads about the incident with his father, David, and the 'posh man' and the undisputed fact that his sister saw them.

"Do you think Dad was bi-sexual?" he asks Nora who is silently weeping from the little girl's story - so recently told, so long-ago written.

"I don't know for certain, darling, Beryl has never said anything about it to me but I do know that he loved her and both of you; he just couldn't find the words to say so. Maybe he had his own secret, quite apart from Jane, and maybe he and Barry got on a little too well which Beryl did suspect? I really don't know.

He may just have been happy to have someone to talk over the past with, which he thought Beryl didn't deserve to go through all over again.

Your father must have rewound the film of his daughter going overboard every day – probably several times a day. He didn't want to inflict that horror on anybody else. Beryl has certainly spent a lot of her time alone these last years and that's why she has got out of the house when she can and, yes, sometimes going for a drink.

Have you any idea how much courage that actually took for a married woman of her age? I guess she preferred to be lonely in a group of people than in her own house. And another thing, Nick…"

But Nick has finally succumbed to sleep and those are the waves that, having crept up so quietly, now flow over him and drag him away from her, from here, from now.

\*\*\*

He wakes just after eight. Nora is drawing back the curtains and, of course, a steaming cup of tea sits on the bedside table atop one of Gideon's Bibles.

"I didn't want to stain the white cloth" she explains, rather incongruously.

"How long have you been awake?" he asks, sleepily and basking in both her and the room's warmth.

"Not long. There was a bit of a commotion

outside just after seven. Apparently, de Criel has disappeared and so has his boat. Oh and I think you should read this."

"What is it?" he asks stupidly as she hands over the laptop.

"It's the blog post that Gladys wrote yesterday."

He skims through a short piece below the title: 'Back from the dead and exposed at last!' It talks about justice being served but it is the final line that grabs his attention: '...the man you all looked up to; the landed squire in our midst was nothing more than a fairy in his own pantomime world.'

He looks across at Nora who has already put the kettle on again. "Do you think this is why he disappeared? Because of the loss of face or do you think someone went after him?"

"Like Leslie Pickett you mean?"

"He was soaked through when we found him."

"So would you be if you'd been sitting at the end of a breakwater for half of the night. It's possible but I think Leslie just needed time to sort his head out – some quiet contemplation that others do in church. The breakwater would have been better than any pew for him and he could be quite alone there.

No, I think Leslie had already had his revenge in the pub when confronting de Criel with the truth – the whole truth. Even de Criel must have realized that he and Gladys together were a potent force in such a small community as this one. They could dismiss Gladys as some kind of witch but Leslie was liked and respected – almost admired for putting up with her eccentricity all these years."

"She's certainly that but Mum seems to adore her."

"They have been good for each other."

"Did Mum know about the diary?"

"Gladys faxed pages through to the library in Littleport when she first found it – she didn't think it right that she should keep it all to herself. I think she also felt that it would help your mum."

"So Mum knew about Dad. Barry just confirmed it when he told her his story in the hospital?"

"I suppose so but, as I said last night, it didn't bother Beryl. She wanted to protect Barry and if he was company for your father it made it easier for her to leave the bungalow when she needed to get away for the evening."

"And she will also have seen the reference to de Criel's boat."

"I'm not sure if she would have remembered it or not but she was suspicious of de Criel after seeing him in the church late on the night that Jane drowned - was drowned."

"Yes, she told me about that. The trouble is we can't place him in the boat, can we? Dad talked about someone else being the murderer but doesn't name him. And now he can't give evidence…"

Nora stops stirring milk into her tea and kneels on the bed beside him as he continues.

"I suppose even then – right at the end of his own life - Dad was frightened: not for himself anymore but for Beryl and maybe even me? I'm pretty sure now that de Criel must have made the connection with me on that first day I went and met him in Waxling.

He kept staring at me intensely which I thought at the time might be his way of putting people at their unease, once Jack Saunders had told him my name; it would certainly explain why he didn't want me working on their account at Prindle Massey."

"There was no 'summer of love', Nick. It was a summer of conflict and death – here, in Vietnam, the Middle East and Biafra just around the corner. I located each of these places on my map and it felt at the time like all of humanity was at war.

This man tried to come between you and me – to break up our family - again! No other person should ever be able to do that. He must have been frightened when he saw you again as a grown man, if not for himself then definitely for his reputation."

"I didn't recognize him at all and Dad wouldn't have known that I had even met him – even you didn't know that. So Dad was still seeking to protect us, assuming it really was de Criel who was responsible for Jane's death."

"And presumably he needed to get rid of Jane because of what she had seen the day before? Yes, that fits, doesn't it? His reputation was on the line then as well and he's been doing whatever has been necessary to protect it ever since." She shivers.

"He must have blackmailed your father into silence, threatening to ruin his own family, his marriage, if he ever muttered a word; except that he needn't have worried because your father would have done anything to protect what remained of his family because of love, pure and simple. The Beatles definitely got that bit right."

"At least we have him in the frame for the lifeboat rescue being delayed nearly thirty years later. We have Barry to thank for that one."

Nora is about to reply when the 'phone rings. It is Mike, the pub landlord, 'phoning up from the main bar. "Mr Golding? Sorry to disturb you sir but there's a lady here to see you!"

Nick dresses quickly and runs a comb through his hair. He glances over at Nora's paraphernalia of books and papers across from his solitary wash bag. She is engrossed with an article on her laptop and does not see him move the top sheet over slightly to reveal more of the legend 'Wright Moves' with an address in Sheringham.

The bar is empty, save for a middle-aged couple in one corner. They are wearing 'holiday' clothes of garish orange t-shirts over jeans with perfectly-ironed creases along matching blue chinos. The man's self-importance is obvious as he reads a tabloid newspaper at arm's length which provides full frontal coverage of his bored wife - sitting dutifully behind it and whom he had coveted so long ago now it seems.

Nick's mind drifts back to the room upstairs. Is Nora looking for somewhere else to live then? Will there be room for him?

"Mr Golding?"

He had expected the visitor to be his mother - or maybe even Gladys - but it is neither of them. The lady before him is slim, grey-haired and in her late sixties at least. With fine cheekbones in a handsome face, she still cuts a striking figure, he thinks. She holds out a pale hand.

"Indeed," he takes it and shakes it gently as though her arm might break right off if he is too forceful.

"My name is Frida Thomasson. My brother was once the pastor here."

"Jonas? Yes, yes, please do sit down." Thrown completely out of his stride, he nevertheless manages to lead her to a table by the nearest window, looking up at the street. How long ago it seems since he watched as assorted individuals bared their soles without even realizing it.

Nora soon joins them and, after the introductions, Frida continues.

"I sent you an e-mail. Mr Savory contacted me about my late brother's death and asked if I could help."

"I didn't receive it I'm afraid…" Nick begins but is cut short by Nora.

"George must have assumed that Nick used ngolding as his Googlemail address whereas in fact, he uses nigolding. I use ngolding and received your message and attachment which I passed straight through to the police?"

"The police? Hudson?" Nick is all at sea, and not for the first time by far since he came to Waxling.

"You seem a little surprised Mr Golding? It is true that we do live in a remote little community but the Scandinavian peoples have generally been ahead of the technology curve for years – especially when it comes to online communications. So much of our territory is otherwise inaccessible."

"I'm sorry, I didn't want you to assume that…"

Nora jumps to his rescue. "I didn't want to raise your hopes, Nick, but it looked pretty conclusive to me. I mean, it must have been because that's why they're holding the press conference here today."

Frida sees the need to explain and, after requesting coffee, they watch Nora head over to the bar.

"She is very lovely, I think?"

"Nora? Yes, she is beautiful in my eyes." Nick realizes how proud he is to say those words, especially to a relative stranger.

"I sent her a copy of a letter my brother wrote to me just before he died."

"I was sorry to read about his death. It seemed that he was well liked here in the community, especially by younger people."

"The Youth Group? Yes. I believe he was happy

with them also. He and I would play folk music back in Eidsvoll when we were so much younger. He wanted to bring that joy to the youth people here in England. It was a time of colour and music I think?"

"Tell me, did Jonas like it here, I mean truly like it?"

"He did. He fell in love you see so, even if there had been things that would hurt him, he most likely would not have noticed."

"He fell in love with Audrey?"

"Audrey. Yes. Ms Bracken as she has become? I visited her yesterday but it seems she had to go away. A taxi was seen waiting for her just before darkness came."

"And the letter. Did it talk of her?"

"Not that letter, though I have others that did."

Nora returns with a round tray containing tea and coffee paraphernalia which she carefully sits on an adjacent table, shuffling around it to join them once again and joining the conversation.

"I was so sorry to hear the circumstances of your brother's death."

"It was a shock. Even now it is a shock. After so many years you'd think the pain would become less so. I never married myself, though, so was not to be comforted. Jonas was the only family I had you see."

She pauses then continues quickly, as though if she waited any longer she would lose her nerve completely. "Some illegal substances were found in

Jonas's cupboards in the Kirke ... Church? He was not a bad man, my brother, and he wrote to tell me that he had no idea how they had got in there.

Some days later he was approached by a big man – an important man. His name was St John de Criel. He wrote that Mr de Criel told him he had placed the tablets in the cupboard and would do so again if Jonas did not do exactly as he asked.

My brother told his wife – Audrey – all of this but she did not believe him. This matter was not mentioned between them again until almost a year later when Mr de Criel burst into the church late one evening and demanded that Jonas help him."

"What did he want him to do?" Nick's thinks he has never been so beguiled by the power of storytelling as he is right now.

She turns away from him and looks to Nora as if to receive permission to continue. Suitably reassured she does so but in an altogether quieter voice. "Mr de Criel told him that he had killed a girl - a young girl - and wedged her body in the stone wall remains of the ancient Waxling church off the coast from here. He needed Jonas to row out there with him to collect it before burying it in the old vault in the church."

"The church vault where Jane's body was found!" Nora's eyes are shining. "He couldn't risk her body just being washed up on the beach. I'm sorry Nick but this must be what your mother saw that night that Jane died. She said she had surprised de Criel and Jonas over on the windowless side of the church where the old de Criel tomb was. That's exactly what they were doing."

Frida catches hold of Nick's arm. "This is very bad. I know that there is nothing I can say or do – and neither can my brother of course – to bring back your little sister but you must know that I am truly sorry. Jonas would have been too but prayers could not save him."

Nick turns to face her. "I am sorry for your loss too. I have not had to spend so much of my life grieving in the way that you have and my mother and father have; even Nora to some extent on my behalf.

Everything has happened so quickly, and I know that there will be days when I shall feel strangely bereaved, but I thank you from every part of my being for having the courage to come forward now. Finally, that man will be prosecuted and sent to his own dark place below the ground, out of sight of human kindness and decency."

\*\*\*

A short while later, he and Nora are walking back to Gladys's house. Children are running excitedly to the edge of the waves before hurtling back with buckets of escaping water to the castles in the sand which will one day mark the edges of their innocence.

"Do you think it was the loss of reputation or potential loss of freedom that caused de Criel to 'disappear?'"

"History might never tell us," Nora is almost skipping along in a carefree way he remembers seeing only once before, on the way to their very first date in Exeter.

"Or we may have to wait forty years to find out!"

"Or four hundred" We can strongly infer, though, that this de Criel thought he was going to finally get caught in the net. He must have realized that the police had discovered something – some piece of missing evidence that they had never had before - for them to call a press conference right here in Waxling.

Also, Barry was careful to keep out of sight as best he could but who's to say he wasn't spotted by one of Audrey's spies. If that was the case, de Criel would have known that Barry felt safe enough to return."

"But why did Barry feel safe enough to return when he did, do you think? I mean he couldn't have known about George tracking Frida down and certainly not about the letter from Jonas?"

"I think Barry knew that he was safe provided he stayed close to Gladys. De <u>Criel</u> was powerless to stop her posting her comments online and though he pretended that this was detrimental to the campaign for better flood defences it was really only his own defence he was concerned about.

He could try and influence all of the locals – from the lifeboat station backwards – but the power of social media enabled people to debate it for themselves. This is where you come in. You can really help people express themselves now with the skills and insight Jane knew that you possessed even then. Free speech is a privilege and a gift; woe betides any individual or any organization that tries to artificially affect it."

\*\*\*

Rowena runs towards them as they approach Gladys's cottage. The day is overcast and somewhat thundery to reflect the turmoil experienced by the principal characters but with the promise of cooling, refreshing rain to come.

"Granny says she might move up here?"

"Up here?" Nora tries not to mock her mother-in-law's wishes or let her daughter down.

"You mean: just for a while?" Nick tries to help out.

"She isn't sure yet but you'll never guess what?"

They look at each other, both of them determined not to say 'what?'

Rowena is thankfully impatient to supply answers to her own questions

"She's thinking of living in the old mill. Mr Thirling – Barry - who we all used to call Harry, owns it but is moving into the cottage next door to Gladys."

"Why on earth would he do that?" asks Nora, laughing.

"I think it may be something to do with tax!" Nick offers.

"Oooh, get you, 'Mr Financial Director'" she teases as they all head inside.

"So what's this about you renting the old mill, Mum?" Nick asks as he sits down opposite her. Barry and Leslie are seated together on the settee discussing, literally, the price of fish these days, while Nora joins

Gladys in the kitchen for a good clatter.

"Once I've squared things up at home – back in Ely – I might consider it, yes. It all depends."

"On what?" he laughs easily, expecting her to joke back.

"On you – on all of you?"

"On us?"

"Me too?" Rowena is standing beside Beryl, her hand on the back of her chair.

"Yes, darling, the whole family."

As if on cue, Nora appears at the kitchen door but doesn't say anything, just waits for Beryl to continue which, after examining the faces of each of her family members gathered around her, she does:

"The mill and the cottages have been in Barry's family for generations and have been passed down to him. Barry has no other family."

"Nor likely to have now!" he butts in and they all laugh: uncomplicated, spontaneous laughter.

"Gladys and Leslie rent one of the cottages…"

"And may God bless you for that" Leslie's turn to join the interruption game.

"And the other one was up for rent, as was the mill."

"I couldn't see myself coming back here, you see," Barry explains, "not to live. Not while de Criel was still around. In any case, the mill would have been too big for me on my own."

"Is there any news of him this morning?" Now Nick interrupts.

Gladys reports: "Breaking News Online just reported on the press conference. They held it at the lifeboat station apparently. Jack Saunders thought it might help to remind people of the flood defence campaign at the same time!"

"Genius!" Nick admires out loud and they all nod in agreement.

"But they just said that they were looking for St John de Criel with a view to arresting him for the murder at sea of Jane Golding in July 1967. They didn't say whether he had been sighted yet or what leads they were following. I suppose they can't really, can they? Transparency is no match for operational needs?"

Once again, Nick is forced to admire not only the thought process but also the sophistication of old Gladys Pickett who had been so falsely painted as a woman living in her own little bubble, when really she was more connected than any landed gentry could ever have been.

"Tell us more about the mill?" Rowena pleads, leading them quickly back to Beryl's story.

"Barry pretended that the second cottage had been let to someone else when he intended to rent it himself – just to put de Criel off the scent if he or Audrey or some other acolyte came to nose around. He left the mill boarded up."

Barry picks up the thread once more. "I sensed that things were on the turn with de Criel and Gladys urged me to come up and live low here, once she heard that Beryl and poor David were having to move out of their bungalow. So that's what I did – not that I ever intended to move back into the mill."

"But the cottage had been vacant since those artists you'd let it out to moved on," Gladys smiles at him benignly, "though Heaven knows why they thought they would get a better light on the Lincolnshire coast…"

They laugh again and then Beryl takes charge once more. "Gladys has always kept in touch with me and told me that Barry would never want to live in the mill again so I kept it at the back of my mind.

She also told me that, if ever the de Criel situation changed, she would try to persuade him to move into the cottage next door instead and that got me thinking. The mill would be too big for me too but, at the same time, I would be near to my oldest friends and also my daughter at last.

She breaks off again as Barry heads over and gives both Beryl and Rowena a hug.

"So it depends on whether you would like to join me here."

For the first time that morning, the cottage is momentarily in silence. Nick takes longer to compute what she is asking than his wife does. Nora, though, he has to admit, has had a head start in most of his family affairs all along.

"You mean for all of us to come and live here, with you, in the mill, next door to Gladys and Leslie and Barry?" she can barely control the excitement in her voice and Nick allows himself to be swept along.

"I do think we could be happy here."

Rowena leaps into his arms before he can go on. "Oh Daddy, I've always loved windmills. I can't believe we could actually live in one."

"And the schools on either side of here are very good, seemingly," Gladys adds triumphantly, "so you'd have a good choice for Rowena – that's if the Ofsted PDFs I downloaded are to be believed."

"What about the house in London?" Nick is forcing himself to be pragmatic but he knows in his heart that reality is no real match for romance.

"You could rent it out." Beryl is allowing herself to get excited too. "You'd get far more for that in London than I expect Barry would charge you here?"

"I wouldn't be too sure about that" Leslie joins in, "have you seen the price of fish these days?"

They all laugh out loud while Rowena looks at each of them for some kind of confirmation.

"There would be a lot to do," Nick concedes but continues to smile. "I'd have to work out the financials."

"But I could help." Nora throws her arms around his neck, unashamedly. "I have rediscovered my mojo here and have all kinds of history projects of my own I want to explore much more of this coast and then write the papers up – maybe even a book.

John Squires mentioned an old airfield at Horsham St Faith – there's a castle there that sounds really interesting. It's not specifically a marine project but this whole county is a marine project – it's 'Nelson's County' after all. Where better?

Given the publicity this has generated I'm sure I'd be able to find a publisher – two have contacted me already as the 'face of the History and Mystery dig' they'd rather deal with."

"Shall I be the one to inform the suave Mr Squires?" Gladys throws back her head and roars with infectious laughter.

"If you both found you could work up here you could always sell your house in London after a while," Beryl's eyes are twinkling, "and one day you'd have the mill all to yourselves – maybe even buy it outright."

"Oh Mum," he cannot ever remember seeing his mother, wife or daughter so happy. Here, where it all began to go so badly wrong.

"Mind you," Beryl continues quickly, "I'll fight you for the top room. The view over the sea is wonderful – ideal for a writer."

"But I'm the writer, Mum!" he protests.

"I think you'll find that you are in the presence of a critically acclaimed poet, darling," Nora assures him, still with her arms around him.

He is confused, and looks from face to face until he sees his mother smiling, knowingly.

"Of course: Jane Standing!"

"A combination of the two females I loved the most – no disrespect to anyone here present of course." Beryl is talking softly but proudly and he can see that he is the only one in her audience who does not know the truth. "My daughter's and my mother's names."

"I've read some of your poems; you were the lady who sat in the bar in Upware sometimes?"

"And other places but not to drink – though of course I sometimes had to have a proper drink or they'd have thrown me out – rather, to think. Your father was totally against my writing any kind of fiction, even expressing myself in rhymes rather than reasons.

I think it was partly because it made him feel even more of a failure (though of course, that was never my intention at all). Also, because he feared I might inadvertently let something out about de Criel – hence the pseudonym for extra cover. Obviously, I didn't know the whole story until now, but he couldn't be certain, could he? It must have worried him."

"Especially with me living in your house." Barry acknowledges his old friend's point, sadly.

"He once saw my writing pad on the kitchen table and put it on his bonfire. It was at that point that I knew I had to find somewhere else to write. I didn't court company – find me a poet who does – so I moved around from location to location but I remain largely anonymous; it works better for me that way you see."

"I never knew you were such a gifted writer, Mum; I am so sorry."

"No need to be sorry," she reaches her hand out

to him, "I'm not, but everyone has their story to tell – whatever they may look or sound like. I'm just grateful for the gift I was able to pass through to both of my children. You both loved poetry when you were little; I think it helped you to see beyond mere words: like a torch in a big dictionary!"

He reaches out and hugs her, neither of them seeking to break away for fear of breaking the moment.

"It will be so much better now," Beryl whispers at last. "As a writer, you can choose the characters you want to be in your life and take control of it. It is a lot more fun that way, I can assure you. Once you find out and understand the truth about yourself, only then can you be the author of your own story."

\*\*\*

That afternoon, Beryl and Barry settle down to a game of Canasta with Gladys and Leslie.

"We could play every day now if we wanted to," Gladys beams, "and Barry is going to teach us Bridge aren't you dear?"

"And that's when we'll all fall out again," he is also smiling, a twinkle in his old eyes that have seen so much, "I've never known partners come under such pressure as during those particular battles!"

"We'll take the risk." Beryl places a hand on his arm as Gladys pours fresh tea for each of them.

\*\*\*

And so it is that later, Nick, Nora and Rowena leave the cottage and make for Waxling Beach. It has rained since they were last in the open air but the clouds are beginning to clear away to the south now, leaving the hazy sun to grow brighter with their every step.

Rowena is like a little girl celebrating Christmas and Easter and every birthday she has ever had. She runs down to the ancient breakwater and back to them again. Like Leslie on the previous evening, the thinking has been done, problems solved and plans for the future made.

"I can't believe we're going to live by the coast, Daddy. Do you think I'll be able to have a real rabbit? I think he'd like it here."

"Sounds like he's already settled in!" Nick laughs. "What will you call him?"

"He's called Snuffles."

"So it is!" He understands now that he has been listening throughout the lesson. He looks down at the flashing light on his 'phone and knows that he will never again rush to read its messages; to return the calls from those whose tails he no longer needs to hang on to.

He turns back to the child. "Don't ever stop reading, writing or telling stories, because they are what history will make of all of us in the end!"

She gives his hand a quick squeeze and races back down to the water's edge.

Nick and Nora are holding hands, swinging them high in the air as they once did with the small girl who now dawdles behind them, knowing beyond her years to give them some space of their own. They don't need to talk; their body language is the only communication they need at this moment in time.

Suddenly, Rowena catches them up, a piece of what looks like old driftwood in her hand.

"Look what I've just found!" she declares, breathlessly.

Nick takes it gently from her and notes that it is not as old as it first appeared. Several strands of dark kelp and an old bluish-grey razor shell are entwined around it. He turns it over and sees part of an inscription in dark, italic letters: *nabu*.

"How interesting," Nora turns it over and back again, "Nabu was worshipped in Babylonian mythology as the god of wisdom and writing I think."

"It also forms part of the name: Barnabus!" Nick hands the piece back to Rowena but not before he spots a faded piece of ribbon wrapped around it, red against the green seaweed.

## The End

# MAILING LIST

If you enjoyed this book please rate it on Amazon.

Please also join our mailing list for the latest writing news, including about forthcoming books.

# ABOUT THE AUTHOR

## Mark Rasdall

Mark Rasdall was born in Peterborough in 1960 and brought up on the edge of the Cambridgeshire Fens. A writer of fiction and history, with a professional background in content creation, curation, and online search in London's advertising sector, he is based in the UK, in a small village on top of a hill in the beautiful Worcestershire countryside. For a few years he ran a sweet shop on Worcester High Street with his wife Michelle.

Now retired, he tells stories and writes fiction and history books.

Other fiction titles by Mark include:

The Proofreader
Water, Slaughter Everywhere
Family Fiction

You can visit his website at www.markrasdallwriting.com and follow Mark on

Facebook, X and Instagram.

Printed in Great Britain
by Amazon